Praise for *Calling the Dead*

"*Calling the Dead* is a timely historical novel exploring the spaces between religion, science and spiritualism. Join traveling medium Eusapia Palladino (1854-1918) on a fascinating journey to the indeterminate realms that have come to dominate the postmodern era. Love, politics and science collide in what, ultimately, is a rumination on human being."

–John M. Gist, Founding Editor, *Red Savina Review*

"*Calling the Dead* is an impressive achievement. It is a straightforward biographical story yet full of suspense, a firmly grounded account with a dreamlike quality, an intensely feminine exploration of self in a predominantly male environment, a historical narrative with contemporary immediacy. An excellent book."

–Jose Havet, Professor of Sociology, Ret.,
University of Ottawa

"In rich and fluid language, the novel explores a plethora of feelings and situations. The reader can't help but be swept up as if under the spell of a real séance. A must read."

–Marie-Andrée Donovan, author of the award-winning
Les soleils incendiés, and *À l'ombre du silence*

Calling the Dead

R.K. Marfurt

New York
Harvard Square Editions
www.harvardsquareeditions.org
2014

Published in the United States by
Harvard Square Editions

ISBN: 978-0-9895960-2-2
Front Cover photographs
'Cosmic Clouds' © Sergey Nivens
'Circle of unity' © Yuri Arcurs
Back Cover photograph
'The Table in the Air - A Typical Table Levitation with Eusapia
Paladino.' The man on the right of Eusapia Paladino, is the French
Professor and Astronom, Camille Flammarion, on her left side, in
front of her is the Italian researcher Dr. Cesare Lombroso © Kristján
Einarsson, The Nordic Spiritual Research Center

Harvard Square Editions web address:
www.HarvardSquareEditions.org

Printed in the United States of America

FOR RAY, WITH LOVE

Historical Note

Eusapia Palladino was born in the Italian village of Minervino in 1854. Only a few facts are known about her early years: her mother died while giving birth to Eusapia; her father was murdered when she was a young girl; and she had a miserable childhood. After being sent to Naples, spiritualists helped her develop her talents and she became famous. Her adult life as a medium is better documented. Famous people like William James, Cesare Lombroso, Nobel Prize winners Charles Richet and Marie and Pierre Curie participated in her séances and investigated her. Many people believed her to be genuine. Eight years after her death in 1918, Arthur Conan Doyle praised her psychic abilities in his *History of Spiritualism*. Numerous books and articles have been written about her. Even today, she has her believers and remains alive in articles online.

This book is a work of fiction set in the second half of the 19th century and the beginning of the 20th at the height of spiritualism, an era of tension between religion and science. While the main character is based on a real person and her relationships with actual scientists and other famous people of the time, I have taken great liberty in telling this story. References to real people, events, establishments, organisations, and locales are intended to provide a sense of authenticity, but are used fictitiously and portrayed according to my own interpretation, understanding and intuition. I have changed the first names of a few lesser known people. Incidents, dialogue and all other characters are drawn from my imagination and are not to be construed as real. As in the world of spiritualism itself, lines between facts and fiction are blurry.

Minervino, Italy, 1854-1866

1

INSIDE HER MOTHER'S WOMB, Eusapia felt the serene calm of the last nine months end abruptly. She tried holding on, relaxing one last time in the comfort of the warm fluid, stretching once more in the familiar sea of love that, small as it was, had offered her plenty of freedom to move. Suddenly she felt yanked around, squeezed and then stuck. She struggled. She needed to get out. Instead, the pressure around her mounted, bringing her movements to an uncomfortable halt.

Her mother's beautiful voice stopped singing, it screamed, Save the child, just save the child.

Eusapia fought frantically to free herself. Every instinct inside her pushed her to move. But an adverse and unyielding force held her in place.

Sapia, my beloved child, the woman pleaded.

The little girl used her tiny foot. She kicked and kicked, straining to follow her mother's call. Kick. Kick again. Her foot became heavy. She couldn't move it any longer. Still, she tried. She sensed her mother's tears. She felt her mother's prayers float through the room and, over interminable hours, contract into desperate gasps.

In the name of the Father, the Son and the Holy Spirit, don't let my baby die. Let her live. Please, let her live.

Eusapia couldn't move. She too wanted to pray. But she did not know the words. So she just said, Mammina, I need you. Don't leave me, Mamma.

Between the woman's legs, the young midwife Lucia worked steadily, urging, Don't you give up, Michela.

But confronted with Michela's out-of-control blood pressure, Lucia's own confidence dropped. She wiped the woman's swelling face. When a violent seizure shook Michela's body, Lucia was reduced to providing little more than comfort.

Fight for this child, Lucia whispered, trying to calm Michela and herself.

The woman relaxed for a moment. Lucia positioned her hands on the womb to turn the child whose buttocks blocked the entry to the birth canal. Her fingers sought the outline of the body. Despite a sudden anxiety that accelerated her pulse and breathing, both hands worked instinctively as if they knew, as if destiny willed them to give this child a chance. Bit by bit, the body shifted. Lucia felt the child take strength, a tiny foot kicking hard, kicking for dear life, but moving too slowly, way too slowly.

Only drastic measures might bring the child into this world alive. Lucia took from the bottom of her bag the instrument her brother had given her in secret after their most difficult delivery when he was forced to use forceps.

Don't let anyone see them, her brother had told her, no one besides us doctors is supposed to use them. But I'd never forgive myself if we lost a child that could have been saved! If I can't be around, use them if you need to. You were born with the mind and hands of a doctor, just like me. It's your duty to save lives.

If Lucia was ever going to use this thing, now was the moment. Carefully, she pushed the tongs up through the fully

2

dilated opening of the birth canal, unable to heed her brother's instruction to use them only at the end of the canal if at all possible. Already she had to accept that she would not be able to save the mother, but she would never give up on the child. Prevented from placing the ends of the forceps on the baby's cheekbones since the head had only partly moved into the right position, she clamped the pincers around its head wherever she could find a grip. Tentatively, but with her usual persistence, she pulled. With minimal success at first. She increased the pressure, clamped down slightly harder and pulled more firmly. Finally, the baby started to move, and Lucia thanked God when at last she was able to pull her out. She had to slap the squashed blue body several times before an anguished wail rippled through the air and was immediately swallowed up by Lucia's mourning the mother's tragic death. Lucia knew that besides saving the baby's life, she had plunged the child into instant grieving for the mother she would never know.

The next few years became confused in Eusapia's mind. The people in her life appeared removed like characters in the story of a stranger. Before her world caved in on her at birth, it had been lit so intensely that Eusapia thought the sun itself brightened her mother's womb. Michela bequeathed this memory to her daughter in her last hours, imprinting it in her child so that Eusapia grew up remembering things no other child could possibly know about her own birth, things adults only talked about in oblique language. As her last gift, Mamma let her keep the light, making sure it shone whenever her child wanted to see her. In its magical rays, Mamma would appear full of life, healthy and strong, with a glowing ruddy face, black wavy hair,

3

large eyes, and an encouraging, warm smile. Eusapia was able to recall her mother talking and singing to her. When sorrow and loneliness became unbearable, Eusapia would take refuge in the period before she was dramatically separated from her mother and, in intense flashes of improbable memories and happiness, recover some of the love Mammina had given her during her pregnancy. On the occasions when Michela came to comfort her, Eusapia took strength from the promise that Mammina's love would carry her through life. Her mother's every gesture, every expression was as fresh in Eusapia's mind as if she'd seen her yesterday.

Throughout the years, Lucia told Eusapia over and over: She loved you more than anything in the world. Her last thought belonged to you.

And Papa? Was he happy when I was born? Eusapia asked one day, a question she had been pondering for months.

Lucia said she couldn't say because she had left the house when Rocco Palladino finally arrived home. Eusapia knew Lucia was lying but didn't press the matter because she knew that Lucia lied out of love.

What about great-aunty Rosalia who took care of me, did she love me?

She did, Lucia assured the girl. Rosalia did love you.

Eusapia grabbed the tuft of white hair that was sprouting like a ghostly flower out of her thick black hair in the front left part of her head.

Lucia, is it true what people say, that Rosalia dropped me on a stone? That she made my hair turn white on purpose?

What does your heart say, Sapia?

I remember her holding me in her arms for hours and hours and trying to sing to calm me down no matter how much her voice shook. Papa said she bleated like a dying goat. But I liked her lullabies. When she sang, I could see the stars and feel the night breeze on my face. I could fall asleep.

You're right, Eusapia, whatever you needed, she tried to give you. Yes, she dropped you a few times when she had her weak spells. I've seen how she fretted over those mishaps and pleaded with the Madonna to keep you out of harm's way. She would have given her life if that meant better care and happier circumstances for you. She never dropped you on a stone. People make mountains out of molehills to give weight to their own sad stories and hard lives. To be honest, Eusapia, I might be the one to blame for your white hair. Lucia continued as if she were talking to an adult and not a child, since she was fully aware that the child had pieced together from whispers and furtive gossip vivid visions of her birth, made real and more poignant through an abundance of imagination and neediness. I think the forceps are to blame for the dent in your head, the little berth for your tuft of white hair. Far from being a curse, that white hair singles you out as the exceptional person you are. Never forget that. Being special will help you march on in life when most would give up.

Where did Rosalia go? Eusapia wanted to know.

Your papa thought it better to hire a young woman to take care of you.

The one he smooched and pawed all the time?

Eusapia, he hired her because she had energy and he believed that's what you needed.

Where did Rosalia go? Wait, I remember her crying. And saying she had nowhere to go. I have this image in my head of her sitting on the ground outside the house.

Are you sure you remember that time? You were only three.

Slowly, it comes back to me. I was woken up during the night because I heard my papa scream, I never want to see your stupid face again. Then there was a noise like a scuffle, and I knew he had shoved Rosalia out the door. Seconds later he left the house cursing non-stop. I was afraid alone in the dark rooms. So I squeezed by the curtain at the front door and looked outside for Rosalia. She sat crumpled against the house wall in the dark without moving. I thought if I brought her some food she'd come back in. I couldn't find bread or cheese. So I had to go outside with nothing. When I sat down beside Rosalia, I saw that her face was wet. But she smiled at me.

Thank you, my angel, thank you a thousand times, she said, even though I had no food to give her.

Rosalia then got another of her weak spells. She toppled over. I took the corner of my shirt and dipped it in a puddle nearby, and I dabbed her face the way you wiped the face of Mammina. Rosalia did not move. I kept sitting beside her, holding her hand, until Papa came back hours later. None of the neighbours must have noticed us out there in the middle of the night. That's why no one came out to help. Papa was angry when he saw us. Couldn't the old cow have waited to die someplace else, he said. When I responded that I wanted Rosalia, Papa told me to shut up and go inside, that the old woman was no good anyway. I didn't see Rosalia again. I soon stopped asking for her since Papa got mad every time I mentioned her name.

To Eusapia it was clear that her father liked the tall, kissy woman Belladonna better. He hit her only a few times, not like Rosalia who was always covered with bruises.

I love you Rocco, Belladonna said, squeezing her cheek to his, her wild waves of dark hair intertwining with his greying curls. I want to swallow you alive, she added so voraciously that Eusapia was afraid she'd actually go ahead and do it.

Half the time they were in bed naked acting crazy, a jug of wine and two cups beside the bed, sometimes toppled over, once even smashed. Then there was Papa's pipe, which Belladonna snatched from him to fill with tobacco, making sure she got the first puffs. Sometimes Eusapia saw them roll tobacco into paper or into some strange leaves. More often than not, the room was blue with smoke. Eusapia mostly stayed outside because the smoke made her cough, and that ticked them off, especially her father.

Belladonna never talked to her and even pretended the child didn't exist. Eusapia had to grab her own food if she wanted to eat. She learned to climb on the kitchen table or the counter to get a hold of anything edible that might have been left there. First she was afraid of climbing back down because twice she fell when she wasn't used to it yet. After that she watched her steps and acquired the appropriate moves. The best moment to find food was right after Papa and Belladonna had eaten. The woman never got around to cleaning up for hours.

As soon as Papa and Belladonna left, Eusapia used her new expertise to climb on the counter and scratch together every last crumb of bread, or on a lucky day bits of meat or pasta. When she was weak with thirst and couldn't find a drop of water, she ventured into their room without fear of enraging Papa with her coughing fits. She sat down beside the jug and the cups and licked the crusty dregs of leftover wine. Who else had a papa who didn't know you had to feed and clothe children? Their parish priest once dropped by and shouted that if the child died it would be on her papa's head, and even if he hadn't really meant to kill her, he'd rot in hell for what he did. Papa wasn't afraid of hell. He just laughed and gave the priest wine until the old man stopped shouting and preaching.

Weeks before Belladonna left, Eusapia woke up screaming every night, expecting to be face to face with terrifying witches and monsters. Drenched in sweat, she stayed awake for hours trying to figure out where in the sparsely furnished rooms she could hide if the need arose. In the morning, she burrowed into corners and niches to verify their suitability as hiding places. She practised punching invisible enemies and threw her family's three spoons and two knives until her aim was perfect. To learn to outlast pursuers, she ran nonstop around the two chairs in her house, through the labyrinth of narrow alleyways in her neighbourhood, under the arches that connected the houses, up and down the countless steps of stone. As young as she was, she became strong and fast.

When Paola moved in the day after Papa kicked Belladonna out, Eusapia was glad the merciless pursuits in her nightmares had trained her to deal with danger. The intense training probably saved her life because when Paola arrived, Eusapia had to hide for real and stay motionless in tight corners or remain outside for hours if she didn't want to be beaten to a pulp. Paola might be a head smaller than Papa, but boy was she strong! Like an ox! When Papa beat her up, she never cried like Belladonna, but beat him right back. They chased each other, then wrestled on the ground. Eusapia could hear the slapping and screaming even though she fled the scene the moment the fights started. The second time her father ended up with a black eye was the last time she saw Paola inside their house.

By the time Bianca arrived two months before the child's fifth birthday, Eusapia had had enough. It might have been different if Bianca had come before Paola or even better before Belladonna.

This new woman, who was short and round, pressed Sapia to her breasts and said, Poor motherless one, I'll be your mamma.

But Sapia recoiled, frightened and overwhelmed by the smothering embrace. Unable to breathe, Eusapia elbowed herself out of the woman's arms and fled outside where to her relief the air hadn't been sucked away, and it was possible to refill her lungs. Haltingly, she calmed down.

Bianca persevered in her attempts for a while. Let me brush your hair. Let me wash your face. On Eusapia's birthday, Bianca gave her a pretty red blouse that her niece had recently outgrown.

Come sit beside me, she called out. I cooked macaroni and beans for you, my girl.

Sapia stayed away. She never ever wanted to be caught pressed against those sour-sweet smelling breasts again. She watched Bianca from afar and couldn't be coaxed into having supper with her and Papa. Even the garlic and tomato smells from the kitchen couldn't entice her to join the adults. Bianca was kind enough to leave a plate of food out for her on a chair. Eusapia waited to grab it until she was sure she couldn't be cornered.

Fortunately, she did not let her desperate need for love draw her close to the woman. Only four or five months after arriving,

Bianca walked out of the house without saying goodbye, and never once came back or even acknowledged that she had known Eusapia and her father.

No one came to replace Bianca. Papa declared that Eusapia was old enough to take care of herself. It's about time you learned what life is about, he said and followed up with a rough slap on the back.

Now that Bianca was gone, Eusapia missed her, especially the cooking. Apart from a few pieces of old bread, there was rarely much around to eat these days. Her father must have started taking his meals elsewhere. On the rare occasions when he brought home a chunk of meat or cheese, he ate most of it himself. If Eusapia begged for a sliver, he'd scream at her, though he did part with a few scraps. It was seldom sufficient to stop the growling and craving in her belly. A few times she managed to distract her father long enough to make off with the package of food as soon as he came home. The two sausages and the morsel of cheese would go a long way.

Her father bellowed with frustration. What the bloody devil, where is my stuff? Never suspecting a small child but assuming the package to have disappeared on his way home, he cursed and whizzed about like a crazed wasp, threatening to kill the scoundrel who stole his food. You won't get away with it, he screamed.

A wicked smile crossed Eusapia's face. Won't I? she sneered soundlessly as she sat crouched in a ball, safely hidden away from her father's fury, munching miniscule portions of sausage and cheese to draw out over days the luxury of not hurting with hunger.

Yet her stomach never felt full. On good days, neighbours gave her bits of the little they had. According to the seasons, Eusapia picked wild asparagus, stole into olive and almond groves for generous helpings, gorged on whatever fruits, seeds, nuts or vegetables she could get her hands on without being caught. She searched under trees and among thistles for a treat of mushrooms to supplement her meagre rations. Since nature didn't always cooperate, the child learned to sneak into other people's houses, figuring out quickly that the best bounty could be found in the imposing buildings of the city centre. There, food and hiding places were less scarce. The dexterity she had acquired getting away from Paola, and her ability to disappear and remain hidden away over long periods of time, came in handy now. It was an advantage too that she could talk to the dogs, donkeys, and even chickens and roosters of her area and that they seemed to understand and like her. They drew close without giving her away when it counted. She much preferred them to the hordes of boys and girls in the neighbourhood who, just a tad better off, mocked her clothes and called her names, shouting that her father was a scoundrel who kept whores in his home.

All the children goaded her. They pelted her with rotten tomatoes. A despicable young boy named Ugo joined in and once even smashed a particularly juicy fruit right into her face.

But Emilio was the worst. With the authority of a boy two years older than her, whose house was the best kept in the immediate vicinity, he cruelly mocked her, repeating what he had heard at home, You'll end up just like your papa's worthless whores.

In her rage, Eusapia could think of nothing but to get even. I'll pay your family a visit they won't forget, she decided right then and there. I'm not afraid of the whole vicious pack of you. No one will catch me. Eusapia snuck into Emilio's kitchen in the middle of the night to avoid detection. She quickly opened the big cupboard and in no time discovered a chipped pot hidden behind other pots on the top shelf, and in it a few small coins that Emilio's mother had squirreled away. Without hesitation, Eusapia grabbed the coins and stuffed them into the ripped-off sleeve of an old blouse she used as a bag for these occasions. She secured her loot with a strong knot, ran home and hid the coins in a shallow tin box she had taken from the house of a rich family. For complete protection, she stowed the valuable box in the hollow below the loose plank of wood under her bed of rags.

She had to laugh when she heard Emilio's mother scream and whack her son over the head just as Eusapia knew she would. In a house with nine disgustingly saintly sisters, he was the only suspect. But no matter how much the woman threatened him and beseeched Sant'Antonio, the money would not reappear. The poor woman could not even confide in her husband who knew nothing of her little stash of money. All those years of hard work and scheming to create this small measure of security — for nothing!

When Eusapia saw the woman's face turn bitter over the following weeks, she had moments of regret, never strong enough though to put the money back. Someday, these coins might save her life.

The person Eusapia liked most in the whole town was Lucia. Every time Eusapia saw her walk briskly toward a house to help deliver a child or assist in emergencies of one kind or another, Eusapia caught up with her. No matter how busy or how serious the task Lucia was rushing toward, she always made time to ask Eusapia how she was.

Can I come live with you, Lucia? Please. I won't bother you. I'll do whatever you say.

Oh my beautiful child, Lucia would respond, it's not possible. I'm never home. People call me day and night.

You won't even notice I'm there, Lucia, Eusapia pleaded, and her large eyes burned with eagerness.

You have your papa.

What could Eusapia answer to that?

I'm sorry, Sapia, Lucia added gently. You know there is no one else here to help deliver babies or carry out the more complicated tasks for the sick. Whatever time is left, I need to search for solutions for the many problems women here struggle with every day. That's the job I'm called to do. One day, you too will discover your passion and purpose in life. You're the most resourceful child I've ever met. Trust me, your life will be interesting.

Lucia gave her an encouraging pat on the back, then disappeared into a doorway that opened as soon as she approached, several hands pulling her inside with an urgency that made the six-year-old shudder. In her desperate need, Sapia concentrated on the closed door until she could see right through it and sensed the dying Signor Pellegrino stare back at her. He was half sitting half lying on his bed, supported by three pillows. Lucia began sponging his forehead, murmuring encouragement and prayers, trying to provide comfort. But Signor Pellegrino continued staring at Eusapia.

Do you want me to give a message to your mamma? he asked.

Yes, please. Tell her to come back.

Signor Pellegrino's lips pulled upwards as if in a smile. He trembled slightly. Then his head fell backwards. Eusapia lost contact with his eyes.

I'll never be able to thank you enough, Signor Pellegrino, Eusapia whispered, hoping that a message delivered directly by a soul passing over to the otherworld would be more effective than her daily pleas to her mother.

One day Eusapia broke into the empty house of Angela and Carlo, two children her age who lived near the centre of the town. It was like entering a wonderland. The sun shone timidly into the dark, smoky kitchen. The room seemed to say hello, come on in, sit down, make yourself at home. So did the whole house. Eusapia stayed longest in Angela's small space, separated from her brother's by a big cupboard. She buried her face in Angela's blanket and pillow. Who would believe it!? Barely a flea or bedbug and no horrible smell! A little cloth doll lay on the pillow. Eusapia pinched its arm. The doll didn't cry out as she half-expected it would. It was the first doll she saw up close. Angela's grandma had stitched it together from old rags and even made a blouse and a skirt for it.

Eusapia had been dumbstruck when she'd first heard about the grandmother and the doll a few months ago. Imagine sewing clothes for a doll. No one had ever sewn anything for Eusapia who was a living person. Lucia brought her second-, third- and mostly forth-hand clothes every so often from the richer houses in town. Those were the only clothes Eusapia ever owned.

She held the doll a while longer, but couldn't imagine what she'd do with it if it were hers. The brown rag ball appealed to her more. She threw it up in the air twice and caught it with surprising dexterity. She then fingered a few chalks and a slab of slate. She saw two books, which she picked up to examine. The one with the cross on the cover had to be a Bible. The other with a picture inside of a woman holding her own eyes on a small plate must be the story of Santa Lucia whose eyes were gouged out. Eusapia knew little about saints, but had always been eerily drawn to a painting in the house of Don Carmelo that depicted this saint holding in her hands a dish with her gouged-out eyes. Eusapia wanted to know how before her death Santa Lucia was given the gift to see without eyes and how in her afterlife she restored the sight of hundreds or even thousands of people. But the letters in the book meant nothing to Eusapia.

Looking at the books and holding them in her hands, Eusapia became curious. She guessed at the secrets they contained and marvelled at the lifelike drawings. She must have stared at the letters and black-and-white pictures for over an hour, too absorbed to notice the family return home. When the stairs creaked, she realised that Angela and Carlo were on their way up. She dove to the floor and disappeared under the bed without a second to spare. Rolled into a tight bundle to avoid detection, she listened to Angela hang up her school bag on a wooden peg.

Something stinks in here, Angela murmured. Luckily, supper was ready and Angela did not get to check out the source of the foul odour.

As soon as it felt safe, Eusapia crawled out from under the bed. She squeezed into a shaded corner of the staircase, making herself very small. In that way she could clearly see the mother,

15

father, children, grandmother and grandfather without being detected. Their quick prayer rang up toward her like a bell. She would have liked to be part of the noisy chatter and laughing that followed. No cursing. No swearing. A small heap of food for each and every one, and sounds that Eusapia associated with her mother and the angels in heaven, not with living people and certainly not with men. She couldn't get enough of this scene even though her stomach growled with hunger. When everyone had scraped their plates clean, the women cleared the table and washed the dishes.

Eusapia, who had lost track of time and danger, was forced to rush back under Angela's bed and stay there until the girl was fast asleep. Only then could she sneak out of the house and under the cover of darkness run back home, where she pretended the dirty, smelly rags on the floor were a bed as nice as Angela's.

Angela's grandmother made Eusapia think of her own nonna, who lived in the neighbouring village. She knew her face, but had never talked to her. When did Nonna last come to town to sell produce? Eusapia couldn't remember.

Stay away from that woman, her father had ordered so savagely that Eusapia didn't dare disobey him. Why did her father hate Nonna that much?

Don't go near her. Don't look at her. Don't ever smile at her.

So Eusapia hadn't. In time she only vaguely remembered she had a grandmother, especially after the trips to town stopped about two years ago. Sometimes Eusapia wondered if her grandmother had died but never tried to find out. Even now, she didn't want to know for sure.

Eusapia could handle the days. The nights were tougher. Even if her father's buddies didn't show up at the house, she slept in nervous fits. Monsters chased her without mercy up and down the stone steps through the ancient alleys of her neighbourhood. The place she knew inside out turned against her. Eusapia's legs buckled. But with just split seconds to spare before being torn to pieces, she'd suddenly find new energy and a way out into the hilly fields surrounding the town. She'd zigzag, barely ahead of sheep dogs and monsters through herds of sheep, and finally crash through underbrush. With the monsters still behind her, intent on finishing their job, just about to grab her, she'd vanish into the thick of a forest where she'd frenziedly burrow into holes, caves or hollow trees. Eusapia would wake up drenched in sweat, the salty liquid streaming down her body like storm water. Even awake she was not safe, eyes would stare out of the dark at her.

What do you want? she'd whisper, paralysed with fear.

We want you, the eyes told her, you, Eusapia. We will get you.

Go away. All of you, just go away. Please. Eusapia thrashed her arms about to make her body look scarier. Go away.

But the eyes remained, sometimes menacing, sometimes mocking. We'll get you, Sapia. You wait and see.

As much as the eyes frightened her, Eusapia was even more alert to sudden and immediate danger from real-life people. She trembled when she heard her father's distant cousin and his buddy drop by the house whenever they felt like it even if her father wasn't there and mostly at night. Eusapia tore herself away from the phantom eyes and immediately darted into one of her most secure hiding places just in time before one or another giant shadow made its ominous presence felt.

Little Sapia, yoo-hoo, where are you? She heard a thud where her bed of rags was, then angry swearing. Where are you, you little whore? Come out here. Now!

Eusapia held her breath, terrified that the thumping in her chest would give her away. After what seemed like an eternity, she heard heavy footsteps, then felt the vibrations of the floor become more distant until the door slammed and a scary quiet fell over the place. She remained in her corner for the rest of the night just to make sure. Some nights she was too tired to watch out for monsters and strangers. It happened that she woke up all naked on top of another naked body, sometimes underneath, big paws squeezing every part of her. She couldn't cry out for help. She'd gasp for air. Mamma, her heart would scream. Mamma, get me out of here. Most of all she hated the slimy substance she had to wipe off her face and body afterwards. Little crusty smears remained and reminded her in the morning how dirty she was. The rare time, she was able to block the monsters and heavy bodies out of her mind and transport herself into the safety of Angela's and Carlo's wonderland, joining the family at the supper table as if nothing bad were happening.

While Angela, Carlo, Emilio and a few other children in the neighbourhood went to school, Eusapia ran loose. At one point she had intended to go to school too. People had said that the teacher was boring and cruel at times, but that she made sure you learned how to read. So Eusapia had scrounged up her courage, put on some of her least dirty clothes with the fewest holes, and joined the kids in front of the school. As soon as the unnaturally light hawk eyes of the teacher met hers, Eusapia knew that there was no point trying. She might not be able to read books, but she could decipher thoughts swooping down on her as if they transformed into signals or pictures. The teacher's unspoken words pierced her heart and ripped her brain apart: You stupid foul-smelling little vermin. Without a second thought, Eusapia turned around and walked away.

Hey you, the teacher screeched after her, you there, come back here, learn something.

And then Eusapia heard Emilio, who had become friendlier lately, Give it a try, Sapia, it's not that bad.

But Eusapia knew it wouldn't work and bolted out of the school yard. That was as much as she ever saw of a school.

Roaming outside, she moved like a ghost, invisible to all but the most eagle-eyed people. She spent hours exploring houses, listening to hard-to-understand adult conversations, fascinated by the chorus of voices with their undercurrents of anger, passion, madness, outrage, love, faith, forgiveness and pity. Those feelings would wash over Eusapia, whip up her emotions, until she needed to seek relief in the open air, a good distance away from the town, among olive and almond trees. The branches of a few strong oaks, solitary remnants of forests from bygone eras, gave her much needed refuge.

Except for Lucia, who would never betray her secret, no one knew that Eusapia spent most of her time in trees. Life had taught the child many lessons early on. Don't let others know your business. Remain undetected. Trees provide the best hiding places. No one would expect anyone, especially a girl, to be hiding away on branches. Nobody had time to look either. Eusapia would always be thankful to Lucia for providing her with boys' shorts, which she wore underneath her skirt. This way, she could swing from branch to branch without her dirty or torn underwear showing. On days when she felt more confident and audacious than usual, she'd take off her skirt to hang it, out of sight, near the trunk on one of the higher branches. Nothing hindered her then to move freely, her small compact body whirling about with the agility of a monkey. She hung from branches and pulled herself up, manoeuvred into handstands and, while standing on her hands or head, snipped off leaves and twigs with her toes. Perfectly balanced and motionless for long intervals, she watched the world from places no one else dared to go.

No matter the pains she took covering her traces, she found her match in Emilio who, almost as agile as herself, began joining her on the branches.

How come you like me now? Eusapia wanted to know, focussing on his calm, determined eyes under remarkably strong, dark eyebrows.

But Emilio didn't know what she was talking about. He had long forgotten the nasty insults he had thrown at her without thinking. Just like her, he loved the breeze and freedom up in the trees. That was reason enough for him to seek her company.

Why aren't you in school? she asked.

There wasn't much to learn anymore, he responded, and they looked longingly out over the region toward the invisible ocean where they presumed mystery and action to begin.

I want to see the world, Eusapia said enthusiastically, after Emilio had described boats that crossed oceans, and told her about lands where elephants and tigers lived.

Me too, Emilio responded, I want to see the world. And I will see it because I'm going to make toys out of wood and sell them in big cities.

He broke off a dead branch and started carving.

I will make a present for you, Sapia.

A doll?

No.

Sapia watched him as little splinters flew in all directions.

Finally, he handed her a small cross. It's because your mother died. You should have something to remember her by. You can wear the cross on a string around your neck. See here, I made a hole on top for a piece of yarn.

From that day on Sapia always wore the cross, except at night when she wasn't sure what the monsters and heavy bodies would do to it.

Several days had passed when Eusapia asked, Did you ever make a doll?

No, but I will carve one for you.

Emilio made good on his promise. The doll he handed her a few weeks later had bulgy eyes, a funny pug nose, big lips and hard wavy hair. He had carved a jacket and skirt and high shoes.

She's a miracle, Emilio.

Eusapia threw her arms around him. It was the first time she touched someone voluntarily.

Thank you, Emilio, thank you a thousand times.

What impressed her most were the doll's limbs. Emilio had found some wire and made joints out of it. The doll could move her arms and legs and even sit down. You're a good toymaker, Emilio. I'm sure you will see the world.

Eusapia got hold of some fine string in Angela's home. She cut it into sections and attached those to the doll and to the crossed sticks Emilio had prepared for her. After a few weeks, she had learned to make the doll stand, bow, sit on a limb, walk along branches, and lie down.

It's called a marionette, Emilio told her as he admired the ease with which Eusapia got the doll to move. One day, I will make giant marionettes.

Dolls that come alive, Eusapia suggested and in her excitement already began to imagine the stories they would tell.

A few months after Eusapia turned ten, as she was sitting high up on a tree branch late in the afternoon, her stomach suddenly contracted with spasms and cramps. Her insides twisted into knots, and it seemed they were about to explode. The expected big boom never came. No unexplained hard cannon ball shot out of her. Instead, she suddenly felt this sickly warm liquid seeping out between her legs. When she checked, her boy's shorts were red. Eusapia gasped.

Blood! I'm dying. My God, I'm dying. I'm dying and I'm not even eleven. The thought was so frightening that loud wails escaped her mouth and hot tears spilled out of her eyes. She tumbled to the ground.

Where is Lucia?

It took what seemed hours to find Lucia across town where she attended another birth. When Eusapia banged at the door to talk to Lucia, people screamed at her. How dare you! They shut the door in her face and forced her to wait outside, even though it was night already.

When Lucia finally emerged, Eusapia was reduced to a whimper.

Over here, Lucia, behind the wall, quick, please. I'm dying.

Lucia, who had spent the last eighteen hours at the house with barely a pause, didn't hesitate a moment.

Sapia, what's wrong?

I'm dying. I'm bleeding to death.

Lucia examined the miserable child. Oh Sapia, you're not dying, you're becoming a woman. I didn't think there was any urgency telling you. Come back to my house, Lucia said, knowing that Rocco Palladino wouldn't miss his daughter. We'll clean you up and you can spend the night.

With this invitation, a bleak day turned into a special night. Eusapia felt as if she had a mother not only in heaven but one on earth as well.

When the boys started whistling behind her, Eusapia did not turn around or stop walking. Despite supposedly having turned into a woman from one day to the other, she continued climbing trees. She felt best high up on some sturdy branch away from the stares of men and boys. She wondered where this sudden attention was coming from. Why weren't they fawning over Angela like the women in the neighbourhood had done since she was an infant? There was a beautiful girl, taller and more delicate than her, with shimmering black hair and a complexion as smooth as silk. Eusapia looked at her own solid body. She would have liked her legs to be longer and stronger, but at least the constant practice from climbing had made them as deft as her arms and fingers. She wanted to grow more but knew she would remain short. She loved her large black eyes because everyone told her she had her mother's eyes. Her mouth, on the other hand, was just like her father's, with strong almost angular contours, sharp, unexpected, and somewhat questioning the rest of her which was soft and inviting. The women still fussed over Angela, and Eusapia would have joined them if that were in her nature, because Angela was the prettiest girl she had ever seen and also the sweetest. Not once had she made fun of Eusapia's clothes. She never called her names.

Many of the women had always felt a bit sorry for Eusapia, but when it came right down to it, they were wary of her and their uneasiness grew when she matured much earlier than their own daughters. The sudden stares of their husbands and the whistling of brothers and sons didn't escape them. Like her father, Eusapia seemed up to no good. It certainly wasn't her beauty that put a spell on the men's hearts and groins. As the power of the young girl grew, the women instinctively drew a protective circle around their own and prepared to defend it no holds barred. For the moment, it was easier for Eusapia to sit up in trees.

Though Eusapia liked it best when she had a tree all to herself, she didn't mind Emilio joining her. He could sit beside her for hours with a piece of wood he had brought with him, whittling it down into an animal or a bowl and minding his own business. He didn't turn when she swung through the trees and missed a branch or lost her balance trying to reach a sprig with her toes, nor did he call out when she crashed a few levels down through the leafage and branches. In his presence, her confidence grew. She moved more daringly, stretched more vigorously, knowing that she would succeed. Should the unimaginable happen and she were to fall, Emilio would be there to help without fuss.

Emilio climbed up beside her frequently, but not as often as he could have, now that he hardly went to school anymore. He had started making furniture at home and people gave him food or clothes and the rare time even money for the chairs, tables and other items they asked him to make or fix. Up in the trees was the place to create marionettes, utensils and jewellery. Eusapia, who was fascinated by his creations, loved to watch him.

One day, Emilio attached the doll he was working on to a branch beside him. He turned to Eusapia and said, You have the biggest and most amazing dark eyes I've ever seen. They look like craters of volcanoes just about to erupt. I can see the fiery golden lava deep inside them. As Emilio talked, her eyes darkened for a moment and then the lava at the bottom started to mount and spew golden sparks.

I love you, Emilio said. He could not take his eyes off her.

His glowing face warmed some ice-cold spot in Eusapia. She moved closer to him and pressed a small kiss on his lips. That small kiss started an explosion of joy and horror in her, a swirling storm of pictures, Emilio's gentle eyes and the hurtful shadows in the nights that left traces of slime and humiliation on her. She started shaking.

But Emilio put his arms around her and said, It's okay, Sapia. You don't have to be afraid. I love you.

Eusapia relaxed, and when she felt his lips again, she was able to push the unsettling memories out of her mind for at least a few moments.

I'm going to marry you, Emilio said before he went back to carving, and Eusapia swung from branch to branch, her strong mouth softened by a rare smile.

When the news came a few weeks after her twelfth birthday that her father had been killed by brigands, Eusapia did not join in the wailing of the women.

She tried to close her ears to the incessant whispering around her. Yes, it's true they killed him. They wanted revenge because he betrayed them. They blame him for the incarceration of several of their peasant collaborators. Rocco was the one, they say, who gave their names to the authorities.

Eusapia didn't care what anyone said. Not a single tear ran down her cheek. Nothing could add to the heavy sadness she carried around since she was separated from her mother at birth. She barely noticed Angela's mother coming by with black clothes for her to wear at the funeral, and some almonds and dried apples to munch on so she wouldn't faint from weakness and hunger. The woman took the girl into her arms, full of pity, and held her for what seemed a long time, even though Eusapia stood unresponsive and stiff as a board. At the funeral, Eusapia was pulled along and stood, sat or knelt like the people around her, paler than usual but without feeling. It's not normal the way she acts, the wailing and agitated women said. Immune to their judgement, Eusapia only started to panic when they speculated that her father had taken her soul with him. Maybe that's why she couldn't say goodbye to him. In the craters of her eyes, the sad shimmering turned into angry brooding without words, without precise thoughts, but so intense she could scarcely move or see. She only noticed being brought to a house that wasn't her own when she arrived and was pulled into an unfamiliar room.

Your nonna will take care of you.

Her nonna? So she was still alive.

When Eusapia looked into Nonna's bleary, crusted eyes and saw only resentment at the extra burden being placed on her, Eusapia knew at once what a terrible mistake this was. Old age had lodged in the woman's joints, causing such pain and inflammation that she dragged herself around like a cripple. Her rattling, raging bones refused to obey, turning the simplest tasks into challenges. The years seemed to have filled every inch of her with bitterness.

The only place for Eusapia to sleep was in her grandmother's room. Lucia had collected some old but clean blankets and helped the old woman lay them on the floor near the window. Nonna spread two patched-up covers over them and placed a small sack of hay as a pillow on one end, which certainly beat the dirty pile of rags Eusapia was used to. But the unfamiliarity of her situation left her desolate. The stink and squalor of her father's lodgings had not prepared her for the sweetish urine smell in the room or the rasping breath beside her.

Lying sleepless on the blankets, the events of the last few days finally hit her. She felt as if someone had knocked her out. No tears came to provide relief. If truth be told, she did not miss her father much. She couldn't miss him because he had been absent most of the time, and when he was around behaved as if she didn't exist. But he had been her father. Until a few days ago, she at least had a father. Now she was alone. The grandmother didn't really count. With her father's threats still ringing in her ears, Eusapia felt guilty just talking to the woman even while living under her roof. So she kept out of her way. All of a sudden, she remembered her treasure box with the money she had taken a couple of years ago from Emilio's house, and the other little mementos she had lifted from places she inspected: two shiny rings, a silver spoon with a swan at the end, a small mirror, and different types of buttons.

She had to get this box before someone discovered it. She got up without a squeak and tiptoed by her grandmother whose noisy snoring reassured her. Quietly, she opened the door, grabbed Nonna's woollen shawl and started out toward her old house. It would be a long journey. She knew her grandmother's village because over the years Eusapia's wanderings had brought her to all the neighbouring villages. Just outside her grandmother's village were a few strong old oak trees she liked and visited when she felt up for some vigorous exercise. To get there, she had to use a good part of the morning just for the trip. It would take her at least three hours to go back to her home, then another three hours to return to her grandmother's. Luckily, Eusapia was not scared outside. It was in closed rooms that harm came to you, not in the open air where you could run, and trees and bushes offered cover if you needed it. She sprinted through the night for fear someone might discover her box before she got the chance to retrieve it.

When she finally arrived at her old place, she went directly to the nook where she had hidden her treasures. There was the box, untouched and in all its secret splendour. Eusapia clutched it to her chest as if it were her twin soul in need of protection. Her treasures might keep her alive someday. After a hurried journey back to her grandmother's, she stopped close to the house and caught a glimpse of Nonna shuffling about the kitchen. Curses exploded through the slightly open door. Even though an octave higher than her father's barks, they sounded just like his. Eusapia slipped into the house without being seen and stowed her box away out of Nonna's reach, high up on a beam. Once the box was safe, she almost cried with relief. She didn't care that her grandmother screamed at her when Eusapia entered the kitchen.

Where have you been? the woman screeched. Then without waiting for an answer, she ordered, Make the coffee.

I don't know how.

The old woman slammed her iron pan around. When Eusapia didn't move, Nonna growled, Then prepare the dough for the bread.

But Eusapia didn't know how to do that either.

By now the woman was shrieking. A stray dog is worth more than you. Is there anything you know how to do?

After a week of daily escapes during which Eusapia ran off to find comfort in her trees, the old woman had had enough. Why should I feed a lazy mouth like you? You're just like your father. Get out of my house and don't come back.

Eusapia snuck one more time back into the house to recover her box. She also took her grandmother's only necklace and two small old knives with her.

Through Emilio, Eusapia was informed that a new family had moved into her father's house.

Crap, where am I supposed to live? Eusapia screamed, walking instinctively toward Angela's house.

As she had learned from spying on neighbours that crying could be more effective than cursing, big tears began to nestle in the corners of her eyes. She could only hope that Angela's mother would again take pity on her as she did after Eusapia's father died.

When Eusapia knocked on the door and the mother answered, Eusapia looked at her with moist eyes and said, Nonna doesn't want me to live at her house anymore.

The mother invited Eusapia in, and the compassion in her voice loosened a hard spot in the girl and unleashed floods of tears.

Angela, the mother said to her daughter who had joined them, Why don't the two of you go to your room until it's time to eat?

Eusapia didn't let on that she had been in this room before. Strangely, it felt like the first time. Angela showed Eusapia her doll and her books, and read the story of Santa Lucia to her. Eusapia then confided to Angela that Nonna had kicked her out. When tears started forming in Angela's eyes and Eusapia saw the shattered pieces of her life mirrored back, her own tears began flowing again, and this time all the pain and grief of the last years and days poured out. The girls sat beside each other weeping disconsolately. Despite being caught up in the moment, Eusapia, who had learned to remain aware of her surroundings at all times, caught the serious undertones in the low voices of the mother and grandmother downstairs.

Just when the girls were called for supper, Lucia arrived at the house and Eusapia had to tell her that Nonna didn't want her anymore.

Why? Lucia asked.

Because I can't make coffee and I don't know how to cook, and I don't know how to do anything.

Angela's mother could teach you.

I'm not going back! Eusapia howled. I'm not going back to that horrible woman.

Eusapia started shaking and her face turned blue. As the fit progressed, she remembered that it might be better if she cried. But she couldn't cry anymore. She just shook and turned blue and white.

Let's have supper, Angela's mother said. Why don't you stay, Lucia, if we all share, there should be enough for everyone.

Eusapia couldn't believe that her dream of sitting down at a table for a real meal with people she liked came true. For once she was not looking in from the outside. A smile crossed her face. She wanted this supper to last forever. But when the father pushed his chair back and stood up, there could be no clearer signal that her moment of happiness had come to an end. Everyone got to their feet and the women started clearing the table. Once again the girls were sent to Angela's room. The whispered discussions floating up the stairs left no doubt in Eusapia that the women were about to determine her fate and set a new course for her life.

Do you want me to show you how to write? Angela asked. She didn't wait for Eusapia to respond. Here. She drew a very neat and clean letter on the blackboard, This is an E. That's how your name starts, and then she continued writing the whole name, E-u-s-a-p-i-a, sounding the letters out for the girl beside her. Now you copy it, she said and placed the chalk into Eusapia's hand. Look here, this is how you're supposed to hold the chalk with the middle finger, the index finger, and the thumb. See.

Eusapia's first try was a screeching failure. But she persevered and wrote, painstakingly, one letter after the other.

Not bad, said Angela, after it had taken Eusapia ages and an enormous effort to complete her task. Now do it again.

Eusapia, who did not like to be told what to do, hesitated for only a second before starting over again. E-u-s-a-p-i-a. She examined the letters. They were less crooked than in her first try. In fact, they were passably straight. Write Palladino, Eusapia said, and marvelled at the neat writing that Angela produced before her eyes. Eusapia copied. She wrote her name a second time. Then first name and family name together. She memorised the letters, the image of her name. She wiped the blackboard clear and filled it up again. Eusapia Palladino. Still a bit uncertain, but without mistake.

You're a good student, Angela said, and Eusapia wished she could make up for all the lost time. She suddenly wanted to be able to read and write.

The lesson ended when Angela's mother called the girls down.

Eusapia, Lucia said kindly, remember the Migaldis who lived in our town until about three years ago when they moved to Naples. You certainly knew Ugo. I don't think he is more than a year younger than you. They mentioned in their last letter a nice couple, the Cattalanis, who are looking for a young girl to take in. I'll see what arrangements can be made. In the meantime, you can stay at my place.

Thank you, Lucia, Eusapia said, and was relieved, although now that she had spent a few hours in an actual family, a seed of hope that Angela's mother might like her enough to keep her had taken root in her and grown out of proportion. She tried not to show her disappointment. She was lucky to be allowed to stay at Lucia's. No one treated her better.

When Lucia was out working, Eusapia went roaming as before. But she also spent time practising her letters on a slate that they retrieved from Lucia's bedroom cupboard. Her name started to look better and she wrote it faster and faster. She asked Lucia to write other words for her. Mamma. Lucia Trapani. Heaven. Trees. Emilio. Napoli. Angela. Dog. Cat. Bird. When Lucia wasn't too tired and had a few minutes, she would teach her how to read. She also taught her the numbers and to those, Eusapia caught on as if she were born knowing them. Within a short time, she could write down without hesitation any number Lucia mentioned, and was able to add and subtract as fast as Lucia.

Some days, Eusapia was invited to Angela's house for supper. With Angela's help, her reading improved. Eusapia's almost perfect visual memory and her talent for filling in blanks were of great help. After a few tries, Eusapia haltingly read the story of Santa Lucia and her gouged-out eyes that Angela had read to her on their first evening together.

Eusapia wanted life to continue just as it was. But the preparations for her move to Naples progressed. With the unstoppable approach of her departure, she became apprehensive. She snapped when Lucia asked her to help sort through clothes that acquaintances of hers had donated. Eusapia didn't want the clothes because she didn't want to pack. She didn't want to leave. This town was the only place she had ever known. The few people she cared about lived here.

I don't want to leave, she screamed.

Eusapia, Lucia said seriously, I know it's hard, but believe me, your future is not here. It's in the city. One day you'll understand.

What's there to understand? Eusapia shouted back. You don't want me.

You don't belong with me. There is no future for you here.

Emilio is going to marry me.

Emilio!?

Eusapia could see the thoughts running through Lucia's head. She knew that Lucia had a soft spot for Emilio. She had overheard her say to his mother that Emilio's heart was made of gold and his hands worked miracles.

You don't want him to marry me?

My dear child, it doesn't matter what I want or think. Life can be very complicated and very cruel.

Lucia didn't say that it would be over Emilio's mother's dead body that Eusapia would marry her son. But even at twelve, Eusapia caught the drift. Unable to close her eyes and ears any longer, she absorbed truths she had been confronted with all her life but had never accepted until now.

When am I leaving? she asked with as much dignity as she could muster.

The day after tomorrow, first thing in the morning.

Eusapia spent the next day in her favourite tree. When Emilio climbed up beside her, she forced herself to smile. From her pain, heavy golden sparks shot one more time into her eyes, jumped over to Emilio and ignited fires in his dark pupils.

Don't go, Sapia.

You know I have no choice.

When their lips locked, their kiss left a burning seal of love in their hearts that would soothe and hurt for months to come. As much as their young bodies clung to dreams of certain reunion in the future, they could not push away premonitions and glimpses of a grimmer reality. This goodbye was final.

It was still dark when Eusapia hoisted herself up on an old cart the next morning and was carried away in the midst of crates filled with earthenware. She knew that Emilio was up in the tree they called their own, watching her leave. Though she didn't look back a single time, his face and his body were the only images she saw and took with her on her journey into the unknown.

Naples, Italy, 1866-1868

2

EUSAPIA LOOKED UP AT THE SKY as the old driver directed his mule and cart through the countryside. The miles and miles of brilliant blue sky and the rattling motion of the cart almost hypnotised her. The only white spots in the stretch of blue, two small gauzy clouds, floated down to cover her. As they grazed her face and body, her remaining tears evaporated and the heaviness that had squeezed her lungs lifted away. Eusapia yawned and stretched on the sack of hay that had been placed in the cart for her. Before she closed her eyes, she saw Emilio's face one last time and took it as a sign of good luck. Naples would turn into the adventure they had been waiting for all their lives, and she would be the first to embark on it.

When sleep finally overcame her, the customary nightmares didn't rear their ugly faces. Far from sending her back to dreadful moments of her past or propelling her into adventures for which she wasn't ready, her dreams unexpectedly opened doors to a blissful universe where her mother took care of her. Eusapia slept so soundly that night fell and the cart stopped without waking her. The driver lifted down the one crate he had to deliver at this out-of-the-way place, then drew a cover over her and the rest of the crates, relieved to save the money for a bed. By the time she woke up, they were already on their way again.

Remembering the small basket of food Lucia had handed her just before leaving, Eusapia devoured the chunks of bread and cheese with such greed that within minutes she had nothing left for the rest of the voyage.

She pulled the cover to the side and continued to lie on her back, staring up at the blue sky and daring it to bring her peace, her journey interrupted only for pee breaks and sips of water. For a few more hours, the air smelled fresh and familiar as if she were still in Minervino. But insidiously the air changed. The houses multiplied and stood closer together. The wind gained strength, whipping together smells and stinks that alternately tantalised and repelled her. Shadows from rows of houses fell on her. When the cart entered further into the city and the walls tightened around her, Eusapia wanted to throw up. Even now though, the tears did not come.

The Migaldis were waiting for her. Two young round-faced boys came running to the cart as soon as it stopped. The older brother Ugo whom she had known in Minervino followed close behind.

Sapia, Sapia, they shouted, dragging her eagerly by her arms and hands through the courtyard and up the stairs to the Migaldis' third-floor apartment.

Did you bring the soul of Minervino with you, Sapia? And the golden heart of Lucia Trapani? Signora Migaldi asked the moment she laid eyes on her and gave her a big hug.

Eusapia wondered why the woman had tears in her eyes.

You must be hungry, Signora Migaldi said and brought her to the table where she placed a heap of macaroni. But before Eusapia could take a bite, Signora Migaldi, starved for news from her home town, continued with her questions. How is everyone in Minervino? Did Signor Pellegrino really die? What about the Foggettis? Did they leave for America?

Eusapia hadn't heard of anyone moving to America or even just to the next village in the last months. Except for her, everyone had stayed put. But wanting to give some news, she said eagerly, The school has been hit by lightening. And, my God, Signora Bevilaqua gave birth to the fattest baby girl anyone has ever seen in Minervino. And did you hear that fearsome ghosts are haunting the Rubino house, and twenty sheep disappeared in one single night from the fields just outside town?

At bedtime, Eusapia jumped into bed without washing herself. Signora Migaldi didn't intervene though her sons had strict instructions to wash their hands several times a day since the cholera had taken so many lives the year before. Nothing bad could come from Minervino. She stood lost for a moment, an unexpected wave of homesickness rolling over her, then, recovering, she dunked a small cloth into the water basin and wiped the worst grime off Eusapia's face, hair and hands, relieved that the girl didn't object. Good night, my girl. Sleep tight.

Eusapia lay in a real bed, the one usually occupied by the second youngest of the boys, Antonello, who was bunking with his brother for the night. Despite the tiring journey, she was wide awake. She wanted to stay forever in this house where everyone knew Minervino and the people who lived there. Even Ugo, whom she remembered only for throwing a rotten tomato into her face, treated her as if she were part of the family. It occurred to her that she might have to pray if she wanted her wish to stay with the Migaldis to come true. Angela had told her that you had to say your prayers every night. Angela wouldn't even think of going to bed without kneeling down to pray. Eusapia, who had prayed only a few times in her life when nothing but a miracle seemed able to save her, left her bed and knelt down as she had seen Angela do.

Holy Mary, Mother of God, she said. If she had to pray, she wanted to pray to the Virgin Mary because that felt like talking to her mother. Let me stay here, she pleaded. But even as she prayed she recognised the foolishness of her hope. She would be sent to this other couple, Gennaro and Grazia Cattalani, whether she agreed or not.

As if to console her, the voice of the Virgin Mary — or maybe it was her mother's — said, My dearest Sapia, don't worry, I'll watch over you. Eusapia was happy to hear her mother's voice. She stretched almost dreamily. She wondered whether everyone who lived in nice houses and had real beds could hear beautiful soothing voices.

The minute the Cattalanis entered the house, Eusapia tensed up. Her skin bristled. The tall, elegant figure of Grazia Cattalani caught her off guard. As soon as their eyes met, she knew that Signora Cattalani had hoped for a girl like Angela. In one split second, the disappointment of the signora swept down with a quick movement of her eyelids and lashes, covering the woman's eyes for that brief moment before she looked at Eusapia with forced excitement, as if nothing had occurred.

My sweet, sweet doll, she exclaimed in a melodious Italian instead of the Neapolitan dialect that was so much like her own in Minervino. She embraced the girl with the awkward effusiveness of women not used to children but desperate to gain their approval. In another dimension, Eusapia sensed the probing eyes of Signor Cattalani in the background. When he came to greet her, he extended a smooth hand that glistened with droplets of sweat. She winced. She did not dare look up into his face for fear of finding a treacherous glint in his eyes. Her increasing alarm triggered memories that she wanted to remain buried in the past. Her heart throbbed and the blood raced through her arteries and veins in a turmoil she had not experienced for a while. In her panic, she whirled around and stormed away from these strangers into the bedroom where she threw herself on Antonello's bed and tightly wrapped herself into the blanket. It took interminable rounds of supplications from Signora Migaldi before Eusapia would allow her to pull the blanket off her face.

I don't want to live with them, she snarled.

No argument convinced her otherwise.

Only hours later, when the youngest boy Pietro went up to sit beside her, did she slowly calm down.

Why don't you join us, Eusapia?

The girl sighed and the boy threw his arms around her.

Come on, Eusapia. We have macaroni with meat, Pietro said, not dried cod or tripe, but beef, he added as if that explained everything.

Maybe it did. Unable to resist the warmth in his voice, she finally stood up, pulling and stroking her hair into place with her hands. When the two arrived at the supper table, the conversation stopped for a moment, but immediately swelled up again to cover the tension that eerily rose from the silence. Eusapia sat down. Contrary to her voracious appetite the day before, she listlessly picked up a single macaroni with her thumb and index finger, then dropped it again. She continued this for a while before the rare piece found its way into her mouth. Gone

41

was the animated laugh and talk of the previous night. She sat as if under a dark spell, waiting for more bad things to happen.

The next morning, Eusapia refused to open her eyes even when Signora Migaldi pleaded with her.

I told you I don't want to see them again, she muttered.

Please, Sapia. Think of Lucia who went out of her way to find a home for you. Open your eyes, please.

Lucia's name brought Eusapia back to reality. Lucia would have given her the moon if she could. But no one can give the moon. The Cattalanis were the best Lucia could do.

Remember, life is not easy, she had cautioned Eusapia in preparation of her move to Naples, and to boot had added, It's good you're so strong, you'll manage. Eusapia liked the fact that Lucia thought she was strong.

Okay then, she said to Signora Migaldi and determinedly sat up. I'll go with them.

Signora Migaldi looked at her with a mixture of approval and apprehension. Your mamma Michela would be proud of you. Did you know what her favourite saying was? No? God helps those who help themselves. Don't ever forget that.

Eusapia looked at her in dismay. Then why did Mamma die, Signora Migaldi? She didn't help herself?

For a moment, Signora Migaldi was left speechless. After composing herself and praying that her spiritual instinct would not abandon her now, she said with a conviction that precluded contradiction or a request for additional explanation, When God calls, you follow his call. Amen.

Eusapia tagged dejectedly along behind the Cattalanis and let herself be pushed into their carriage. She answered their questions with yes or no, nothing else.

She needs new clothes, Grazia Cattalani said to Gennaro Cattalani, staring at the shapeless calico dress that at one time must have been a specific colour, but had turned a washed-out grey long before Eusapia first received it.

She needs a bath, Gennaro answered.

First thing when we get home, Grazia agreed.

Though catching the drift of their fast-spoken Italian, Eusapia listened impassively as if the person who didn't measure up was a stranger.

The doors of the Cattalani home had scarcely opened and closed again behind them when the two housekeepers were asked to prepare a bath for the signorina. It didn't escape Eusapia that the two women secretly made faces and winked at each other, with one of them making a show of holding her nose behind Grazia Cattalani's back.

The younger housekeeper started boiling water.

I'll wash your hair, Grazia said.

But Eusapia wouldn't budge.

Come on, Eusapia, Grazia coaxed, with a touch of impatience that gave her voice an unexpected edge. She reached for Eusapia's hand.

No, screamed Eusapia, who had never taken a bath in her life. No, no, no.

Everyone stared at her in shock. The housekeepers gawked with open mouths, Grazia with tears of exasperation in her eyes, and Gennaro Cattalani with cruel curiosity.

Move it, Eusapia, he ordered. Now!

43

There was nowhere Eusapia could run. The trap had slammed down as if on a rat.

Now! Gennaro repeated with a sharpness that finally jolted her into moving.

The older housekeeper made an attempt to take the girl's blouse and skirt off her body, using rags like gloves so that she wouldn't have to touch Eusapia's stained garments. It took both housekeepers to finish the job and force Eusapia into the tub. Without warning they pushed her head under water to make sure she got a thorough washing. Eusapia screamed and thrashed about until the strong arms of the older housekeeper pinned her down. She went limp. With an expression of revulsion, the younger housekeeper started scrubbing.

Grazia fussed over the well-washed and dried girl. What beautiful hair! She petted Eusapia's head with an air of satisfaction. Look at you, all neat and clean, and smelling good. Don't you feel much better? Grazia asked.

Eusapia, who still felt violated and humiliated, didn't respond. She hid her eyes so that the woman in front of her wouldn't see the rage in them.

Look at me, Eusapia.

Stubbornly, the girl stared at the floor. Grazia sighed. She decided to show Eusapia her room. They went up the stairs and turned left. The room was bright, the walls painted full of pink roses on a gold and light-yellow striped background, the most beautiful room Eusapia had ever seen. It didn't matter. From the moment she first laid eyes on the Cattalanis, she knew this arrangement could not work. The more she had to deal with them, the more she hated them. Why, she couldn't explain, and she didn't care. Since she couldn't stand the Cattalanis, Eusapia took no pleasure in anything to do with them. She looked gloomily around the room. Pictures of saints hung on the wall on both sides of the bed just like in Angela's room, only these saints were unfamiliar.

Following her gaze, Grazia said, San Gennaro and Santa Restituta. She handed Eusapia a clean, white nightshirt and motioned for her to put it on.

Without anywhere to hide or disappear to, Eusapia changed, her face flaming red and her fingers stiff with embarrassment. Grazia bent down to press a kiss on her head, then proceeded to hug her. But Eusapia couldn't bear to be touched another time. Brusquely she jerked away.

Good night, Grazia, she said in an effort to appear less rude. Thank you.

Slightly mollified, Grazia remained beside the bed as the girl slipped under the sheets. Eusapia clenched her teeth to avoid another explosion that would cause more upset. But she wanted nothing more than to kick this woman out the door. At some point, she'd have to scream to release the mounting pressure in her. Go away, she wanted to shout. Just leave me alone. Grazia sat on the bed wondering what there was to say to a child like this. She trembled with a sudden sense of dread. Eusapia, who watched her through half-closed eyes, saw disappointment and rejection settle in the woman's eyes. She wanted to pull the sheets over her head, but was afraid to cause another scene.

Good night then, she heard Grazia whisper, sleep tight.

A few seconds later, she saw the woman stretch to her full height, turn slowly, leave the room and close the door without a sound.

At seven thirty in the morning, Naples was alive. Carriages and carts rumbled over the cobblestones. Horses neighed. Whips cracked through the air. Men's voices spurred on the horses and donkeys, shouted greetings, told jokes, gave orders, related news. Here and there a song took flight and floated up to the rows of windows above, teasing those Neapolitans who couldn't tear themselves out of bed, or echoing down to those sleeping outside in the midst of all the ruckus on steps or stretched out near walls. The sun squeezed through the cracks of the wooden shutters into Eusapia's room.

She suddenly felt wide awake. Life was calling from outside. What was out there? What stories did the noisy voices want to tell? To her surprise, Eusapia heard the cackling of a chicken. And did she actually hear cows mooing somewhere not too far from her building? She would need to explore and uncover the secrets of this city. Emilio, the world is big. There is so much to learn. At that moment the door opened with a bang. The older of the two housekeepers barged in. Brusquely, she grabbed Eusapia by her right arm and dragged her through the room to the water basin. She took a rag, plunged it into the water and then got to work on Eusapia's face.

Don't touch me, Eusapia screamed.

The housekeeper held her tight, but had not counted on the ferocity of the girl. Eusapia yanked herself loose and grabbed the basin with both hands. In one well-calculated movement she splashed the water at the woman, who was unable to dodge fast enough. The dripping housekeeper, livid with rage, took hold of Eusapia's hair and pulled it with all her strength. By now the girl was completely incensed. She threw the empty wash basin on the bed. With her second arm free, she extricated herself and went on the attack like a fury, her nails digging into the woman's flesh until blood ran down her arms and face. The racket brought the second housekeeper, as well as Grazia and Gennaro running into the room. Gennaro tore into the tangle in front of him with surprising strength to pull woman and girl apart, an almost impossible task since neither was willing to stop what they had started. The second housekeeper held on to the first and Grazia, with the help of her husband kept the girl from storming back. Grazia sent the two women and her husband downstairs.

Get dressed, she said to Eusapia, who mechanically changed into her clothes.

With her appetite destroyed, the girl stared at the food on the table sick to her stomach. But having gone hungry too many times, she was unable to leave anything edible uneaten. Under Gennaro's and Grazia's astounded stares, she stuffed her mouth full of bread and almost choked on it. Her mouth went dry. Her occasional responses to the Cattalanis' questions would invariably be received with a rather curt Excuse me? What did you say?

Don't talk with your mouth chock-full, Gennaro finally snapped. How is anyone to understand a word you say!

When Eusapia defiantly continued stuffing her mouth, he stood up, threw his arms up in disgust, and left the table.

Rot in hell, Eusapia thought. And you, Grazia, join the bastard wherever he goes.

But Grazia said quietly, Wipe off your mouth with the napkin.

Red-faced, Eusapia complied. She had secretly watched Gennaro wipe his mouth after the meal with a strange piece of cloth, something she had never seen in Minervino. So instead of wiping her mouth on her arm or sleeve, she dabbed her lips just like Gennaro had done moments earlier.

When the housekeepers finished clearing the table, Grazia said, I have to arrange schooling for you. How good is your reading?

What was Eusapia supposed to answer to that? Except for the few lessons from Angela and Lucia, she'd never had any occasion to read.

Not good, she answered sullenly.

Grazia had already installed herself at the table with the newspaper and a rather large book she called the Tale of Tales, surprised that Eusapia had never heard of it.

You prefer news or stories?

Eusapia bit her tongue. How was she supposed to be able to read whichever if she struggled to understand Gennaro's and Grazia's foreign-sounding Italian no matter how exaggeratedly slow-spoken? Even in dialect, she'd be unable to piece the sentences together because she couldn't read, period, except for the smidgen she had been taught back home.

Why don't you read the first paragraph to me? Grazia interrupted the girl's brooding.

Eusapia stared at the letters. True, she had been able to read Angela's book in Minervino, but only by relying on her sharp memory and recognising the words that Angela had taught her. Thanks to her quick and intuitive mind, she had pieced together the rest. In contrast, Grazia's book was an incomprehensible jungle of black roots and leaves. The first sentence stumped her.

I don't want to read, Eusapia protested. I want to see the city.

Grazia, whose patience was stretched thin by now, lost her cool. What is wrong with you, Eusapia? People have to work.

People have to learn. Let's start over, she continued with a determined effort to regain her composure. Start reading, she ordered.

Eusapia bit her lips, scowling. She wouldn't start stammering in front of this woman.

It's a stupid book, she said after a tense few seconds and shoved it away.

Grazia gasped.

Tell me the truth, Eusapia. Can you read what's written here?

Eusapia wouldn't answer. Mind your own business, she mouthed silently.

Let's wait until tomorrow, Grazia said to cut the tension. Tomorrow, we'll start afresh

The older housekeeper had no intention of putting up with Eusapia. That girl will be the death of us all, Signora Cattalani, Eusapia overheard her screeching voice. You'd be so much better off without her. Please, plea-ease, think about it.

As Eusapia peeked unseen into the room, she caught the housekeeper demonstratively scratching her hair.

There are already more lice and fleas in this house than I've seen in my entire life. She's a hopeless cause.

After a short silence, Grazia said, Give her a chance. She had a hard life.

The girl, who listened carefully, decided that Grazia was trying to convince herself that the effort was worthwhile.

Eusapia snuck away. She quietly left the house. She had to see if the outside world was more tolerable. First, she memorised the façade and location of the Cattalani house, including the number, then the two houses beside and the three across to make sure she found her way back. As the street to the left of the house appeared livelier, she chose that direction, eagerly proceeding down the street. It didn't take thirty seconds before she was caught up in the hustle and bustle of the city. Finally, she could breathe. The pungent smells around her intoxicated her. She hadn't paid attention to the men whistling from the corners of the streets and from their carts.

I love you, Bella, one of them shouted, his arm up in the air to attract her attention, his smile exposing a mouth with most teeth missing. Hello, Baby, make me happy.

When she became aware of his calls and others, she reacted totally out of character, unchained almost. She waved at the men, then stuck out her tongue, and the men laughed as if she had paid them a compliment. Eusapia walked ahead, turning right and left. Suddenly there seemed to be less light and more shadows. She looked upwards, examining the high walls on both sides of the narrow street. She marvelled at the rows and rows of windows and balconies on walls that towered commandingly over narrow alleys. Catching occasional flecks of sky and rays of sun between the heavily hung clotheslines crossing the street from balcony to balcony, she frowned at the notion that people survived on streets with just fragments of blue and yellow. But no matter how much she missed her home town on its small hill and its open blue sky, ancient dwellings and alleys, and the simple elegance of the town's centre, a sudden exhilaration grabbed her and made her smile and chuckle. She skipped down the street like a child who had just received her favourite treat. Yet it was at this very moment that she shed the last bit of child in her, or maybe it was torn right out of her. This other person who suddenly sprang into action must have been cocooning in her for a long time without Eusapia knowing or understanding her. Who was this person who boldly entered into a foreign world and resolutely removed the last shackles of childhood? Where would her path lead? Who was she to become? Naples has been waiting for me, she declared as she plunged into her explorations.

It was dark when she found her way back to the Cattalani house without too much difficulty. As she had never been required to account for her whereabouts, she was unprepared for the uproar she had unleashed.

Where have you been? Grazia screamed as soon as she caught sight of the girl. Her eyes were red from crying. Gennaro is out looking for you with his driver. What were you thinking? It's not safe out there for a girl your age. Look at your shoes and clothes. They're caked with dirt. What happened?!

She waited for Eusapia to explain herself. But stubbornly, Eusapia kept silent. There was no way to explain to Grazia that she had always felt safer outside and that without sun, rain and wind she was not alive. Here in Naples, she was already in the thrall of new experiences. The faceless throngs of people, the multitude of horses and dogs, even the mountains of garbage, mud and refuse on streets or alleys held a precarious attraction for her. Grazia looked at the girl in despair, and for a moment, when Eusapia looked up into her red eyes, she wished their relationship could be different.

I'm sorry, she said, as she had heard Angela say to her mother after she'd chipped a plate by accident. I'm so sorry.

She saw Grazia's face soften a bit.

Go wash yourself in your room and get ready for bed. I will bring some bread and milk up.

Noise from the door drew their attention.

Go, Grazia whispered and, in an attempt to protect Eusapia from the wrath of her husband who had spent hours searching for the girl, sent her scurrying up the stairs.

Eusapia woke up with the first sounds of the city. It was as if the clamour were calling her out into the open. Within seconds she became fully alert. The house was still quiet. Eusapia slipped into her last change of clean clothes. She quietly made her way down to the kitchen, grabbed a piece of bread and a few grapes, then left the house without anyone noticing. When she felt the first timid rays of the morning sun on her, she screamed with joy. She hurried along the same path as the day before, trusting her unfailing memory, recognising each corner, each post, each gas light. If she had stayed at the house, she would have been forced to read in front of Grazia. Luckily, she was spared another round of humiliation.

At least someone has something to cheer about! a stranger crossing her way muttered. Did you win the lottery?

No such luck!

Eusapia wished she had won or at least had the money to buy tickets. But she felt grateful all the same because any day spent outside the Cattalani home was a great day. To move freely and push boundaries lifted her spirits. She could leave fear and frustration behind and trust that she'd find a place where she fit in. If the street turned out to be that place, so be it.

Through unfamiliar smells and territory, Eusapia advanced like a soldier, a heady feeling of conquest spreading from her heart to the extremities of her limbs. If her hometown had spit her out into this new world, she deserved at least to get the full taste of the strange excitement that filled Naples. The further afield she strayed, the noisier the streets, the bigger their lure. Women traded gossip, jokes and insults from one side of a street or one row of windows to another. Half-naked boys chased each other through the streets. Men and women crossed themselves for protection and good luck in front of the city's abundant shrines to the Madonna, and Eusapia followed their example. To keep the devils away, she said out loud to make it count. Small bakeries and stores selling leather goods, hats, or second-hand clothes lined the streets. Water, fruit and coffee vendors wandered about, taunting her with offerings she couldn't afford. Eusapia, who by now had eaten everything she had brought, slapped her stomach to dull the pain inside.

For the next several hours, and in honour of Lucia who she sensed watching her, she fought a mounting temptation to snatch food when she spotted a chance to do so undetected. Eusapia wanted to make Lucia proud. It was only when she saw a girl in rags, five-years old at the most, with eyes hollow from hunger, moving like a shadow, a lost soul already, staring at loaves of bread, that Eusapia questioned her noble intentions. Some circumstances call for intervention. She identified with this girl whose belly was so used to being empty it hurt without noise. In contrast to herself, this child would not challenge her fate. Unprepared to use her wits to get by, the girl would die, too weak and starved to put up a fight against disease. Hurts from past and present combined with Eusapia's rising indignation and, together with an intense compassion for the starving child, propelled her into action. With the agility of a seasoned thief, she grabbed a loaf from one of the stands in the street and made it disappear in a fold of her dress as if she had practised this manoeuvre all her life. Smiling brazenly at the shoppers and walkers around her, she strolled toward the girl without appearing to single her out.

Come with me, I have food, she whispered.

The child, who would have trusted a monster if it promised food, eagerly followed Eusapia into a quiet alley where few people passed through. They huddled together against a wall. The girl's eyes lit with wonder when she saw and smelled the bread. Eusapia broke a piece off for her.

What are you doing with my sister? the voice of a girl her own age rang accusingly through the alley. The girl approached rapidly, ready to fight, her eyes aflame with contradictory impulses of protectiveness, suspicion and plain hunger.

There is enough for the three of us, Eusapia said, pointing at the loaf.

The girl sat down beside her.

God, I need this, the girl said, surrendering, as Eusapia handed her a piece of bread.

Again it was dark when Eusapia arrived back at the Cattalanis. Another salvo of noisy reproaches descended on her, all originating from Gennaro's mouth, while Grazia's tight lips pressed together in punishing silence. Eusapia noticed right away though that the plate with her share of food had not been cleared from the table. Without explanation, she wolfed down the few morsels. With two pairs of eyes boring into her, she felt at a loss of what to do next. Despite sensing the need to give some sort of justification for her behaviour or at least an apology, Eusapia remained glowering silently, an angry burst of heat in her cheeks.

54

She had taken care of herself her whole life. Why after all those years was she required to justify her behaviour? What did the Cattalanis want from her?

Questions and accusations continued pouring down on her, infiltrating her skin, filling her to the brim with despair and rage. She knew she was supposed to answer, but she could not make out the meaning or even just the words of their questions. If she wanted to avoid doing something drastic, she had to get away. With a brisk movement, she spun around and raced up to her room, slamming the door behind her. Yet agitated spikes of conversation pierced through the heavy wood. Eusapia clamped her hands on her ears to block out the sounds. She had stomached all she could. Throwing herself on her bed, she found no peace. In vain she sought refuge in a world without distress and interference. Grazia did not come up to talk to her.

With the first hints of morning noises, Eusapia jumped out of bed, her toes and fingers prickling with the expectation of new excursions. An irrepressible urge to start moving overcame her. She rushed to find some clothes. Except for what she had worn the day before, not a single piece of clothing was in sight. The suitcase in which she had hidden away her treasure box under her few pieces of clothes was gone as well. It took her a few seconds to recover from that jolt. She would need to extract her box from wherever the Cattalanis or their housekeeper had hidden it. She put on yesterday's dress, trying not to notice how splotched and torn it was and that it needed washing and mending before being fit to be worn again. For a moment, she thought of Grazia, whose eyes would be red by the time Eusapia came home in the evening. If there were a way to avoid it, she would not hurt this woman. But to explain why she acted the way she did, she would have to look deep inside her heart and find words for emotions she didn't understand herself. I don't want to upset you, Grazia, she felt like saying, realising instantly that those words would never cross her lips. Why say them if she then charged ahead and did things that Grazia couldn't possibly condone or understand? Without noise, Eusapia went down the stairs. Like the day before, she entered the kitchen and crammed any fruit and bread she could find into the small basket Lucia had given her before her departure. She crept toward the main door. But there, on the red brocade chair beside the front door, sat Grazia, looking straight into Eusapia's eyes. To her left stood the suitcase with the treasure box.

I can't allow you to go out, Grazia said. We have to talk. Come on, we'll eat and talk.

But Eusapia was finished talking. Anything she'd let out of her mouth would only offend and upset.

I want to leave, she uttered curtly. She hadn't meant to sound rude, but she did.

Grazia's face was as pale as that of Emilio's mother when Eusapia had taken her coins.

For the last time, please, be reasonable, Grazia pleaded.

Despite knowing that the woman meant her no harm, the trapped-rat feeling came over Eusapia like a fever. Leave me alone, she shrieked.

Grazia shrunk into herself, then got up from her chair as if in pain and looked at the girl in despair and horror.

If you leave now, take your belongings with you and don't come back, she said in a choked-up voice.

But Eusapia heard the words as if they had been screamed at her. Slowly, she advanced toward the woman and the front door. She picked up her suitcase.

Eusapia . . . , she heard Grazia's voice in a feeble attempt to hold her back.

Without answering, without looking back, Eusapia walked by the chair in the entry, out the door, and away from the place that was supposed to have been her new home.

The girl hastened to find a hidden corner to make sure she still had her treasure box. Beware of thieves, she told herself, don't let anyone see you, hurry before anyone realises you have money. Luckily the box was inside the suitcase, seemingly untouched. None of the money was missing. Forgetting her caution for a second, Eusapia threw her arms into the air in relief. There was also a new dress, neatly folded on top of her freshly washed old clothes. Grazia must have picked it up for her and bought the few pieces of undergarments at the bottom of the box. At the sound of voices close by, Eusapia slammed the suitcase closed. After just a few days in Naples, she was already suitably impressed by the sheer number of pickpockets and their highly developed skills, not like in Minervino where she would have been hard-pressed to name anybody besides herself who stole in open daylight. You can't be too careful in this city. If you have any possessions, protect them.

She proceeded carefully down the street, set to defend the money in her box if necessary. Even a beaten-up old suitcase could be a temptation to someone. Cleverly, she swung it to and fro like a toy of no importance, a ruse she had to abandon after a few steps since the box was too heavy for that. While walking, she weighed her options. The only viable possibility was to find the Migaldis. As friends of Lucia's and former citizens of Minervino like herself, acquaintances of her mother to boot, they would not turn their backs on her. How would she be able to find their house? She had no sense of direction yet. When she was brought from Minervino to Naples, she had felt so dispirited on the last portion of her trip that her eyes were stuck to the floor of the cart or closed. There were no buildings or street corners for her to remember because she had refused to see any. She had a vague notion that the name of the street was Cairoli, with maybe another word attached. On her way to the Cattalanis, the surroundings again failed to register. That's why she had no way now of knowing where to go.

Eusapia charged ahead blindly, hoping it was the right direction, but feeling it wasn't. A sudden cold gust of wind made her shiver. She looked up. The sky was black. She was still watching the clouds when big drops of rain began to fall.

She found shelter in a church, remaining close to the entry, crossing herself several times like the woman beside her, but without following her to one of the wooden benches for the poor where you could sit without having to pay for your seat. Standing there with barely a shred of hope, she clung to this shred until unsteadily but with surprising tenacity it grew again and her survival instinct took over. I'm alive, and I'll stay alive, Eusapia proclaimed as if to challenge her fate.

She left the church, studying the to-and-fro. She hesitated to ask any of the men for directions. Their whistling and calls made her suspicious. Not even the women could be trusted when you had valuables but no place to go. Nibbling on a piece of bread, she continued walking as if she knew where to go. She marched determinedly for five, six miles without recognising a single building. Suddenly, though, she was back at buildings she had seen before and realised she had been walking in a circle. But entering some grimy, putrid-smelling alley, she stopped. Instead of taking special precautions, she perked up. This must be close to the place where she had met the two girls the previous day. Again she rushed ahead almost blindly, hurried now, hopeful. Yes, there was the place! Eusapia started running. And yes! There was the younger of the two girls, Maria, rushing toward her. She looked at Eusapia with huge happy eyes, but without asking for anything. Yesterday had been her lucky day. At five years old, she had already learned that luck didn't come two days in a row.

You've come to visit me? she said, grabbing Eusapia by the hand.

Sort of, Eusapia answered. I need to talk to your sister Anna.

I'll find her for you, Maria offered and disappeared. A few minutes later, she came back with Anna.

I have some food, Eusapia said.

The two girls gaped at her as if she were playing a trick on them.

Where did you get it from? Anna asked.

From where I live.

You don't look that rich, Anna stated, examining Eusapia's clothes, which were almost as bad as her own. Are you?

I wish! I do have some food today but nowhere to go. The people I lived with have thrown me out.

The three girls found a sheltered corner to eat and figure out how to go about the next steps.

It's a fea-east, Maria chanted, smacking her lips contentedly and full of wonder. There was enough food for the three of them, very small portions to be sure, but not rotten and not mouldy. Thank you Father God, Maria called out, thank you Virgin Mary, thank you, Baby Jesus, thank you Sant'Antonio, thank you Santa Teresa, thank you dearest Eusapia.

The girls talked and laughed together as if they hadn't a worry in the world.

But after a while, Eusapia started to get restless.

What is it? Anna asked.

Do you know a Cairoli Avenue, Anna?

I've been in the neighbourhood, but never had a reason to go there. I'm sure I could find it though. It is at least an hour from here. We can walk with you, she proposed.

Even with her suitcase, Eusapia preferred walking rather than spending a few pennies of her money to pay for a ride. She could imagine plenty of more urgent occasions for using her money. Better not waste the coins.

Fortunately, Anna took turns carrying the suitcase, but Eusapia had to refuse Maria's help because she was just too weak. With frequent rests, they made it to Cairoli Avenue, where the girls said goodbye. Eusapia promised to visit them again if she wasn't sent away to some godforsaken place.

Ugo was the first to notice Eusapia.

What are you doing here!? he exclaimed, beaming with excitement.

His surprise and pleasure at seeing her gave her hope.

They don't want me, she said.

The Cattalanis? he asked. What did you do?

Eusapia groaned. I don't fit in there. I want to see the city. I need to know what's around me.

Ugo stared at her. What does that have to do with anything?

Before she could explain, Signora Migaldi who was returning from running an errand caught sight of her and joined them.

Eusapia? Heavenly Father! What happened? Signora Migaldi almost shouted, eyeing the girl's filthy dress and the suitcase on the ground. Did they send you away? How did you get here? Come into the house. Tell me what happened.

As Eusapia remained standing in front of the building, trying to describe the events of the morning, she realised that there was no valid explanation or excuse for anything she'd done. Enormous, hot tears began spilling over her cheeks as if someone had opened a water gate. By now she was sobbing so loud that the windows and balconies close by filled with people curious to find out what the latest drama was about.

Come inside, Signora Migaldi repeated. She put her arm around Eusapia and guided her up the stairs.

Even inside, no useful information came forward. New outbursts of tears were the only response to any question.

Explain later when you're less upset, Signora Migaldi suggested. She poured water into a glass and put pieces of dried fruit in front of Eusapia when a shout from the nearby window made them both jump.

The Cattalanis' housekeeper is ploughing down the street, young Pietro yelled at the top of his lungs.

Eusapia started to tremble.

Don't worry, said Signora Migaldi, who went to the door to invite the housekeeper in. Eusapia got up from the table and positioned herself behind Signora Migaldi to prevent the housekeeper from feasting on her misery.

That girl, the housekeeper screeched, her index finger pointing like a dagger to the right side of Signora Migaldi where a part of Eusapia's dirty green dress waved back and forth, that girl is no good. Signora Cattalani wants to let you know that she had no choice but to turn her out. She is a savage, this one, dirty, cheeky, and without morals.

The housekeeper could not stop herself.

Signora Migaldi tried to interrupt her. Thank you for bringing me Signora Cattalani's message, which she was sure had been made in a very different tone.

She brought the housekeeper to the door, realising that she would have to wait for a more objective assessment of what had occurred at the Cattalanis from Grazia herself.

The housekeeper turned back, again pointing her dagger index finger at the part of Eusapia that was exposed, How dare you upset Signora Cattalani who is the most saintly woman I've ever met, how dare you . . . you . . . you incarnation of evil! Find your way back to hell and if Heaven has pity on us, the devil will never let you loose again.

With that, the housekeeper stomped away, muttering a curt goodbye to Signora Migaldi who in her eyes was sheltering the devil's brood and therefore equally beyond saving

What are we going to do with you? Signora Migaldi wondered aloud, looking at Eusapia puzzled but with her habitual warmth.

She can sleep in my bed, Pietro shouted. I want Eusapia to stay here. Mamma, do you know that she can stand on her head? he asked, his voice filled with admiration for the unbelievable stunts Eusapia had shown him during her last stay. She can walk on her hands.

A smile crossed Signora Migaldi's lips. Don't worry, Eusapia, we'll keep you here for the next few days until we find a more permanent solution.

With this one sentence, Signora Migaldi took a load off the girl's mind. It gave Eusapia a few days to come up with her own plan. She remembered Lucia mentioning the convent at some point, and had to make sure they wouldn't bury her there alive. If she couldn't make a go of it at the Cattalanis, she certainly had no chance of surviving a convent. The quiet rooms and hallways and the total lack of control over her life would kill her. Without sun, wind and nowadays these new chaotic crowds of people, she would not stay alive. Pleas to be liberated would be the only prayers to fill her heart. She had to find a more suitable arrangement. What about working as a household help? With no training, talent or inclination for cleaning, cooking or sewing, she'd be fired before the end of the first day. Her strong and agile hands might be useful for laundry work. Slapping pieces of clothes around to loosen dirt and grime looked doable. Anything she saw being folded, she could fold faster and neater.

Eusapia? Signora Migaldi called out, giving her a friendly shove to bring her back to earth.

Wha-wha-what? Eusapia stammered.

Signora Migaldi laughed. What's the matter with you, girl? Wake up. My two sisters are coming from Rome tonight to stay with us for a few weeks. You must have some clean clothes in your suitcase. Put on your best dress.

At the supper table, the voices of Signora Migaldi's two older sisters dominated the conversation. They had left Minervino and settled in Rome the year after Eusapia was born. They had seen

Pope Pio in person, blessing them from his window on St. Peter's Square.

Yes, it's a holy city, they declared, you feel it in the air. Angels are around us all the time.

You see angels? young Pietro asked, his dark eyes about to rise out of his full-moon face in wonder.

We both sense the comforting presence of angels and of our departed, they answered. We wish we could see them, though, and that they'd talk to us.

Eusapia, who had listened attentively, butted in with odd intensity, The departed talk to me. My mother always came to me in Minervino. She will not abandon me here in Naples.

The women, who got to know Michela when she moved to Minervino after marrying her husband Rocco, looked at Eusapia with mixed emotions, annoyed at the interruption, but intrigued as well.

You see Michela? they exclaimed. Do you have a picture of her?

No, I never had a picture.

What does she look like? the sisters asked.

Short like me, in fact, exactly the same height. She has the same large black eyes. Her hair is wavier than mine and when she appears to me, she wears it open, letting it hang down to below her shoulders.

The women and the boys hung on every one of Eusapia's words.

Yes, the sisters agreed, that's Michela all right. God bless her soul. Poor, beautiful Michela.

Gratified by the attention, Eusapia continued, Mamma's voice is deep and full and when she sings, the notes warm your heart.

Does she really communicate with you? the women at the table asked, and added, Her voice was pure gold, she could have been a singer. Our priest asked her to join the church choir and she sang a solo once, but then she stopped coming because Rocco got into a fight with the priest and forbid her to have anything to do with him.

Eusapia cut them off, When she sings to me, she never sings church songs, she makes up the words. She gives me messages.

Again the women nodded.

She loved to improvise.

What messages does she give you? the younger sister asked.

Eusapia's mouth fell open. Her blood shot into her cheeks.

They're private, she snapped, heavy shadows darkening her eyes.

Of course they are, Signora Migaldi smoothed over the tense moment. Let's just give thanks for being together after so many years! Hail Mary, Mother of God. The visitors joined in, Hail Mary, full of grace. Ten seconds later the two sisters were again busy recounting strange and wonderful episodes from their life in Rome.

Time and again that evening, the women raised the possibility of contacting the otherworld. What likelihood was there of getting through? Of hearing once more the voices of their dearest friends and relatives who had passed on?

While most of Naples struggled for plain survival, clusters in the more prosperous circles fluttered with spiritual energy and yearning for otherworldly presences.

It's just a matter of time before the human brain has expanded enough to allow us to fluently communicate with the souls on the other side, Signora Migaldi said. Not just in Naples, people on all continents search to open the channels to the world beyond us.

Her sisters nodded emphatically and stated excitedly, We had visitors from England a few weeks ago. It's hard to believe what's happening there. Friends of ours witnessed objects move by themselves. They witnessed actual levitations. They heard raps.

Signora Migaldi, whose emotions ran wild at any mention of the supernatural, added, We have reached new levels of consciousness. Our knowledge of electric currents and magnetic fields has increased drastically in this century. So why should we be surprised that today's spiritualists are able to experience currents no one has been able to detect in previous centuries? Just months ago we wouldn't have dared to imagine such possibilities. Did you hear of Taddeo Scarlatti? When he is in trance, he inscribes roll after roll of deep revelations inspired by saints who hadn't had the opportunity to transmit all their messages during their lifetimes.

Eusapia listened with curiosity. The incomprehensible talk about invisible physical currents bewildered her less than the weird occurrences in England. Why would objects have to move to prove that the souls of departed loved ones wanted to talk to us? Why levitate to demonstrate that communication had been established? She only needed to concentrate and her mother was there. Eusapia could sit on a tree branch, doing absolutely nothing, and her mother would start talking to her. The girl needed no proof that communication was possible. She communicated all the time. Afraid to offend or attract negative attention, Eusapia kept her views to herself. She needed to give Signora Migaldi a reason for keeping her. Moving objects? If her mother did nothing but shuffle objects around, she'd never forgive her.

Signora Migaldi said eagerly, I heard that quite a few people might have the gift to be mediums without knowing it. Once they recognise their latent potential and acknowledge it, they can start developing their special abilities. It is possible that the supernatural powers needed to establish contact reside in one or all of us sitting here at this table.

Her sisters nodded.

I wonder whether the strong sensations I often have to endure are not a sign, the younger sister whispered. The more humankind develops, and with it our spirituality, the better the chances to reconnect with the people we lost. One day, we might be able to converse with our dear mother, God bless her soul. I can't believe she was our age when she was called to the Heavenly Father. She would want us to know that she keeps watching over us. Of that I'm convinced.

The older sister added, She is familiar with the pain we suffer. We don't need to explain the problems we're having with our husbands (and at this moment the younger sister crossed herself three times fretting about the fortune her husband was squandering again this week at the lottery), our mother understands the worries about our children that keep us awake at night. She knows without judging that our hopes for great love and fulfilment, for doing good in the world, the hopes we carried so confidently through our twenties and thirties have evaporated, that now we're just trying to cope with the everyday heartaches that are thrown at us. No matter how strong we are, we continue to crave the type of love and encouragement only mothers seem able to provide.

The women forgot about the young ones around the table. Eusapia absorbed every word they uttered. She knew exactly what these women were talking about. She craved the same acceptance. She too felt that only her mother could soothe the pain inside.

Mamma, come and see us, Eusapia implored her absent mother. Give us your blessing.

She stared in rapture at a spot on the wall close to the ceiling. She perceived dim outlines. But her mother would not appear. Where are you, Mamma? Eusapia cried out and the desperation in her voice brought tears to the women's eyes. Talk to me, Eusapia tried again. But there was no answer to her call. The silence in the room was so commanding that even the visitors held their tongues for a moment.

Tomorrow, we will put our inner strengths and currents to the test, Signora Migaldi promised. We'll see if any of us can cross the threshold to the other side and convince one or two of our beloved dead to make their presence felt by raising a table.

Eusapia awaited the next evening with impatience. Because she had impressed the three women with her ability to see and hear her own mother, she was asked to join the séance. Expectantly, they sat around a light table in the back corner of the drawing-room. They placed their hands four inches above its top, palms facing down. The older women reached deep inside themselves, trying to tap into their psychic potential. But the table did not move. Their intense desire for a sign from their mother touched Eusapia like a fifth presence at the table. To her, nothing about that need seemed pathetic. She had learned from experience that an everlasting connection to loved ones on the other side helped you stay alive. If her own mother hadn't remained with her,

68

Eusapia would not have survived her childhood. Fully in tune with the women, she fervently hoped for a sign. The sudden revelation came to her that adults too needed encouragement and that sufficient food and a place to stay did not guarantee happiness. As Eusapia waited for the table to rise, she wondered, Why the hell doesn't it move? Souls on the other side, she pleaded silently, why don't you give consolation to those in need? Nothing happened. Eusapia, who had a strong instinct for the dramatic, assumed that too much light drove the dead away.

I think that our loved ones in the otherworld would prefer less light, she suggested, almost hesitantly because she did not want to upset anyone.

You're right, Eusapia, Signora Migaldi concurred, why didn't I think of that?

She dimmed the lights. Again, the women sat anxious with expectation, their hands spread stiffly above the small table. In vain. The table remained solidly stuck to the floor. Eusapia couldn't stand their disappointment any longer. She gave a deep sigh and stared straight up to the ceiling. The women followed her gaze. At that moment, with one quick twisted movement of her foot and leg, Eusapia, like a snake-woman, placed her leg unseen under the table top. Then balancing the table on the inside of her right foot, she slowly raised it up into the air.

The table, the sisters cried out. Mother, you're here. Please talk to us. Impart your wisdom to us. Mother, they whispered, overcome by a powerful exultation.

Eusapia gave the table another push.

Mother, the older sister asked. Is it you? If it is you, please rap three times.

As if compelled by ghostly hands, Eusapia secretly followed up with three raps that sounded hollow through the room.

It is you, Mother! Signora Migaldi sighed, and it felt as if a great weight had been lifted from her. You're here. Thank you for coming back to us.

At that moment, the table slowly descended. No one spoke a word for a very long time.

That evening, new doors opened for Eusapia.

You're the special one, my child, Signora Migaldi said the next morning. You have the gift to contact the world beyond. Yesterday, contact was established. Through extraordinary manifestations, our mother sent us signs of comfort. This is your vocation, Eusapia. You are in this world to receive messages from the departed.

Carried into the future by her own speech, Signora Migaldi caught satisfying glimpses of Eusapia with her powers fully developed. She anticipated hundreds of visitors to her house, and those visitors, shaken by unexplainable phenomena, coming back, over and over again. Signora Migaldi's expectations swelled into irresistible visions. Her house would become a centre for spiritualists. She beamed at the thought of such honour being bestowed on her and her family.

A great responsibility has been placed on your shoulders, she told Eusapia. You'll have to work hard to be worthy of it. We'll have to work hard every night. Only the best will do.

Eusapia felt all eyes turn toward her, the three women's with an almost pious glow, the three boys' in excited awe. When she quickly glanced at Signor Migaldi, she detected a smirk that made her blush. He refrained from any comment. A shrewd businessman, he recognised at once the financial potential in his wife's beliefs. Eusapia wavered for a moment. She could put a stop to this right here and now. If she did, what would happen? Nothing good, for sure. They'd ship her off to God-knows-where, most likely to a convent. So what if she had to raise a table and produce a few raps, convincing everyone they came from the beyond? Suddenly her lips curled into a smirk, as if in imitation of Signor Migaldi's, but she immediately corrected herself. She could ill afford to show contempt without jeopardizing her future. With terse resolve, she ironed her lips into strong, non-committal lines. If she wanted to stay at the Migaldis, she had to pay for her keep in some way. It was in her best interest to fulfil their spiritualistic expectations.

At first, twelve-year-old Eusapia worked herself into a rage about the nightly nonsense.

Idiotic stupidity! she complained when no one could hear her, but she was thankful that Signor Migaldi let her keep a modest portion of the fees that he charged for her séances.

Eusapia made certain she drew the attention of the guests around the table to each other or to the wall or the window whenever she started her levitations. At the beginning the women were easily satisfied. But with habit, the emotion of their experience wore off. To succeed, Eusapia had to be more careful, more inventive. She listened intently when the Migaldis and their visitors discussed trances, raps, and other phenomena. When she heard that in other countries mediums fell into a trance for the dead or for spirit guides to manifest themselves, she immediately went through the motions of what she understood to be a trance and loudly offered her body as a vessel for messages from the beyond. Her sitters, as the people participating in a séance were called, needed to be impressed. Eusapia barely talked when she gave a séance. Instead, she used facial expressions to convey meaning and answer questions. Building on the conversations of the visitors, she instructed her sitters seriously, as if the subject hadn't been discussed at length earlier, that rapping three times meant yes, rapping once meant no, and rapping twice meant not sure. Raps echoed in rapid succession all over the room in answer to a series of questions. Are you a relative? Did you cross over recently? Do you have a message? From the corner of her eyes, Eusapia could see Signor Migaldi smiling.

At the beginning, she tried to make a believer out of him. But he saw right through her. Only complicity between the two of them could save her. They never talked about it. But she started to trust him. Once or twice in dicey situations, with her act in danger of falling apart, he spontaneously turned into an accomplice. He drew the attention of suspicious sitters away from her by talking about shadows he'd seen that shouldn't be there or unexplainable hands that touched him. He continued his performance until she had recovered and the moment was right again for new manifestations.

When two youngish women were watching her like hawks one evening and, at some point, to her horror touched her right leg, which she had pulled back in preparation for one of her more difficult manoeuvres, Signor Migaldi's quick-thinking quelled sudden rumblings of fraud.

Keep in mind, he seriously informed the sitters, that according to all accounts, psychical forces have the power to redirect the movements of the medium and often do so to challenge or test her.

Coming from a man whose derogatory comments on psychic phenomena, religion and spiritualism had upset many of the attendees in the past, his comments carried weight.

It might well be that we're dealing with such a test here, he suggested nonchalantly.

If a sceptic like Signor Migaldi was ready to give Eusapia the benefit of a doubt, who were they to question her authenticity?

Realising that in times of doubt it was best not to give the sitters extra time to think and re-evaluate, Signor Migaldi immediately went to turn up or down lights or hooked the sitters with stories, suggestions or novel theories in an attempt to distract them.

Aunt Eugenia! he exclaimed at one point when he was in a particular prankish mood, sticking his hands up in front of his face like small shields, pretending to hide behind them, you haunted me when you were alive. Don't pretend you're here now. You know I don't believe in that stuff. You'd need to bring a more charming and trustworthy person with you to convince me.

Can't you see, his wife interrupted, that by talking to someone you don't believe is in the room, you acknowledge that person?

No, I don't, but I must say it's fun pretending to be part of mystical episodes. I can't remember talking to Aunt Eugenia so frankly before and without the risk of being cut out of her will.

As all eyes were glued to his face, the table rose, higher than ever, and then, with a very slight swish, a wilted rose came flying from out of nowhere and landed in the middle of the table amidst cries of astonishment. Eusapia who looked directly into

Signor Migaldi's eyes wanted to burst out laughing, but catching his unspoken warning, restrained herself. The table slowly descended to the jerky rhythm of Eusapia's out-of-control sighs, her hands vigilantly above it as if to tame a wild beast, directing it with non-verbal but effective commands. When the table reached the floor with just the slightest of thuds, Eusapia's head dropped down on the wooden tabletop. Her heaving body and anguished moans scared Signora Migaldi.

Come back to us, Eusapia, she pleaded. Souls from the otherworld, set her free.

Eusapia decided this was a good moment to end the session. Slowly, she sat up, and even more slowly, she opened her large black eyes, as if trying to find her bearings again in the world of ordinary mortals. It was Signor Migaldi's turn to stifle the laughter that was building up in him and threatened to ruin the enormous progress they had made in the last few weeks.

In spite of her success, Eusapia grew tired of her performances.

I've had enough, she told Signor Migaldi.

Oh no, you haven't, he responded, you just got started. Your psychic powers are growing.

Eusapia stared at him too exasperated to reply.

He continued seriously, Creating an evocative, dim atmosphere by covering the lights with red paper in the séance room, as most mediums do, was a brilliant idea. You must be aware how extremely auspicious this is for phenomena to occur. Greater things will happen.

Enough! Eusapia insisted. You want to burn the house down? Anyhow, I can't do this anymore. I want an ordinary job like other people, no funny business, no tricks, nothing of that sort.

Compose yourself, Eusapia, how else do you propose to make a living? The spiritualist women friends of my wife already seek you out. But it's the men that will become your gold mine. Make your red lips smile, promise things you'll never give. They'll eat out of your hands. When they sit beside you, brush against their legs. Touch them as if by coincidence, the closer to the groin the better.

Eusapia turned white. Her eyelids twitched. Horrible memories from her father's house broke loose to torment her. Visions of naked body parts threw her into a state of agony as if in revenge for having been suppressed so long. White and trembling, she held on to the chair beside her. Signor Migaldi watched her closely.

What's wrong? he asked, suddenly wondering about his tactics. In front of his eyes, Eusapia regressed into a young child in the middle of a nightmare.

Eusapia, he called.

She snapped out of her dark mood. A slow, mean smile crossed her face as she opened her eyes fully on the man before her, and when he started to squirm, she continued to gaze at him, slowly realising the full extent of the power she could wield if she set her mind to it.

Regardless of her growing reputation in the large circle of the Migaldi family and their acquaintances, Eusapia found no peace of mind. Thoroughly disgusted, she was set on quitting. It upset her to pretend that she could contact the otherworld when she couldn't. The only person who was there for her from either paradise or heaven, it didn't matter which, was her mother, who seemed not pleased with the current developments. What are you doing, my child? she appeared to say. Eusapia, who was rarely at a loss for words, had no answer. She herself didn't know what she was doing.

Show me another way, Mamma, she begged.

Again, laundry work presented itself as the only solution and Eusapia took this as a sign.

Signor Migaldi, Eusapia said, my mother tells me to do laundry work.

Your mother? he asked mockingly.

Yes, Eusapia answered, Mamma tells me to do an honest day's work.

Her eyes shone with such sincerity that despite his cynicism, Signor Migaldi hesitated. He looked at the miserable girl in front of him and couldn't help but feel sorry for her.

All right, you find a job and work every day. Three quarters of your money will go for your keep here, the other one belongs to you, the same arrangements as for the séances.

Full of relief and gratitude, Eusapia threw her arms around him. You won't regret this.

Signora Migaldi, her sisters, and even the three Migaldi sons were beside themselves with disappointment when Eusapia announced her decision.

Laundry, they shouted, when you have psychic powers! What a waste! Eusapia, what an unforgivable waste!

The girl responded seriously, It's Mamma who wants me to do this.

Michela wants you do to laundry? But why? Why would she want you to break your back? Do you know how hard doing laundry is? You think you can do this work at twelve years old? Do you want to die? You wish to die to join your mother? Is that it? Why, Eusapia, why, when you have special powers and a clear mission in life?

I don't want to die, Eusapia responded. But I have to listen to my mother.

Of course, Signora Migaldi acquiesced. Of course you have to follow advice that comes from the beyond. Did Michela tell you why she wants you to work in a laundry shop?

No, she just showed me the way.

Two weeks later, Eusapia started working as a laundry woman near the bay, with the only good thing about this arrangement being the location. Each time she looked over the water towards Mount Vesuvius, she stood in awe. But Signora Migaldi had not been exaggerating about the hardship of laundry work. After twelve hours toiling and sweating, Eusapia couldn't stand straight. She walked home in pain, doubled over like a prisoner after months or years of hard labour. All she wanted to do was quit her wretched job, but, no, she would persist if it killed her. Under the pitying stares of the Migaldis and their friends, her resolve remained strong. Not a single complaint came over her lips.

I still have to get used to the work, she conceded.

Signora Migaldi gave her a warm hug. I'm sure you're doing a fine job.

From that day forward, Eusapia, who had run wild her whole life, knuckled down and forced herself to endure the heavy loads that almost ripped off her arms, the heat that drew the water out of her body and left behind a dry shell, the stench that caused her to gasp for air. After only a few weeks, her body started to crack under the pressure. Mechanically, she pushed her sore feet one in front of the other. Too proud and stubborn to give up, she continued working even though her legs threatened to buckle and her aching arms nearly refused to move. In a new attempt to persevere, she let Neapolitan songs run through her head to bring some rhythm and facility to her work. To her dismay, they dried up after the first few sounds. She struggled to keep her unshed tears from spilling. No, she would not cry. Mamma, I want to make you proud. But with each passing day, the work took more of a toll on her weakened body, and she expected her chafed hands to burst into flames. The circles under her eyes darkened. The light in her eyes faded. She stared frowning into a world she did not understand anymore. One day when she was about to faint, she heard her mother's voice, You did your best, my beloved daughter. If it is necessary for you to raise tables to survive, go ahead, do it.

The Migaldis couldn't have been happier when Eusapia announced that she would resume her séances.

What about Michela? Signora Migaldi asked. Would she give you her blessing?

Mamma was the one to suggest it, Eusapia responded. Because she understands that in the world the way it is, the only way for me to survive is to become a medium.

Signora Migaldi beamed with satisfaction.

Then that's what you will do, she exclaimed and smothered Eusapia in an enthusiastic embrace.

From under Signora Migaldi's arms, Eusapia heard Signor Migaldi's voice, Are you sure, Eusapia, that's what your Mamma wants? That's what you want?

Eusapia felt touched by his concern. She extricated herself from Signora Migaldi's embrace and turned toward him with an honest and open expression.

Yes, she answered, It's all right. I will make my living with the help of the departed.

Signor Migaldi searched her eyes for her true feelings. Reflecting on how he had tried to exploit her supposed psychic powers and the naivety or plain stupidity of his family and guests, he felt ashamed. But the girl looked at him with composure, nodding almost imperceptibly. My God, he thought, it took just a few short months to wipe away any trace of the child in her. Who is this girl-woman? What is her future?

Don't worry, Eusapia said with unexpected warmth in her voice, This is what I have to do.

Again she nodded reassuringly, and Signor Migaldi turned away, unsure whether his collusion did not add to the heap of sins he had already accumulated.

To celebrate the renewal of Eusapia's mediumship, the Migaldis included her in a large gathering of family and friends. During the event, she caught a glimpse of Signor Migaldi and an attractive man huddled together in a conspiratorial discussion. At some point, they both turned, Signor Migaldi searching her out from across the room, talking to his partner all the while, and suddenly the other man's eyes settling on her with a disconcerting intensity, then turning away quickly as if in fear of being found out. Eusapia was dumbfounded. What was going on? The men disappeared into the crowd. Eusapia was left with the face of a stranger imprinted in her memory.

Soon, the séances restarted. Eusapia's powers and maturity appeared to have grown during her absence. Though she was careful with words, she used every nerve in her face to convey messages and moods. She never gave explanations, leaving all interpretations to the sitters around her. She stored every comment, encouragement and criticism in one of the many compartments of her brain, where she dissected them until she completely understood how her movements, words, grimaces, moans, and smiles affected her sitters. She figured people out quickly: Signora Migaldi's need to be loved and popular and the centre of attention, Signor Migaldi's penchant for mischief and his contradictory traits of greed and generosity, the visiting sisters' religious fervour and feelings of superiority.

One day, a visitor from England mentioned the celebrated medium Florence Cook, who was supposed to be controlled by John King, the spirit of the infamous buccaneer Sir Henry Morgan, pardoned and knighted by Charles II and then sent to become governor of Jamaica. The spirit had come through so strong that he guided Florence Cook's thoughts and actions and transmitted his messages through her. This John King was also the father of the spirit girl Katie King who materialised through Florence Cook.

If Florence Cook could channel Katie King, maybe Eusapia could attempt to do so as well. Mediums were not very different from each other. They all needed cunning means to produce their phenomena. Right then and there, Eusapia decided that she would surpass them all.

She listened carefully as the visitor elaborated further: I've never witnessed a medium so infused by the power of a spirit control that, channelled through her, his daughter not only materialised in the séance room but walked about like a flesh-and-blood person.

But what are John King's intentions? Eusapia interrupted the visitor, burning with curiosity.

Gratified by her interest, the visitor enthusiastically expanded, When I had the honour of seeing this spirit control during the séance, John King was helping his daughter find roots on earth.

In line with this logic, Eusapia thought, his next goal must be to solidify his daughter's presence on earth, which could mean reincarnation, another big word she had become familiar with in the last few weeks.

During meetings with visitors from many different countries, Eusapia learned to identify their origins and backgrounds within seconds. She unerringly spotted depression over recent losses, insecurities and sexual frustrations, and recognised vanity, hypocrisy, and meanness as soon as she met people. Their yearning for revelations from saints and loved ones became as visible to her as a sculpture. Armed with this new knowledge, Eusapia wasted no time to put every bit of it to use. Sometimes she revelled in her own power, other times she reeled from the bitter aftertaste her trickery produced in her mouth. But she accepted the séances as her fate despite wondering what that meant and where it would lead her.

Naples, Italy, 1870

3

EUSAPIA ADJUSTED THE RED LIGHTS in the dimmed room, wondering why Signor Migaldi had arranged this meeting with such urgency. After three years of developing her skills and working as a medium, nothing surprised her anymore. But every now and then, events took an unexpected turn. Never assume you had people figured out. No matter how easily she read people in general, Signor Migaldi's intentions mystified her. He acted as if her future depended on the success of this meeting. According to the sparse information he provided earlier in the day, a Signora Damiani had contacted him the previous night, asking to see Eusapia in private.

In response to Eusapia's questioning look, he said, No, she hasn't given any explanation for her request. But he turned away for fear of revealing more than he intended.

When Signora Damiani arrived, Eusapia detected an almost feverish animation in her eyes. The two women sat down at the séance table.

I've been given a sign, Signora Damiani said immediately.

Eusapia took in the quiver of exaltation in the woman's voice with astonishment and even suspicion. Strange, she thought, especially as she inferred from Signora Damiani's accent that she was English and not a hot-blooded fellow Neapolitan. Few foreigners attempted to speak the Neapolitan dialect, let alone mastered it like this woman. She had to be married to a Neapolitan, though her mannerisms made this hard to believe. Her controlled way of talking and acting was so contrary to the southern temperament that Eusapia wondered how Signora Damiani survived with a Neapolitan husband. Maybe there was truth in the saying that opposites attract. Eusapia continued observing the woman, struck most by the restrained movements of the body, the pale white face, and the doleful eyes of a woman desperate but unable to conceive.

You're the reincarnated daughter of John King, Signora Damiani exclaimed, grabbing and squeezing both of Eusapia's hands.

Eusapia, who took the most outrageous statements with barely more than a slight double-take of breath, emptied her eyes of all expression, a trick she had acquired through experience, an easy way to extract additional strings of words and sentences that put meaning in the most incoherent babbling. Turning into magnets of sorts, her blank eyes drew in the bits of information that her sitters let go without noticing. The little pieces jiggled and pushed each other until they fell together in a powerful mosaic. Like other sitters, Signora Damiani stared into Eusapia's eyes, and seeing her own life mirrored back, could not hold back her pent-up feelings.

You must help me, she cried.

Still Eusapia did not respond. The daughter of John King?

Eusapia again gazed at Signora Damiani, still puzzled at what the woman had in mind. Reincarnation, she continued her musings, that's probably where her own role was to start. But did she really want to be Katie King's reincarnation? There was one

84

good aspect with letting Signora Damiani's claim stand. It would allow Eusapia to call on John King as her spirit control. He had the potential to be useful, and after what she had endured in her childhood, she'd have no qualms erasing the memories of her own biological father and adopting a new one. No danger of conflicting loyalties here! Replacing him with the powerful John King undoubtedly had its advantages. All the same . . .

You must tell me where the child is, Signora Damiani begged, her voice ringing into Eusapia's thoughts, calling her back to the meeting and the hysterical woman in front of her. As if scorn toward her sitters had never awoken a relentless fury in her, Eusapia now felt almost dazed by an unusual compassion. She took the woman's hands into her own. Her pity warmed the deadly cold fingers. It thawed the woman's frozen spirit.

I cannot be with my husband as a wife should, Signora Damiani confided. Any time he tries to get intimate, I go into convulsions. But I can feel the child waiting to be conceived. Every day, I feel her eyes pleading, Mamma, let me be born. I want her in my life. I try. But as soon as Giorgio approaches, the convulsions start.

Eusapia looked straight ahead through Signora Damiani into the future. With a sudden feverish but sharp and intense intuition, she saw the girl, smiling at her, waving. I'm glad you found me, I'm Celestina, the girl said quietly, her eyes lit with joy. Eusapia stared at her, incredulous and shaken, then turned to Signora Damiani. Celestina's complexion was much darker. She displayed no trace of her mother's polished Englishness. In fact, Eusapia mused, it's almost like looking into a mirror or into the face of my mother. She has Mamma's eyes. She has my eyes. Eusapia stopped.

Celestina, she murmured. What's the meaning of this?

Celestina? Is that her name, Signora Damiani barged in. What an exquisite name! When will she come into our lives?

With the first sound of Signora Damiani's words, the child faded away.

I don't know, Eusapia said, perplexed. I don't know the meaning of it.

Ask your father John King for insight. You're his daughter. He'll enlighten you. We need to set up another meeting.

We'll see, Eusapia replied slowly.

Next time, I'll bring my husband. He'll want to know about Celestina.

As soon as Signor Damiani entered the room with his wife, Eusapia knew she had seen him before. He was the handsome stranger who had stared at her across the room at the Migaldi family gathering.

My wife believes you can help us, Signor Damiani said. It's an enormous honour to meet you. I myself have trained many mediums in the last few years. So I can appreciate remarkable abilities when I see them. From what I hear, your powers are impressive. How odd that it had to be an English medium who led my wife and now me to you here in my home town!

Eusapia just smiled. It was never a good idea to reveal more than necessary. Whatever was developing in front of her, it would evaporate if she mentioned having seen him before. She was intrigued. What kind of a game was this? Signor Damiani couldn't take his eyes off her. Thinking suddenly of his wife's frigidity, Eusapia felt a moment of deep sympathy for her, an almost sisterly protectiveness that turned into cold fear when unsettling images from her own childhood caught her off guard. Eusapia forced herself to concentrate on Signor Damiani with a single-mindedness that left no space for his wife or the dark memories she evoked in Eusapia. There was nothing repulsive about him. Eusapia actually wondered how any woman could resist his almost frightening magnetism and penetrating eyes. Who wouldn't be charmed by his good looks and sensuous smile?

Celestina? he said, looking at her with a glint in his eyes.

Eusapia didn't respond.

She can see our Celestina, Signora Damiani chirped in. Eusapia knows she's out there.

Signor Migaldi, who stood a few steps aside watching the three people, had caught the split second of recognition in Eusapia's eyes. He looked at her, his expression clearly cautioning not to ruin whatever was being hatched right in front of them. Give it a chance, he seemed to implore her. Give this couple a chance.

The four of them sat around the séance table. All lights were dimmed. Signor Migaldi asked Eusapia whether candles ought to be lit in the back of the room in honour of San Gerardo Majella and Santa Marina, patron saints of pregnant women. Not exactly sure why he called on those saints at her séance, she nevertheless granted permission immediately. It was clear from the charged atmosphere that something was up. Even the sad eyes of Signora Damiani fluttered with nervous anticipation, with a strange combination of hope, calculating expectation, unease and guilt. What is it they want from me? Eusapia wondered with sudden apprehension.

To hide her emotions, she rocked herself into one of her semi-trances from the very beginning.

What do you want? she heard her voice boom out, deep and unrecognisable as her own. It must be John King speaking. What do you want from me? What do you want from my daughter?

Who is Celestina? Signora Damiani asked nervously.

John King refused to respond.

He might prefer to respond by rapping, Signor Migaldi ventured. It's his preferred mode of communication at this point in time.

Is she our daughter?

Three raps for yes.

My wife will conceive? Signor Damiani asked breathlessly.

After a pause, one rap indicating no.

Signora Damiani pressed her hands to her face in despair.

What are you saying? he exclaimed. Is Celestina my daughter, yes or no?

Three loud raps rang through the room. Then with insistence, another three raps, and then another three.

Suddenly, as if placed there by spirit hands, a single candle appeared on the table, its flame radiating with promise. Signor Damiani, who knew what it took for a medium to perform at such a level, was enthralled. He grabbed his wife's hand on one side and Eusapia's on the other and encouraged the two women to join hands, which left Signor Migaldi to sit outside the circle.

Together we shall find you, Celestina, he whispered.

All four, even Eusapia, gave in to the emotion of the moment. It wasn't just her mind racing into unfamiliar regions. Her body was quickly learning an unknown, passionate language.

Together, she murmured. Together we shall succeed.

She noticed with an unnerving excitement that the pressure of Signor Damiani's hand intensified.

And? Signor Migaldi asked after the Damianis' departure when he succeeded in cornering her alone, Can you handle it?

Eusapia blushed. As she felt Signor Migaldi watching her closely, the red on her cheeks deepened. He did not need to spell out the implications of continuing séances with the Damianis. She understood.

Are you sure you want to continue? I would hate for you to get hurt.

I'm sixteen now, Eusapia answered haughtily. I can take care of myself.

As long as you're sure. Financially, it would be to your advantage. If you accept this project and complete it successfully, Signor Damiani would pay you three times what you'd have made as a laundry woman in a year.

Eusapia almost fainted at the thought of so much money.

Signor Migaldi quickly grabbed the girl to steady her and was fast to warn, Yes, you do have to make money, but don't ever think that money can buy happiness.

I like Signor Damiani, Eusapia said, turning beet red.

Signor Migaldi looked at her with concern. As long as you don't get too attached. You know that, Eusapia, don't you? He has a wife. Never forget that.

We'll see, Eusapia answered wistfully. Life is unpredictable.

Signor Migaldi took her firmly by her upper arms. Not as unpredictable as that, Eusapia. Look at me. I've lived a long time. I know.

But Eusapia's eyes were lost already in faraway worlds where dreams begin and can come true.

That night, Eusapia lay wide awake. Sweet memories of Emilio's kisses lit her face. Every time she opened her eyes though, instead of Emilio, there stood Signor Damiani, his fiery, demanding eyes on her as if to swallow her whole. Behind him, Emilio paled away, the very essence of him drawn into the black hole of his four-year absence. She was a woman now. She needed a man, not a boy. Not even her nightmarish memories diminished her sudden need to lean against Signor Damiani, to feel his arms around her, stronger, more powerful than any father's, different from any kindness she had known, so exciting that she became dizzy.

When they met next, Signor Damiani said, Eusapia, I can make you rich and famous.

However at this point, not even a full stomach and a safe roof over her head carried the slightest importance. In this context, rich and famous held no attraction for her. Her whole body ached with longing, with impatience, with a passionate desire she had not known before. She suddenly turned red again.

You'll be giving me my wife back! Signor Damiani exclaimed elatedly.

Eusapia winced.

Explain the meaning of Celestina to me, Signor Damiani requested.

She has my eyes.

Signor Damiani stared at her.

Are you sure? he asked, a slight tremor in his voice.

Yes, Eusapia said and let his eyes sink into hers, waiting for his strong arms to finally hold her so tight that she would never feel alone again.

She called him Lover, Banger, Paps, Giorgio. Every minute away from him was torture. She wanted to feel his hands on her at all times. She needed to feel his passion.

You're getting careless, Signor Migaldi warned her. You have responsibilities as a medium. You can't afford to tarnish your reputation. If you're not more careful, people will find out and start talking. Worse, Eusapia, you've fallen in love, and it will break your heart. Get out while you can.

Eusapia shrugged as if to push his concerns away.

Signor Migaldi, she finally said with as much composure as she could muster, not many people find love in their lives. Once you find it, you don't give it up.

Poor child, Signor Migaldi said, and once again feelings of guilt gnawed at his conscience, You must see that he has an unbreakable bond with his wife and, in spite of their problems, he does love her.

He loves me.

Signor Migaldi sighed. How could he explain to a lovesick teenager that the great love of her life considered his involvement with her as little more than a passing infatuation and business arrangement? Giorgio Damiani was not a bad guy. But he was starved for sex and that made almost any man unpredictable or rather too predictable. At this point in time there was nothing on his mind but sex and having a child. Unable to find the right words, Signor Migaldi sighed again.

He loves me, Eusapia insisted fervently. No one has loved me like that. Don't try to destroy the only happiness I've ever known. Don't you remember what it means to love someone with every fibre of your being? It would do you good to remember. It would do Signora Migaldi good if you remembered. Don't talk to me about love.

Without another word, Signor Migaldi turned away and left.

Right, go sulk, Eusapia growled after him. What's wrong with you? Can't you recognise when two people truly love each other?

Amazing, the sitters exclaimed and marvelled as Eusapia's talents developed in leaps and bounds. Her reputation grew steadily. But Eusapia cared little about accolades. She craved praise from one person only. For the first time in her life, she took pride in her work and put her whole being into improving every aspect of it. She wanted to make Signor Damiani proud of her. Nothing gave her more satisfaction than seeing how much he appreciated her stunts. He saw her for what she was, a superb entertainer, a contortionist, a prodigy when it came to putting together clues, hints, stored-away memories, and detective work. Whatever she wanted and needed to know, she knew.

You're brilliant, Giorgio said. I've never worked with a medium who had that much talent. You're going to go far.

Signor Damiani showed her every trick he had seen or heard about, and Eusapia made them her own as if she had invented them.

Even with her temper as hot and uncontrollable as ever, she grew more and more accomplished as a medium and became less rough around the edges as a person. Everyone noticed the changes in her.

Signora Migaldi said, My God, Eusapia, you've matured so much in the last few weeks. You seem happier now.

I am happy, Eusapia responded.

I'm glad you find fulfilment in your vocation, Signora Migaldi said, I knew that you couldn't throw such a talent away.

Her son Ugo gave the older girl an enthralled, lovesick look.

Eusapia, who loved the Migaldi boys like brothers, gave him a little shove, Let's go explore the city before my next lesson with Signor Damiani.

No, shouted the younger brothers, tell us a story.

Eusapia knew that the stories they wanted to hear over and over were the stories about the ghosts that had haunted Minervino, the ghosts in her house, in each one of the many shadowy corners along paths and streets, lurking behind every bush and tree, even threatening from behind, underneath, the sides and tops of shrines to the Madonna and other saints. She could see and experience them as if they had followed her to Naples. Invariably, the boys got caught up in her emotions. Tell us again, they would say as soon as she finished. Even if she told her stories a thousand times, they wouldn't tire listening to them.

The sitters participating in her séances tried to catch moments alone with her. To make these meetings profitable, Eusapia squeezed undetected into the smallest corners to listen in on confidences and gossip. She heard about abuse, quarrels, infidelities, sickness and death, then combined this knowledge with her unerring instinct for sorting out the sad and sordid affairs. Sometimes, she comforted people in distress by bringing sweet messages from the recently departed or by announcing that a seemingly unmarriageable daughter would find a good husband in the end. Other times, when she was in one of her bad moods, she froze her sitters blood with terrifying warnings, and if she observed that they brutalised their animals and servants, predicted their death or that of a close relative. She foretold their imminent ruin if they continued gambling away their family's future on the weekly lottery. Nothing she did was without effect. Her gestures and fierce eyes left lasting impressions, preoccupying her sitters during the day and haunting them in their dreams.

During this otherwise rather happy time in Eusapia's life, one event occurred that left her desolate. She had decided to pay a visit to sweet five-year-old Maria and her sister Anna. When she couldn't find Maria, who always stuck around the food stalls, she asked, Where is she? Where is Maria? The vendor she asked wouldn't look at her, but rolled his eyes heavenwards and plunged into a woebegone litany to all Italian saints. The helper at his side was sniffling and looked even more disconsolate than his boss.

The vendor's wife wailed in a harrowing voice, Little Maria is dead.

Eusapia cried out, No, not Maria.

Yes, Maria, the woman lamented, how was the poor, malnourished child supposed to fight disease? How is any child around here to fight disease? Yes, we gave her crumbs when we could, but we struggle to keep our own children alive. What are we to do? When the fever grabbed Maria and ravaged her body, she became delirious within hours. Even adults who are sick can't survive in the dank, mouldy cellar rooms in this neighbourhood. A weakened child has no chance. Maria's mother and two neighbours kept vigil day and night sponging her burning body, and dribbling water and melon juice into her mouth. What help is that when the water is contaminated and the melon rotten? Every hour, the girl got sicker and two days later, she was dead.

The woman stopped speaking. Everyone seemed to relive those horrible days and prayed that their child wouldn't die next. Eusapia ran off, sobbing and shaking. As no one had seen Anna for days, Eusapia left without talking to her. At night, she lay awake with grief. She tossed around, pale and distraught, wondering what she could have done to save the girl. Celestina would not suffer the same fate. But Eusapia shuddered thinking of all the mothers who must have made the same vow, then ended up wasting away in cellars or caves with their children.

Fortunately, serious training with Signor Damiani started. Learning from him every trick in the book of the so-called mediums he had met and taught in the past, how to use the newest props and change her expression and demeanour to elicit the reactions she intended, distracted Eusapia from her sadness. When she went to his apartment, she tentatively allowed hope to find small footholds again. The heartbreak of Maria's death slowly lost the worst of its sharp edges. Eusapia began breathing lighter. She was convinced that Signor Damiani's apartment saved her. It became her favourite place after Signora Damiani left to visit family in London for a full three months, and Eusapia became the queen of the castle. As soon as she arrived at the apartment, she grabbed Giorgio, who didn't need encouragement, and they raced to the bedroom.

I love you, said Giorgio.

I love you more, Eusapia responded.

Wrapped in his arms and swayed by his body, intoxicated by his odour and sweat, soothed by the incredible softness of the sheets, she seized her little happiness with greedy arms and legs, trying to hold on to it with desperate bravado.

One day, as she vaulted happily out of bed, she felt a warm jolt in her body, some jubilant occurrence that seemed to open the skies and light up the rainbow where Celestina had been waiting for her call. Eusapia watched spellbound as the girl leapt eagerly to her feet and lightly jumped down to earth.

Finally, she said to Eusapia. You made me wait a long time.

Celestina? Eusapia enquired, Is it really you?

Is it her? Giorgio interjected. Has my daughter arrived?

Don't you see her? Eusapia asked. Can't you see our precious child?

As much as he tried, Giorgio saw nothing. But he quivered with hope.

I should write to my wife, he said. Lillian needs to be told that in nine months' time, she will become a mother. She'll be so . . .

Don't tell her, Eusapia cut him off. I don't see the girl anymore. I might be mistaken.

But Eusapia saw Celestina clearly right in front of her. The girl even took her hand. She looked sad now. Why? she seemed to say. Why do you lie about me?

Eusapia didn't dare answer. What would happen if Giorgio knew for sure that Celestina had sprung into existence? Without the reassurance that he'd stay with her, Eusapia refused to give him a definite answer. Her destiny had led her to Giorgio and his apartment. What for, if not to remain here, to find happiness and an abundance of love and money? Eusapia sighed with hopeful expectation as she resolutely pushed unsettling images of Giorgio's wife out of her mind.

What are you thinking about? Giorgio asked.

Nothing, Eusapia responded. Nothing much. Isn't life magnificent, Giorgio?

Yes, Giorgio agreed. He already saw Lillian coming back. Her face was aglow and in her arms lay their child smiling up at her. Now she knew how much he loved her. He gave her the child she had always wanted. Her face softened. And when he touched her lightly, there were no convulsions.

Giorgio, do you love me? Giorgio? Eusapia's voice pulled him out of his dreams.

Yes, yes, I do, Giorgio said reassuringly. He had to make sure Celestina had truly arrived.

When Eusapia missed her period, she hid it from Signor Damiani. She wanted nothing in their relationship to change. That's why she could not tell him. She found excuse after excuse to avoid going to his apartment for several days.

What about Celestina? Signor Damiani would ask from time to time.

It's bad luck to talk about Celestina, Eusapia grumbled. It bothered her when he talked about the girl. The sudden catch in his voice roused her suspicion. He was making plans that didn't include her. She could feel the change in him.

You love me, Giorgio?

Don't you know, Eusapia?

Tell me.

Don't you feel it in your body?

Tell me, Eusapia insisted, her eyes blazing with insecurity and rage.

I love you, Eusapia, he finally uttered.

The second time Eusapia missed her period, she was more careless. She hadn't counted on Signor Damiani keeping tabs on her.

Aren't you four days late with your period?

I'm often a few days late.

I don't think so, Eusapia.

Are you spying on me?

No, I just know you. Are you aware how pale you look?

Because you want me to learn everything at once, she almost shouted at him. It's too much. By now she was desperate to shut him up. She could not afford questioning of that sort. Giorgio was sly. But even though she was convinced he knew, there was no way she would confirm her pregnancy before he was committed to her. She had to make sure no one noticed how sick she felt most mornings, how the mere sight or smell of food could turn her stomach.

Are you pregnant? Signor Migaldi inquired one day. Since she had carefully hidden any sign that could have given her secret away, she knew that Signor Damiani had asked him to get the truth out of her. Are you? he insisted, watching her closely.

That's none of your business, Eusapia shot back angrily.

You know I care about you.

So what? You don't own me.

Giorgio has a right to know.

I'll tell him when I'm sure.

Is there a possibility?

Eusapia escaped, slamming the door behind her. Signor Migaldi was not going to ruin her chances with Signor Damiani. I can't live without him, she thought wretchedly.

She fled to the maid's room freed up for her because the Migaldis could no longer afford a second household hand. Instead of calming down, Eusapia panicked. Her stomach started heaving. She ran to the basin, where she threw up without making noise, as she had learned to do over the last few weeks. Before anyone got a whiff of the smelly brew, she snuck outside to dispose of it in the gutter.

The daily sessions with Signor Damiani degenerated and revealed her neediness in such a crude manner that she herself cringed in humiliation. Don't leave me, Giorgio. Her panic wrapped itself around her body like a big sign. She could not silence the pleas thrumming mercilessly inside her. Stay with me, Giorgio. I need you. Don't steal Celestina away from me. Eusapia's desperation made Giorgio so nervous he couldn't make love to her anymore.

Don't worry, Eusapia, everything will be all right, he said meekly.

But she wasn't fooled. She knew it wasn't going to be all right.

Giorgio, you don't love me anymore, she said, her misery screaming sharp and accusing.

I will always love you. You're the mother of my child.

Our child!

Don't scream, Eusapia.

But Eusapia continued screaming, Our child, our child, Giorgio. She started punching him on the chest, in the face. Giorgio staggered backwards.

Don't do that, Eusapia. It's bad for the child.

What child?? There is no child. Don't ever think there will be a child. You bastard son of a bitch.

Don't talk like that. I beg you.

Don't talk like that??? You beg me?? For Christ's sake, just shut up.

I do love you, Eusapia, Giorgio said quietly.

You love me about as much as my father loved me. You're all the same.

That's not true. Remember how happy we were.

Right! Stupid me, your act was so convincing I believed you. I thought our love was real. Everything was just a horrible scam. You conned me, Signor Damiani.

Where does this sudden bitterness come from? You're sixteen years old, Eusapia.

The world seemed set against her. Giorgio would never belong to her. He would go back to his wife. He would give their Celestina to Lillian. Eusapia was too young and alive to give in to depression. But with the same passion she had loved, she now boiled with rage.

If under the calming influence of the Migaldis and the strict guidance of Signor Damiani, she had sweated and laboured to purge herself of the foul language picked up from her father and his buddies, she now reverted back to spewing out curses and obscenities. No more restraining herself until she was blue in the face! Why shouldn't the idiots and son-of-bitches be called the names they deserved? The filth she spit out released at least momentarily a bit of her tension. Shocking her sitters who swallowed the nonsense she dished out, and insulting the men who behaved like groping imbeciles as soon as the séance room darkened, brought urgently needed temporary relief.

What's wrong with you? Signora Migaldi asked after a séance during which Eusapia had made everyone blush with embarrassment when she panted and writhed as if she had an orgasm and her spirit control called the sitters pathetic and stupid. Where is your smile? How is it possible for the innocent and generous good-heartedness in you to disappear like that?

Eusapia refused to respond. She didn't want to hurt Signora Migaldi, who had always been good to her. If she opened her mouth, nothing good would come out. Everything soft, tender, and loving in her had hardened to a sharp-edged rock. Since she couldn't rip it out of her body and bang people over the head with it, she used it as a launch pad for pitiless pronouncements that brought tears to the sitters' eyes and made others faint. Lashing out and inflicting pain kept her from falling apart. She wanted to see others suffer like herself.

Eusapia, let me help you, Signora Migaldi tried again, with as little success as earlier.

Later, it was Signor Migaldi who took her aside. This has to stop, he said. How could you have turned into the vulgar monster you pretend to be?

Goodness never worked for me. So there, Eusapia answered and stared defiantly into his face. I want to keep Celestina.

You know that's not possible. How could it when you barely make enough money to pay for your own expenses? Giorgio and Lillian will provide a good life for your baby. They will love her with their hearts and souls.

I love her too.

I don't doubt it. But you know what's best for Celestina and for you. You understood perfectly well what the deal was.

I changed my mind.

You can't do that, Signor Migaldi said, sharper than he intended. He could see the girl's misery. He understood how much she suffered. Worse, he was fully aware how wrong it had been to push her into this venture, and that behind the back of his wife! But he also was determined to do whatever was necessary to save face. I'll be there for you, he said lamely.

Eusapia looked at him. Even though she could have punched him in the face right now, she knew that despite all his faults and crazy schemes, he did care for her.

If you were there for me, you'd help me, she retorted.

As he looked at her, Signor Migaldi had to blink away a tear. For a moment, he put his arms around her. Don't worry, Eusapia, he said. You'll be all right.

His voice calmed her, and she almost believed him. Exhausted, she pressed her face into his chest, and was able to relax for a moment.

You'll be all right, she heard his voice again. She breathed easier. If only he were right!

On the days when Eusapia gave séances, she tried to put a few small coins away to prepare for the arrival of Celestina. She had found a perfect hiding place for her savings. In the maid's room where she slept stood an armoire that, after meticulous inspection, revealed what she had been hoping for, a forgotten secret compartment. Perfect, she muttered, coughing several times in a row as the heaps of dust and the musty odours inside seeped into her nose and throat. The next day, Eusapia furtively snatched a rag from the housekeeper and cleaned the compartment the best she could. The treasure box itself was too bulky to fit into the hole. But there was more than enough room for the coins, watches, bracelets, Nonna's necklace, and all the other trinkets, which she poured onto the large surface area with relief. No one would sniff out this well-concealed hideaway. Who had used it last? Maids had no valuables to hide. Since only a few very educated people could read and write, it's unlikely someone would have concealed love letters here either. For a moment, Eusapia tried to imagine the person who needed to keep secrets, but her own precarious situation robbed her of the energy necessary to continue thinking about anything else than her own problems.

A few centesimi and a lira from time to time accumulated painfully slow among the treasures she had brought from Minervino and never amounted to a confidence-inspiring sum. Regardless of how hard she worked, it would never be enough to feed and clothe a child.

Celestina, tell me what to do, Eusapia pleaded. But there was no response. Over the weeks, her little girl had withdrawn more and more until she was swallowed up by her new role as a foetus. Eusapia was keenly aware of Celestina's presence in her belly although no outward sign gave her away yet. She talked to her child every night, but Celestina, the spirit companion, had vanished, leaving behind nothing but a vague memory as she waited to be born. Radiating from this memory was her special brand of goodness and wisdom, which left Eusapia bewildered. What use was goodness in her situation? For Celestina's sake, she tried to hang on to it. She wanted her daughter to be proud of her.

She wanted Giorgio to realise what he was missing. But Signor Damiani started to keep his distance. He seldom showed up now at the Migaldis and what training he provided always took place outside his apartment. When he came to the Migaldi residence, his first glance was at her stomach. Was she or wasn't she pregnant? Eusapia was glad her pregnancy was still so unnoticeable that Signor Damiani was left with traces of doubt. Giorgio, she would think, concentrating all her energy on him, come back to me. Her wishing and scheming had no other effect than to prolong his uncertainty. She wanted to hit and punch him, but that would ruin the last of her chances.

You'll never get the child, Giorgio, she served notice into the dark when her anguish kept her awake. Sleep, which had come easier to her since she roomed at the Migaldis, became elusive again. Night after night she lay awake pondering her misery and her future. One night, she sat up in her bed with a frantic inspiration, You won't defeat me. I'll show you!

It was after the next séance that an elderly gentleman started shouting that his watch had disappeared. Another sitter added to the general mayhem by insisting that his pouch of coins was missing from his wallet.

How is that possible? Signora Migaldi exclaimed.

By now, the sitters were on their feet. Signor Migaldi flooded the room with light to make even the darkest spots visible. People searched every corner. They lifted the chairs. They moved the table. Despite feeling dizzy and headachy from the aftereffects of her trance, Eusapia took part in the search. But watch and pouch had disappeared into thin air.

Are you sure you wore your watch this morning? Signora Migaldi asked. Isn't it possible that you left it at home?

And the pouch? someone reminded her.

Let's check in the entry and in the dining room for both of them. Or maybe they fell to the ground on the way.

The Migaldis and their guests spent two hours turning over every object in the rooms the sitters had come in contact with. Signor Migaldi watched Eusapia with concern.

When he could grab her alone, he almost hissed at her. Give the stuff back, he commanded, making sure no one could hear him.

What are you talking about? Eusapia responded, staring at him in a show of disbelief, her eyes bulging with outrage. She registered with satisfaction the flicker of doubt that crossed his face. At this point they were interrupted by Signora Migaldi.

Do something, she beseeched her husband.

Signor Migaldi hesitated for a moment. With uncertainty lingering in his mind, he asked everyone, including Eusapia and the members of his family, to join him in a search along the way to the hotel of the sitter whose watch was missing. He knew that the man had taken shortcuts to their home, paths that few people set foot on. This allowed for a slight chance that the watch could lie undetected, at least for a short period of time. The group began its search in some disarray. No sign of the watch along that path. Either it had never been there or someone had found it and disappeared with it a long time ago. The Migaldis and their group went to the sitter's apartment and started moving and turning every piece of furniture in an attempt to find the lost object. All of a sudden Ugo screamed, Here it is. He had removed one of the cushions from the sofa and couldn't believe

105

his luck when the gold watch lay innocently toward the back of the seat. It must have fallen off this morning, he said more calmly. Relief swept through the group. Not long after, the sitter who had claimed to have lost his pouch, said in a rather embarrassed voice, I just noticed that my pouch is in my coat pocket. Even though I never put my pouch there, I could have sworn I checked the pocket when we left your house, he added, looking self-consciously at Signora Migaldi. He opened the pouch and counted the few copper pieces. He was sure it had contained a large sum of money, including four silver and four gold coins, instead of the measly pocket change lying inside like an insult. But he did not dare to mention it. He couldn't risk making a complete fool out of himself.

Thank God, Signora Migaldi cried out, her hands still slightly trembling from the scare the apparent theft had caused her.

Signor Migaldi threw a last glance at Eusapia who pretended not to notice, but gleefully took in his bewilderment. He liked to be in charge of things and would not take kindly to finding out that he had been duped. Well, Signor Migaldi, she thought, trying to hide her smirk, One day you'll find out who you're dealing with.

The séances never recovered their untroubled atmosphere. Somehow they had lost their innocence. Uptight sitters nervously guarded their possessions. Yet, small valuables and coins continued disappearing. Instead of a serene expectancy infusing the sitters before a séance, disturbing currents of mistrust chilled the room.

Watch out, everyone. Hold on to your precious objects, a sitter warned during an especially unpleasant séance.

Now wait a minute, Signora Migaldi tried to placate the different groups. Remember how the watch was found on the sofa and the pouch with the coins that was supposed to be missing turned up in the gentleman's coat pocket.

But where is my necklace? a distraught woman cried out.

I'm sure it will turn up just like the other items, Signora Migaldi continued. When you get home, check all your drawers, check beside the bed and under tables and chairs. It's bound to be somewhere within your own walls.

The discouraged woman began whimpering. She clearly was not convinced.

Let's cut the séance short for today, Signor Migaldi suggested. I'll give you back your money and you'll be able to reschedule another sitting at a later date. Even his warm smile couldn't wipe away the general unease.

I smell a rat, an older gentleman repeated over and over.

Dear friends, Signor Migaldi addressed them in an unaccustomed grave tone, I believe the presumption of innocence must prevail until there is proof of wrongdoing. Think twice before making accusations. Doing so without cause is not conducive to psychic phenomena. You must be sure your allegations are true before bringing disrepute on anyone in this room. His passionate sermon seemed to reach his guests and re-established a certain calm. They rid themselves of suspicions and worries for the moment. By the time coffee was served, conversation and laughter wafted through the room at a good-natured pitch.

At night, when Eusapia could be certain everyone was asleep, she'd sneak into her armoire. Without noise, she'd open her hidden drawer to contemplate her possessions in the sheen of the lamp close by. After depositing new pieces, she'd drink in the sight like an addict, unable to think of anything else, unable to stay away for more than a day. Inside the armoire she'd do nothing but stare at first until every one of her senses was completely intoxicated. When her initial high had lost its power, she'd start touching each of the coins she had accumulated. She would hang the two watches she had pickpocketed on the crowded streets of Naples on her nightshirt and the gold and pearl necklaces around her neck, completely oblivious to the world yet strangely ready to pull the door of the armoire closed at the slightest sign of danger, prepared to make herself and her treasures disappear within seconds without a sound.

She never talked to Celestina when she was in the armoire, and she avoided thinking of her mother and Lucia. But it took great effort to keep their shadows from pushing through into full consciousness. If she'd allowed them to reach her, she'd fall apart, unable to deal with the alarm in their eyes. They did not understand how the world worked. Her mother had been dead too long, Lucia only saw the good in people, and Celestina was too innocent to realise that virtue and noble sentiments might lead straight to starvation. She'd die like poor Maria. That, Eusapia could not bear thinking about. But the thought was too strong to be ignored. How long would her loot last? Ten months? Two, three years maybe?

No matter her misgivings, life seemed still more or less controllable. Eusapia saw herself moving about Giorgio's apartment with Celestina in her arms, Giorgio standing across from her, smiling, cooing happily to their little daughter. The room looked bright and cheerful. But in Eusapia's heart, growing doubts started to cast shadows on the picture. She was dismayed.

What am I all worked up about? she asked herself. Giorgio would never abandon me. She clung to this belief in sullen desperation. Slowly, though, her confidence frittered away. While she might enter the séance room smiling, she found it difficult to keep up appearances. As soon as the séance began, she was unable to keep her turmoil and unhappiness in check. Like gales, they swept through her soul and thrust her into a state of frenzy and gloom so distressing that she barely held it together. Objects disappeared persistently. What's happening? shouted the frustrated sitters. Signor Migaldi dispatched an urgent message for Signor Damiani to join them.

You need to work this out, Signor Migaldi said to Eusapia and Signor Damiani in his office. You stay in here as long as it takes. With an emphatic, take-charge gesture, he left the room. Eusapia glared at Giorgio, but was unable to hide the intense longing that mixed with her rage. Why did he have to torment her? Why be so cruel? All of a sudden she lunged at him and punched him with a passion that she thought had died over the last few weeks.

Giorgio, you swine, get out of here.

Are you pregnant?

What do you think, Giorgio?

I know you are. Don't worry. I will take care of you.

How??

There is this wonderful place up in the mountains. The woman who lives there is a cousin of mine and worked as a midwife before she got married. She is the most able and kind person you'll ever meet. You will love her, and she'll give you the best of care.

Will you be there?

Don't be silly, Eusapia. You know that's impossible.

Then get out and don't come back.

Eusapia grabbed Signor Damiani by the collar of his jacket. Again she hurled insults at him. Swine. Thief! Get out. She pulled him along to the door, yanked him around and gave him a kick in the ass that propelled him into the hallway with surprising force.

There! Now leave me alone.

Hours after Signor Damiani had left, Eusapia remained exasperated and subdued. She punched the air with her fists. She swore. Son of a bitch, she spat out under her breath. The worst insults didn't seem strong enough. Still, they exploded out of her with such wrath that their heat dried up the lakes of tears in her, leaving nothing but deserts behind. Swine. Bastard. Consumed by her emotions, she was unaware of the changes in her. Acts of revenge destabilised her séances as soon as she sat down at the table. She shot out arrows with no regard for what or whom they hit. Lashing out was her only way to continue breathing. Her explosions kept her alive.

You will not get Celestina.

The sitters watched her with mounting mistrust. Steadily, their numbers declined, though she was still in demand. It became increasingly difficult for her not to heap ridicule on the men and women around the table. Didn't they know how ludicrous they were? Couldn't they see how foolish they sounded, clamouring for contact with the other side? Who would want to listen to their constant begging: Spirits make your presence felt, bring us this memento or that, bless us with one object or another and lay it neatly on the table in front of us, give us proof of your existence. The sitters' stupidity galled her. Yet she was aware that her anger had only drawbacks. More anger, less money. If she didn't want to lose the only income she was able to make, she'd better regain control of her emotions. In her condition, returning to work in a laundry shop or as a housekeeper was out of the question. It might kill her and the child. Fully aware of her limited options, she continued to produce the phenomena her sitters asked for. When they requested flowers, roses and camellias would appear as usual except that they were wilted and missed petals because she took no care when she picked them and purposely squashed them into her hidden compartments, sleeves and the folds of her dress. That was on a good day. A few times, dirty rocks appeared instead of flowers. Signor Migaldi had to take her aside for a serious talk several times.

When she cursed in a particularly appalling way one day and small rocks drew blood on a sitter's cheek and on the forehead of a family friend, Signor Migaldi said, Pull yourself together, child! This has gone beyond anything acceptable. Can I help you in some way?

Can I help you in some way? she parroted, and the sneer on her face made her look grotesque.

Honestly, Eusapia!

Yes, there is something you can do. Shut up!

Signor Migaldi cringed.

Let's remain friends, he said trying to recover his even temper.

Let's remain friends! Eusapia again mimicked him, more sarcastically than the first time.

111

She pushed passed him and ran out into the street. She drew in the smelly air emanating from rotting garbage that had accumulated left and right. Two rats gnawed on chicken bones. Suddenly she stopped, staring at the stiff corpse of another rat. A sick gleam came into her eyes and her half-crazed mind whirred in uproar. She gave the corpse a quick shove to make sure it was as dead as she thought it was. Then, wilfully ignoring the danger of her actions, pushing thoughts of plague and cholera out of her mind, she wrapped the dead rat decisively in some of the paper she always carried with her and hid the package in her purse.

Eusapia rushed back into the house and, after a few extra preparations, literally stormed into the séance room. She didn't greet anyone. She didn't even acknowledge anyone.

When a woman, who had lost both her parents in the last three months, asked the spirits to bring a pink rose as a sign that they were happy, a dead rat dropped onto the table. At its sight, the woman shrieked, then fainted, falling off her chair to the floor with a thud.

God help us, Signora Migaldi exclaimed and started praying aloud, crossing herself. Appease the spirits. Bring comfort to this poor woman. Forgive us our trespasses.

Forgive us our trespasses, the others joined her pleas in an out-of-sync chorus. Everyone was standing around the woman on the floor.

Our Mother of Perpetual Help, have pity on us sinners.

It was Ugo who had the presence of mind to send for water. When the housekeeper finally brought it, he started reviving the woman by wetting her face.

An odd combination of stunned silence and fearful agitation filled the séance room.

Is she all right? a voice from the back of the group inquired.

She hasn't regained consciousness yet.

The housekeeper brought more water, while Signor Migaldi sent an employee to fetch Signor Damiani who was said to be the most knowledgeable when it came to psychic phenomena.

For the first time, Signor Damiani lost his cool.

Get that rat out of the house, he shouted as soon as he arrived.

The housekeeper rushed to the table and swept the stiff little corpse into a pail, quaking at the sight. This wasn't an ordinary rat. It had been sent by the dead. A bad omen. A curse maybe. When someone yelled, Hurry up, the poor woman broke down bawling. It was Signor Migaldi who took the pail and disposed of the rat, throwing it into a heap of garbage on the street, a safe distance from the house.

Signor Damiani fought to regain his calm, but failed. His thoughts, his breaths, his gestures raced in frenzied loops. Life itself was spinning out of control. How could this happen? He was always in charge of things. He glared at Eusapia. She was bent on ruining his plans.

Ladies and Gentlemen, he finally said, dangerously close to losing his cool altogether, but determined to win this round. Our medium is possessed by a gang of low spirits. They control her actions. No matter how hard a medium tries, it's too difficult for her to fight off their dubious attacks. We'll have to cancel Eusapia's séances until further notice. We shall ask advice from the spiritualists in London who have more experience in such matters. I will sit down to write a letter immediately. Ladies and Gentlemen, like you, I deplore this turn of events. But rest assured that, with the right type of guidance, this whole episode will have been a catalyst for the awakening of new powers. In the future, better and purer phenomena will occur as a result.

The letter was sent off to London the same day, and unbeknownst to the other spiritualists a second letter by Signor Damiani made its way to England with clear instructions as to the formulation of the response. The Migaldis and their friends waited while Eusapia was left to her own devices. She did not give any séances and spent most of her time brooding in her room. Finally, the response came back.

Take Eusapia away, it said, Bring her up into the peace of a mountain where she can rest in fortifying solitude without demands on her. But make sure she is in a house full of love and caring, and in the company of a good-hearted and spiritual person, who will help her find her way back to the purest state of mediumship.

Where could we send the girl? Signora Migaldi asked anxiously as none of her acquaintances lived near a mountain.

Don't worry, Signor Damiani responded, one of my cousins lives on a mountain. She is the kindest person you could wish for and a true spiritualist.

Then she is the godsend we've prayed for, Signora Migaldi said and bowed her head in silence for a moment, thankful for the grace that God in his generosity bestowed on them.

What do you think, Eusapia? she asked the girl, who had sullenly kept to herself since the rat dropped on the table. Signora Migaldi received no answer. The mountain air will calm your nerves, she continued and wondered whether Eusapia was conscious of the plans being made. The girl sat on the floor in a corner of her room, hugging her knees to her breasts, rocking slightly back and forth, staring as if haunted by unspeakable visions of darkness.

It was Signora Migaldi who packed Eusapia's clothes and led her to the carriage that would bring her to the mountain.

I wish I could go to the mountain with you, Ugo said in a soft, warm voice.

Come back soon, shouted his younger brothers.

But Eusapia seemed to have disappeared into a world of her own where nothing and no one else existed. She didn't respond to the warm goodbyes and heartfelt wishes. She didn't wave or even look up as the carriage started rolling away.

"Heaven-on-earth" Mountain, Italy, 1870-1871

4

SITTING SMALL AND SQUASHED in the back of the carriage, Eusapia continued hugging her knees as she had done for hours at a time since the letter from England arrived. She had lost all notion of time or place. Dazed by the events of the last few days, she could conceive of only one thought, Giorgio, Giorgio, Giorgio, the name repeated beseechingly to the monotonous turning of the wheels. Giorgio, Giorgio. A relentless blaring, a plea sent back to Naples, spanning over the increasing distance to prevent the connection between her and Giorgio from breaking. She would never accept a rupture. Every time she chanted his name, it would ring in his ears and hopefully reach his mind. There was no way he'd dare to ignore her desperate summons.

Hours into the journey, she vaguely perceived climbing down from her carriage and squishing into a small, uncomfortable cart more suitable to the narrow mountain path and drawn by a skinny donkey. Though eerily conscious that the weight of the cart, luggage, driver, and herself was beyond the capacity of the animal, Eusapia had no energy to object. The mountain wind tousled her hair, but she hardly noticed. She was unaware of ascending and had no idea she was halfway up a steep mountain already. She wasn't conscious of either the sun or the suddenly darkening clouds. Sunk into herself, she couldn't hear the welcome messages of the mountain: the bleating of goats and sheep, the chirping of crickets, the whistling of birds, the murmuring of the wind. She didn't see branches and flowers waving as she passed. Giorgio. Giorgio. Giorgio. The pain ripped her heart in two.

Celestina, help me, she exclaimed. The collar of her dress was wet as if it were raining already.

The path became impassible even for the small cart. Eusapia and her driver were forced to continue the last forty minutes of her journey on foot. She stumbled unseeingly over rocks and patches of grass and arrived at the home of Gianina DeNatale, oldest cousin of Giorgio Damiani. Eusapia was too exhausted to notice the striking family resemblance. Gianina had to take the girl by the hand to lead her into the house.

You must be hungry, Gianina said. She put water, bread, and a sliver of cheese in front of Eusapia, who did not see it despite having gone without food for hours.

You'll feel better after a good night's sleep, Gianina cooed. She brought Eusapia to a tiny room with a small bed. When Eusapia sank into the bed and closed her eyes, kind words chanted from somewhere above her, Just sleep, my child. Dream of happiness. This mountain will make you whole again. A sad note entered the unfamiliar voice, Believe me, I know. When sickness took my husband and sons, this mountain promised peace and made good on its promise. I'm alive. Do you understand, Eusapia? I'm alive. And you will live too.

Eusapia heard without understanding. She let herself fall into a deep sleep and slept through the night and the morning, into the early hours of the afternoon.

Wake up, Gianina called gently.

For a moment, Eusapia thought she was a little girl again and her mother was calling her. A timid smile crossed her face. But when she opened her eyes and saw a woman with the eyes and mouth of Giorgio in front of her, she cried out, startled, and in complete panic grabbed the hands of the older woman.

Who are you? Eusapia asked.

I'm Gianina, Giorgio Damiani's cousin. He asked me to take care of you.

Giorgio's cousin, Eusapia repeated in her mind. Maybe he'd be coming too. Her hope soared.

Is Giorgio coming?

No, Gianina said. You know he won't.

I don't know that. He is the father of my child. He loves me.

He is married, Eusapia.

I don't care whether he's married. He loves me!

The girl's pain stared up at Gianina as if it were alive, a wounded animal still strong enough to attack if you came too close.

Come, she encouraged Eusapia. You have to eat and get your strength back for whatever life holds in store. Gianina quietly left the room and went downstairs.

Eusapia's eyes remained fixed on the ceiling. All of a sudden, she heard the twitter of a bird. She glanced toward the window. The afternoon sun poured in. Around the rays, specks of dust followed the rhythm of a leisurely dance. Slowly, Eusapia sat up. She pushed her legs over the side of the bed. With a little jump, she lowered herself to the floor and like a sleepwalker moved to the window. Blinded by the sun at first, it took her a few seconds before she saw four scraggly pines a short distance from the house, and further down two beech trees. She breathed in deeply. In contrast to the smelly and heavy concoction in Naples, the air was crisp and refreshing. Greedily, she drank it in. More, she mumbled, more, more. I need to breathe. She smelled the flowers and trees and herbs. She smelled the wind. All of a sudden, she stopped. I smell coffee, she said. God, do I ever need a strong cup of coffee. The smell wafted up to her with a temptation she could not resist.

This should perk you up, Gianina said, placing a steaming cup of coffee in front of her. What's good for your body is good for the spirit too.

Eusapia looked at the odd, elderly woman who asked Eusapia to call her Gianina, not Signora, but Gianina pure and simple. She liked the face whose wrinkles pointed upwards in a smile that said, I have gone through the worst that life can throw at you, and I have survived, and so will you. It was Gianina's quiet strength and positive outlook that touched Eusapia most. Everything about her said, You can survive. Life is worthwhile.

You're smiling, Gianina said.

Maybe it's not so bad here after all.

Let's make the best of our time together, Eusapia. Look at the trees, the flowers, the stars. When you can see them, there is hope. Eusapia, don't forget, there is always hope.

Eusapia stared at the woman. It was like being around Lucia. She wanted to reach out. Mother, she wanted to say.

As soon as the word formed in her mind, the silhouette of her mother appeared behind Gianina, slowly drifting into focus, a smile forming on her lips. Yes, Eusapia, her mother confirmed, nodding, Gianina is the real thing. Trust her.

We're on a mountain?

Yes, we are, Eusapia, Gianina responded, on "heaven-on-earth" mountain. When I was at the lowest point in my life, I unexpectedly found hope here.

I want to see the mountain, Eusapia replied and stood up.

Go ahead. You won't be disappointed.

Eusapia left the house. She looked up and down, then walked ahead and climbed the first pine tree with a heavy enough branch to support her.

To Eusapia, it seemed as if she had known Gianina all her life. Gradually she forgot Naples and the harsh judgement it had meted out after the rat had landed on the table. She started to feel better too, with the bouts of morning sickness diminishing daily. When she did have to vomit, Gianina understood and would say, Your baby is doing well.

Look, Gianina, Celestina is growing.

Eusapia took the woman's hand and let it rest on her stomach. See the little bulge. It's not much yet. But if you look closely, you can see it.

It seemed natural to feel the woman's hand on her belly, like extra protection for Celestina. Gianina's love would carry them both through the next months.

Thank you, Gianina!

What for? the woman asked.

For being here for us. For being kind and generous.

Gianina never asked Eusapia for a séance. But the same way Eusapia talked to her mother, Gianina had never stopped communicating with her husband and sons after they died. There were even days when she set the table for her whole family and laid out a plate for Michela Palladino as well. Eusapia got to know the family as if they were her own relatives. She especially liked the two handsome boys, who, at eighteen and nineteen, were just old enough to make them intriguing. Contrary to her tempestuous nature, both boys seemed happy-go-lucky fellows with big hearts just like their mother's. Gianina's love made them so real that Eusapia thought she felt their breath on her. At times, Eusapia was tempted to flirt, but they treated her like their sister. As her big brothers, they didn't hold back with their opinions, convinced that it was their duty to give advice.

Eusapia, take Giorgio, for example. Don't you realise by now that he is way too old for you? Look at him and then at our Papa. Giorgio looks older than him for heaven's sake. Doesn't that tell you something? For sure, he is charming and good-looking, but Eusapia, wouldn't you have more fun with guys our age?

I wish they were my brothers, Eusapia said to Gianina.

They are your brothers now.

Eusapia took strength from her new family. Even during times when she wanted to tear out her hair and the absence of Giorgio darkened her moods, their love pulled her out of the black holes in which she sank more often than was good for her and the baby. To see her own mother become best friends with Gianina, her husband and sons gave her special satisfaction.

We're all connected, Gianina said more than once.

On occasion though, Eusapia couldn't stand seeing any of them, not even her mother, least of all Gianina whose resemblance to Giorgio poured salt on her wounds and nearly drove her insane. It was Giorgio who had made Eusapia a woman, if she didn't count the terrible nights in Minervino. He was the one who made her realise that she needed a man, a strong hot body beside her. When she sat on the branch of her pine tree to find refuge, Giorgio was there, naked and energetic, ready to plunge into her, the way she wanted and needed him. While the mountain gave her peace and Gianina warmed her with motherly love, there was a craving in her that neither could fill. With no close neighbours, there was no one to break her isolation or bring relief to her feverish longing. Yes, there were the ghosts of the dead keeping Eusapia and Gianina company in their solitude. They might have saved Gianina, but they weren't enough for Eusapia. Over time, the mountain transformed into an unbearable prison.

Where are you? Gianina inquired from across the table.

Eusapia didn't blush, but her greedy passionate look gave her away.

There is nothing to be ashamed of. You're young, you're healthy. I understand.

How could you? You probably haven't been with a man since your husband died, Eusapia growled scornfully.

That's why I empathise with you. Do you understand the hell I went through in the years following my family's death?

This time, Eusapia blushed, but did not apologise. Gianina looked too withered to even remember what it felt like to have just one thing on your mind.

I'm not that old, Gianina said in response to Eusapia's unspoken thoughts.

What do you know, Gianina? Eusapia asked with the disparaging desperation of a sixteen-year old cruelly separated from the love of her life.

I know that you're hurting, the woman replied.

I want Giorgio.

Gianina didn't respond. She sat quietly across from the girl, her love flowing toward Eusapia in an attempt to reach and comfort her, but unable to find an entry into her heart.

As winter approached, Eusapia's misery deepened. Not once had she heard from Giorgio. Even her tree withheld its comfort because of her rapidly growing belly and the freezing weather. What was the point of risking the climb if she couldn't sit on a branch longer than two minutes, if the biting wind forced her to return to the house in a hurry so that the cold didn't go right through her body to the child who needed all the warmth she could get?

Moping around won't help, Gianina said as Eusapia lay listless on the sofa.

I'm not moping, Eusapia muttered without stirring as much as a finger or a toe, without a trace of a smile. She wanted to be back in Naples. That was the only place where she and Giorgio had a chance. She even missed the silly and overbearing men and women who had come to her séances. Anything was better than being snowed in on a mountain with just one person — a person that wasn't Giorgio.

Are you all trying to hide me?

That's not it, Eusapia. But you weren't happy in Naples. You found it too hard to give up Giorgio.

Why should I have to give him up if he loves me?

He loves Lillian. He would do anything for his wife.

No one wants an ice queen for a wife, Eusapia shouted, her own desperation rapidly dissolving the compassion and understanding that had filled her when she first met the woman, destroying the connection that came from common experiences and unspeakable memories.

She isn't an ice queen, Eusapia. That's what you don't understand.

Oh yeah?!! She doesn't even let him touch her!

She is getting treatment for her problem.

You can't cure something that isn't a sickness.

How do you know, Eusapia? Lillian is being treated by a doctor in France who has helped other patients with similar conditions. From what I hear, she is getting better. There is hope for her and Giorgio.

Screw them all. They don't know what they're talking about.

But that night, when Eusapia wanted to fall asleep, Lillian showed up, looking radiant.

See, Eusapia, she said softly, there is a cure for everything. I'll be a good mother to Celestina.

You'll never get her! Never! Ever! Eusapia shouted so loud that Gianina came running into her bedroom.

What is it, my child?

No answer came forward. Worried, Gianina kept sitting beside the bed until hours later Eusapia's droopy eyelids became too heavy to keep open.

When Eusapia woke two hours later, worry lines crossed her forehead. If she didn't hand over her baby at the end of her pregnancy, Giorgio's promised money would not materialise, that much she had understood from the beginning. Her worry lines deepened. Only the thought of her treasure box cheered her up a bit. She jiggled it just enough to hear the unmistakable tinkling of her coins. Carefully she opened the lid and looked at the goods inside with almost smug satisfaction. Despite the turmoil during her departure, she had had a presence of mind that shocked even herself. She didn't remember packing the box. How on earth could she have thought of it, let alone managed to recover the items from their hiding place! But here was the box, its contents more than just money and small valuables. This loot was her ticket to freedom.

Coins, watches, brooches, necklaces, earrings lay on her left hand with promising reassurance. With her right hand, she picked up one piece after another, dangling each in front of her eyes, taking in the sight voraciously as if it were food and she hadn't eaten in days. In a way this box was nourishment. It gave her love-starved body strength and a potent infusion of hope that the treasure would be her means to buy her way back to Naples where Giorgio was waiting for her. Anytime she wanted to leave, she could do so. It might have to be after the birth. They were snowed in almost completely. She had to think of Celestina. That was the most important consideration. She would never allow any harm to come to her daughter.

From time to time, a man stopped at their house and brought Gianina packages of food to keep the two women healthy and make sure the foetus was progressing well. Gianina would give a letter to the man in return. Once, the man, a very young man, a boy almost, arrived as the blackish clouds suddenly tore apart. Out from nowhere, a terrifying winter storm gathered force. The wind whipped the snow through the air and off the ground with such turbulence that nothing but sheaths of snow, ice and fog were visible.

You can't go on in this weather, Gianina said. Come into the house until the storm calms down.

The man accepted and sat down at the table with them. He talked about his wife who was expecting their second child.

Eusapia stared at him. She didn't see a stranger, no, his young face turned into Giorgio's. When Gianina went to her room to get the letter she had prepared, Eusapia gazed at the man as if mesmerised. He shifted nervously.

You're expecting a child too? he asked timidly.

She will arrive in two months.

She??

Oh, yes, Celestina. She can't wait to see us all.

How do you know?

She told me.

The man looked at her with open mouth, suddenly ill at ease.

Come on, put your hand on my stomach and feel her.

The man did not move. He sat taken aback and self-conscious.

Impatiently, Eusapia walked over to him and stuck her belly right into his face. Then she grabbed his head and pulled him up from his chair with amazing strength. Before he could object, she slung her arms tightly around him and pressed her mouth on his. Her excitement was so strong that it transmitted itself immediately to the man. If he had wanted to flee at the beginning, he was now helplessly caught up in the tension-filled lust between them. Eusapia was triumphant. He loved her. Giorgio loved her, and he would never stop.

By the time Gianina came in with her letter, the two young people were sitting on their chairs, red-faced and quiet. She picked up on the charged atmosphere in the room at once. Eusapia kept staring at the man, who refused to look at her. Gianina turned to get coffee. Though it was too hot to drink right away, the man gulped it down, wincing when the hot liquid seared his mouth and throat. Yet no matter how much it hurt, he continued drinking.

I really have to be going, he said, clearly anxious to get away.

Be careful. It's still bad outside, Gianina cautioned.

The man almost fled out the door. Eusapia scarcely noticed. She had retreated into her own world back in Naples where Giorgio made preparations for her return and the arrival of their daughter.

We need to talk, Gianina said.

What about?

The future.

The future? There is no need. It's all set.

Eusapia, I'm serious. You have to come back to the real world.

Don't worry, Gianina. I know all about the real world.

Gianina shook her head, worry lines furrowing across her forehead.

Your daughter is going to be born in February. Decisions need to be made. You have to come out of your fantasy world. Lillian is back in Naples with Giorgio. They're waiting for their daughter, for your child.

128

You're lying, Eusapia screamed, and ran out the door into the freezing rain without coat or shoes.

Come back, Eusapia!

Gianina chased after the girl. Despite her age, she caught up with her near one of the pine trees, where Eusapia had stopped, wondering whether to climb up.

Don't be a fool, Eusapia. You're going to kill the both of you. You love this child. Come on back in before we all get pneumonia.

Gianina waited. The minutes seemed to drag on for hours. Finally, after endless pleas, Eusapia followed her back in. She threw herself on the sofa, not realising that Gianina helped her get out of her wet clothes and put blankets over her. When Eusapia appeared to get warmer, Gianina changed her own clothes and sat by the fire, shivering for a long time before her old limbs started to thaw in the warmth of the room.

Within a few minutes, they both fell asleep, Eusapia on the sofa and Gianina on a chair. Gianina never once woke up until the next morning, when the room resounded with three consecutive sneezes from the direction of the sofa. Eusapia was sitting up, sneezing and blowing her nose. Before Gianina could say anything, she too started to sneeze and cough. A headache held her head in a vice, and when she tried to stand up, her bones were stiff and heavy. She shuffled about as if she had to pull along a weight that would be too much even for a strong young adult, let alone herself.

Gianina pushed herself to brew coffee for the two of them.

I'm sorry, Eusapia said.

I know, Gianina responded simply. Let's get better and then continue our talk where we left off.

Their colds lasted longer than expected. It wasn't just the sneezing, coughing, wheezing, and sniffling. It was the debilitating fatigue that affected them most. Despite her pregnancy, Eusapia bounced back faster than the older Gianina. As soon as they felt a bit better, Gianina again took on the task of sitting Eusapia down to have that talk she had postponed for too long.

Now listen, Eusapia. What is it you want? You have no means to keep the baby. Giorgio won't support you if you keep the daughter he so badly wants. I don't have money to help you, but I do have this home. It could be your home and Celestina's, and we could get by on the little I have, Gianina said, fully aware of the strain that such a decision would put on her relationship with Giorgio.

But who could survive on this goddamn mountain with no one around?

You might be able to find work in a household or store in the valley and come for visits, at least during the summer when it is less strenuous and dangerous.

Eusapia said nothing.

My child, I know it won't be a picnic. But it would allow you to keep your child. I would look after her during the times you can't be here.

That's depressing . . .

It might not be what you'd hoped for, but it's a viable option.

You might as well stow me away on the moon.

Oh, Eusapia, one day, you'll learn that this place can give you peace.

Did you want peace at sixteen, Gianina? Didn't you want men and excitement?

Gianina looked at the pregnant girl sadly.

You're right. I wanted it all. Big passion. Happiness. Excitement. It's only after I lost my family that I found solace in the little things the mountain has to offer.

Don't take this the wrong way, Gianina. I love you with all my heart. You have been like a mother to me.

Then trust your instincts, Eusapia. Stay with me.

You know I can't. You know me better than I know myself. That's why you know I can't stay here.

Then give your child to Giorgio and Lillian where she will be loved and has a chance.

Not on my life!

When after the long winter months the snow started melting in the unusually mild January weather, and the water rushed down the mountain, wild and unpredictable, Eusapia felt a surge of hope. Soon the paths would be passable. The mountain would release her and give her back her life. In the last days of January, she saw the first few blades of grass pierce through the hard mountain earth in spots where the snow had melted away early. The sun, sending a gentle wake-up message, let its rays dance joyfully over Eusapia's big belly.

Celestina, we're ready, Eusapia said, wrapping her arms around her body. It's time to start moving.

Sooner than expected, in the first days of February, a sudden shift in her body stopped her in her tracks. A river of water rushed out of her and down to the kitchen floor. Gianina, who watched her closely these days, knew that there was no time to lose.

Here we go. We'll get through this no matter how much it hurts, she said and prepared clean sheets and pots of boiling water.

In the back of their minds, Eusapia's birth and the death of her mother flickered nervously and threw sinister shadows on every twist and turn of the labour. They tried not to think about it, but it was no use.

Neither Gianina nor Eusapia was prepared, though, for the speed and ease with which the child arrived.

My God, Eusapia, I've never seen anything like it. This one popped right out as if she had trained for this moment all nine months.

As soon as Celestina caught her first breath of air and blinked into the daylight, she screamed at the top of her lungs.

Well hello to you too, Gianina said, cradling the newborn for a moment, full of memories of the births of her own sons, then placing her tenderly into the arms of the young mother.

Eusapia couldn't take her eyes off the child.

Suddenly, her mood darkened. She looked anxiously at Gianina.

What's going to happen to us, Gianina?

You have to trust in God and the protection your mother in heaven gives you, Gianina answered quietly. Most of all you have to rely on your own strength. Life doesn't just happen. You make it happen.

What are you saying?

You know what I'm saying. It's time to make a decision.

Thinking wasn't really Eusapia's thing, but she decided she had to see beyond her own nose. Up till now she had acted on impulse, following a very vocal inner voice that pushed her along.

132

Where had that led her? Into big trouble. Nothing turned out the way she had imagined. She wasn't stupid enough not to know that Giorgio had dumped her, but her silly hope kept surviving like a strong weed. When finally her heart told her to uproot that weed, she refused to listen. She simply couldn't. What were her options? I will have to think my way out of my predicament. I'm done trusting my heart, she kept telling herself, knowing full well that she'd put herself on a slippery road.

Decisively, Eusapia went to get her treasure box and plunked it in front of Gianina.

I have prepared for hard times since I was a small child.

Gianina took her time examining the bounty in front of her. She glanced at Eusapia curiously, without judging and almost with pity, not asking where those watches, brooches, rings, necklaces, and coins had come from. She just looked at Eusapia as if she saw her for the first time.

I can provide for my child, Eusapia insisted.

Even if you sold every single piece, the money would last one, maybe two years, and then? What would happen then? Remember the stories you told me about Anna and her sister Maria who died? It's very hard to make it on your own.

I'm a medium. I can make a living.

With a child in tow and no husband, I don't think so. You would have a hard time finding someone to manage your career. Without rich mentors, you'd make a pittance that would lead right into disaster.

I want to keep my child.

I have offered you my home, Eusapia.

But I'd die here . . .

Gianina was able to keep Giorgio away for a while. She didn't inform him that the baby had arrived three weeks early. When his messenger came up to get news, she told him that the child couldn't be separated from her mother for at least another two months. She wanted to give Eusapia the maximum time possible to sort out her life.

Eusapia held Celestina in her arms.

What am I going to do?

The child looked up at her mother with big dark eyes.

Don't leave me, she pleaded.

If Anna were around, maybe I could arrange something.

Anna?

You know, little Maria's sister. She disappeared two months after Maria died. No one knew where she had gone, not even her parents. And the police said, No body no case. She must have run off to a better life, Eusapia thought. Yes, Celestina, Anna has found a better life. This was the only notion Eusapia could entertain.

Why are you talking about Anna?

Because she could have helped take care of you. Apart from Gianina, she'd be the only one I'd trust with my life and yours.

She's gone, Celestina said sadly. Who will take care of me?

I will.

I don't believe you. I can feel it. You're already gone. In your mind, you said goodbye a long time ago.

Don't say that, Celestina. I love you.

I love you too, Mammina.

In Eusapia's heart though, the word goodbye started swelling up, breaking free, sounding down into the valley and echoing back stronger and stronger, Goodbye, goodbye until it came crashing into her world like thunder. The sky turned black and the mountain became muted except for one terrible noise hitting her from all sides, Goodbye, good-byyyy-eeee.

I'll never give up my child, Eusapia shouted to counteract the screams around her. I might be only sixteen, but I am able to take care of her. I'm her mother.

An accusing voice came out of nowhere, a voice she had never heard before, You heat the milk so much you've burned the child twice already. You almost dropped her a few times. You wouldn't even notice if Celestina had a fever or a sore tummy. You're not a mother, you're nothing but a girl with no knowledge, no experience and no means. What do you think you're doing to your child? You want to ruin her future?

She belongs with me.

What about her father? Doesn't she belong to her father too?

We could be a family, Eusapia whispered. As she said it, the sentence imploded into a miserable heap of nothing.

See?

Why does life have to be cruel like that?

You have the power to make it sweeter for your child.

By giving her to Lillian?

You know she'll love her.

What about me?

This is about your child, not about you.

Eusapia didn't dare look at her mother who also appeared in the back of the room, silent and serious. It certainly wasn't her mother's voice giving her instructions, but who was it? Who was this voice that seemed to be all around her asking questions about her child, pushing her to the limit and beyond? But

135

Eusapia knew full well what was happening. Her own bad feelings and anxiety, the darkness in her, were crystallising, as often when she was at her most vulnerable, into a voice that was stronger than all her good intentions put together.

Mamma . . . ?

But Michela ignored Eusapia's questions and worries.

Mamma, you won't help me?

I have to let you decide for yourself. You're the one who knows what's in your heart.

The almost inaudible whisper hung for a moment in the room. When Eusapia tried to read her mother's expression, Michela had disappeared. Only the slight fluttering of her last sentence was left behind.

Intuitively grasping Eusapia's thoughts, Gianina put her arms around her.

Your mother is right. Only you can decide what to do.

But . . .

No ifs and buts. You took on the responsibility of carrying a child. It's your responsibility to make provisions for her. I have offered you my house and my help. Giorgio and Lillian desperately want to raise this child and will love her with all their hearts. You know your own strengths and needs. I'll support you in whatever you do.

Eusapia abruptly jumped to her feet, pressed the baby into Gianina's arms, and left the house. Up on a chilly tree close to the house, she tried to calm her nerves and throbbing arteries. As a few sunbeams started to shine soothingly into her dark uproar, and the light breeze caressed her gently, the fear that had taken hold of her slowly vanished. She tried to pray like Andrea prayed in Minervino. But it didn't work for her. She still wasn't able to find the right words, or even the right feelings. Somehow though she felt she wasn't alone. A while later, her mother sat down on the branch beside her and put her arms around her the same way Gianina had held her earlier in the day.

Taking care of Celestina was a challenge for Eusapia. Gianina let her do most of the work so she would learn how to take care of the child. But Celestina, who at times talked like an adult to Eusapia, could turn into an unreasonable screaming baby without warning. She had the exasperating habit of waking up at all hours of the night, clamouring for food and attention with an intensity that could tax the patience of even the most placid person. But Eusapia, who was the opposite of placid, coped poorly. The howling incensed her so much that she was left shaking. As soon as the screams started, she had to rush outside and rub cold snow into her face to put out the angry fires that threatened to engulf her. I'm calm, she chanted quietly, I'm calm. I'm calm. I'm calm enough to take care of my beautiful baby daughter whom I love more than anything in the world. She would rock Celestina for an hour or two, continually putting out fresh flames of anger. But no matter how close she came to exploding, she rocked her child with tenderness. I love you, Celestina. I love you, my child.

Despite the baby in her arms, despite Gianina's generous and companionable nature, despite the constant presence of her dead mother and Gianina's husband and sons, and despite the soothing memories of Lucia, Eusapia was consumed by loneliness and overwhelmed by an ever more oppressive routine. The days dragged on, uneventful and boring. The sun could beam its most brilliant gold down on the snow-covered mountain and the sky glitter in its shiniest blue, but Eusapia only saw grey, as if her eyes were covered with murky lenses. There was no one to break the monotony unless Eusapia found refuge in hallucinations. On an especially good day, Giorgio would make love to her until she was too exhausted to stay awake. Most of the time she was left to touch herself to calm her over-stimulated, frustrated nerves. In that state she was even tempted to seduce her new brothers. But she knew it wouldn't be right, and the young men had too much integrity to get involved in her games. When Gianina tried to put a comforting arm around her, Eusapia shook her off.

Leave me alone, she screamed, you don't have a clue what being cooped up on this stupid mountain does to me!

With the end of winter, her pent-up feelings of imprisonment started to break apart. Like snakes, they slivered into every part of her body, heading straight for the extremities: fingers, toes, hair, nipples. Eusapia squirmed under their wiggling and pushing. She was on edge. Something was about to happen. Every few minutes, she'd run out of the house and climb up one of the cold trees. After staying just a few seconds, she'd climb another one and then another to survey from every angle the valley where all the life was. When she set foot on the ground again, she ran in all directions, spinning and unruly like one of the cows out of the barn for the first time in spring. Only the thought of Celestina screaming for milk would bring her reluctantly back into the house and the responsibilities of motherhood.

I love you, Celestina, Eusapia told her child, barely containing her raw and overwhelming emotions of love and guilt. I love you, my wonderful daughter. Over and over she repeated it as if to reassure herself. She imagined herself pack Celestina's clothes, her own belongings, her box of treasures, then leave and lock the house as if no one else lived in it, holding her child tight, walking slowly and carefully down the mountain, trying to figure out where they could find a place in the valley, how they could survive.

There is a way, she told herself as in her mind she descended the mountain. There has to be a way.

Celestina started crying for milk at that point. Eusapia sat down to feed her. She always sat on the same rock about half a mile down the path where the sun could easily reach and warm them. She stared down into the valley and all she could see was herself. What about Celestina? She tried to find a spot for her as well. But the more she tried, the stronger the valley seemed to refuse her a home for her daughter.

Think of Maria. She had to die. If Celestina comes down to this valley, she'll face the same danger. Is that what you want? the unknown voice challenged her, increasingly insistent.

But, Eusapia said, I won't let her die.

How are you going to accomplish that? Even now, with Gianina's help, you are struggling to care for your child. You can't cope with the sacrifices a baby entails. Without money, you'll be stuck. You'll be stuck forever. No fun, no excitement, no life.

That's not true, Eusapia countered, life will be different. I'll be able to manage. Other women manage.

You're not other women, Eusapia. You crave freedom. You want action.

It was always at about this time that Celestina's gluttonous sucking stopped. Eusapia would wrap up her child tightly in her blanket and gaze at her wistfully before getting up.

This was the most painful moment of her daydream. She would look down to the valley, tears dropping on Celestina's face. Every time, she would finally turn around and drag herself back up the mountain to Gianina's house.

I can't hold off Giorgio any longer, Gianina said one morning in early April. I need a decision, Eusapia. His letters have been arriving every second day for the last two weeks. He'll be coming up himself any day.

Eusapia glowered. She refused to answer or even acknowledge Gianina's statement.

My dear child, Gianina said, you've made a decision a long time ago. It is time to admit it and live with it.

Don't pretend to know what is going on inside me!

Didn't you make the decision, Eusapia?

No!

I'm on your side. Eusapia, never forget that. We're both on Celestina's side.

Eusapia stomped up to her room. She threw herself on her bed, but couldn't relax. She jumped up again, pulled out her suitcase from under the bed and started packing.

One last time, she allowed herself to think of Giorgio, to see him, herself and the baby in a beautiful house, a happy family lovingly taking care of each other. That's all she had ever wanted. Finding a home. Being loved by the man she had so desperately fallen in love with, and raising their daughter together.

But no, it wasn't going to be like that. And she was unable and too young to take on the responsibility of a child by herself.

When Eusapia brought herself to go downstairs again, her face was drawn and sallow, the light had vanished from her eyes. She picked Celestina up, pressing the child to her chest as if to receive an imprint that would remain forever. Her voice broke when she finally spoke.

Celestina, for once I hope to do the right thing. As much as I hate to admit it, I know that Giorgio and Lillian will be able to provide a better life for you. Until now, I have refused to accept this, but now the time has come for me to do what is right. So instead of carrying you in my arms, I will carry you in my heart, always. Call out to me if you need me. Wherever I am, I will hear you and come to you. I won't say goodbye because we will be together again.

When Gianina gave Eusapia Giorgio's envelope with the promised money, Eusapia shrank back.

I can't, she said in a small voice. As much as she wanted and needed that money, she couldn't accept money for her child. Never! She might have made a mistake getting involved with Giorgio, but she was not the type of person to sell her child.

Eusapia's face was wet when Gianina folded her one last time into her arms. Neither of the women talked for a long time.

Here, Gianina finally said, and handed Eusapia two pieces of paper, one with an address, the other with a note. Go to this place first. It's the house of Signor Cammarata, my husband's childhood friend. He'll help you adjust to the valley again.

Thank you, Gianina, for everything.

Thank you, Eusapia, for making me feel alive again.

We too will meet again, Eusapia whispered. She hastily grabbed her luggage and left.

As she took her first steps down the mountain without looking back, without hesitation, Eusapia heard Gianina's faint but clear voice behind her, Please God, guardian angels, Michela, my husband, my sons, accompany and protect her, let her be happy.

Down in the Valley, Italy, 1871

5

EUSAPIA SPED DOWN THE MOUNTAIN without noticing the first spring flowers, the bustle of mice and insects, or the thickening growth of trees. To make it down to the valley, she had to shut off her senses. If she were to acknowledge her loss, regardless how bold she had been in making her decision, she would give in to the call of the cliffs with its promise of immediate peace. So she closed her ears and put blinders on her eyes. Single-mindedly she pushed herself forward, clinging to life, seeking whatever future was available to her.

When she reached the valley, she asked for directions to Signor Cammarata's village, a good fifteen miles to the east. Eusapia continued her journey without taking a break. The April sun shone down on her hotter and more oppressive than was usual for this time of year. She was unaware of sweat pouring down her body, and of her clothes sticking to her arms, trunk, and legs as if glued to them. She was oblivious to her nose turning a painful red and didn't feel the blisters forming on her toes and heels. Move, she said to herself. Just move. Go.

After inquiring where Signor Cammarata and his wife lived, Eusapia was on her way to a small house some distance from the village. Signor Cammarata opened the door before she could knock, curious why an unknown young woman would seek out his place. Eusapia handed him Gianina's note and waited anxiously for his reaction. Signor Cammarata stared at the letter without comment, but Eusapia could see his emotions surge to the surface and settle in the darkness of his pupils.

Come on in, he finally said, his voice cracking.

Signor Cammarata served her big pieces of bread with sausage. He didn't mention Signora Cammarata, who seemed absent from the house.

You could sleep in our son's room, which has been empty since he moved to Canada twenty-nine years ago.

Thank you, Eusapia responded, not daring to look at his face because of the strange catch in his voice.

In the morning, there was still no sign of Signora Cammarata.

My wife is sick, Signor Cammarata said, explaining the liquidy mush he was preparing. Do you want to say hello to her?

Eusapia followed the old man into the bedroom.

Hello Signora Cammarata, she said, covering her shock at seeing the woman Gianina had described as vibrant paralysed in bed with a blank stare, rasping through her parted lips, coarse white hair sprouting over her chin.

Eusapia watched silently as Signor Cammarata supported his wife's back with extra pillows and fitted a large cloth over her chest. With a little spoon, he carefully fed her minuscule portions of mush. Even then, the bits of nourishment irritated her throat, causing her to cough and choke. She did not seem conscious of eating. Eusapia stared at the Cammaratas with open mouth. She had never seen a man feed a woman or even a child, and wouldn't have believed it possible. The task didn't fit the category of things men were supposed to do. But then why not? Why should it make her uneasy?

144

Julia, my treasured wife, Signor Cammarata said, his voice fraught with love and sorrow. Try to swallow. We need to put flesh back on your bones.

Julia, my delicate rose, think of this watery food as honey dew or full-flavoured red wine. Please take a sip.

Julia, my glittering sun, don't fade away on me. Let me bring you back into our lovely home.

Eusapia, who had never heard anyone talk like that, listened spellbound. That's how love must sound and look, she thought as she witnessed the man's desperate attempts to keep his wife alive, although it perplexed her that anyone could use such extravagant language. While Eusapia had experienced the love of a few women, her dead mother, Lucia, and Gianina, she had not thought much about men in this way, or associated caring and conversation that sounded like poetry with them. Passion, yes. Giorgio was proof of that. But love that gives and continues giving, unselfish and without treachery? No, she didn't think so. She pinched her arm to make sure she wasn't hallucinating. But there was Signor Cammarata, devotedly spooning tiny bits of food into his wife's mouth for over an hour without a sign of impatience until her choking fits became too unrelenting to continue. He took a bowl of water and washed her face, neck, arms and hands, even her feet, with a tenderness so foreign to Eusapia that she blushed. Lucia's and Gianina's down-to-earth, no-nonsense generosity was the only kindness she had experienced and was comfortable with.

Julia, my charming shower of raindrops.

Eusapia cleared her throat. Can I help you with anything?

Oh, you'd be an angel if you'd shave the stubble off her chin. She'd want that more than anything else. My hands are too shaky. I'm afraid of hurting her if I tried.

Carefully, Eusapia removed every single hair.

Thank you, Signor Cammarata whispered, so delighted and grateful that Eusapia felt a reluctant surge of warmth.

Within a few hours, the feeling of warmth had peaked, then fizzled out. Nothing remained but a miserable mixture of loneliness and frustrated longing. Eusapia refused to see Celestina, who appeared without warning, looking expectantly down from the ceiling. Unable to acknowledge her child's clear hope that this home might welcome the two of them, Eusapia stared out the window into the rapidly approaching darkness of the night.

I need to go out, she said to Signor Cammarata, her voice grating with stubborn determination.

Signor Cammarata looked at her with concern. My dear child, it will be dark in a minute.

I'm not a child.

I didn't mean it like that, Eusapia. Why don't you stay and go out tomorrow?

But Eusapia had already grabbed her jacket.

I just need to go, I'm sorry, Signor Cammarata.

Without waiting for his response, she opened the door and ran into the night toward the village. She had seen a tavern when she first arrived. There must be people somewhere. There had to be young blood. Someone to hold her. Someone to bring her back to life.

When she slipped through the door of the tavern, the conversations stopped as if she were an apparition. The smoke in the room triggered a coughing fit that should have erased any doubt that she was real. It didn't occur to her that she looked out of place in a room full of men.

No women allowed, a burly man behind the bar yelled, the rough authority in his voice an obvious indication that he owned the place.

Yes, yes, yes, women are allowed, the men heckled, young ones, for sure, no old crows, oh, but a young one like this, oh please, keep her here.

Eusapia could feel the men size her up. She was unfazed. In fact, their lewdness filled her with a sense of power.

Aren't you the one staying at Signor Cammarata's? asked the owner, who knew everyone's business the moment it occurred. Without waiting for an answer, he said, Walk her back, Guido. Make sure she's safe.

A man in his thirties got up and walked toward her and the door.

The men cheered. You lucky son of a bitch.

Another man started to make his way to the door.

Hey, you there, the owner shouted, get back. Sit down. You're not even from here. Leave her alone, you.

But the man followed Guido out the door.

You heard the boss, Guido snarled.

It's all right, Eusapia interjected. We all go together.

My name is Raphael.

Raffaele? Raffaello?

No, Raphael Delgaiz.

147

Where the hell are you from? Guido almost shouted at him. Who in the world is called Raphael Delgaiz?

I am, the man said sternly and without further explanation. Now let's go, he added with a firmness that propelled everyone forward. He put his arm around Eusapia, who did not withdraw. She slightly pressed against him. She looked up to see how much he towered over her. A head and a half!

I'm the one supposed to bring her home, Guido grumbled beside them.

It's okay, Guido, Raphael will take me there. One is enough. It can't be that dangerous around here. Thank you for offering though, Eusapia added to make the brush-off less offensive.

You're sure? Guido asked, enraged that he wasn't able to impose himself, but uncertain how to handle the situation.

Yes, I'm sure.

Good night, then.

Good night, Guido, thank you.

Raphael and Eusapia walked on in silence, slower and warmer with every step until Raphael stopped and drew her close. Eusapia looked up at his face, expecting to see Giorgio, but the eyes that bore into her were definitely not Giorgio's. They were darker, moodier, almost brooding, and impatient, a starved, hot impatience that set her on fire. Oh yes, he needed her, and he needed her now. Eusapia closed her eyes.

When she felt his lips on hers, their heat seared into her with such force that she almost fainted. Raphael, she thought, we belong. It's a miracle we found each other in this tiny village at this time of the night. She sensed his hands on every inch of her body. His hold would never let her free again, and she was exactly where she wanted to be. Here was her survival.

Tomorrow, I'll pick you up in the morning. I'll make you my wife. You're mine, Eusapia.

Yes, Eusapia responded, drunken and ecstatic from the passion that bound them. I'll be there. Raphael, you and me, we'll travel the world as man and wife.

You don't know him, Signor Cammarata said. Why don't you stay here and get to know him better?

But I do know him. I know him as much as I'll ever know a person. We belong together. It's as simple as that. Waiting would be a waste of time. I can't waste time any longer.

Signor Cammarata sighed.

At this point, Eusapia didn't care whether he understood. Looking into his face, she found his usual good-natured smile, but also noticed the pain he tried to keep buried. Signor Cammarata, who liked her from the moment she arrived, had allowed the young woman to fill his heart with her vivacity and drive some of his loneliness away. Now that Eusapia would vacate that little spot she had warmed and filled with hope, sadness was preparing to sweep in and add to the misery his son had left behind when he turned his back on the village and his parents to make his living in a faraway country. Eusapia's departure would open wounds that should have been healed by time. Once again, Signor Cammarata would be haunted by memories.

Godspeed, my dear child, Signor Cammarata managed to say before his voice broke.

The knock at the door spared Eusapia from a prolonged goodbye that was more difficult than anticipated. But she also didn't have to cover up her excitement anymore. Since Raphael had proposed to her, she barely controlled her impatience to start her new life and to experience to the fullest everything she had been missing for so long. She wouldn't be alone any longer. She'd have her man. He would fill the void that her mother left behind when she died. He would make her forget the unbearable emptiness that the absence of Giorgio and Celestina created. Already Raphael had turned her child into a gentler and vaguer memory. Yes, surrendering her to Giorgio had been the right decision. Eusapia was sure of it now. Her life in general left no room for a child, and life with Raphael was an adventure too much removed from the stability required for raising a child. No matter how hard she tried to picture the three of them together, it was impossible. As soon as she conjured up the image, Celestina got sucked into a black hole. To Eusapia, this clearly confirmed that Celestina was better off with her father and his wife. She never considered another interpretation. There was no way she'd jeopardise her relationship with Raphael. He was her destiny, the man she had been waiting for.

With an easy leap of faith, the couple was on their way, bursting with passion and exhilaration. In their need for privacy, they sped along, they ran. A thicket of large trees finally offered what they were looking for. There, Eusapia came back to life under waves of passion and semen, as if a powerful storm had unleashed torrents for the sole purpose of satisfying her pent-up emotions. Don't let it stop, she screamed. Go on, Raphael. That's what we exist for. These moments. This wildness, this adventure!

After hours in the thicket, Raphael said, Now you're my wife. I have wandered the world just to find you.

And I came down from the mountain, I gave up living close to the sky, so that we could be together.

You're my wife.

You're my husband.

Raphael took out of his pocket a gold ring with an enormous yellow topaz. Eusapia gasped with wonder.

To the most intriguing woman. Let the sky, the sun, the wind and these trees be witnesses of our union. With this ring, handed down to me from my mother who received it from her mother, I now take you for my wife.

Eusapia took out of her pocket a small hand-painted snuff box with dancing women on it, the only appropriate present for a man in the loot she had collected over time, apart from two watches she didn't think would appeal to Raphael, who was naturally tuned into the cycles of the sun and the moon.

With this token, she said solemnly, I now take you for my husband. I wish for us a life of happiness, excitement, and never-ending sex. This last piece she said with such exuberant gusto that Raphael laughed out loud. Then he became serious. He took her face in his hands, with his strong fingers resting gently on the sprouting white flower in her black hair.

Amen, he responded cheerfully. You're now Signora Raphael Delgaiz.

I am now and forever Signora Raphael Delgaiz, Eusapia called out, and her voice had never sounded more content. She had never been as happy as at this moment. Everything in her arranged to cling to this happiness over days, months, years. Not once did Eusapia think of Giorgio. Raphael was all she needed: strong, greedy, ruggedly handsome Raphael!

As they walked along to the rooming house where Raphael stayed, Eusapia had no idea what her husband did for a living. Apart from being in love, happy and healthy, nothing mattered. She still had her treasure box hidden in her suitcase. If worst came to worst, it could carry them for at least a year, maybe longer. Between the two of them, they surely would find a way of making enough money to survive.

I have an engagement for one of my shows scheduled in three days in a small village, a twelve-hour walk from here. Are you up to it? Raphael asked, watching her carefully.

Am I up to it? What kind of a question is this? I'm up to anything that involves you and me. What show, Raphael?

I'm a magician.

You are?!! That's beyond my wildest expectations. Raphael, it's perfect. Can I be part of the show?

Sure. You have what it takes. Your eyes are magician's eyes.

Magician's eyes? But Raphael, I'm a medium.

Raphael laughed. Exactly, Eusapia, a born magician!

Did you ever see a woman magician?

Not really, but you'd be a great assistant.

I'd rather be a medium and have my own show.

One day, Eusapia, you will. For now, let's get the show on the road and earn enough to fill our stomachs and have fun. There is plenty of time for you to live the life of a medium. Any training you can get from me will save your hide one day. Honestly though, I doubt you'll need me for long. I see your cleverness, your shrewdness, your well of knowledge. As hard as it is for me to admit this, you'll surpass me in no time. You think you're the one to predict the future? I can do that too. I predict that you'll leave me within a few months.

152

What a horrible thing to say, Raphael. We've been married for one day.

To which Raphael responded, And what a fabulous day it has been, Eusapia! He said it with his eyes blazing as he grabbed her again, their clothes flying off in all directions. What a fabulous day it continues to be!

After a few hours of sleep, they ate leftover macaroni and beans from his supper of the night before. They loaded her suitcase on top of Raphael's cart, which contained his few belongings and his magician's clothes and tools, and they were ready to start out on their journey with the first rays of dawn. Pushing or pulling the cart to negotiate rocks, ruts, overgrown grass, and creeks along the way, racing along the main roads, juggling between tree roots and bushes, along shortcuts and small paths, they advanced at an impressive speed. In the few months Raphael had spent in this area, he had travelled every road and trail, sketching each on an invisible map he seemed to carry with him at all times.

Because it was their honeymoon, Raphael chose the most picturesque route.

Have you ever seen anything more beautiful than these lemon trees in bloom? he asked and stood still, drinking in the view before him with joyful wonder.

Not as impressive as these ones, Eusapia said as she walked along. She smiled until she saw Celestina balancing in the whitish pink bloom of one of the trees, unconcerned about the many thorns, expectantly waving to her mother. Eusapia stopped in her tracks, the full guilt over abandoning the child crashing down on her.

Celestina, Eusapia wanted to shout, but kept quiet. Celestina, she thought, the intensity of her call alarming the child, whose eyes turned serious. In the throes of conflicting emotions, which reared up, sharp and unnerving, too strong to keep in check, Eusapia was pulled toward the child, then yanked back to Raphael. She held on to the flimsy bit of consolation that at least she had done right by the child, that a good and stable life was awaiting Celestina.

Helplessly, Eusapia staggered toward the child in the tree.

It's okay, Mammina, Celestina seemed to say, and her face wasn't the face of a baby but the face of a wise old woman. It's okay.

Eusapia stretched out her hand, beckoning, but the child disappeared.

What's wrong, Eusapia? Raphael asked.

Eusapia was too distraught to confide in him. She grabbed her husband and pulled him close. Never leave me, Raphael. Never ever leave me.

Without answering, Raphael cupped her face with his large hands and said, My fabulous bride, chase those black thoughts out of your head. Let's enjoy the time we have together.

Eusapia, rocking Celestina in a hidden corner of her heart, put her to sleep and out of her mind, then ran ahead. She ran until she found a tall, sturdy tree unknown to her, a tree that wasn't in bloom, reaching out to her with green intensity. She accepted its invitation, climbing the tree with a desperation that hung on her like extra weight, but could not slow her down. As soon as she was on top, Raphael showed up beside her no less agile than herself. When they made love on the branches of the tree, Eusapia knew that she had met her match and that they were husband and wife for real.

Raphael had just enough money to pay for a honeymoon meal at a restaurant along the way. With their hunks of beef, he ordered a bottle of wine that generated even greater affection and noisier happiness. They gulped down their drinks and let their laughs yap out with the exuberance of puppies. They held each other's hands so that no one would ever be able to pull them apart. Celestina, looking like an angel, sang for them from the top of the ceiling, clapped and wished them well.

Thank you, Angel, Eusapia said.

Thank you, Angel, Raphael repeated full of enthusiasm, though he didn't see Celestina or hear her song.

In an attempt to somehow silence doubt and guilt, Eusapia broke out into unnaturally loud laughter, turned up the volume of her voice when she spoke, and dug noisily into her food.

She would not allow anything to dampen their enjoyment of the moment. For how long had she been deprived of passion and exuberance? The mountain had isolated her. No, healed you, she heard a faint voice, so gentle but firm that she knew it could only belong to Gianina.

Trying to break away from the heavy shadow of the mountain, Eusapia declared, We belong to the valleys and the cities. We belong to the world.

Together, we will find our way, Raphael chanted into her ear.

To Eusapia, it sounded as if all the bells of the world were ringing to announce a new era in their lives, one in which they wouldn't be deprived, one that delivered happiness and riches, or at least enough food not to go hungry.

They spent the night in a small house belonging to a young couple who rented out their small child's room for extra income. Raphael had stayed here before, and the couple welcomed him like an old friend. When Eusapia looked at the baby who was cooing then screaming, she had the strange sensation that the baby had Raphael's nose, but she banished that thought at once. After a helping of pasta, Raphael and Eusapia went to their room, which was so narrow that the bed almost touched the side walls. What did it matter! The only thing they needed was a mattress and privacy.

In the morning, they left again at the crack of dawn. They still had many hours of travelling in front of them, and Raphael had to prepare his show. So no more honeymoon escapades! Instead, the disciplined undertakings of performers who need to make a living. And performers they were, both of them. They felt no drudgery when they charged ahead single-mindedly, determined to impress each other, to make a success of the upcoming show.

Raphael, what's your family like? Eusapia asked out of the blue.

Don't ask, Eusapia.

Eusapia looked into his face and shuddered as colours of pain changed its aura. His eyes clouded.

What is it? Eusapia asked again.

Raphael tried to talk, but the words stuck in his mouth.

Don't shut me out. You need to get this pain into the open, Eusapia said soothingly as she burrowed herself into his body.

There was no response at first, but after many long minutes, his arms folded around her. Raphael and Eusapia stood impassively except for moments when tremors shook them as if in response to explosions deep inside him.

Apart from my father, they're dead, Raphael finally answered.

Eusapia waited.

Nothing else came forward.

You must talk about it, Raphael. Whatever you feel, it needs to get out.

They were circus people.

Eusapia waited again.

They had a number with dogs.

The minutes ticked away without another sound.

As Eusapia had almost lost hope of reaching her husband, he said, My brothers needed more than the dogs. They were hooked on dangerous stunts, walking, running, and flipping on tightropes higher and higher up in the air. Nothing held them back. They walked from one tall building to the other and over rivers and streets.

Another silence.

Then . . .

Raphael's thickening breath drew a sheath around them that threatened to smother them both.

Shshshsh, my love, Eusapia murmured, trying to get air.

Then . . .

What Raphael?

They invented this spectacular flip on the rope . . . I watched them every day. I wanted to join them. But they laughed at me. Grow, little shrimp, grow up first, then we might consider the possibility. They were ten and seven years older than me. They were my heroes . . .

Yes?

One day, when a big crowd was there to watch their newest stunt . . .

What happened that day, Raphael?

They fell.

Eusapia squeezed tighter into his body.

They fell right in front of me. I didn't even recognise them anymore. I just heard my mother scream and scream and scream. I still hear her scream.

I love you, Raphael, Eusapia said helplessly.

My mother never was the same after that. She couldn't eat anymore. My father and I tried. We begged her, Please eat, we need you. My mother couldn't hear us. Her soul had joined my brothers. When we tried to feed her, she lashed out. She wouldn't let any doctor touch her. My father called out to her, Teresa, return to us. Don't leave us too. But the shock had stolen her from us. My mother's decision was made the moment my brothers' bodies hit the ground: my father would remain with me and she would take care of my brothers. She never ate again. She stared with big black eyes up to the ceiling. When we brought her outside where it was sunny and the smell of flowers and the songs of birds were supposed to draw her back, she stared up at the sky straight through the clouds where my brothers were waiting for her. Even I could feel them waving and trying to pull her up. Someone must have given them a magic rope. The day my mother left, I knew she was climbing that rope. She folded my brothers in her arms as soon as she arrived up on top. And then the three of them walked away . . .

The hair on the right sight of Eusapia's face clung in damp tufts to her temple and cheek.

Let it all go, my love, she murmured, and in a sudden impulse focussed all her concentration toward the sky. And there they were, the three of them.

Raphael, look, Eusapia said and pointed to the sky.

It took a while before Raphael pulled himself together and looked up. He couldn't see his mother and brothers, but felt a familiar and comforting presence.

Our families are with us, Raphael, Eusapia suggested. Their blessings protect us from the evils of this world.

Blessings?

They do want us to be happy, Raphael. That's their blessing for us.

Slowly, a hopeful smile spread over Raphael's gloomy face. He grabbed his cart. They resumed their march without another word, knowing that neither of them would ever mention this episode again.

This is it? Eusapia asked in disbelief when she saw the run-down place where the show was to take place. It looked bad even in the dark.

This is it, Raphael replied as if there were nothing wrong with the shabby building, the dirt, and the smell that reminded her of rotting fish. He had seen worse. At least fellow performers had already constructed a stage with solid walls on the sides and the back, and a full roof. There were even movable boards to adjust the daylight. You had to be thankful for any one of those unexpected extras! Quite often, he had to build his own enclosures and figure out how to darken or lighten the place to make his magic work.

Eusapia, don't worry. When the sun comes up tomorrow, you'll be surprised how transformed everything is. You'll see flowers, hear birds, and breathe in the fresh smells of the morning breeze. For now, let's eat a bite and then go to work. It'll take most of the night to get ready.

You must be kidding?!

Why would I do that?

It's our honeymoon for Christ's sake, Eusapia shouted, her voice quivering with outrage. It's not the work, Raphael. I can work as hard as anyone else. But can you blame me if I had other plans for tonight?

If we work hard enough, it's possible to accomplish both. Let's get going.

Since it was Raphael's show, he was the one in charge. But Eusapia balked at following orders. She was her own boss and intended to keep it that way.

Put the small wooden boards in that corner over there, Raphael barked as if she were his little assistant, not his wife.

Do it yourself, Eusapia shot back.

Raphael bristled with indignation, but kept his cool. Come on, Eusapia, don't be like that, he coaxed, but she wouldn't be placated. All right, you win, he acquiesced, screw first, work after. He almost shoved her from the stage, along the path towards the old building, up the stairs and into the bedroom, where he threw her on their bed. Despite his earlier resistance, nothing could stop him now. A one-second vision of her naked body, and there was no turning back! Working seemed suddenly absurd. Any reminder was driven firmly into a hard-to-access corner of his brain.

Half an hour later, though, they were back at work, determined to make a success of his show. Since it was so late, most of the other performers were asleep. Raphael and Eusapia could hear noises from a few of the open windows, but didn't dare to knock on any doors and ask for help at this time of night.

So Eusapia worked hard to arrange the boards in the corner as Raphael had instructed her earlier. She would have liked to ask questions, Why did the boards have to be assembled in exactly this manner, why was there a long pipe dug into the ground just beside the stage? As his wife, she deserved to know the secrets of his magic, all of them, right here and now. Looking into Raphael's eyes, she read reluctance, or worse, complete unwillingness to part with his knowledge. Since her body was still luxuriating in the passion that had washed over them just moments earlier, Eusapia felt in a conciliatory mood. Tonight was not the night to insist. She smiled, and Raphael smiled back.

They worked through the night. No magician could leave his performance to chance. Every detail had to be planned. Raphael verified mirrors, angles, secret chambers, collapsible poles, and all sizes of black magnets. He checked and re-checked.

I don't pretend it's the greatest show on earth, he said to keep the expectations of his new wife reasonable. One day, maybe, I'll go beyond the usual tricks people expect and pay for.

I'm sure you're great, Eusapia replied, I can feel it.

I just don't want you to be disappointed.

I won't. I promise.

After catching a few hours of sleep way past midnight, they knuckled down again right up to show time at two o'clock on this warm, part sunny, part foggy Sunday afternoon. Eusapia had just enough time to find a seat among the spectators before a seven-foot giant made his entrance on stage, a four-foot dwarf in tow. They ceremoniously introduced the first act: a German ventriloquist named Dietrich who hacked his Italian into harsh splinters that could have pierced your eardrum if he hadn't softened the little daggers with clear and bright vowels. The rather rotund German held out his arm. Ladies and gentlemen, meet Lydia, he said, introducing his sidekick, a busty drunk barmaid puppet. When she started burping and making googly eyes toward the men, the performer reprimanded her sharply, Behave yourself, Lydia.

But the spectators defended her, half seriously, half jokingly. Shut up, Dietrich, leave her alone.

In appreciation of their support, Lydia curved her back to show off her puppet assets, waving and winking so invitingly that some of the men left their chairs to get closer.

Keep your hands to yourself or rot in hell, Dietrich rebuked them. Despite his staccatoed Italian, he paradoxically reminded them of their own Monsignor Mosca whose hellfire sermons they tolerated at church, but surely not here where they wanted to have fun.

Go home, Dietrich, and leave Lydia with us, they roared in an attempt to drive the unpleasant thoughts away. Then, even livelier, the men chanted, Come on down, baby.

Dietrich would not let his woman walk about among the men, which left Lydia trilling, See me after the show, boys. I might give you my key.

Don't believe her, Dietrich barged in, she's a good woman.

That's right, Lydia responded, I am very good (wink, wink, nudge, nudge), No key for anyone (wink, wink).

This odd couple from Germany was followed by a pair of Siamese twins looking like a two-headed woman with three breasts and four legs. Everyone pointed. A hired musician started to play the harmonica and the two-headed woman danced with a grace that took everyone by surprise. Even the cruelest of the spectators kept their noisy comments down as they were drawn into a roller coaster of emotions, laughing and crying tears at the same time. Thunderous applause showered down on the stage.

Finally, it was Raphael's turn. Introduced as Signor Rapido, Raphael dashed onto the stage and stood there impressively, even taller than usual with his top hat. Eusapia wondered what his stage personality would be like. Smiling and sensitive? Brooding? Or impatient and commanding? For all she knew, Raphael could as easily turn into a fun-loving prankster as into a scary black-magic trickster. Eusapia waited while around her the spectators gaped expectantly at her husband.

Signor Rapido bowed slightly. All of a sudden oversized cards moved around him, first without design, then in circles, zigzag lines, up and down, from left to right in an exuberant dance to the sounds of a harmonica. Everyone wondered how the cards floated above the floor. But Eusapia had seen Raphael negotiate with a whole many other performers, most of whom he seemed to know from previous shows. She had no trouble seeing through this trick. Thanks to her sharp eyes and her own experience with assistants, she was able to detect the outlines of the legs and arms of at least two other people responsible for making this performance a success. The cards followed the lead of the instrument, enjoying a few lively measures of a polka. When the music stopped, the cards hung for a moment aimlessly in the air, then scrambled to get in line, from the ace or one up to *Re,* the king, with the knave, *Fante,* stubbornly trying to take the top spot until the horseman, *Cavallo,* brought him back in line. Bravo, the spectators shouted. The cards bowed and when they turned back up, they had miraculously changed orders. The ace was now to the right of the line and *Re* to the left. After much applause, the cards bowed again, and this time they had all turned into aces when they straightened up, except for *Fante* who ran around in seeming humiliation trying to fit in but unable to do so until Signor Rapido said Abracadabra, and the knave turned into an ace as well.

Eusapia smiled wistfully when Signor Rapido invited a little girl up on stage.

Pull a card out of my deck, Signor Rapido said. The girl eagerly pulled out a card, which turned out to be the King of batons.

Isn't he a bit small for you? Signor Rapido asked.

Yes, stammered the girl.

Do you want a big king?

Yes, answered the girl timidly.

Then you'll get a big king. Abracadabra, Signor Rapido called out.

The instant he said it, a giant cardboard king of spades turned up hopping toward the girl. He bowed, then flipped around and greeted her courteously.

Do you want to dance with King *Re?* Signor Rapido asked.

When the girl nodded shyly, an arm reached out to her, took her by the hand and twirled her around twice. The big king and the little girl danced a few steps to the right, and a few steps to the left.

Thank you, Signorina, Signor Rapido said as the king blended into the background and suddenly disappeared without a trace.

Where did he go? the girl asked.

Back to his kingdom, Signor Rapido answered and sent the girl back to her proud mamma and papa, and into the large crowd of cheering spectators.

All of a sudden Signor Rapido abandoned his cards to pull flowers out of his hat. With his never-ending supply, he created a magnificent garden. To go with the garden, he lifted a dove out of the hat.

The audience clapped.

Where did he find it? Eusapia asked herself. Before Signor Rapido could set it free, a scratched-up black cat shot out of the hat, lunging viciously after the bird.

The audience booed and hissed.

Signor Rapido raised his arms and let the dove fly to the sky. The cat stormed off the stage into the audience where some boys chased her.

Eusapia was furious. Never ever would she let Raphael use animals again. This was pure cruelty. Infuriated, she jumped out of her seat and left.

After the show, Raphael found his wife huddled in a chair in a dark corner inside the restaurant, hanging on to her cup of coffee as if it contained her life.

What's the matter? Raphael asked, still pleasantly warm from the enthusiastic applause of the audience.

What's the matter!?? You have to ask, you animal hater, you bone breaker, you abominable no-good hooligan!

What are you talking about? Raphael asked, taken aback by her outburst, but still reasonably happy, trying to kiss her to calm her down.

Get away from me, she hissed.

That's enough, Sapia. I just finished a good show. I bring in money and you treat me like your worst enemy?

Don't you get it, Raphael? I can't stand by and say nothing when you hurt an animal.

I didn't hurt the cat. I love animals. I want to have tons of animals — doves, rabbits, bears, tigers, elephants. If I had the money I'd have a whole circus.

Without me you would!

I don't understand.

Didn't you see how roughed up and scared that cat was?

No more than usual. She is the biggest fighter in the neighbourhood. From what I'm told, not a day goes by that she doesn't get herself into one scrape or another. The fur that's missing on her back and those horrid scratches on her right side, that happened way before I used her. By God, Eusapia, I'm a magician, not some vile torturer!

Well . . .

Come on, wasn't the show a little bit praiseworthy?

A bit.

Just a bit?

A lot. It was good, Raphael, said Eusapia, but the disturbing image of the cat would not leave her until the next day when she saw the animal jump up on Raphael's lap to be petted and spoiled with a small piece of sausage.

Can you believe that this cat likes me better than you do, Raphael teased his wife. And you'll see how much all the animals

I'll own in the future will be drawn to me, every single one of them.

Eusapia relented. She couldn't stay mad at Raphael. But when she saw the cat being chased and kicked by two teenagers, she drove them away with her screams. No one was going to mistreat an animal in her presence. She was even more enraged by the way people acted toward the Siamese twins. When children paraded around imitating them with cruel excitement, she pulled them away from the restaurant by their ears, threatening to turn them into frogs if this nastiness didn't stop. When men started groping the twin's three breasts as if that were their right, she tore them away from the sisters. At the sight of the twins crammed together with the giant and the dwarf in a filthy, flea-infested room, commonly referred to as the freaks quarter, with just a bit of mildewed straw on the floor for beds, she cried with fury and frustration. She went to her room, took a few coins out of her treasure box, and gave them to the four people for a better room.

You're a lifesaver, they said, but remained in their miserable room, saving the money for times when they weren't offered even the shabbiest roof over their heads.

What kind of a world is this!!? Eusapia shouted into the night. Where is the justice?

That night, the unfairness of life kept Eusapia awake. She knew there were people out there working to improve the fate of the weak and vulnerable. She had heard about such people and had met a few. Lucia and her doctor brother did their part as best they could. Eusapia could imagine gentle and pretty Angela from Minervino turning into a protector of the helpless. As for herself, Eusapia had no illusions about her own contribution.

167

She'd be lucky to survive. But at this moment, she pledged to use whatever small talents she had to make a difference in some poor souls' lives and equal things out to the tiny degree she was capable of. She had heard Giorgio talk about government and about big changes that would affect the whole city of Naples, even the whole of Italy, maybe the entire world. He'd talked about the "promise of the future". She had always thought that he talked a lot of impressive nonsense, though "promise of the future" was one of the expressions she hung on to. Thinking of the freaks quarter, she decided that no one deserved to languish in poverty while others had more than they needed. It was up to her to take what she could from the rich and give it to the poor.

At Raphael's next show, she placed herself strategically behind the few people in the audience who showed off their small wealth. She would have felt better getting to work among Giorgio's rich acquaintances and the more well-to-do sitters that came to her séances in Naples. But even here the difference in wealth was unfair. When the audience concentrated on Raphael's special effects on stage, Eusapia worked her own magic, glad to see another layer added to her treasure box.

Raphael watched his wife's indignation with bewildered admiration. She looked like an avenging angel, eyes glowing, sword, no, torch in hand. He almost believed that real magic was about to supplant trick magic and the thousand flames of her passion had the power to burn everything in their path to make room for a new and better world. Raphael sighed. Sure, he too knew the difference between rich and poor. He had always known it. But he had accepted it as a given that could not be changed. It had never occurred to him to do something about it, especially not concerning others. As long as he wasn't starving –

168

and up till now he had survived – he saw no reason to lose sleep over it. Still, Eusapia's determination awed him. He had found out about her treasure box as well. Did she think she could keep it from him? She had to know that any true magician would be aware of any unusual object at once! If this man-and-wife thing was to work, she would have to trust him.

It took a while before Eusapia and Raphael settled into married life. When you had been your own master for so long, adjusting to someone else's ambitions and routines did not come easy. Details like when to get up and when to eat provoked endless discussions and bickering.

You wash your own clothes! It's your turn to clean up! No, we can postpone it until the evening! Eusapia's voice was louder and shriller than Raphael's, quickly drowning him out. He was in general more easy-going, smiling broadly after a fight, agreeing obligingly to Eusapia's demands.

Okay, don't worry, I'll do it, he'd say, making a valid effort to scrub, brush or wash.

While Eusapia welcomed his attempts at keeping the peace when it came to domestic arrangements, his don't-provoke-anyone attitude drove her nuts when principles were at stake. What galled her most was his uncritical acceptance of the sorry state of the world, as if everything were as it should be. To her, Raphael had no solid beliefs and zero capacity for outrage, and this was beyond her comprehension. Luckily though, no matter how serious their disagreements and bad moods, their young bodies could not keep apart. They drew each other like magnets, generating such heat that their frustrations went up in flames in an instant and left space for new beginnings. After each spat, they started over.

I didn't mean to upset you, Raphael would say, and Eusapia would respond, I shouldn't have lost my temper like that. Let's try to make our marriage work. Worse than their fights was the drudgery of everyday life for which neither of them had any patience. Yet they remained optimistic. It helped that Raphael's shows took them wandering from village to village, where at every turn they encountered new faces and situations. And the workings of Raphael's magic tricks fascinated Eusapia. With his hints and advice, it didn't take her long to figure some of them out.

Intriguing! she would exclaim, truly astonished at all the mirrors, angles, holes, hidden compartments and pockets she had failed to notice at the outset. When he was sleeping or talking to friends, she took his key from one of the many hiding places she had discovered and secretly inspected his paraphernalia. She practised and practised, but found it hard to replicate his feats. Despite working with all his pots and tins and different magic wands, none of the tricks went smoothly until she also used his giant jacket with its innumerable pockets and hidden slots, and realised that each of his rolls of strings had its own purpose. It was during this learning process that she started to appreciate his talents. Understanding the mechanics of at least some of his tricks was one thing, perfecting them another. It would take years and special skills to achieve his dexterity, and to be effective, a person also had to be able to direct the audience's attention far away from the actual action. Raphael used noise and lights, even smells, to confound his audience, and deployed his supreme mastery of body language to keep the spectators in the realm of magic. I will learn every aspect of his craft and adapt it to my mediumship, Eusapia thought, her ambition adding new purpose to her life with Raphael.

During a stop in one of the bigger villages, Raphael introduced her to a friend of his called Mario, who was a performer in his own right, but had also been of assistance to Raphael in several of his shows. That evening, the three of them and a group of colleagues sat together to drink, sing and catch up on news. Mario made her laugh out loud with his jokes and quirky stories about his three-year-old son Felice trying to juggle like his Daddy, and two-year-old Emilia blowing kisses. They'll be arriving soon, he said, you're going to adore them.

Life was good until the next day when it seemed that Mario had disappeared into thin air. Hours later, Raphael and some other performers found him floating face down in the river, stuck between two high rocks. Why hadn't she seen it coming? She would never understand!

Mario's death was another blow that Raphael would not talk about, and after a few failed attempts to broach the subject, she followed suit, pretending that nothing had happened and this was just another ordinary day in their new life together. They left the village in a hurry, but advanced slowly as Raphael barely dragged himself along and beside his grief seemed to be coming down with something.

Suddenly, a lively figure came charging down a side path, waving happily, his enormous mop of copper brown hair bouncing to the rhythm of his steps.

Raphael, he shouted, and Eusapia could hear the joy of seeing an old travelling companion in his voice.

His joy turned to concern as soon as he saw Raphael close up.

You're sick, my friend, he said decisively. You can't go on like that.

Raphael trembled on his legs by now and looked as if he were about to fall to the ground. He was unaware of his old friend.

Eusapia watched the stranger in front of her with astonishment, but also unexpected trust, which he seemed to reciprocate.

It's Tomasso, Raphael, remember, he tried again.

But there was no response.

He can't walk, Tomasso said to Eusapia.

Without asking permission, he hoisted Raphael on his own cart. Eusapia took hold of Raphael's cart and they were on their way, Tomasso taking care to avoid the rocks and roots to make the journey as painless as possible.

When they arrived at their destination, Raphael was shivering and barely responsive. Without thinking twice, Tomasso searched in his travelling bag and finally pulled out a small bottle from his supply of medicines, his latest endeavour to make a living.

Give him ten drops every hour, he said, and Eusapia did.

Soon, Raphael felt at least strong enough to talk. You have to take over, Eusapia, he decided.

How? How am I supposed to do that after you've withheld your secrets from me? Eusapia whined. Now you're too sick to teach me!

I've seen you practising, Raphael blurted out. Did you really think you could hide it from me? Every time you touched my tools I knew.

So what if I did?!

I know you figured out the flower tricks, Raphael responded, suddenly almost too tired to continue this conversation.

Yes, I could handle the flowers, Eusapia admitted, but not with your flair. And it would be ludicrous for me to attempt any of your card tricks.

You wouldn't have to do the show alone, Raphael proposed in a voice so slowed down and feeble that Eusapia looked at him with alarm. Sickly pearls of sweat formed on his forehead as he painfully continued, I could lug myself up on stage with you for the flower act, sit on some fancy, elevated chair, point at you as if you were performing magic under my control. But you'd be the one in control.

We couldn't get away with just doing the flowers. People want more for their money.

No problem, you'll give some sort of a séance. You always wanted to be a medium.

Don't be crazy, Raphael. I've neither the ability nor the experience to work with your sophisticated lighting arrangements and tricks. Have you ever seen a medium produce phenomena while the afternoon sun illuminates every corner of the stage? The dead are afraid of the light.

Despite his debilitating weakness, Raphael had to laugh, only to stop immediately when a new attack of pain took his breath away. I guess they would be, he managed to whisper and, as if in defiance of the fever chills that almost killed him, a mischievous smile remained on his lips. If objects can't fly and the table won't rise in daylight, there is always mindreading or clairvoyance.

Mindreading or clairvoyance?

Raphael tried to answer, but was too weak. Vacillating dangerously between feverish convulsions and increasingly frightening periods of unconsciousness, he left Eusapia to wonder how he could possibly hang on to life.

Wake up, Eusapia called softly. Please, Raphael, wake up.

Water, Mario, water, rock, dead, brothers, Raphael called out from the dark space between reality and nightmarish visions where he kept hovering.

Come back, Eusapia begged, wiping his hot and trembling face with cold water. Don't do this to me.

The other performers brought whatever blankets or spare clothes they had and piled them on Raphael.

You have to break his fever, Tomasso said and gave her additional medicines.

Eusapia hummed to her husband, soothing like a soft breeze.

Raphael?

He didn't seem to recognise her.

The show was to take place the next day.

Water, water, rock, she heard Raphael moan, with sad and crazed insistence.

She continued wiping his eyes and lips.

He wants me to act as a mind-reader or clairvoyant tomorrow, she confided to the Siamese twins who had dropped by to check on Raphael.

That's a good idea. Do you need help? asked Carmela, the twin with the bigger head.

I don't know how to do either.

You've never seen acts like that? They've become popular lately. I don't think there has ever been one in this village. We

174

can help you prepare for it. Without previous experience, you're better off going for clairvoyance, it's harder to get tripped up.

How would I do this?

If you want your act to work, you have to know as much as possible about the people you want to use as your subjects. We have been here for three weeks, even though the show starts only tomorrow. We know what's going on in this village. The villagers don't watch what they say around us because to them, we're more like the nearby cats and dogs than human beings. Except when focussing on our deformity, people don't notice we're present. It doesn't occur to them that we're able to feel, think, and understand what they say, and that we might remember when it's convenient.

After just a trace of self-pity, the twins shared the information they had collected, Take for example the large lady in the green hat with its growth of lilies, Signora Maddalena Zolotti, said Carmela's twin sister Concetta, you'll know her because she is the only one with such a hat, which, from what I heard, she wears even inside her house. More interestingly, she's had three husbands, Aldo, Sergio and Angelo, who all died within a year of being married to her. Aldo succumbed to a massive epileptic seizure, Sergio was killed by a runaway carriage, and Angelo fell victim to gangrene after he cut himself with a knife while skinning a rabbit. According to the doctor, they died of natural causes, but the village never forgave her. The families of her husbands' never forgave her. They still believe that she had something to do with their deaths. Now that's rich fodder for a clairvoyant.

Eusapia learned quickly. A person with the talent to make tables rise could become a clairvoyant with the flick of a hand. Eusapia started to feel excited. Her friends filled her in on the most important events and tragedies of the village. They described some of the more recognisable characters and repeated what they had heard about noteworthy deaths in the previous ten years.

Even Tomasso provided a few tips and additional gossip.

At last alone with her husband, Eusapia sponged off the sweat from his forehead. His fever seemed to be breaking. His shirt and the rags and sheets were drenched. Eusapia was able to extract new sheets from the hotel owner without having to dip into her treasure box, and one of the other performers lent a shirt until Raphael's could be washed and dried. The giant, who was not only tall but also strong, lifted Raphael up when Eusapia was ready to change the sheets. Raphael moaned, but barely stirred. A few hours later, his breathing became less raspy and he fell asleep, almost peacefully this time. When he woke up, he forced his eyes open despite the tiredness that threatened to pull him back into semi-conscious darkness. He looked up at Eusapia with a faint, crooked smile.

Luckily, dashing Tomasso is not interested in women, Raphael said.

Eusapia sighed with relief that Raphael had at last noticed the presence of his friend. He must be on his way to recovery.

You're going to be all right, Eusapia said soothingly. We're going to be all right.

Ladies and Gentlemen, Eusapia greeted the audience when it was Raphael's turn the next evening. As you can see from the intense white face of the great magician Signor Rapido, the magic inside him is so strong that despite a terrible flu that has robbed him of his voice and strength, it needs to come out. It wants to be transferred. I'm honoured that on this special night I have been chosen to present his magic to you. Signor Rapido, let the show begin.

Overcoming his morbid fatigue, Raphael lifted his arm in style and with a sweeping movement pulled a magician's hat from out of the air and set it on Eusapia's head, then transferred his own prized jacket to her. As she stood there, the jacket hanging to her knees, the long sleeves folded back, Carmel and Concetta waltzed in pushing a high-backed velvet chair, something like a throne with three steps in front, for Signor Rapido to sit down and direct the show. Beside him, Eusapia started the magic with flowers. Soon, plants bloomed around her in all shades and sizes. Apart from the intoxicating love-making with Raphael, she hadn't felt such intense pleasure for a long time. She wanted the ooooh's and aaaahs of the audience to continue forever.

It was during the clairvoyance session that she was fully in her element. Raising both her hands just slightly, palms toward spectators to stop the conversations, she commanded complete silence. The spectators sat hypnotised. Her own power surprised her. I can do this, she thought. She had noticed with relief that Signora Zolotti sat as predicted in the front row and that other characters described by the twins were present as well. Eusapia forced herself to concentrate. Her eyes darkened. Out of that darkness, miraculous beams shot toward the men and women in front of her. She swayed back and forth. No sound came over her lips for several seconds. The swaying became stronger until she seemed in a full-blown trance.

Suddenly, her voice sounded out ghostly and unrecognisable, Flowers, yes small flowers, white, snowdrops, no . . . lilies. I see lilies, very small lilies. I see a face, a name, Ma . . . no, Magda?

no . . . it's becoming clearer: Maddalena. There is also the colour green. What does it mean?

Eusapia saw Signora Zolotti shift uncomfortably, almost frightened.

I see men . . . three men.

Slowly, Eusapia directed her gaze toward Signora Zolotti. With satisfaction, she realised that many of the people had already turned to look at the woman whose eccentricities and story were known to the entire village. Some pointed. Some just stared.

The letters A . . . A . . . S . . . come to mind. Does that make sense to anyone?

Yes, yes, Signora Zolotti shouted, yes!

Eusapia now looked at her directly.

I see the three men floating around you. Now two of them are holding your hands, and the third, A . . . An . . . Angelo is putting his hand on your shoulder.

Signora Zolotti, who held out her hands, recognised the touch of her former husbands. She could feel Angelo's hand on her shoulder. Tears started streaming down the woman's face.

The men, Eusapia continued, they're smiling.

A startled gasp swept through the audience.

They want to give you a message. They want you to know that they don't blame you.

Another gasp.

They love you and want to help you. Yes, I hear it very clearly, it's a plea to their families. Are there any family members here?

Many hands shot up. Yes, yes, the voices came from all across the audience.

The message says: Give us peace in the otherworld. We need to know that Maddalena is taken care of, that she is treated well.

I promise, a high-pitched voice sounded from the back of the audience.

We promise, yes, we promise . . .

Thank you, Eusapia said, the men say thank you. They'll remember your kindness. They're fading. They're slowly disappearing.

A sob interrupted her speech.

But Eusapia continued solemnly, Their faces are at peace.

Then suddenly, with a change of voice, I see a brown spotted dog. Eusapia recoiled from her own vision, her voice roared, It's growing . . . its face is covered in blood. There are welts all over its thin, starved body. It has been beaten. The poor animal has been beaten to death. Look at its eyes. Even in death, they show suffering, fear, and sadness. There is a name . . . wait . . . it's becoming clearer . . .

The spectators sat paralysed with fear.

The name is . . . the name . . .

Wake up, clairvoyant, came all of a sudden the still sickly, hoarse, but commanding voice of Signor Rapido.

The spell of anxiety and fear was broken. Feet shifted. Murmurs and whispers started up. Eusapia was annoyed. Behind her back, Raphael hissed, Stop it. Stop it now. Keep it light. For Christ's sake, keep it light.

Eusapia, who made it her mission to avenge the mistreated animals in the world, bristled with resentment. Please, she heard Raphael say. Don't ruin it.

Slowly, she gained control of her emotions. She waved her hands, rubbed her eyes, then opened them slowly, wiping away the last traces of her trance, assuming her normal appearance, shuddering dramatically, then getting up, waving, moving toward Raphael, pointing toward him.

They both bowed.

And this is the show for today, Eusapia said. Thank you for coming.

Amid the outburst of excited conversation and spontaneous applause, Raphael and Eusapia left the stage.

When the owner of the establishment suggested that Raphael's flower tricks be replaced with clairvoyance sessions for the remaining two performances, Eusapia's heart skipped a beat. But Raphael said in a serious voice that left no room for contradiction, No we stick with the Signor-Rapido show as agreed months ago.

But . . . , Eusapia tried to intervene.

Raphael pulled her away before she could say more.

I don't deny that you're good, Eusapia. But if you don't learn to keep a lid on your emotions, you'll destroy our chances for work. We have to make a living before we can afford to save the world.

If you aim that low, that's where you'll remain, at the bottom, always scrambling for survival. I want to go beyond survival and live what I believe in.

You don't know what the world is about, Eusapia, or you wouldn't talk like that.

Wouldn't I?!! Eusapia replied in a huff and turned to leave.

Wait . . . Eusapia, please wait . . .

But his wife stomped off.

Oh, I'll be your little assistant, she shouted back, yes, Raphael, don't worry, for now I'll continue, I'll be what you want me to be. But don't think you can keep me down forever. Who do you think I am?

Don't get mad all the time. I know you're good.

Good? Try exceptional!

You're exceptional, Eusapia, but believe me, you're better off learning more about this cut-throat business before throwing yourself into it. If you want to make a living, you have to be astute enough to know what's appropriate and acceptable. Even if you're first rate, you can be replaced in the blink of an eye. So don't burn bridges. Don't go on crazy crusades unless you're sure as blazes you can win them. Say things that make people feel good. Be nice, Eusapia.

Screw you and your sermons, she screamed.

Screw you too, Raphael shot back, and this time, his anger almost got the better of him.

For Eusapia, living and speaking the way she felt was as necessary as breathing, whether Raphael agreed or not. While small things in their everyday life raised her hackles, his general attitude bothered her most. How could anyone keep quiet when evil stared you in the face? Eusapia almost exploded with moral superiority, just for an instant, but this short moment was filled with unexpected contempt for her partner. Such meekness! No, she would not tolerate his attitude.

Snap out of it, Eusapia, Raphael called out, trying to wrap his arms around her to put an end to her brooding.

Leave me alone, Eusapia snarled, and brusquely wriggled out of his hold.

But Raphael grabbed her back and clung to her in a tight embrace until the warmth of his body filled hers and pushed aside her contempt in one commanding swoop. The power of his body had not diminished.

Yes, more, deeper, she screamed before their frenzied love-making wiped away any feeling other than the need to satisfy their feverish bodies.

Yet, in a hidden corner of her heart, an imperceptible seed of doubt had taken hold.

Now that Eusapia could see through the workings of most of Raphael's magic, except for his specialty, the card tricks, which she was unable to reproduce, the performances lost their interest. In front of her eyes, his magic frittered away little by little. Vague feelings of boredom seeped into their daily life and took away much of the excitement.

You have to understand, Raphael defended his work, My show might repeat itself, but every audience is different. Can't you see it, Eusapia? It's not the tricks that make the magic, it's the interaction with the spectators. Just like in a séance, he added with a hint of a smirk.

Eusapia knew he was right and that his performances were way beyond anything she'd be able to produce and probably less monotonous than her séances. But how was she to learn without hands-on experience and what would be the point? Who would hire a woman magician?

Well, said the Siamese twin Concetta whom she consulted, one good thing about being a freak, it doesn't matter whether you're male or female, as long as you're different enough for people to stare at you. They always hire freaks. People flock to see the abnormal because it makes them feel better about themselves and their shortcomings.

Come on, Eusapia, learn more, Raphael exhorted her, as he had done so many times before. Very few succeed without paying their dues first.

Eusapia rolled her eyes.

You want a cheap assistant, she growled. It makes you feel good to order me around.

Cut it out, Sapia. You've become such a pain in the ass.

A pain in the ass? That's what you're calling me nowadays?!!

You know what I mean.

Get the hell out of my face, she snapped.

Who is earning the money around here?

I could easily earn my own money if you didn't hold me back.

You still have a lot of learning to do, Eusapia, Raphael responded, this time in a more conciliatory voice. You will make it as a performer, I guarantee you that.

When?? After slaving beside you until I'm a wrinkled old prune?

Anger shot through Raphael. His hand shook with the urge to lash out, but he walked away.

Yes, walk away. It's the thing you do best when you don't want to admit that you're wrong.

Her words came down on Raphael like a blow before he slammed the door of the rooming house shut behind him. In his heart, he already understood that it wasn't with him that she'd become a successful medium.

What's wrong with the two of us? Eusapia asked herself as she stood alone outside on the street. He is my big love. He loves me. There has to be a way to make it work between us.

What's wrong with Raphael and me? she asked the Siamese twins a while later.

The twins looked at her earnestly, but provided no answer. One thing they had learned over the years is that most people did not want advice even when they asked for it.

I can take it, Eusapia said. I know there is plenty wrong with us. I need someone to tell me exactly what it is.

Still, the twins did not respond.

If there were nothing wrong with us, you'd tell me, Eusapia griped crossly.

Knowing they were in a no-win situation, the twins said, Go find Raphael.

Find Raphael? she screamed, And say what? You're right, Raphael, you know what's best for me, if you can't accept me as a performer in my own right, that's no problem, we still have each other, it's enough that you screw me well.

The twins blushed. They wanted to leave, but fear of an even worse outburst held them back.

I'd be happy to have a man like Raphael, Concetta blurted out.

All of a sudden, Eusapia's anger was spent. How could she be that insensitive! Carmela and Concetta were her friends. So was Raphael. They deserved better! I'm sorry, she said and wondered how she could make it up to them. Your advice is spot on, I will go and find Raphael.

Eusapia walked up to her room intending to say sorry to Raphael. But his soft, rhythmic snoring left no doubt that he was asleep. She did not want to wake him. Quietly, she lay down beside him. After a while, she spooned around his body and slung her left arm over his side to his chest. She calmed down.

This was Raphael who had saved her from loneliness and brought her back to life. And how did she reward him? By knocking him down!

I'm sorry, Raphael, she whispered, knowing that her words could not reach him.

In her dreams though, they were both happy. When they woke up, she saw that Raphael's dreams had been good ones too. He took her into his arms and held her as if someone were trying to pry her away from him.

I was wrong, he said after a while. I so much wanted to keep you for myself that I could not admit that you were ready to become a medium. It's time, Eusapia. I have to let you go.

What are you talking about? Eusapia cried out, shaken by the sadness in his voice. I'll never leave you.

That's the thing, Eusapia. You must. It's not with me that you'll develop your talents any further. Our destinies are separate.

No, Raphael, no, don't say that. I can't live without you.

Yes, you can. And it's your only chance to make your mediumship count.

Not without you.

Then you'd be stuck with second-rate clairvoyance shows. I don't have the means to help you with your career. You need more respectable and richer men.

But I want you.

That's what you think now. But later, you'll resent me. I'm bringing you back to Naples. That's where you need to be because that's where the spiritualists that matter are.

Eusapia didn't respond because she knew he was right. Again, they held on to each other as if this could change their decision.

Before Raphael dropped Eusapia off near the Migaldis' place, he wiped her wet face with his sweater. Eusapia pulled Raphael into a well-hidden corner, and did what she had not been able to do before. She opened her treasure box.

Equal parts for both of us.

Raphael couldn't believe it.

No, Eusapia, you will need this more than I.

But Eusapia wouldn't hear of it. We share our hearts, we share our treasures, she said simply.

You'll always remain my wife, Eusapia.

Till the end of my life, Raphael, I'll remain, Signora Raphael Delgaiz.

I'll come back at the end of my next tour to see with my own eyes that you're all right.

Don't ever forget me, Raphael.

How could I!? Even apart, we belong to each other, Eusapia. You're the one who has my heart.

They knew that they would meet up again and there was no doubt in either of them that they would remain part of each other for the rest of their lives. Yet, Eusapia could not keep at bay a disconsolate emptiness that swooped in on her. She did not dare acknowledge this empty space in her. Besides the loss of Raphael she'd find there, she'd also have to cope with the ever festering absence of her daughter, and that was simply unbearable.

Naples, 1871-1886

6

EUSAPIA STRETCHED OUT HER HAND so that the yellow stone of her ring sparkled in the sunlight from the window.

Eusapia! both Signora Migaldi and Ugo exclaimed. Who gave you this ring?!?

I'm now Signora Raphael Delgaiz, Eusapia answered with confidence, her black eyes sweltering with the new experience.

I can't believe it, Signora Migaldi exclaimed.

Where is he? Ugo inquired with a choking voice.

Signora Migaldi looked at her son startled and with sudden anxiety.

Are you all right, Ugo? his mother asked, and before hearing his, Yes, I'm fine, she knew that her son was jealous. She sighed apprehensively. It shouldn't be like this, she thought. His first love was supposed to be happy. But her son's eyes contained only pain and anger. She wanted to fold him into her arms like she did when he was a small child and she could bring a smile back on his face just by kissing a scratch or a bruise. Now her kiss could only add insult to injury. Ugo had grown up without her fully noticing.

Eusapia, Signora Migaldi tried to say with her natural warmth but could not hide the sudden coldness in her voice.

Yes? Eusapia asked, taken aback and wished she could confide in Signora Migaldi and tell her about the pregnancy, the birth and the loss of her child. But apart from the Damianis and Signor Migaldi, no one in Naples knew about it. Signor Migaldi had not told his wife about the child, and because Eusapia would not betray him, she bit her tongue.

Come and have supper with us, Signora Migaldi said and, determined to smooth over the tension in the room, added, It's good to see you again.

Eusapia felt right at home in the familiar smells of the house. She sniffed. Basil, garlic, cheese. Her mouth watered. It's always the food that tells you that you belong, that a place is truly yours. She smiled.

Signora Migaldi was more quiet than usual. She had loved Eusapia like her own daughter since the girl first arrived from Minervino. And yet, this time, Signora Migaldi looked at her with disquiet, with the painful instinct of a mother. The unfamiliar suspicions alarmed Signora Migaldi, whose spontaneous kindness tended to flow unchecked toward everyone around her. Resolutely, she fought to regain her cheerfulness, flustered that she had to make such an effort.

Tell me all about the last few months, Eusapia, she said. You must have news galore.

I do, Eusapia responded. But too much had to be kept secret, most of all her pregnancy.

How did you like it at Gianina's place? Did you find peace on the mountain? Signora Migaldi asked, trying to re-establish closeness.

She treated me like family, Eusapia said.

Why did you leave?

I needed to see the world. I needed to see young people.

How did you meet your husband?

Raphael is a magician. He gave a show in a village I passed through.

You love him?

I do!

Signora Migaldi relaxed without feeling reassured, wondering why she was so suspicious all of a sudden.

At that moment, Signor Migaldi came back from a meeting. As he saw Eusapia, he stopped abruptly. One look into her eyes and he grasped the full extent of the change in her. He saw the dark abyss that threatened to swallow whatever came its way. He understood its origin and knew its power right away, but refused to put words to it.

Welcome back, Bella, he greeted her, then tore himself away to tousle the hair of his youngest son. Isn't this a surprise!

As jovial as he tried to be, his wife had caught the strange spark between her husband and the girl. Uneasily, she breathed faster.

Yes, isn't it nice to have Eusapia back? she said hastily to cover her unease. Let's all sit down for supper before everything gets cold.

Eusapia has a husband, Pietro told his father excitedly.

Do you? Signor Migaldi asked, incredulous at the unexpected news.

I do, Eusapia said without further explanation.

On the surface, the supper seemed to be a jolly affair full of laughter and cries of wonder as Eusapia told story after story. But the harmony was forced and fragile. Eusapia couldn't stop Ugo's brooding. Signor Migaldi's misgivings remained, and Eusapia

189

had to stand by helplessly as Signora Migaldi's fears pulsated out of the pit of her stomach.

Why don't they trust me anymore? Eusapia asked herself. I'm still the same person I was a year ago. I am, she insisted, covering sudden doubts, Just because I've become Signora Raphael Delgaiz doesn't mean I'm not the old Eusapia Palladino anymore, the same girl I was when I first met the Migaldis. Shouldn't that be the truth of the matter?

Eusapia was allowed to sleep in the guestroom since no guests were expected for the next two weeks. Only the two younger boys objected when she went to her room right after supper. The relief in Signor and Signora Migaldi's faces was visible, though Eusapia had no doubt that Signor Migaldi would corner her at the first occasion to get answers to his questions. She needed to escape before anyone started snooping around in the muddy gullies of her life. Oh Raphael, she sighed when she was alone, we made a mistake. I can't focus on becoming a medium when the only thing I crave is your body in my bed. I'm not ready. It's not going to work.

Frustration and forebodings aside, she fell asleep as soon as her head hit the pillow. Yet her dream granted no bliss. She was caught with no escape. Mountains of debris blocked the way back to her old life, and monsters populated the way forward. Undaunted by adversity, she walked ahead, spurred on by an optimistic breeze that promised a good fate, more acceptable than her horrible childhood would have led anybody to expect. Eusapia's lips curled up in hope and restored confidence. She knew she would wake up refreshed and ready to take on the world.

What is it with you? Signor Migaldi inquired almost rudely when he met her in the hallway the next morning.

Something in her body seemed to talk even when she was silent. Her involuntary language reached him exactly where he didn't want it to reach. Signor Migaldi turned away.

Are you mad at me? Eusapia asked.

No, he said and forced himself to turn back to her. Here lay his goldmine. Isn't that what he had wanted? Dividends from a medium whose every breath and movement promised the forbidden?

Then why are you different with me now? Eusapia interrupted his thoughts.

I'm not different, he answered wearily, still trying to regain his composure. For all his faults and twisted ethics, his conscience would never leave him in peace for long.

Eusapia, be careful.

What are you talking about?

You know exactly what I'm talking about.

No, I don't!

Then figure it out and do so as fast as you can if you don't want to get yourself into trouble, Signor Migaldi snapped, and fled as if Eusapia were about to eat him alive.

Eusapia stood devastated. As she stared into the emptied space, she suddenly saw the outline of something dark and ugly. She squinted. She almost got what Signor Migaldi had insinuated. Maybe loosing Giorgio, giving birth, leaving her child, suppressing the resulting guilt, and marrying Raphael had changed her. For the better, for the worse? When Eusapia overcame her fears of unwanted insights and tried to bring the partly glimpsed vision into focus, it dissolved into meaningless splotches. To be honest, she was glad. Her experiences over the last few months might have pushed her to grow up brusquely. Yet, she still wasn't ready at all to deal with adulthood. I just want life to be like before, she sighed. I want to see the gleeful twinkle in Signor Migaldi's eyes. I want to feel Signora Migaldi's trust and her belief that I'm special and will do great things. And the boys? Please love me, Pietro and Antonello. Ugo, remember the simple fun we had together. Suddenly her mood changed. To hell with you all, she cried inwardly, her curse in painful contrast to the realisation that only their acceptance could bring her a measure of peace.

At the next chance encounter where no one could hear them, Signor Migaldi, regretting the harshness of the day before, put on his most pleasant face.

Really, Sapia, how are you?

What do you care!

Come on, that's unfair. I want to make sure you're okay. You must want to know how Rosa is doing?

Rosa??

Isn't that the name you called your daughter?

Eusapia stared at him as if he were out of his mind.

I guess not, Signor Migaldi said appeasingly. I just thought you might want to know that your daughter is thriving. The Damianis took up residence in England. Don't worry about Rosa. She is well taken care of. In all the time I've known the Damianis, I've never seen Lillian so happy. She is a mother through and through.

Though the words sank deep into Eusapia, she barely understood them.

Are you sure you're okay? Signor Migaldi asked again. He had hoped the news would ease her mind. Instead her body stiffened, then shook in agonising turmoil. This was not going to work.

You did the right thing, he said, you gave happiness to this couple and a wonderful home to your daughter.

Damn you and your sugary talk, Eusapia snarled and bolted out of the room, punching the air to fight off the evil spirits Signor Migaldi had unleashed on her. Doubts and guilt returned with a vengeance. Yes, she knew Celestina had a better life and better opportunities with the Damianis. But what kind of a mother gives a child away? Eusapia stormed into the noisy streets of Naples. She charged ahead between carriages, carts and horses, pretending neither to see nor hear Celestina who tried to draw her attention. When she finally couldn't ignore her any longer, it was Rosa and not Celestina who wanted to talk to her. Why would she talk to Rosa? Rosa wasn't her daughter. She was Lillian's, for God's sake! Why on earth would she want to talk to Lillian's child? Go away, Rosa, she almost shouted, ignoring that two guys to her left gestured that she had a screw loose. Eusapia couldn't bear to watch the child's sad face. Go! she shouted again. As soon as the face faded away, she erased even the faintest trace of this incident. Life goes on, she murmured. Life has to go on.

Eusapia charged ahead blindly. She paid no attention to the whistling around her until she almost barged into a group of young men lazing around and drinking in the dark shade of a narrow alley.

Hello Cara Mia, Honey, hello Baby, they shouted.

Eusapia almost tripped over their feet. They pushed her and shoved her. What did it matter, with Raphael and Celestina gone, what did she care? She let herself drop in the lap of the nearest guy and pushed against him. Right now, any hard prick would do. She grabbed the man's bottle of wine and drank from it before it was brusquely ripped from her hand.

Go ahead, guys, squeeze those hot melons even tighter. It makes me forget things, she mumbled as she was swung from lap to lap. Whenever she could, she swiped another bottle and drank in big gulps before it was pulled out of her hands again. When she looked unfocused up into the air, she noticed that Celestina had come back.

Don't do it, the child mouthed.

Dammit, Eusapia screamed, this isn't even you, Celestina. Only Lillian's daughter would want to scold me. Celestina is different. She would say, Don't worry, Mammina, it's going to turn out all right. But you, Rosa, you think you know what's best for me. Go back to Lillian.

Hiccuping, Eusapia tried to get up from the last lap she had dropped on.

The guys laughed at her. Where do you think you're going?

They taunted her and pulled her down again. For a while, Eusapia lay against a naked chest, hands pawing through and under her shirt. After one especially loud hiccup, she almost woke from her stupor. What am I doing? For a moment, she sobered up long enough to make use of her strength and flexibility to break free. Luckily, her move took the guys by surprise. They tried to hold her back, but stumbled and grabbed after her ineffectually, not even close to where she actually stood and moved.

Come back here, bitch. You owe us!

As unsteady as she was, she managed to get away and find shelter on the steps of a public fountain with dozens of people around her. She plopped down. How she wanted to be back at the Migaldi's house! There was no way she could arrive there in this state.

After a while of half-dozing, the murmur of the old fountain reached her ears. She forced herself to get up. Leaning listlessly over the edge of the basin, she splashed water into her face and over her hands and arms. She drank water even though she was afraid of the horrible diseases it might carry along. When she was done, she found another empty spot to sit down. She bent and stretched her arms and legs to bring them back to their normal agility. Her stomach heaved, but she didn't throw up as she feared she would. Sitting on the steps, she thought of Ugo. As tempting as it might be to rush into experiencing his brand of love and love-making to drown out her own turmoil, she wouldn't give in to temptation. Ugo was her friend. His mother, father, and brothers were her friends. However out-of-control, she would not betray a friend, ever!

Luckily for her, young Pietro was outside the building when she returned.

Pietro, she whispered, I'm not feeling well. Can you tell your mamma that I'm sick and won't come down for supper?

Are you going to die? Pietro asked, his eyes wide with worry. Don't die like Nonna. Please, Eusapia, don't die.

Silly you, Eusapia joked, attempting to keep control over her stomach. I won't die. I just need to rest. Tomorrow, I'll be as good as new. We'll play together, I promise.

Pietro relaxed.

You want me to bring something to eat to your room?

No, thank you, Eusapia answered, hastily entering the house. The mention of food was the last straw. Don't make me throw up, she implored whoever or whatever might have the power to keep the contents of her stomach from spilling out. Despite an uncharacteristic clumsiness, she reached the guestroom without being seen or heard.

Once the door closed behind her, she trembled. She held herself very straight, leaning against the wall. Breathe slowly. It took many tries before the erratic pounding in her chest resumed a more normal rhythm and the churning in her stomach subsided.

Where was Raphael now? She could see places, trees and rivers, but she did not even want to know what he might be doing. She had enough to deal with.

She hoped Celestina would reappear, but she didn't. And why should she? Eusapia didn't deserve her!

At one point the door opened. Though she feigned to sleep, she recognised Signora Migaldi by the whiff of lavender that followed her everywhere. The lavender intermingled with the tempting aroma of coffee. Eusapia did not stir. After a moment's hesitation, Signora Migaldi put her small tray on the table and left quietly.

Eusapia grimly went to examine the items in her treasure box. She wasn't surprised to find that their usual confidence-inspiring gayety had vanished. In days gone by, the treasure had held promise. It had kept her fears in check and brought a smile to her face. Not now. If the Migaldis didn't want to keep her out of love anymore, she would convince them with her money to let

196

her stay. Her fate hung on a thread. Signora Migaldi was afraid of her, ready to protect her family. But why? I won't hurt you. I'm still the girl I was when I first arrived, Michela's daughter, remember? You have to believe this, Signora Migaldi. I love you all, Eusapia fervently formulated her silent speech into the empty room. The coins she had pulled out burned in her hand. She needed a place to stay. And this was the place.

Here, Signora Migaldi, Eusapia said, I don't want to be a burden. I can pay.

Where did you get it? Signora Migaldi exclaimed, her voice full of suspicion.

Raphael and I worked hard.

How is this possible? Signora Migaldi said, unable to believe that the two young people had been able to save a few pennies, let alone the coins in Eusapia's hand.

Eusapia, who could see Signora Migaldi's trust slip further, felt miffed. You don't want me anymore? she asked, her face red with desperation.

Signora Migaldi relented. You can stay until we figure out where to go from here. Keep your money, Eusapia. You might need it one day.

That was close, Eusapia thought. I won't let her get rid of me! This is the only place where I can become a medium. Why give up Raphael if not to start a career that'll make me rich, let me live without worries and make it possible to help those in need? An empty stomach and flea-ridden, bedbug-infested quarters are behind me forever. My séances will be held in comfortable and respectable places. I'll find a way to convince the Migaldis that I'm worth the trouble.

At the supper table, with the glow of an oil lamp softly illuminating the room, Eusapia sat as if turned to stone, her eyes riveted to her plate.

What's wrong? Pietro asked.

Eusapia didn't respond, but kept staring so intensely that everyone at the table turned to watch. It wasn't just that she was preoccupied with her plate. But something heavy and unearthly seemed to seep into the room. Pietro fidgeted.

What's going on? he asked nervously.

Nothing, Eusapia said, but her voice shook. Slowly her hands moved up from her sides, rising as if pulled by invisible ropes. Then, with sudden force, her plate jerked upwards, spinning toward the open window. With a swift movement, Eusapia's hands shot after it, her body lifting out of her chair, the chair flying backwards and landing on the floor with a bang. At the very last moment, just as the plate seemed already out of reach, Eusapia grabbed it and pulled it back onto the table. Everyone stared, too shocked to say a word.

What was that? Ugo asked.

Eusapia stood trembling. As she opened her mouth to say something, no sound came out.

Leave her be, Signora Migaldi said. It's the spirits. They must have a message for us.

It was impossible to continue with supper as usual, though they tried. The strange incident kept everyone transfixed. All of a sudden, Signora Migaldi jumped.

A cold hand touched me, she said, wondering whether she was hallucinating.

I'm scared, whimpered Pietro. But at that moment, a striking red rose started growing and blooming right beside him. Look!

he exclaimed, surprised. Look how beautiful! The family was focussed on the flower when the plate took off again. To everyone's relief, Sapia was able to catch it and keep it in place.

My flower is gone, Pietro cried out. He stood up to search under the table, behind his chair, everywhere. I can't find it, he whimpered. No one could explain where it had gone.

Signor Migaldi looked impressed. I guess your powers have grown, he said carefully to Eusapia.

It's a miracle, his wife added, Michela's daughter really is a medium.

Is she? Ugo grumbled, his face red and livid. Who believes in that stuff?! he snapped and left the table.

They'd better not get rid of me now, Eusapia muttered when she was finally alone in her room. Why do I have to fight so hard to stay with the Migaldis? she complained, yet considered herself lucky for the extra time she had bought. No other place would serve her purposes. She needed backing from reputable people like the Migaldis to realise her dreams. More importantly, the Migaldis' had known Michela, and their reminiscences revitalised Eusapia's memories of her mother. Signora Migaldi provided particulars no one else could, that Michela had sung one song in a foreign language, and could walk faster and with more endurance than any other citizen of Minervino. Eusapia smiled. She had inherited her mother's fast legs, an advantage for any medium. It allowed her to make quick exits after listening undetected to secrets not meant for her ears.

Eusapia worked hard to start making a living, and for that to work out, she depended a great deal on eavesdropping.

From time to time, she was invited to stay at friends of the Migaldis to give private and group séances. In no time did she know every inch of their houses. Hidden away in nooks or behind curtains and thin cupboard walls, she made it her business to learn and understand the secrets of each and every inhabitant in full.

Take your daughters and come stay at my place for a few weeks, Eusapia heard an aunt say to her niece as the older woman applied heavy make-up on her niece to hide yet another black eye.

The niece waved her arms about, agitated and discouraged. I want to kill that bastard, she said.

But to Eusapia it sounded like, I'm going straight home to him. She had seen it before, women bawling, then submitting to more abuse like lambs trotting to the slaughterhouse. True, they didn't have much choice.

Here, said the aunt, pressing a few coins into her niece's hand, at least get food for the children.

Scared for the woman and her children and affected by their predicament, Eusapia said to the niece after that day's séance, There was a loud and urgent voice in my head today transmitting a message from the otherworld, Take your children and live with your aunt. Now. There is no time to lose.

Another day, this time at the Migaldis, Eusapia spied on two shopkeepers in the back alley, one the owner of a supposedly decent pastry shop haggling with the other man over prices for ingredients of questionable quality.

We agree then, the owner said, three hundred kilos of starch and three hundred kilos of bran, delivered after midnight to me personally, at the usual price.

It's impossible, the other objected, That price would ruin me.

While Eusapia couldn't make out everything they said, she clearly heard the owner complain that too many got sick last time. If someone dies, it will come back to haunt you!

When the pastry shop owner sat in the séance room that evening, Eusapia made sure that the psychic forces hit him hard over the head.

Death to you, a voice shrieked through the room in such a menacing way that the sitters jumped.

Again, the owner was whacked over the head while Eusapia's flaming eyes seared right into his black heart. The owner trembled, and suddenly rushed out of the room.

Most information flowed to Eusapia directly from her sitters. I love my husband's brother, a woman confided to her in a private meeting. He comes by every day. Eusapia waited patiently. After a while, the woman blurted out, Most of my children must be his. As if relieved of a heavy weight that had crushed her over time, she sighed. Owning up to the serious transgressions she would not even have admitted to her parish priest during confession made her breathe easier.

To this woman, Eusapia said with the children in mind, Never talk to anyone about your secret again, ever! But stop what you're doing before you get caught and all hell breaks loose.

When the sitters left, Eusapia, who never forgot for a moment how it felt to be hungry and poor, made it a habit to exhort them, Do good, she would say invariably, give food to the poor.

The Migaldis cabled Signor Damiani and received an answer without delay. He was coming to see Eusapia's progress for himself. When he did arrive a month later, Eusapia was struck by how old he looked compared to Raphael. She didn't linger on that thought because with Raphael away, anybody — old, fat, ugly — would suffice. Gazing into Giorgio's eyes, she realised that his sex life must have improved. Not enough though, she thought, to diminish her power to unleash with one quick touch of her hand a desire that would be hard to control. But she had to consider her daughter. Giorgio was now the husband of the woman who was the mother of her daughter, which meant he was off limits. Eusapia would not ruin the child's chance of growing up in a family with at least some sort of stability if not happiness.

Signor Damiani had rented out his apartment to a cousin, her husband and their two small children, but kept one of the rooms so that he had his own place whenever he travelled back to Naples, for which he was homesick during any absence of more than two weeks. Italian food, he sighed, where in the world can you get such tasty food?

Signor Damiani looked at Eusapia with tenderness. She had given him a daughter. And Rosa had given him back his wife.

It's good to see you, Sapia, he said warmly.

Same here, Eusapia answered politely, but curtly.

I hear you still want to become a medium?

You hear right.

Signor Damiani looked at her, trying to read her thoughts. But Eusapia kept her cards close to her chest.

Do you still want me to teach you? he asked with a slight hesitation, as if afraid of being snared into a trap.

I would, Eusapia answered simply.

When they met at the apartment, Giorgio's cousin and all her family were there. After greeting them warmly, Giorgio led

Eusapia into his room to start his lessons. There was one intense moment when Eusapia thought she'd be unable to avoid throwing herself at Giorgio. But she saw Celestina, well Rosa to be exact, and even if it was Rosa instead of Celestina staring down at her with a sad and accusing face, Eusapia could not hurt a child. Messing up her family life, destroying the bit of harmony that might be there — it wasn't something she wanted on her conscience.

How are you, Giorgio? she asked with a reserve that surprised even herself.

I'm fine, Sapia, and my family is fine as well, he answered carefully.

I'm glad, Eusapia said without hesitation and meant it. Her gesture of self-restraint might be the only good thing she would do in her life, the hardest as well, but she would not stumble.

Let's start the lessons, she said, thankful that Giorgio nodded, a shadow of disappointment but mostly relief on his face.

The room however breathed and whispered with still fresh memories of past passion and neediness. Neither Giorgio nor Eusapia could help glance over to the bed which sent out hard-to-resist invitations.

We can't, Eusapia said.

We can't, Giorgio agreed.

But they kept standing close together, the temperature of their bodies rising, the air around them sizzling with the absorbed heat. With an almost inhuman effort, Eusapia pulled her eyes away from Giorgio, drawing away from the magnetic pull of his passion that by now seemed too strong to leave unanswered. But he did not stop her as she walked toward the door and, after one last moment of hesitation, opened it wide.

From the hallway where the cousin's two children ran to and fro, a slight breeze entered and gradually mixed with the hot currents of the room until it became easier to breathe normally.

Why don't we go for a walk? Eusapia suggested.

Giorgio took his hat and jacket and followed Eusapia out the door into the noisy streets of Naples where the complications of their lives were instantly absorbed and disposed of.

I hear your powers have grown, Giorgio said as they walked through a nearby park.

I don't know what my powers are, Eusapia replied, but I've always been able to communicate with Mammina. When I was up on the mountain, all of Gianina's family talked to me.

They did? Who?

Her husband and her two sons.

You saw them?

They helped me put my life back together.

Giorgio was silent.

You don't believe me?

I do, Eusapia. Maybe that's what Signor Migaldi meant when he said your powers had more depth to them than before.

No, Eusapia replied disparagingly, I think he meant the flowers.

What flowers?

Raphael showed me how to grow flowers. I learned a thousand and one things from him. He knew how to talk to his audience.

Do you want to be a medium or a magician?

A medium, Giorgio. That's why I came back to Naples.

When they returned to their room, they left the door open from the beginning. Giorgio set up a spirit cabinet in the corner opposite the bed.

There, just like her magician husband, Eusapia grew flowers and called for the little guitar and a reddish-brown flute in the cabinet to play a few notes.

I have to admit, it's amazing, Eusapia, Giorgio exclaimed. Now concentrate, Sapia, remember the steps I taught you before and you didn't want to follow for fear of losing control, do it now, fall into an actual trance, hypnotise yourself.

After they dimmed the lights, and Eusapia braced herself for the unexpected, she left her fears behind and slowly submerged into something unknown, not quite dark, but a bit threatening.

Giorgio, hold my hand, she begged.

As he did so and she counted down, three, two, one, she sank into a trance. It was Mammina who appeared.

Mammina, why are you here? I don't need a trance to see you.

Be careful, my child, Michela said simply and disappeared.

What do you mean, Mammina? Eusapia called after her, but was left without an answer.

When Gianina's sons appeared, Eusapia hoped for understanding. But neither of them wanted to talk to her. All the other departed remained silent as well. So there wasn't really any point falling into an actual trance. Eusapia emerged back into a conscious state edgy and with a splitting headache.

Giorgio, are you sure I'm on the right path?

It's right for you, Eusapia, he said.

Out of her misgivings grew a stubborn confidence. Everyone has to make a living.

I was given a gift and I'm going to use it, Eusapia said into the air, as she walked down the street by herself. I wish I had the supernatural powers they say I have. Do other mediums have those powers? And what about Mammina, does she really appear to me or do I need her so much that I make her up without realising it? Eusapia pushed the question away. She couldn't deprive herself of her only consolation and reassurance in life. Gesturing wildly, she attempted to dispel her persistent fears.

This is it, she summed up her thoughts decisively. I was born to be a medium. Isn't that right Mammina? she added, anxious for the approval of her mother, but Michela was not around to encourage her.

You would tell me, Mammina, if you didn't want me to do this, wouldn't you? she called out.

If you are that worried, you probably shouldn't do it, a stranger beside her chipped in.

I didn't ask you, Eusapia growled.

As she watched him hurry along, she recognised that she might be able to dismiss a stranger, but her own doubts might prove more of a challenge.

For the time being, Eusapia kept living with the Migaldis. While life on the surface rolled along as usual, happy and noisy, a jarring note rang through their conversations that made her blood run cold. Whenever the whole family was together, Ugo became tongue-tied and sullen. Even crossing paths with Eusapia when no one else was around, he refused to continue the teasing banter they had shared in the past.

What kind of marriage is that? he demanded to know. I've never heard of a husband and wife living apart from each other. You just got married, if indeed you got married. Is he so ugly that you don't dare show him to us? What's wrong with your so-called husband?

It's our careers that keep us apart, Ugo, Eusapia tried to explain.

Are you crazy? Why aren't you with him? Are you already tired of him?

I want to be a medium.

That's more important than being with your husband?? Who would want a wife like that? At least have the guts to admit you made a mistake!

Whatever you think, Ugo, I love Raphael. And he loves me. But this is life.

The two of them were never alone long before Signora Migaldi would show up. In the past, Eusapia and Ugo could have joked together about his mother spying on them. Not anymore. Eusapia sighed. Signora Migaldi acted like a mother hen protecting her young against a predator.

Do you need help with any of the daily tasks, Signora Migaldi? Eusapia asked with forced eagerness.

Oh no, I was just walking by. What are the two of you up to?

Nothing, said Ugo, storming away, a dark cloud in his wake, the same cloud that seemed to hover over him whenever he was around Eusapia.

Signora Migaldi stared after her son. Again her stomach knotted and twisted in fear.

Are you sure there is nothing going on I should know about? she asked Eusapia. Then with sudden resolve, she said, Eusapia, Don't hurt my son.

Signora, Eusapia replied anxiously, I did not encourage his feelings. It's his age. There is nothing I can do about it.

Isn't there, Eusapia?!! You better get this situation under control. This is my family we're talking about. And no one, especially not you, will harm any one of my children.

I won't, Signora Migaldi. I promise I won't, Eusapia said dejectedly, gripped by renewed fears of being sent away. Please, Signora, you have to believe me.

Signora Migaldi looked at her suspiciously and said, It's your actions that will tell whether you mean what you say. I pray to God that you'll do the right thing.

Eusapia was left trembling. I don't want to leave, she thought. Please, let me stay, she begged, trusting unexpectedly in an unreachable God with the face of a Christ statue near the Migaldi's place, hoping that he was more real than Mammina, and powerful enough to help her.

Signora Migaldi's feelings seemed increasingly conflicted when it came to Eusapia. The girl presented a danger to her son, but she was also as a medium with the potential to open gateways to invisible worlds. In the end, Signora Migaldi had no choice but to heed the psychic signals that emanated from the girl, promising possibilities beyond the wildest expectations. Not long after her confrontation with Eusapia, she took her aside.

You must develop your powers. Michela would never forgive me if I didn't assist you in your progress toward full enlightenment.

Though Eusapia was not sure whether she'd manage to remain in Signora Migaldi's good graces, her mediumship saved her for the moment.

Would you like to contact anyone in the otherworld? Eusapia asked, trying to solidify the foothold she had just gained.

Yes, please, I would like to talk to my mother again. Just me. With no one else around.

That evening, after the boys went to bed, Signora Migaldi and Eusapia sat quietly in the darkened living room at the small table used for séances.

When Eusapia fell into a trance, Signora Migaldi asked, Are you there, Mother?

As soon as she asked, the table rose and there were the three raps for yes.

Are you disappointed in how my life turned out?

One rap for no.

Signora Migaldi, tears in her eyes, cried out, Thank you, Mother, I just needed to hear you say so.

Then the hollow voice of one of Eusapia's many spirit controls piped in, My daughter, you give love and warmth to your family. What else could I want? After a silence, the voice spoke up again, Don't forget your husband. You're also a wife, not just a mother. Why come to me for affection? Then louder, with more enthusiasm, Take back your place. Seek new closeness. Let him feel the heat of your body, then wait. He'll notice.

Mother, what are you saying? Signora Migaldi asked, taken aback. She had never heard such things, used as she was to accept without question whatever marriage brought with it. It would have surprised her less if her submissive and fervently

209

religious mother had sent her to Lourdes or some other pilgrimage place to be cleansed of impure thoughts.

Don't neglect your husband, the voice spoke up again, and for a moment, it sounded more like Eusapia than anyone even remotely resembling Signora Migaldi's mother. But the next moment, the voice recaptured its unearthliness and spoke with solemn assurance, You will find love again, my daughter.

As Eusapia woke up from her trance, Signora Migaldi sat speechless in her chair.

When Eusapia looked at her inquisitively, the woman blushed and quickly left the room.

Eusapia smiled when the next morning she saw the satisfied and excited expressions on Signor and Signora Migaldi's faces.

Again, Eusapia had bought herself some time, more importantly, she had Signora Migaldi's blessing. Since the séance, their relationship had improved, though a cautious awkwardness remained when it came to Ugo. Signora Migaldi's mother-hen instinct took over the moment her son as much as glanced at Eusapia. When his infatuated eyes came to rest on her, his mother's protectiveness went into overdrive, but there was nothing she could do to console him. Deep down she held Eusapia responsible for her son's unhappiness. It was the girl's fault that he was lovesick and thrown off balance. She was to blame for his moodiness and sudden need to talk back as if his mother were his enemy.

Ugo, Signora Migaldi said, open your eyes, there are so many wonderful girls out there eager to get to know you. Give them a chance.

Get off my back, he snarled. What do you know about love? Real love I mean?!!

Signora Migaldi could do nothing but back off and watch apprehensively the turmoil in her son's life from afar. She wouldn't confide in her husband for fear he would make fun of their son. Teasing was the last thing Ugo needed right now.

Why do you lead him on? Signora Migaldi questioned Eusapia when she was alone with her.

I don't! Eusapia exclaimed, her eyes blazing. Why do you always think the worst of me? I'm not some sinister villain.

Sorry, Eusapia, but the facts speak for themselves. Make things right. Then I might feel differently about you again.

In the evenings though, the tension vanished, and Eusapia was celebrated as a famous medium. Signora Migaldi first invited family friends, then the wider community of spiritualists in Naples. She intended to make her home a place of awakenings. The dead would bring solace and love into people's lives. Her big heart wanted to make sure that as many people as possible could reconnect with recently or long departed loved ones.

Once again, the spirit guide John King took over, providing information from the otherworld to his reincarnated daughter. He rapped his responses and left many sitters unnerved. While everyone wanted to hear him speak, his voice was rarely heard. The currents in the room had to be particularly propitious. It happened more often when close friends or relatives of the Migaldis were present, people Eusapia was familiar with. Then it could happen that John King's voice slowly came forth, first in barely intelligible noises, later in deep hollow-voiced pronouncements that sent shudders through everyone present. He would give messages that cut to the quick, revealing secrets that couldn't be known by anyone except the person trying to make contact, and possibly one or two of the very closest relatives or friends. Eusapia drew the sitters so deep into her hypnotic and suggestive circle that they recognised in John King's words and manner of speaking their child, father, mother, sister or brother, and through him were enabled to commune with the otherworld. Tears flowed easily at such gatherings. In the exulted atmosphere of the dark room people hugged, comforted each other, and shared their misery and longing. In the circle of supportive fellow sitters, a rare trust developed. Here, feelings could gush out without inhibition. Being allowed to express needs and sorrows was a liberating experience that left many of the men and women in the séance room shaken and with a desire to re-evaluate their lives and values.

Signor Migaldi sat through those séances with mixed feelings. On the one hand, he appreciated a good spectacle and even helped along phenomena that the spirits somehow weren't able to bring about. On the other hand, like tonight, Signor Migaldi looked at the distraught people with discomfort. It was especially at the sight of his grieving cousin Carla that he questioned his role in this charade. She had lost her two-year-old daughter a few months earlier. He remembered the vivacious woman before the tragedy, the hilariously provocative chitchat between the two of them every time they met, her sharp frankness to which he responded likewise, full of mischief. She deserved better. In her grief, she had followed the lead of fellow sitters into an all-consuming fascination with the beyond. Yet beneath this temporarily calming absorption, he could already feel the harsh reality waiting to swallow her up. When he looked at her and at the other sitters, he almost heard deception screaming back at him. Although no one could see him in the dark, he blushed.

What was he to do? Who was he to destroy the illusion that brought her temporary solace? No, he couldn't do it. Carla needed this crutch. Once her sorrow became more manageable, she would find new ways of dealing with it. How do you deal with losing a child? What would he do if anything happened to his sons? He quickly pushed the thought out of his mind. No parent should have to bury his child. Carla was sobbing in the arms of Signora Migaldi, who cooed to her with soothing sounds until Carla's breathing slowly fell in step with her own. Around them, the candles flickered and gave off a faint smell of church. Suddenly, a childlike voice broke free from Eusapia.

Mammina, the child said, don't cry. I'm happy in your heart.

At the sound of the voice, Eusapia woke from her trance with a start, trembling, expecting to see Celestina. But only the pale faces of the sitters stared back at her.

I love you, Giovanna, Carla whispered, and through her moist eyes shimmered a trace of a smile.

Life had too much of a pull on Signor Migaldi to waste it on the ethics of spiritualist activities. Even when it came to a real-life flesh-and-blood person like Eusapia, his qualms lingered for just a moment. She had to make a living. Housekeeping wouldn't work. Her stint as a laundress almost did her in. It was a pity she hadn't received an education. A shrewd person like her could have made something of herself. Was it too late? She showed no inclination for formal learning, although sometimes he wondered whether her reading ability hadn't improved sharply and was much better than she let on. She knew things she could only have read. Why question her right to work as a medium? At least she wouldn't starve. If the present trend continued, she'd be able to make a decent living one day. Signor Migaldi chuckled when he thought of how expertly flowers appeared in the séance room or how otherworldly the sounds of instruments jingled from the spirit cabinet, not a treat to his musical ear, but an amazing feat of showmanship. That's that then, he decided, he was not the one to stand in the way of her future. With his mind put at ease, the last of his scruples were swept away for good, never to bother him again. In fact, he looked forward to some exciting and innovative entertainment.

While Eusapia held on with both hands to her new opportunity, she could not relax. She was granted an extension of sorts at the Migaldis, but for how long would they put up with her? Days, weeks, a month or two? Even Pietro seemed to pick up on the tension in the house.

Why is Ugo always mad at you? Did you do something to him? he asked, hoping for an explanation that would let him continue to love both of them.

If I did, I didn't mean to, Eusapia said. I want Ugo to be happy, Pietro. I want him to laugh and smile like before.

Does Mamma still like you, Eusapia?

I hope she does, Pietro. There is nothing I want more. I don't know what it is, but I always do things that get people upset.

You shouldn't have gotten married, Pietro stated.

And why is that?

You don't love him

Eusapia grabbed him.

Why would you say a stupid thing like that? Do you have any idea what you're talking about?

Ugo said you're a whore, and whores aren't capable of loving anyone.

What are you saying!? Eusapia seized Pietro by the neck this time and slapped him across the face.

Whore! Pietro screamed.

Whack, whack!

You stupid whore!

Eusapia crumpled. What was happening? Why did everyone hate her? Giant tears dribbled down her cheeks.

I didn't mean to slap you, Pietro.

The boy ran over to her and threw both his arms around her neck.

You aren't a whore? he asked breathlessly.

How could you even think something like that?

Pietro held on to her.

What's a whore, Eusapia?

This time, Eusapia had to smile.

It's not something you want to know, Pietro. It's enough to know that I'm not a whore. I love Raphael. We just can't be together right now.

Eusapia is not a whore, Pietro stated earnestly at the supper table.

After a split second of shocked silence, Signora Migaldi responded, Of course she's not. Only a pure person can be a medium.

Eusapia caught the flash of a smirk on Signor Migaldi's face, but couldn't respond without making the situation worse.

Furiously, she stabbed the beans on her plate. One, two, three, and shoved them into her mouth as if in penitence for some awful deed.

Don't you like the food? Pietro asked, watching her with astonished curiosity.

I do, Eusapia answered and forced her voice to sound as sweet as she could, which didn't mean much since she felt like smashing her plate on the floor.

Why couldn't her life go smoothly like other people's? Besides becoming a medium, she just wanted a place with a family of her own that would make her feel she belonged.

Not long after this episode and following a long talk between Signor Migaldi and Giorgio Damiani, Giorgio offered to pay for a small apartment for Eusapia, one that wasn't too far away. Eusapia would continue holding her séances at the Migaldis to ensure respectability. And Signora Migaldi, who was convinced that Michela's daughter possessed an extraordinary gift, wouldn't have wanted it any other way.

She said, A place of your own won't affect your mediumship since I'll do everything in my power to make sure you're able to follow your vocation. That's my duty.

So much for Eusapia's dream of being part of a family! The proposed arrangement felt like a slap in the face, and only started to look brighter when Raphael came back to town to check on her.

I was worried about you.

Don't, Raphael. I can take care of myself.

But their three days together in her little apartment revived her body and soul. When he left for another tour, she knew she was ready to tackle whatever life would throw at her.

Eusapia often wondered why her rapport with most women was tenuous and strained. She knew they called her lewd and shameless behind her back. Only her mediumship redeemed her to a certain extent. It was a different story for men, who let her cast spells on them with greedy pleasure. Especially the older ones whose sexual energy had declined, the ones who wanted to relive the power of their younger years when the mere whiff of sex sent them into a frenzy, and the bodies of their wives were young and fresh. Men expected her to turn back the clock. Not that they would ever admit that they needed help. No, they ostensibly participated in séances to search for a purpose in life, to look for a more immediate spirituality than their formal religion permitted, and to try to deal with loss and sorrow. In the darkness of her séance room, where ancestors and dead children brought them new insights, and ghosts seemed to touch them in unspeakable places, men received what they came for, spiritual awakenings, physical solace and satisfaction.

Somehow, I'm able to fulfil their needs, Eusapia thought, wondering about the exact nature of her contribution. Men came alive in her presence. She freed them from the notion that life was over. Life is never over. Life is what you want it to be. In her generosity, she gave men back the confidence in their own strength and sexuality. It's something their wives should do, she often thought. But who knew what crises of their own these wives were going through. It was left to her to save fragile egos, it became her duty and her destiny to do so.

Under the clever guidance of Giorgio, who informed her of new trends in spiritualism around the world, Eusapia steadily developed into an accomplished medium with an uncanny knack for absorbing whatever was advantageous to her career, especially adapting to any scenario instantaneously. If a conciliatory and good-natured response was called for, her eyes became dreamy and soft. If an aggressive action was needed, she shrieked, punched, and scratched. Either way, her sitters fell under her spell, and her reputation grew. Over the months and years, her financial situation slowly improved. She put money aside, though much less than expected because in Naples, she almost tripped over the many children and old people too weak from hunger and sickness to stand upright. She wasn't able to walk by without buying food for them. Every day she wondered how a city like hers could abandon the poorest and most vulnerable to their horrendous fate. I want to do my share, she promised herself, and did so, clearly aware that her generosity did not bode well for her own financial security.

During Giorgio's recent visit to Naples, Eusapia had picked up disquieting hints about Gianina's health. Something wasn't right. Suddenly, the only thing she could see when going into a semi-trance during her séances was Gianina's face, her big eyes.

What do you want, Gianina? she asked.

Who's Gianina? the sitters asked, annoyed that the person in the room with them wasn't anyone they were familiar with.

There was nothing Eusapia could do. Gianina's eyes were all she could see.

What's wrong, Gianina? Eusapia asked, but Gianina remained silent.

The next morning, Eusapia sold some brooches and watches from her treasure trove, more than enough to pay for a trip to the mountain. She packed extra coins and money from her séances. The Migaldis did not think it was a good idea for her to leave while she was still establishing her career. But Eusapia could not do otherwise. She had received a call and she was going to heed it.

She left early the next day and arrived at Gianina's the night after. No one rushed to the door when she knocked, calling, Gianina, are you there? Impatiently, Eusapia entered.

Gianina, it's me, she shouted.

Still no answer. Suddenly anxious, she ran up to Gianina's room and found her emaciated and unresponsive on her bed.

I'm here, Gianina, Eusapia said. I'm here to take care of you.

Gianina did not open her eyes.

Are you dead? Eusapia shouted. As her frightened cry filled the room, Gianina's eyes fluttered open. A small smile seemed to transform the hollow eyes. For a second, a glimmer of life shone out of them.

Don't die on me, Gianina, Eusapia begged.

But Gianina had already fallen back into unconsciousness.

Eusapia soothingly washed the old woman's face and her body. She dragged the mattress from the adjacent room into Gianina's, then lifted her out of the bed and lowered her onto the clean mattress. She took the soiled sheets, washed them and hung them outside to dry even though it was night. She used an extra blanket she found in the cupboard to warm Gianina's cold body.

Just as Signor Cammarata had fed his wife, Eusapia mushed together pasta beaten to a pulp and a skinned, finely crushed tomato that she found in the garden.

Here, Gianina, she said invitingly. She pried open Gianina's mouth and dribbled some water on her tongue. To her surprise, Gianina swallowed. After another small amount of water,

Eusapia spooned a bit of mush into the mouth. Again, Gianina swallowed.

Good girl, Eusapia said, and carefully continued feeding her. You're coming back to life, Gianina, she said, I can feel it.

When Eusapia checked out the kitchen cupboards, she saw that except for the bit of pasta, the cupboards were empty. After a good night's rest, she washed Gianina again, changed her clothes, and fed her a few more spoonfuls of mush and also some water.

Gianina, I have to go to the village and get food and medicine, Eusapia said as she was brushing strands of hair back from Gianina's forehead.

As if in response, Gianina's eyelids quivered.

You don't want me to go? I won't be long, Eusapia promised. I will just pick up the most important items. I'll be back in no time.

All of a sudden though, Eusapia knew that besides getting food and medicine for Gianina, she also had to go to the Cammaratas' house. She didn't know why exactly, but it was like a summons that she could not ignore. The extra mileage would not set her back too much since she had money to pay for a ride. She found Signor Cammarata in mourning and almost beside himself with grief. She was not sure whether he understood what she was telling him about Gianina. He just stared at her, almost accusingly, as if her presence would have made all the difference.

By the time Eusapia arrived back at Gianina's, the old woman hovered between life and death and barely hung on. Eusapia had spent a great part of her savings on food, medication, and a nightshirt. She began brewing a broth, added tiny pieces of broccoli, cooked and mashed them, and spooned the liquidy mixture into Gianina's mouth. After several mouthfuls, Gianina opened her eyes. She looked up at Eusapia without recognising her, but grateful for this touch of kindness. A few seconds later, a flicker of recognition crossed her face before she fell back into a coma. All around her, Eusapia heard increasingly urgent calls for Gianina to start on her new journey. Under the grateful watch of Gianina's husband and her sons, Eusapia sat beside the dying woman holding her hand.

Four days later, Signor Cammarata arrived.

I understand you need help, he said simply.

Together, they kept vigil around the clock. In the few moments Gianina regained a semblance of consciousness, they tried to feed her bits of nourishment. Half of it dribbled down the stiff left corner of her lips. Eusapia saw that Gianina wanted to say thank you, but was reduced to a few muffled sounds.

Rest, Gianina, Eusapia whispered, get back your strength.

An almost imperceptible tremor slivered through the paralysed left end of Gianina's lips, and Eusapia wondered whether she would ever get her spontaneous, heart-warming smile back.

When a sudden gurgling and rasping made Eusapia jump in fear, she had to accept that Gianina had begun an intense and drawn-out goodbye.

I'll go down to the village to cable Giorgio who is presently in Naples, Eusapia said.

Relieved to know that Gianina would be in good hands with Signor Cammarata, Eusapia left for the village to send an urgent plea for medical assistance.

With this errand behind her, Eusapia sped back up the mountain as fast as her strong legs would carry her. When she arrived, she saw right away that Gianina's health had deteriorated. Silently Eusapia sat down opposite Signor Cammarata, on the other side of the bed.

Did you call the priest? Signor Cammarata asked. Eusapia shook her head, embarrassed that the thought had not even occurred to her. Signor Cammarata sighed, but did not scold her. He held one of Gianina's dried-out hands in his. Again, Eusapia tried to feed her, but was unable to do more than moisten her lips and the end of her tongue.

Gianina . . . , Signor Cammarata's faltering voice came forth.

I love you, Gianina, Eusapia said.

Beside Gianina stood her husband and her sons, providing loving assistance. Despite gasping for air and barely able to breathe, Gianina seemed at peace with herself, God, the Virgin Mary, the world and her impending death. Eusapia held on to her hand. Across from her, Signor Cammarata started to pray. Eusapia was glad he was here because it was important to give Gianina a proper send-off with sanctioned rituals.

They took turns watching over her, relieving each other for short naps through the evening and the night and the next day.

In the afternoon, Signor Cammarata called Eusapia to the bed where she listened to his murmured prayers. She could see now that Signora Cammarata had joined the bedside as well, fully restored to her former beauty. Eusapia hoped that Signor Cammarata would see her as well. But for the moment, he was concentrating on his prayers for Gianina. Eusapia moistened the sunken face. When it became too difficult for Gianina to breathe, Eusapia lifted her up and held her in her arms. The breathing appeared to become less painful, more quiet until, after a last rattling gasp, Eusapia couldn't hear anything at all anymore. She kept holding on to Gianina until Signor Cammarata lifted the body gently out of her arms, laid Gianina on her back, and after a last look, closed her eyes.

At that moment, voices from the outside disturbed the stillness. Neither Eusapia nor Signor Cammarata moved when the door opened and Giorgio entered with a doctor, who could only certify that Gianina had joined her family.

Eusapia had not the heart to stick around any longer. After an emotional hug with Signor Cammarata, she left to find her way back to Naples. She knew that Giorgio would give Gianina a decent Catholic burial and arrange whatever business was left to be arranged.

The losses added up to a weight that almost crushed Eusapia. Back in her small apartment, she choked up for a moment before outrage and sheer will to overcome adversity took hold of her. She threw open the window.

Take everyone away from me! Let me fend for myself, she berated the God she only knew from paintings and sculptures. You made me grow up without a mother. Lucia lives far away. Celestina is gone. So is Gianina, good, loving Gianina. Why did you have to take her?

But her imagined God had no voice, no justification for the pain he inflicted on people. Eusapia saw that Gianina wanted to say something. Probably something like, Everything happens for a reason or Our Heavenly Father's wisdom will prevail. But Eusapia was in no mood to understand or accept such nonsense.

The Heavens love you, she heard Gianina say.

No, Eusapia answered. You love me, Gianina. And my mother Michela loves me. You're the ones who need to watch over me. Right now, I don't give a crap what happens to me.

Eusapia stared crossly at all the dead people who entered the room. Despite her immense sadness and sense of loss, she was luckier than most people in her situation. At least, the dead were not lost to her. She was able to talk to them when she needed them.

You won't be alone, her mother said.

We'll always take care of you, Gianina added.

Why should I believe that the dead will not abandon me as well one day? Eusapia uttered confrontationally.

Eusapia stood listless. As if sent by the dead, a sudden memory of Lucia fluttered into the room. Lucia dealt with sickness and death day in and day out, not complaining, not whining. So Eusapia decided to learn to be courageous too. Lucia's example gave her the strength to at least try to cope with this new loss.

Yet, another wave of grief washed over Eusapia and threatened to drown her. It took four nights and four days before the noises of the streets called up to her again and pulled her out of her suffocating room into the open, where tentatively, she started to breathe more freely again.

Eusapia wished for Raphael to come back. She needed to hold his body. But Raphael was a magician, not a medium. He could not hear her silent pleas. For him, it would be business as usual. She had never explained to him how she felt about Gianina because she did not want to tell him about Celestina. That part of her life, she had locked away and would never let out except as fragments of tall tales with only flimsy connections to reality. She herself could only stand short flashbacks if she wanted to keep her sanity.

Shortly after Eusapia had arrived back in Naples, Signora Migaldi beseeched her to contact Gianina.

You were close to her. She will talk to you.

But she already does, Eusapia responded. I don't need a séance for that.

Then how is it over there?

The dead don't talk about that. They don't need a place. I don't think they're very much aware of their environment. The only thing they want is a sense of connection. When I die, I will be together with my mother and with all the people I loved. The same way, Gianina is with her family and all the other people she was close too. Over there, it's possible to have complete awareness of everyone you ever loved. There is nothing to explain about it. It just is like that.

Signora Migaldi stared at her.

Did Giorgio tell you this? she inquired, looking doubtful and taken aback.

I don't need Giorgio to figure out the afterlife, Eusapia answered, trembling with indignation.

I just mean it would be nice to have Gianina confirm what it is like.

You don't believe me?

I do, Eusapia. But here is a person we all trust. I would so much like to talk to her.

It's not through séances that you really communicate with the dead, Eusapia explained.

225

What do you mean?

If you really want to know what the dead have to say, listen to your heart.

You don't want to share Gianina with us!

Ahh!! Eusapia almost screamed. Don't you get it?

What?

Oh forget it. Maybe I'll try. But I won't promise.

Eusapia stomped away in a huff. She had enough of this séance business.

Why don't people get it? It's not raps and spirit controls that bring you knowledge from the beyond. I wish Signora Migaldi would understand this, but explaining it to her would be shooting myself in the foot. Eusapia could not afford to sabotage herself. Very few people do so intentionally. I have a right to make a decent living like everyone else. I'm finished with poverty and humiliation!

Eusapia was not a defenceless girl anymore. She had power and was going to use it to become famous and never be forced to worry about a roof over her head again.

So Eusapia finally agreed to contact Gianina. When the séance got under way that night, the room was filled with excited anticipation. Despite Eusapia's best efforts to tone down the expectations of the few distant relatives of Gianina's and especially of Signora Migaldi, the sitters were convinced that Eusapia would transmit messages from Gianina. This woman had always lived for others. She would continue to reach out to them from the other life.

The table rose at once, higher and wilder than during any previous evening. Eusapia fell into a trance, but brought too much anger into it. Yes, she felt grateful to Gianina. But damn those sitters with their crazy demands for signs! One of those days she'd kick them all in the ass. Her agitation ran through her body in violent tremors. Instead of playing pleasant melodies, the instruments screeched. The flowers barely unfolded their petals before they flopped to their sides and disappeared.

Are you angry with us, Gianina? a meek second cousin of Gianina asked fearfully.

Eusapia looked into the corner where Gianina stood quietly, accepting of everything that came her way, as Eusapia had seen her day after day.

Talk to us, the cousin demanded, a bit louder and bolder this time.

Eusapia couldn't take her eyes off Gianina whose husband and sons had thrown their arms around her and held her close, her smile radiating like a sky full of stars.

Are you happy? an older gentleman asked.

As much as Eusapia wanted to respond, yes, yes, yes, three raps, she held back.

Are you, Gianina?

As the questions repeated themselves and became increasingly insistent, Eusapia started moaning, foam dribbling down the corners of her mouth.

She is having a seizure, someone whispered. Signora Migaldi rushed over and wiped her face with cold water until, slowly, Eusapia calmed down and finally woke from her trance. Signor Migaldi looked at her with alarm. He gestured to the sitters to pick up their purses and leave the room. He went out with them, explaining that the emotions had become too much for Eusapia, who had lost in Gianina a woman who was like a mother to her.

Eusapia went to her room without looking at anyone, without saying a word. She lay on her bed.

Come back, Gianina, she begged, but as much as she stared into the dark room, she couldn't see anything. Staying awake half the night, she pleaded with Gianina. To no avail. Toward morning, Eusapia fell into a fitful sleep and found herself walking through Gianina's eerily empty house on her mountain.

When Eusapia woke up, she felt overwhelmed by grief.

You will see me again, Gianina whispered in her ear and it felt soothing, giving Eusapia the strength to make it through another day.

Though Gianina had not come through at the séance in a tangible way, the sitters were convinced that she had been in the room. They all had felt her presence. Behind the rambunctious table and the screeching instruments hid the gentle presence of this loving and giving woman. If only Eusapia had been granted extra time for her trance, she might have been able to open the channels of communication with her. In the aftermath, the sitters could almost hear the raps of her answers and their faint echoes. While elusive, answers did float around and otherworldly presences manifested themselves. Eusapia had awakened such powerful feelings in everyone present that her reputation soared and spread throughout Italy, and her fame grew with each day. Eusapia became the medium to see in Naples.

Naples, Italy, 1886-1891

7

THE FIRST THING GIORGIO ASKED Eusapia after being summoned urgently from London by Naples' spiritualists was, Did Gianina contact you? He looked concerned, even caring, but made no attempt to hide the amused quivering in his voice.

Eusapia eyed him as if she saw him for the first time.

Talk to me, Giorgio said, fully expecting her to confide in him.

But in stark contrast to her customary outpouring, she responded with a wilful silence. His power over her was gone. Sure she wanted to grab him even now and find out where the hot waves rolling over her skin would lead, but she only had to recall Celestina and Raphael's muscled body to bring her residual lust under control.

Eusapia . . . ??!

Without looking at him, she turned to leave.

Why are you acting this way? I'm still your teacher. How will you learn without me? Do you understand how important it is for you to be up to date on everything to do with mediumship and its latest developments?

Eusapia hesitated. True, not even her magician husband could provide her with the inside information Giorgio accumulated left and right. Giorgio was connected with spiritualists all over the world. He had attended innumerable séances with the most diverse mediums and was friends with scientists who investigated psychical phenomena.

Let's start, Giorgio said encouragingly, taking advantage of her hesitation.

As you like, Eusapia muttered, still in her stubborn-as-a-mule mood, but her curiosity getting the better of her. As Giorgio was her best source for learning everything there was to know, she ignored the flash of triumph in his eyes.

Anything new? she asked brusquely.

Ectoplasm, Giorgio responded and watched Eusapia almost choke on the unfamiliar word. Materialisations, he added mysteriously.

Once they settled down to work in Giorgio's apartment under the rumble of foreign-sounding words, the teacher in Giorgio took over. Adapting to Eusapia, who had no patience for fluff, he stuck to practical, to-the-point explanations.

The last three mediums I visited in England were able to grow extra limbs. Spirit limbs, they call them. A substance extends out of a medium's body, sometimes it grows out of her mouth.

What is it? Eusapia asked, cutting him off impetuously.

Ectoplasm, which means spirit energy oozing out of a medium's body.

But what is it really?

Eusapia! I don't believe you'd ask such a question. Spirit energy is just that: spirit energy, no ifs or buts.

They looked at each other knowingly.

I'll try, Eusapia promised. Her thoughts raced. Spirit energy? How was she going to accomplish that?

You better try hard, Giorgio exhorted her, if you want your career to take off. Wait, he added, I brought you a surprise.

What?

Two spirit photographs.

I don't believe it! Eusapia exclaimed as she closely examined the pictures Giorgio put in front of her. On each was a medium producing ectoplasm, in the first case a gigantic tongue protruding from the medium's mouth, in the second case six limbs growing strangely out of her body.

You look as if you rediscovered the wheel, he said.

What are you talking about? Eusapia asked innocently.

Never mind. As long as you apply yourself to producing the new phenomena.

Eusapia kept staring at the photographs. If someone were to ask her what spirit growths looked like, she might describe them as whitish, soft, cottony or gossamer-like limbs, though she also noticed the more rigid quality of some bulges, especially the rather coarse, enlarged tongue of the first medium.

I've even seen full-blown materialisations, Giorgio continued. Actual spirits stepped out of the séance cabinet and walked amidst the sitters.

Eusapia's eyes opened wide.

Were they made up of this same whitish substance? she inquired breathlessly, as a sly glint ignited her dark pupils.

Pretty similar.

The sitters don't touch the growths?

No one in his right mind would try. Sitters are warned that interfering with spirit energy by touching the ectoplasm could bring irreparable harm to the medium and destroy any chance of special occurrences.

231

The glint in Eusapia's eyes intensified.

You're right. I'd have to make doggone sure no one dares to touch me.

Giorgio nodded, appreciating the speed with which she processed new information.

Mammina never looks anything like those ghosts when she appears.

What does she look like? Giorgio asked, suddenly compelled to understand Eusapia's visions. Did she actually see her mother or at least think she did — or was this just another ruse to draw attention to herself and create intrigue?

Eusapia looked straight at her mother in the corner of the room and started describing her. She is luminous and transparent, dressed in clothes made of coloured lights, looking exactly as Mamma must have looked on this earth. But if I were to touch her, my hand would go right through her. I think it's her soul that reveals itself.

Giorgio waited for more, strangely affected by Eusapia's obvious emotion.

Well, he finally said, I guess you'd have to possess a special gift to see actual souls. I'm afraid that most ordinary sitters would require something more substantial, just like it shows in the pictures.

Eusapia snapped back to reality.

You're right, Giorgio, she said, aware of how important it was for her future success and material security to heed his advice.

Can I borrow these? Eusapia asked, pointing to the pictures.

Keep them, Giorgio replied grinning, they're all yours.

When Raphael visited a few days later, as he always did when he was near Naples, Eusapia wanted to show him the pictures first. But their bodies had other intentions. Goose bumps spread over Eusapia's skin in frantic waves. Raphael grabbed her. Within seconds, their naked bodies melted together, and in frantic rhythms drove towards a momentous explosion, a glorious tangle of delirium. As they finally caught their breaths, he kissed her again and again, and twirled her and turned her. She followed the unfamiliar touches with ease, awe and an occasional burst of jealousy. Where had he learned these moves? With a new lover? A very experienced wild woman? My God, what's he doing now? Partly shocked, but mostly driven wild by his passionate love-making and spurred on by her own overheated fantasies, she greedily submitted as he took her from behind. After a dreamy interruption, she blinked in disbelief as he placed her on top of himself. Moments later she enthusiastically engaged in an exhilarating and liberating ride she hadn't known was possible.

So what did you want to show me when I arrived? Raphael asked after they resurfaced from a few hours of sleep.

Eusapia put the pictures in front of him.

You want me to help you with this?

Would you, Raphael?

He studied the photos with the extreme concentration he reserved for professional puzzles and secrets: a jumble of images, ideas, and suggestions buzzing and flashing through his brain, sending electric charges into his hair. His hands and arms gestured in obsessed fascination for over thirty minutes. Unintelligible grunts and snorts sputtered out of his mouth, but the occasional flicker in his eyes spoke volumes of the feverish activity in his head.

Eusapia knew him well enough to leave him to his thinking. She sat across from him, biting her tongue to keep from talking. She forced herself to keep as still as possible, suppressing hot remembrances of the night before. Now keep your appetite under control, she exhorted herself. A new bout of sex would delay the answers she sought from Raphael.

When he started to come out of his spell, slightly disoriented, stirring tentatively, his natural lively allegro rhythms flowing back into his gestures, Eusapia eagerly took his hand.

Do you need money?

You're afraid your ghosts might not come cheap?

Well . . .

It won't take that much, as far as I can see.

Eusapia grabbed a handful of coins from her box.

Here, she said.

Business must be booming . . . , Raphael responded, eyeing the coins.

Money does roll in at times, Eusapia admitted. But it rolls out as fast as it comes. You too wouldn't be able to walk by the misery around here without sharing.

You're too generous, Sapia! Look at me, Raphael said, weighing the coins in his hands. One or two of these will be sufficient for your ghosts. But . . . , he said, stuffing the coins in his pockets, it's a relief not to have to worry for a while.

Husbands and wives always take care of each other!

Even husbands and wives like us??

Especially husbands and wives like us, Raphael!

He tried to concentrate again on the business at hand. But Eusapia's eyes and body would not allow it.

I guess this can wait, he murmured before he grabbed her once again and they both forgot about ghosts for the next few hours.

Raphael did not let her down.

The next day, late in the afternoon, after scouring the little shops in God knows what neighbourhoods, he huddled with a heap of gauze, white cotton, strings, clasps, collapsible mechanisms, starch, glue and needles in a corner of her apartment. He would not let her near him. Although he thrived on noise and action, distractions drove him crazy when it came to professional challenges. He worked like a maniac, moving material around, measuring, cutting, walking about, throwing his hands about. Eusapia thought it wiser to get out of the apartment and leave him to his own devices. Outside, she imagined how Raphael would make a ghost come alive. Their minds worked similarly, but she knew better than to butt in. Give him space to get results. Only once he was done would he be approachable again and eager to accept suggestions to improve his work.

Eusapia raced through the streets, too wound up to take it easy or enjoy the sun and crude energy of Naples' smells and noises. She too had her pride. If she was to be a medium, she wanted to be the best. She might not have gone to school, but so what? If going to school meant ending up like her sitters, she must not have missed much. Did education make them smart? No! Did it make them logical? No! What on earth did school do for them? What was the point of being able to read when you couldn't think for yourself? But then Eusapia thought of Giorgio and his intoxicating way with words. Would he have been able to talk like this without school? He was a natural entertainer, a born storyteller and teacher, with an abundance of ideas in his head. Other ideas, though, Eusapia knew he took them from books. He spoke of his books as if they were friends or family. There was a connection that didn't escape her. In those moments, she resented her lack of schooling. She too wanted to dig out secrets and revelations from books. If she could give the sitters more than her own limited ideas, she might have an impact on the world as well. But her priority was to earn a living, not make up for lost opportunities. Forget about that! At least she had Giorgio to learn from.

On impulse, she bought a small book to read, with minimal writing and easy words instead of the complicated texts that on occasion she spent hours deciphering. Brief messages attracted her most: newspaper headlines, street names, hotel names or personal letters she found lying around and attempted to read. She had mastered the basics and got by quite nicely, but fluency and ease in reading would definitely be an advantage for any medium.

Time passed quickly. Eusapia didn't notice that the sky had darkened until all of a sudden, torrents of rain plummeted down on her and the wind whipped her along. She rushed home, arriving at the apartment a miserable bundle of wet clothes and rapid breathing. Raphael must have finished his job. He sat relaxed in a big chair, his long legs stretched out, the room smelling of freshly brewed coffee.

Here, he said, handing her his cup. Drink.

He went to brew more coffee. When he turned back and found her standing in a puddle of water, he lifted the cup out of her hands, took off her clothes, towelled her dry and warmed her with his big body.

Are you feeling better now? he asked when they had recovered enough to begin serious work.

Much better. What about the ghosts, Raphael?

Her husband grinned.

Let's see now, he said playfully.

They talked and practised through the night until, finally, the next day, she was able to present her first materialisation to Giorgio: three limbs growing out from different spots on her body.

You did it, Giorgio said. I knew you had the gift, he added enthusiastically, sending his big laugh frolicking into the room until it enveloped both of them in their private world of exhilaration. Eusapia couldn't wait to tell Raphael how well the ghostly apparitions had gone over. At the same time, she made sure the two men did not meet. Her husband's presence in town was best kept a secret.

Word of the materialisations spread and even caused a line-up in front of the Migaldi residence.

No more space, Signor Migaldi announced apologetically. He had learned that séances worked best with a restricted number of people.

A disappointed roar rose into the air.

Come back tomorrow, he encouraged the waiting men and women, then added that unfortunately he'd have to double the price. Despite outraged objections, next day's séance was booked out so fast that Signor Migaldi was sorry he hadn't tripled the admission fee. The higher price actually increased demand, with people reasoning that only special séances could command such amounts. Shrewdly, he again raised the fee but kept the number of sitters to a minimum.

When Signor Migaldi mentioned the hike to Eusapia, he also told her bluntly to make sure to meet expectations if she wanted to get her forty percent of the money.

With feet tapping and shuffling, and hands flung about the air, the séance room vibrated with a suspense that was barely kept in check. Suddenly, whispers started up and took on an ominous hiss until Signora Migaldi silenced them, belting out her favourite hymn. Signor Migaldi joined her immediately. Music, that's it, he thought, music facilitates trances, it leads to the most intense phenomena. Eusapia, you better perform if you don't want to be knocked off your pedestal.

Only perfection will do, he cautioned her when no one could hear him, as he walked by the back of her chair. Eusapia didn't react, but he knew she had heard him. In an eruption of moans, the trance seemingly took hold of her. Signor Migaldi wanted to plug his ears so much the sounds she emitted bombarded him with unwanted images. Maybe it was his dirty mind playing tricks on him. Catching the piety in the eyes of his wife and the fervour in her singing, he got hints of a more religious experience. Her expressive Catholicism had room for nothing but God, angels, her departed relatives and friends — and what she considered the heavenly gift of communication from the other side.

If Signor Migaldi were the blushing type, he would have blushed. Since he wasn't, he shrugged, then immediately pledged to himself or some higher power an unspecified good deed to atone for his more dubious behaviour.

238

Eusapia's moans intensified, though underneath her frenzied exterior, she was in control of every aspect of her manoeuvres and fully alert to the response in the room. Her body jerked around as if grabbed by ghostly arms and hands. Some sitters shrieked. His weak-hearted cousin fainted, and it took skill and persuasion to bring her back to the reality of the séance room. Signor Migaldi bit his tongue to keep from swearing. His face turned purple. He shouldn't have invited his cousin. If she were to take a turn for the worse, she could ruin it all.

Signor Migaldi's strain lessened as the hymns picked up again. That's a good sign, he reasoned, but why such neediness? Still, the longer they sing, the easier the sitters' minds open up to the mysteries of psychic forces. Let them take their sweet time. Spun-out expectations make for fertile ground. He realised that two hours had passed already. Good! He turned off two more lights. The songs now swirled around in quasi-darkness. Droopy eyelids and heavy limbs gradually lost touch with reality, and sensitivity to apparitions and touches grew.

Eusapia quieted down. Calmly, she analysed the two male sitters beside her. No luck with the one to her left. He looked incorruptible, a solid husband and family man, his clear eyes open to new insights but closed to anything improper. The sitter to her right was another story. Eusapia snapped forward, then fell to the side into his arms. She remained there for over a minute, shifting to the rhythm of unnerving sighs.

Signor Migaldi blushed as the charged atmosphere started to get to him. Luckily, Eusapia couldn't see him. But he knew that she was conscious of every breath in the room. To cover his vulnerability, he intoned another hymn, immediately pumping up the volume to drown out less uplifting sounds.

He only looked at Eusapia again when his wife screamed, They're here, they're finally here. Then he saw it, a luminous third arm extending out of Eusapia's body, waving tenderly, moving in front of the man to her right. In the dim light, Signor Migaldi saw pearls of sweat form on the man's forehead.

Red light, Eusapia commanded suddenly, and Signor Migaldi obeyed without delay.

Half a minute later, another sort of extension slowly rose from between Eusapia's legs. For a moment there was complete silence until Signora Migaldi burst into song again. With her first notes, instruments started to play. A trumpet tooted, and the strings of a mandolin added to the noisy chaos.

The whole performance must have lasted less than five minutes. All of a sudden, the ghostly emanations disappeared. The instruments lost all sound. Eusapia lay in her chair exhausted, without moving.

Signor Migaldi took his cue and lit the room. The light brought the animated sitters into sudden focus. They had received their money's worth. The dead had spoken.

Signora Migaldi hugged Eusapia, her wet cheeks glistening in the sheen of the lamp.

Thank you, she whispered. You opened the doors.

Eusapia kept silent.

You're the portal to the otherworld.

Again, Eusapia said nothing.

Your mother must be proud of you.

Eusapia stared into the corner where her mother stood watching.

Are you? she wondered, Are you proud of me?

Michela, who had been the most vivacious person when she was alive, remained expressionless. Eusapia had hoped for her blessing. But it wasn't forthcoming.

Silently, she defended herself. They're happy to find some connection to their departed children and parents. It consoles them. It gives them strength.

But Michela looked at her daughter without a sign of approval or encouragement.

I give them hope, Eusapia continued the conversation with her dead mother.

Are you helping them or yourself? Mammina inquired.

Eusapia did not like the turn the conversation took. She squeezed the hefty body of Signora Migaldi as if her salvation depended on it.

Will Gianina talk to us? the emotional voice of Signora Migaldi finally reached her ear.

I don't know, Eusapia murmured, I really don't know.

As she thought of Gianina, she had to ask herself whether the simple, loving woman wanted to be part of this circus. She would want to bring comfort to her relatives and friends, to all those who experienced the darkness of loss and knew what it meant to be paralysed and destroyed by pain.

Gianina, Eusapia asked, will you reveal yourself?

But the chatter in the room rendered any answer inaudible.

Giorgio, who had continued paying for Eusapia's apartment out of a sense of obligation to the mother of his and Lillian's child, thought it was time that she was introduced to scientific men with the power to open new doors and help her become fully independent. First on the list was Professor Ercole Chiaia

241

who had been a schoolmate of his, and had remained a close friend.

Chiaia almost waltzed into Eusapia's apartment at Giorgio's side. His lusty energetic eyes took in the sight of the woman in front of him, darting from her face to her bust, waist, legs, and back up again without restraint. A short, stocky man, just about an inch taller than Eusapia, he seemed to fill more space than five taller men together, his arms flailing about in animated talk, marking his territory, but inviting anyone he liked into his sphere with an impatience that Eusapia found irresistible. She entered his circle on her own momentum without extra pull.

I request a private séance for the two of us, Giorgio said, knowing she would jump at the opportunity.

Within a few minutes, Eusapia had prepared the room and the cabinet, more avid than in a long time.

Lights down, she commanded. Giorgio obediently turned down every single light except for a small lantern with panels of red glass that stood in the opposite corner farthest from him. The room took on a life of its own with everything possible and nothing forbidden. For a second, Giorgio wavered. Wherever he looked he encountered Lillian's gaze, mirrored back tenfold, a thousandfold by his guilty conscience. He wanted to stand up and turn the lights back on, but he sat unmoving, prisoner of a strange power he could not shake off. One more time, he tried to tear himself away.

You're disturbing the ghosts, Eusapia shouted at him. Keep quiet.

But her own body moved and squirmed, emitting highly suggestive sounds.

Control my feet!

As Eusapia was assured that both men's feet rested firmly on the hard top of her easy-to-slip-off shoes, her outbursts became rowdier.

Make sure you don't let go of my hands!

She gloated when she felt pearls of sweat forming on their skin. It was time to start her show.

While the table rose, a trumpet played. Sounds from a small guitar reverberated through the room.

For Eusapia this was just a warm-up. She reached the height of her power when she had both men panting beside her, incapable of following further action with any intelligence, and she could find her own gratification without danger to her professional dreams.

When the lights came on, she hollered with merry laughter as she caught the confusion in the suddenly hooded eyes of Professor Chiaia.

Ercole, she shouted merrily, the ghosts must have liked you.

Incredible, Professor Chiaia managed to say.

Giorgio, who had regained his composure, added, Didn't I tell you, Ercole? Do you believe in her special powers now?

Oh yes, Professor Chiaia exclaimed. She is special all right. I will work with her and explore every aspect of her phenomena.

That sounds like fun, Eusapia responded, but now I'm starving.

The men brought her to a restaurant nearby and loaded her plate with macaroni and beef, and filled her glass with her favourite Sicilian wine.

The scientific investigation of her powers had begun, and Eusapia immediately recognised the full extent to which her destiny had just made a jump forward into the good life.

Ercole, you're a good man, Eusapia called out when they were finally alone, and pressed him feistily to her body.

You're a good woman, Ercole shouted back, content and raring to go. Their clothes went flying. It was that simple. No complicated high-flying speeches and ever-present guilt feelings like with Giorgio. Not Raphael's demanding intensity. Oh, no. With Ercole, it was fun, plain and simple. She knew he had a wife and didn't care. Their involvement was the happy-go-lucky, here-today-gone-tomorrow type, with no room for jealousy, remorse or shame. Never mind Ercole being a doctor and professor, she recognised him as a pea from the same pod, sharp-minded and quick-witted like herself, always after instant gratification, full of vitality, and yes, vulgar, which suited her just fine and didn't seem so bad after her experience with the weird hang-ups of her high-society clients. When they had food brought to her hotel room or his apartment, they didn't touch any of the utensils. They just grabbed it with their fingers and shoved it greedily into their own and each other's mouths. Why bother using napkins? They licked their fingers with satisfaction. Washing hands or bodies? Not necessary! They burrowed their noses in each other's sweaty armpits and it turned them on. Nothing of that insufferable refined stuff that the Cattalanis had expected from her or Ercole's high-class in-laws and colleagues demanded of him. For once, they could be unselfconscious in their feisty vulgarity for which they would have been ostracised in upper-crust circles. Why give a crap, knowing that they could outsmart almost anyone around them?

Forget about what people say and think, Eusapia shouted. Here you can be yourself. You don't have to watch your language, your manners, your passions. Here you get what you want.

Eusapia gave freely and took like a glutton. With Raphael on the road, Ercole was the perfect replacement.

Again and again and again, she sang, and her voice rang like a delirious clanking bell.

Ercole had no need for encouragement, he grabbed her hard and fast. Like her, he never could get enough sex, and was not at peace unless squeezed and pawed and sucked on all the right places. He was always up for a romp, and that was all she wanted. Falling madly in love was behind her. Giorgio and his betrayal were behind her. She had learned her lesson: betrayal takes more from a person than love could ever give. There she was, still bruised from that experience. If not for Raphael who had given her back her confidence, she'd be a complete wreck. His steady presence in the background, a relationship they both could count on and that survived because of its perfect mixture of freedom, friendship and passion kept her sane. But for the moment, fun was what the doctor ordered.

Ercole, we were made for each other.

My ass you're right.

Their camaraderie was sealed tighter than love because there were no strings attached. This way, neither had to worry about betrayal.

As the scientist and professor in Ercole took over, Eusapia cheerfully submitted to all his measurements and tests. The cold instruments sent shivers up and down her body. Ercole incorporated in paragraphs and in tables and diagrams every detail of her bodily reactions, down to the length and frequency

245

of her burps and farts. Eusapia exploded with laughter, but was flattered that anyone could be interested in her to such an extent.

Who would want to know that stuff? she asked, doubtful about the seriousness of his scientific pursuit.

Academics for sure. If you don't give them figures, charts, footnotes, and lengthy explanations at every turn and twist of a phenomenon, they'd write you off at once. They need to analyse to understand.

Understand what we know without thinking twice??!

Ercole burst out laughing.

You and me, maybe, but don't underestimate our talents. We're more intuitive than most anyone I know.

You must be kidding.

Am I, Eusapia? Is that your experience?

Well . . .

That's what I mean. You don't know how rare your quick mind is. It's what makes you great. You're too smart to get flimflammed. You know what people are about as soon as you see them.

Eusapia smiled. It was rare to be paid a compliment for talents she actually possessed. Ercole had figured her out and liked what he saw. No wonder she enjoyed his company.

With Ercole and his unabashed pawing and lusting came prosperity. The indefatigable professor spread the word about Eusapia's powers. Despite his hearty vulgarity when the two of them were alone, he could ooze accomplishment and sophistication of manners with the touch of a switch. She watched with shocked bewilderment as he conversed with academics and slithered his way into the circles of the refined

246

and beautiful women from high society. At those moments, she was sure he was one of them. If his transformation hadn't served her so well financially, she would have had her fun with him, like making him squirm in public and then parroting his sophisticated apologies to the women to make him look like a total fool. As it was, she made sure not to curl up her lips or wrinkle her nose. Her eyes shone with admiration, not scorn. Whenever anyone, even a child was present, she called him Il Dottore Chiaia or Sir Ercole Chiaia or, especially when visitors from England participated, Lord Chiaia, though not everyone showed appreciation when she assigned that last title to him, but she liked the sound and importance of it. Her regard for Ercole grew in proportion to his influence and impact on others. People sought him out. His vitality was infectious. Rightly or wrongly, he was the person men and women trusted. He could have made them believe that his horses had wings and could fly to Summerland where their beloved departed were blissfully awaiting their visit. But Ercole worked within self-imposed boundaries. His task was to introduce acquaintances and strangers to the most incredible medium in Naples. He would display his amazement at her feats and just barely allude to possible spirit intervention. But his animated face would spread hope, and heighten the already keen expectations.

Nothing could outdo Ercole's flashing eyes and exuberant gestures when it came to creating the right atmosphere for her séances. He was an ideal partner, and she made it worth his while. They shared her profits equally and lived a good life. Ercole didn't mind when generosity toward the poor, old and frail overcame her and she gave away a whole evening's or a whole week's income. When he watched her press coins into the hands of mothers and fathers desperately trying to keep their children alive with scraps of food or medicine, or watching her feed a toothless old woman, he'd say, You've got a good heart, Eusapia. You remind me of my responsibilities on this earth.

Eusapia would dive into one of her furious speeches about the horrible injustices in the world. Only after a thoroughly savage condemnation of the state of the world would she calm down. At those moments, the two of them settled down and drank their last bottle of wine, ate some leftover food, until such time as new money rolled in. Without a break in her sermons, Eusapia often said, Never ever forget where we come from, and he agreed without reservation, asking almost vehemently, How could I, Eusapia? How could we?

A few weeks earlier, Eusapia had overheard a sitter refer to her as a "crooked angel". While she wasn't sure whether to take this as an insult or a compliment, she considered the description fitting. No matter how much she might have liked to be an angel, unsavoury dealings with dubious characters held a stronger attraction for her, as long as the weak and vulnerable didn't get hurt. Maybe that's why she felt comfortable with Ercole. Besides being a distinguished scholar of the occult, he was split like herself, half angel, half devil. He even looked the part. When she concentrated on his aura, she saw a devil's horn on one side of his face, and part of an angel's halo on the other. That was just fine with her. If he were exclusively an angel, he wouldn't have anything to do with her, and that would be a loss she couldn't bear. If he were pure evil, she would avoid him like the pest. But his split tendencies drew them together.

As Eusapia's fame grew, Professor Ercole Chiaia continued quantifying and analysing her phenomena and feats. He filled page after page with exact measurements of every part of her body. He relied on her for the length and widths of her ghostly emanations, as it threatened a medium's life if a human were to touch them. When objects flew through the room, he wrote down the distances they travelled. He recorded the height and speed of elevations, and the incredible fluctuations in Eusapia's weight before, during, and after her séances.

This is all about me? Eusapia marvelled, pointing to his neatly stacked bundles of paper.

Much more will be written, Doctor Chiaia stated, smiling at her wonderment, there is never such a thing as too much information where science is concerned.

It's beyond me that science would bother with someone like me, Eusapia replied.

Well, the professor explained patiently, if you don't want to be thrown back into poverty, and I believe that's your main goal, it's essential for us to make certain that your mediumship is investigated by the most respected and experienced scientists.

Those stupid conceited academicians!

Be grateful, my dear, for every scientist that comes your way and declares your phenomena genuine.

But why do they think they're so much smarter than anyone else when any half-decent magician can pull the wool over their eyes?

Because in other ways they are smarter. The best of them are by nature always looking for the unexpected and unexplained. They're open to new approaches and unlikely realities. Look at all the discoveries they made in the last decades: magnetic fields, electric currents, x-rays, radioactivity — words and worlds you've probably never heard of, Eusapia. These scientists you despise so much, they have minds that see beyond the ordinary. Intuitively they can perceive invisible phenomena. That's their strength. Besides their intelligence and sheer brilliance, it's their best quality. But when they come in contact with lower spheres, where people play by rules of their own, such openness becomes a weakness. Keep in mind that every strength is also a person's weakness. Here it's so obvious that you want to shake some sense back into their overly developed brains. Don't you dare despise these scientists because they can't comprehend that your world is not governed by the accepted laws of logic and respectability.

Eusapia stared at Ercole with open mouth. Am I supposed to learn something from this speech? she finally asked, shaking her head and spitting noisily on the floor.

It would serve you well to take this lesson to heart, Ercole said with unexpected seriousness.

The gravity in his voice gave her reason to pause.

Eusapia, don't forget, he continued, it's not only that they don't understand your world. You don't understand theirs either. We're equal in that everyone has something to teach as well as something to learn.

You should have become a preacher, Eusapia snapped, but added quickly, I do understand, Ercole. I'm not stupid when it comes to human beings. But thanks for reminding me that people are more complex than we give them credit for. We all can use a reminder sometimes. I never forget that you're a scientist, and I do respect your mind. After suddenly hooting out loud, she added, Or did you think your body was your most precious asset? Think again. I too am attracted to brilliant minds. In your case, it's such an interesting jungle of wires it certainly beats what your body has to offer.

It was Ercole's turn to look puzzled. But whatever her outburst meant, the signals coming from her were as boisterously sensual and unquestioning as ever, so that the words in themselves carried little importance.

At Ercole's invitation, legions of his friends, many of them scientists, came to Eusapia's séances.

We're making piles of money, Eusapia said. How come you're not satisfied?

It's not about money.

What then, Ercole?

Respect!

I do respect you.

I'm not joking. I want to be recognised by the scientific community.

What for?

For opening new worlds.

Are you serious?

I'm dead serious. To succeed, I have to get the endorsement of Cesare Lombroso.

Who?

You wouldn't know him. But at this juncture in time, only his recognition confirms a scientist's worth.

Is he some sort of pope?

In the scientific world, yes, yes and yes again, though as a Jew he might prefer a less Catholic term to describe his superstar status.

251

What's holding you back from getting his approval?

He is a skeptic when it comes to contacting the otherworld.

Tell me about him. Maybe I can help.

Cesare Lombroso is a criminologist who believes that some people are born criminals. Not only that, but their traits betray their bad character. By studying people's features you can determine who the bad guys are because their traits are different.

Ercole would have loved to go into detail and expand with scientific terms like *occipital fossetta*, *sagital suture*, and *cerebrogenous character*. Instead he said, The jaws of criminals are large, their foreheads small and sloping, and their ears giant and ugly like cabbage leaves. Their noses are either frighteningly hawk-like beaks or stupidly flattened or upturned. Their eyes are shifty, their beards scanty, and their heads shiny with unseemly baldness. In contrast, their lips bloom with ghastly, unrespectable fleshiness.

Aren't you describing a certain Professor Prenta who gives lectures all over town??

You must be kidding!!?

Am I, Ercole? Most of what you described applies to him.

But he is a good guy! And the traits I listed for you are the signs of born criminals.

Then maybe your hero Lombroso is talking nonsense, Eusapia replied mockingly.

No, never. He is the best, the most famous.

I wonder what he would say about me? I'm sure my tuft of white hair would provide hours of intriguing investigation and explanation!

It might be the sign of your genuineness as a medium.

We better convince him of that! What if he decides I'm the perfect example of a born criminal?

That's impossible. In his view, women are too passive to become criminals. They lack the intelligence and ambition.

Keep that bloody scoundrel away from me, Ercole! I can only conclude he was born an idiot if he believes that. What about you? You probably share his views. Do you think that women can't be as capable as men? Think again or get out of here. Go, go now, Ercole. I don't want anything more to do with you.

Did I say I believe everything he says?

But you admire him!

Because he is famous.

That's no reason for admiration if he is wrong! What is he thinking? Because you're born with a certain nose, or because you're born a female, you're destined to be one type of person? Doesn't he even consider what happens in your life or what good or bad stars cross your path!!? Is that what they teach you at school? What about learning from life?

To emphasise her outrage, Eusapia stomped with indignation.

Ercole, who started to enjoy her fiery eruption, guffawed.

Don't judge him before you meet him, he said good-humouredly.

I don't want to meet him!

That would be a big mistake, my dear! He is the one with the key to the world. Did you ever dream of travelling? If so, then he is your ticket.

Are you sure I have to put up with his nonsense to fulfil my dreams?

It's the only way, Eusapia. Trust me, it won't be as painful as you fear. You'll be impressed by Professor Lombroso.

To Ercole Chiaia's disappointment, he was unable to procure the cooperation of the illustrious scientist. He received no response to written invitations. The busy scientist, medical doctor and psychiatrist seemed to have better things to do than get involved in dubious spiritual experimentations.

Finally, in 1888, Chiaia saw a renewed opportunity when Lombroso concluded in one of his many scientific articles, "Who knows whether I and my friends who laugh at spiritism are not in error, since, just like hypnotised persons, thanks to the dislike of novelties which lurks in all of us, we are unable to perceive that we are in error, and just like many lunatics, being in the dark as regards the truth, we laugh at those who are not in the same condition."

Shrewdly, Chiaia placed an open letter in some newspapers, challenging Lombroso to observe in person the incredible phenomena of Eusapia Palladino before writing her off. This medium, he stated, a woman of extremely humble origins is able to move tables by simply glaring at them. They back away when she warns them off. Her body is able to rise straight up into the air where it remains suspended between heaven and earth. Her spirit control John King materialises and walks around the room bringing messages from the other side. Out of Palladino's body grow new and strange spirit limbs so that nobody knows exactly how many arms and legs she has. Instruments play without being touched. Flowers grow out of the table. Sitters are touched by unseen hands. Who can dismiss such convincing manifestations?

Despite his deftly crafted letter, Chiaia had to wait until 1891 for Cesare Lombroso to come to Naples with some of his colleagues and attend Eusapia's séances.

Ercole, who had seen Cesare Lombroso in a few of his legendary lectures, had described him to a tee, down to the last strand of his pepper-and-salt hair and the exact shape of his walrus moustache and wild goat's beard. But when the professor actually walked through her apartment door, Eusapia realised that the whole was much more impressive than the sum of the details. In front of her stood a man who commanded respect, with his mind stretching over the gulf of differences between them. He seemed to pull her up into a different sphere where more important matters were discussed than she was used to. Under his high forehead and from behind his round glasses, his myopic eyes took on an unexpected and unnerving concentration and reached her in spots she desperately wanted to keep private. She could not allow him to go there. She returned his stare and finally willed the blood that had shot into her face back to its normal course and speed. Slowly, she pulled herself up straight and faced this formidable man and his penetrating eyes. If his theories seemed ridiculous to her, she now realised that the man himself was larger than life. Sapia, she had to remind herself, keep in mind what he said about women. Give him what he ought to have coming to him.

What exactly is a psychiatrist? Eusapia asked Ercole later in the evening.

A doctor of the soul, he responded without hesitation.

What does that mean?

A psychiatrist looks at a sick person, beyond the physical aspects, right into the space where feelings and thoughts are formed. In a healthy person, that space is a perfectly arranged puzzle. But when a person is sick, the pieces of the puzzle have

255

jumped out of their designated places. Everything is out of whack, moving precariously and causing enormous pain. The psychiatrist is the man to put those pieces back in their places again.

Then I'm a psychiatrist too.

Not by a long shot, Eusapia, you need to be a doctor to become a psychiatrist. It takes years and years of studying and experience.

But I put many jumbled pieces of the soul back into place. Do you know how many men and women left my séances changed and able to make their partners and children happier than they'd been in years?

It's not the same.

No??

You know what I mean.

I know only too well. You have to be a man to do great things, just like in my hometown of Minervino where Lucia's brother could become a doctor, but Lucia who was at least as able was destined to be a midwife.

Oh shut up. Concentrate on the task ahead. You're in the presence of a truly brilliant man.

I'm very capable of taking into account the exact nature of my sitters, Eusapia said haughtily, charging out of the room, with the door banging ominously behind her.

Eusapia prepared for her meeting as if she were to climb the steepest wall of a treacherous mountain instead of conducting a simple séance in her apartment. She ran for long stretches at a time to improve stamina and tolerance to pain. Flexing and stretching exercises took up another good chunk of her day. While she slept barely five hours on ordinary nights, she now made sure to sleep at least seven hours. Cesare Lombroso, with his all-seeing eyes, had put the fear of God or Satan in her. If she wanted him to believe in her, she needed to be in full command of her physical and mental powers. She couldn't afford to miss details or clues. Her hypnotic powers had to be up to par. She had only three days to get into top shape.

Equally important, she had to make arrangements with a few trustworthy friends to help her set up the séance room to her specifications when the time came. They'd also be ready at a moment's notice to carry out additional services with invaluable know-how and secrecy.

When Professor Cesare Lombroso began his scientific investigation, her stress mounted to levels she had not known before.

Don't worry, Cesare Lombroso tried to calm her, fully aware of her anxiety.

I've never been investigated by such a distinguished scientist, Eusapia said, her voice shaking with trepidation. How could she measure up to his and Ercole's expectations? To avoid making the enormous amount of hard work she had put into establishing herself as a medium worthless, she needed to erase Cesare Lombroso's doubts. If she failed to make the professor into a believer, Ercole might drop her as well. How would she make a decent living then? What injustice that some people lived in luxury and others just scraped by, or even had to die like Maria! With enough food in their belly and a bed to sleep in, all children could develop their talents and catch up to the rich ignorant fools who held their little accomplishments over the heads of the poor!

Eusapia quivered with fury, then focused all her energy into a smile and the lava of her volcanic eyes. To her satisfaction, she caught a hint of alarm in the face of the professor.

You will find it easier to examine me once I put myself into a trance, she said coyly.

In scientific examinations, there was a part that required a medium to get undressed. She did this in deliberate slow motion, putting one piece of her clothing after the other neatly folded on the chair beside her. She stretched out on her bed, her strong breasts jutting defiantly upwards.

It'll just take a few moments, she murmured as if not noticing the effect she had on her investigator.

Five, fou-our, three, two-oo, one . . . her voice trailed off, and she lay there, splendidly displayed, without a movement.

The professor watched her for a while, then cautiously approached as if she could jump up and bite him. Eagerly, he started measuring her limbs, and wrote the numbers neatly in his book. He did the same with body temperature and pulse rate. He poked and prodded her, but detected no response. Cesare Lombroso examined every trait of her face, every cavity in her body. When — near-sighted as he was — he bent very close to her face to observe her facial muscles, one of her arms automatically rose into the air, swerving slightly toward his head, as if by accident touching his hair, then sliding down the side of his face, pulling his beard, holding on to it when he cautiously tried to extricate himself from her grip. He did not want to wake her before exploring at least some of the many secrets of her trance. But in the presumed subconscious movement of her hand lay a strength that caught him off guard. The hand held onto his beard, and pulled him even closer to her face until his lips were planted stiffly on hers. At first, there was no response on his part, only surprise. Then the heat of the hot lava in her eyes shifted to her lips and seared itself right into his heart.

Cesare, a ghostly voice echoed in the room, Cesare, my love, Cesare.

His lips softened and his body was sucked into Eusapia's world from where there was no escape, his surrender a potent testimony to her powers.

Suddenly, the heat of the burning lava withdrew. Eusapia's arm fell limply to her side.

The doctor's face was coloured in purplish tones of passion and surprise.

He pulled himself up, more insecure of who he was than he had ever been in his life. He stared at Eusapia's motionless body. What had happened just now? Did anything happen or was he hallucinating like the lunatics he was treating? Cesare Lombroso did not know how long he stood beside the entranced woman. It was only when she started moving and seemed to come out of her trance that he was able to get a grip on his emotions.

Eusapia opened her eyes, looking confused.

Who are you? she asked. What are you doing here?

I'm Professor Lombroso, the man answered dutifully.

Why are you here? And why am I naked? Eusapia asked and hastily pulled a cover over herself.

Don't worry, Cesare Lombroso replied, I'm here with the best of intentions to investigate your mediumistic powers.

Eusapia wiped her eyes as if coming back not from ordinary sleep but something she couldn't put her finger on.

Oh, she said demurely, my trance must have been more powerful than usual. I don't remember a thing. I'm trying to come back into this world, but something is holding me back.

What? Cesare asked, his inquiring mind at full alert again.

I don't know, Eusapia said feebly, looking at the professor with frightened eyes. Help me, help me, she implored him pitifully.

The professor, still intrigued by his experience, but relieved that the woman in front of him appeared to have no recollection of anything inappropriate happening, was only too glad to consent, I will, Eusapia, don't worry. Everything will be all right.

Ercole did his part to prepare the professor for supernatural occurrences. Eusapia heard the two men and a group of other professors discuss spiritualism for hours at a time.

No, Dr. Lombroso said, these psychic phenomena are just too rudimentary and quite frankly ridiculous to be pathways to the otherworld.

But, Ercole interjected, don't forget, we're at the beginning stages of establishing contact. We have a long way to go. Progress is slow. Maybe in two years, maybe in twenty years only, we'll be at a level that will convince even the die-hard skeptics.

I doubt it, Lombroso replied, looking dubious.

Then the men plunged into an intense discussion on religion, faith and spiritualism that was so abstract and filled with unfamiliar words that Eusapia lost interest after the first few exchanges.

The small séance room was already hot before the séance started but its temperature increased by a few degrees when

Ercole, Professor Lombroso and his colleagues, Professors Tamburini and Violi, as well as Doctors Prenta and Limoncelli, filed into the room and took their seats beside Eusapia who sat in a splendid black wool dress at her special table. Ercole dimmed the light, and at the medium's request started to sing a hymn as necessary preamble to a séance, regardless of the sitter's faith. Two men joined in after an embarrassed hesitation and repeated invitations, but with reasonably sure voices. To ascertain that the medium did not use her legs to produce phenomena, Ercole and Professor Lombroso had placed their feet on Eusapia's, who let her right leg lean against the professor's with a slight tremble. She had to wait a long time before she felt responding warmth in his calf and hip. It took another hour before the sitters displayed the right frame of mind for her to invoke her powers and display some of her phenomena.

I was touched by a hand in the back, exclaimed Professor Lombroso, who made sure he still had control of the medium's hand and foot. Now the hand tousled my hair. The professor's voice rose a few decibels. I can't believe it.

Eusapia realised that the perfect moment for her phenomena had arrived.

The hand took my glasses, the professor exclaimed and was astonished to hear them land softly in the middle of the table. His time for reflection was cut short when a tambourine throbbed behind his back and a trumpet tooted through the room.

I need to check this out, Professor Lombroso whispered. Eusapia tried to suppress a smile. She had managed to introduce her absolute best assistant in the room and had been able to acquire a few marvellous mechanisms lately that were wonders in themselves. If both she and her assistant performed at their best, she could almost convince herself that actual supernatural manifestations took place. Professor Lombroso tried in vain to light a match. His neighbour to the right handed him another match. Before he could try again, Doctor Prenta called his attention to the medium who was clearly levitating more than a foot into the air. He wondered how long this levitation could last when, all of a sudden, the chair on which Eusapia perched sailed carefully higher until it landed softly on the table. For a moment, there was complete silence. Then, as if in response to a question, raps could be heard all around them, followed by insistent echoes. In the general excitement, no one remembered to keep controlling hands and feet. Everyone exclaimed and talked at once. Reminded by Eusapia, Ercole broke into another hymn amidst the feverish chatter and wild conjectures of the others.

In this turmoil, the medium made a dignified descent to her previous spot on the floor beside Ercole and Professor Lombroso, while both men swore they could feel strange hands on their heads. Whose hands? They could clearly see the medium's profile from each side and her sleeves and hands resting motionless beside her.

Seconds later the instruments resumed their tunes, and a bell rang somewhere above the sitters. This time, Professor Lombroso managed to light his match. There, in the dim light, he could clearly see the bell suspended over Eusapia's head and ringing as if by its own volition and power.

My God, Professor Lombroso exclaimed, caught up in the excitement of the unexplainable scene. I've never experienced anything like it. I would have laughed if someone had described such occurrences to me even yesterday. And here I am, completely stumped, questioning my previous convictions, wondering whether I've gone through life missing out on the mysteries of a dimension I thought could not exist.

For a moment, the room brightened.

Everyone stared at the medium who sat motionless but relaxed, almost smiling.

The sitters waited for a sign.

Ercole again started to sing, and this time two sitters joined in rather loudly as if to calm their nerves and make sure not to offend the powers at work in their midst.

Still mulling over the earlier event, the investigators saw the lights suddenly go out. A single red flame glowed almost piously across the table from Eusapia.

In this red glow, the sitters became aware of phantom limbs growing out of Eusapia.

Materialisations, Professor Violi called out. We're witnessing real materialisations.

No one knew how many limbs the medium had. Two extra ones on each side? Another one growing disconcertingly out from between her legs, and one sticking up from her left shoulder.

A sudden clatter of raps disrupted the sitters' intense concentration on the strange emanations in front of them. Currents of cold air provoked goose bumps on their skin. An icy breeze made straight for the candle and extinguished it. In the dark, you could hear the alarmed breathing of several of the sitters.

When unexpectedly the lamp behind Eusapia came on and illuminated the exhausted medium, she sat there in her chair just as she had before the séance, with the sitters to her left and right holding her hands and their feet resting on hers. There wasn't a trace of the phantom limbs left. The men stared at her.

All of a sudden, she threw herself backwards, and started convulsing.

She is coming out of her trance, Ercole explained.

Eusapia shook more, suddenly collapsed, her head landing in Professor Lombroso's lap. Shocked by the medium's action, the professor stared down at the woman who buried her head into his groin, and he wondered how to react.

She's always like that when she's coming out of a trance, Ercole explained quickly, she'll compose herself in a second.

When Eusapia finally woke up, she looked dazed, and Ercole brought her to her bedroom so that she could recharge her powers.

The demanding physical and mental manoeuvres of her performance had left Eusapia in excruciating pain. Bile and acid churned in her stomach, a torturous headache hammered her forehead, and inflammation from having forcefully regurgitated secret threads and small mechanisms to perform her feats during the séance seared her throat. Through the thin walls of the bedroom, Eusapia could hear the animated discussion of the men. Too exhausted to follow every word, she still got the gist of it, and it was good news. While she heard them argue over whether or how much she had cheated, the men were at a complete loss when it came to explaining most of her phenomena. Lombroso's confident voice seemed humbler than before, as he had to admit that there was no denying that her phenomena were authentic.

Not that I endorse the spiritistic theory, he continued, but facts are facts. As a scientist I have and will always be a slave to facts.

Are the dead talking to us? one of his junior colleagues asked uncertainly.

We deal with undeniable facts, Lombroso responded, but from there to confirm the truth of spiritualism is a far stretch.

You were brilliant, Ercole congratulated Eusapia the next day. We're on our way.

Does he believe in the intervention of spirits?

Well, he isn't quite there yet, but I think you'll be able to convince him.

Cesare Lombroso continued his investigations, describing in detail Eusapia's feelings of numbness before the occurrence of phenomena, the sudden prickling and tingling in her fingertips, the spread of goose pimples throughout her body, and the simultaneous whizzing of a current in the lower portion of her spine. He wrote down that she endures the mounting pressure of this current until it suddenly shoots into her limbs, where it expectantly stops in preparation of the impending phenomena. In his opinion, it had to be the essence of her sexual energy that was redirected to produce the extraordinary phenomena she is capable of. He noted that her menstrual flow was stronger during spiritistic happenings, her pulse sometimes raised drastically, other times low to the extreme.

The professor was stunned when during a séance a full materialisation took place right in front of his eyes, a darkish face looking down at him.

Are you the spirit control John King? Lombroso asked feebly.

To his bewilderment, the figure rapped three times for yes.

Before Lombroso could ask anything else, the apparition had disappeared.

The normally talkative professor was at a loss for words. He had seen John King materialise and dematerialise right in front of his eyes.

I wish my colleagues had been here, he said after a while.

The spirits seem to favour you, Eusapia replied. You are among a handful chosen to witness full materialisations.

Why is that, Eusapia?

Because the spirits want to give you a message. They need your cooperation.

Describing his relationship with spiritualism to a friend a few months later, Professor Lombroso wrote, "I am like a little pebble on the beach. As yet, the water has not covered me, but with each tide, I feel drawn a little closer to the sea."

His conversion from skepticism to curious openness caused a sensation in Italy and around the world. It drew scientists to Naples to see the medium's phenomena for themselves. Eusapia, who had been well known in local circles, became a sought-after celebrity, not only in Italy, but in the whole of Europe. Few participants could escape the spell of her séances, her hypnotic powers and the impact of unexplainable happenings. For a few hours in the darkness and mystery of her room, she reigned supreme. Through hard work and talent, Eusapia Palladino turned into The Palladino.

Her fame brought her the unexpected luxury of plenty of food but, more importantly, new opportunities. She remembered looking out over the Bari region with her childhood friend Emilio and dreaming of travelling. Now, those dreams were becoming reality.

Where do you want to go, Eusapia?

I don't care, she shouted joyously, as long as I go someplace where they have food, wine, and interesting people to keep me company and warm at night.

Be careful, Ercole said, a medium has to protect her reputation.

Don't worry, I know what I'm doing. But let me have fun as well, or there would be no point in leaving beautiful, extravagant and sunny Naples. Lead me into the world, Ercole. I'm ready.

Southern France, 1894

8

FROM THE BRILLIANT BLUE SKY of Southern France, the sun scorched the Golden Islands off the coast of Hyères. The tiny island Île Roubaud lay broiling against the azure. Eusapia didn't mind. For her, the good life had begun. What could beat travelling in style to foreign countries in the company of important, rich men who lavished attention on her and provided heavenly wining and dining?

Eusapia stretched and looked around in amazement. Aside from the mountain to which she had been banished to give birth, she had never seen a place as quiet as this. Sometimes, you could hear the wind whip the waves against the rocks of the small island, but today the water lay eerily still, and the air pressed in on people like a solid mass. The rare sounds came from seagulls circling above the water and from the young lighthouse keeper and his wife bantering back and forth.

Île Roubaud was the island of the famous French physiologist Charles Richet. Apart from his cottage, she counted only two other buildings on the island, the lighthouse and the small dwelling of its caretakers. Eusapia walked several times around the cottage, pausing after every few steps, studying its nooks and crannies from all angles with the fascination of a child and the insights of a professional.

Excellent, absolutely perfect, she sang out approvingly, but immediately checked behind her to make sure no one had caught her outburst. A magnificent house! she now hollered, knowing that no one paid attention to her exuberant satisfaction with the way things presented themselves. Her laugh competed with the dry creaks of a seagull. A wonderful place for a short visit and to advance her career. Would its isolating and monotonous heaviness end up suffocating her as inevitably as the mountain where she gave birth? No doubt. She needed the screaming chaos of Naples. It wasn't true what they said, See Naples and die. Once you got to know the city, you wanted to live forever. See Naples and start living!

Through the pines, she saw Richet down by the beach stare out at the Mediterranean Sea. His two guests from England should have arrived by now. Unforeseeable circumstances had forced them to postpone their departure from London for two days which meant they should have arrived on Wednesday. But Wednesday had come and gone. Thursday had passed. Friday morning was almost over. Still no sign of the visitors. Richet's back looked tense, with a trace of impatience, maybe concern. Where were they? As Eusapia continued watching him through the pines, his unease gave way to natural curiosity. He moistened his finger to test the air even though it seemed utterly motionless. His body would be more accurate than any of the many instruments with which he was fiddling and measuring God knows what. Eusapia hated his annoying tendency to get sucked into his professional pursuits to the exclusion of everything around him. But she relished looking at him. His body soaked up the sun as if it were a gift from heaven, and his skin puckered playfully at the mere idea of a breeze. She saw beautiful words and poems dance away from him, so intense and melodic that she was convinced they were Italian.

At present, though, her main interest was Richet's guest from Poland, Julian Ochorowicz, a philosopher, psychologist, inventor, poet, and publicist, who now came rushing up to Richet. The two men would be lost to the world for hours. They stuck their heads together, bent down to verify their instruments, then looked up again to search the skies. They had to be discussing flying machines. That's when their discussions became so impassioned you could see smoke coming out of their brains. Ochorowicz took sheets of paper out of a brown case he was carrying with him at all times. The men sat down on a rock, staring at the pages, talking and gesticulating. Eusapia was annoyed. They excluded her from their world as if she didn't exist. If at least they spoke Italian! But there they were, discussing in French, leaving her with little to go on apart from guessing the subject and filling in the rare detail. She wanted to know how they planned to get heavy metal up into the air. In her experience, it took great effort and a dose of unscrupulous inventiveness to make simple ghost hands and faces float in the air. Richet and Ochorowicz were convinced that their genius and some magic of their own would lead them to zooming through the air when all logic dictated that they'd come crashing down to earth. They weren't joking either. Was it possible? Or were they crazy? Eusapia had watched the two guys fingering and weighing pieces of metal with a respect normally reserved for precious stones. She saw them write down the results of their tests, plans, and instructions, and watched them draw bizarre pictures of flying ships. There were numbers scribbled on all sides of their images, and more numbers on the back of their sheets of paper.

271

The men never stopped talking. Yesterday, Eusapia had to shout when she wanted to eat. What was wrong with them? Who forgets about food? These two were unreal.

To her relief, she had planned for all eventualities. Raphael had been ecstatic when she asked him to be her invisible travel companion. The chance to go abroad was a dream come true, especially since Eusapia had given him most of her savings so that he could make proper arrangements to follow. She hadn't seen him yet. But she felt that he had arrived on the island during the night. The air was different. Raphael always left an imprint on his environment. Everywhere she looked, she detected familiar particles floating around and teasing her. Come find me. They'd celebrate their reunion as soon as it was safe. She carefully scanned the island. Nothing out of the ordinary either on the ground or up in the trees. Not a sign of Raphael. Good! If she couldn't see him, no one else could. Full of anticipation, she went back to the house. As she opened the door to her room, two strong arms grabbed her.

Be careful, she whispered.

But careful was the last thing on Raphael's mind. His arms grabbed her even tighter. Even if he didn't know that those scientists wouldn't lift their noses out of their papers for at least another two hours, he wouldn't care.

Don't worry, Sapia, I have everything under control.

For an instant, she forgot where she was.

God, am I ever glad you're here, Raphael, she whispered before they fell on her bed.

Raphael's presence infused her with new energy. Thirty minutes of pure bliss, not longer though, safety still had to come first. Eusapia stared at the door, which didn't have a keyhole or a bolt.

You never know who comes wandering through that door unannounced, she said, and Raphael nodded knowingly. We have to stay alert, day and night, she cautioned before he disappeared. She didn't want to know where in the house or on the island he made his lodgings because she'd be tempted to join him on the spur of a moment.

When she left the cottage again, she was smiling. Nothing could dampen her good mood now. She noticed right away that Richet's boat was not attached to its usual pole, which meant that he had gone fishing. Ochorowicz must be on the other side of the island where he had spent most of his time yesterday when she followed him to find out his secrets. He was quite a sight to be sure. In a desperate attempt to survive the blistering heat, he ventured out of the cottage in his light cotton pyjamas and not in his customary expensive suit. He stood on a large rock, uncertain at first, then all of a sudden dove off head-first into the water, splashing around, swimming close to shore with great vigour. Eusapia had run toward the cliff when he jumped, fearing for his wellbeing. But he paddled and continued to paddle as if to get rid of frustration and anger. How unexpected, Eusapia thought, he usually appears relaxed even in stuffy clothes. Well, she concluded, such rage can only have to do with a woman, it must be his wife. Several images flitted through her mind. She let herself remember a curious incident from a few nights earlier that now took on new meaning. The men had been talking about some conference in Rome. When Richet referred to someone called Helena, Ochorowicz winced. Though he instantly recovered, his reaction etched itself into Eusapia's memory. As if by chance, she mixed the name of some woman called Helena into one of her theatrical gossips. There it was again. A flicker of meanness or darkness. Disgust, she thought. He wants to leave her and feels trapped. With a sudden need to scream her new knowledge from a platform, she had vigorously leapt up in a single jump on the table where she gesticulated and shouted in expressive Neapolitan, with the men staring at her in horrified fascination. Men, Eusapia screamed, but immediately abandoned that topic and dramatised for them the murder of her father by brigands. Down she jumped from the table, grabbed some sharp kitchen knives, bounded back up, and juggled those knives in front of them, playing the bandits and playing her father, the knives cutting dangerously through the air until one of them seemed to sever her head. She crumpled into a heap and remained spread unmoving on the table. Richet and Ochorowicz gingerly approached and prodded her. She lay as if dead.

The heat must have gone to her head, she heard Richet say. The woman needs to cool down.

The men opened her shirt, took off her skirt, realising she wasn't wearing much underneath. With nothing else to grab close by, Richet threw the tablecloth over her.

We can't keep her here, he said.

They lifted the inert medium into their arms and carried her to the bedroom. To provide relief, Richet went to get a pail of water and some rags. Luxuriating under their care, Eusapia wanted to scream when the cold water touched her breasts but remained motionless. She should be all right now, Richet concluded after a last glance. Moments later, the men left and Eusapia opened her eyes, a satisfied grin on her face.

Eusapia snapped back into the present. Today, Ochorowicz was in the water again. Just as she looked down over the cliff, he looked up, spotting her immediately. For an instant, his movements stopped. When they resumed, Eusapia saw him swimming toward the shore. She sat down at the edge of the cliff and listened to his approaching footsteps on the rocks and among the gorse and heather. He plonked down beside her.

How are things? How are you? Ochorowicz asked.

Good, Eusapia responded, and how are you?

She looked him straight in the face, her eyes glowing with dark mystery. As he was about to answer, she turned away and stared intently out into the water as if seeing ghosts.

What is it? Ochorowicz wanted to know, What do you see?

Eusapia ignored his question, her eyes following the trajectory of an invisible creature.

What do you see? Ochorowicz asked again, more insistent this time.

There is a woman out there, Eusapia said slowly, seemingly amazed at the sight in front of her, A blond woman, not a French woman, certainly not an Italian woman, a blond curvy figure. Eusapia felt Ochorowicz stiffen beside her. She continued, in a more assured voice, And this blond witch is coming toward us.

The reaction was immediate. Ochorowicz grabbed Eusapia with both hands.

Don't call her that.

Eusapia pretended not to feel his grip. He slowly withdrew his hands. She continued staring.

Helena, she cried out beseechingly, Helena, don't do it. Again Ochorowicz gripped the woman beside him and this time he shook her. As he did so, small rocks started flying all around them, over the cliff into the sea, others hitting their arms and legs.

Stop it, Ochorowicz shouted, stop it right now! Brusquely he stood up and left, without saying another word.

Later, Eusapia watched Ochorowicz and Richet in vigorous discussion. From their gestures, she concluded that Ochorowicz was describing the flying rocks. The two men sat down under a tree, mystified, trying to figure out what force of nature or the universe had provoked the inexplicable phenomenon.

With Raphael's energising injections, Eusapia's séance that night was bound to take on fantastical proportions. Already at supper, she felt her powers soar. She pulled the men back from the sphere of their grand schemes into her world. She didn't have to try hard. Still baffled by the flying rocks, the men watched her and every one of her movements with the same interest they accorded their flying machines. What was at the origin of her manifestations? They were determined to uncover her secrets. In a world where scientists pushed boundaries, obsessed with unlocking the mysteries of nature, on the verge of discovering seemingly inexplicable and invisible currents, rays and fields, they would not rest until they could define and name the perplexing forces behind her mediumship.

Not that I believe in spiritualism, Richet said pensively. Once the brain is dead, the soul is gone. It's unimaginable that it could survive. It's more likely that some extraneous entity incorporates thought vibrations and feelings of the dead so that fragments of a person continue to exist within this other body at least temporarily.

Ochorowicz shook his head.

It's much simpler, he said. Look at the woman.

Both men stared at her as if she were on display. She looked even more voluptuous than usual. For a moment, Richet thought that a smell of semen emanated from her. No, that was impossible, there was only Ochorowicz on the island. Ochorowicz? Really! Was it that impossible? Richet looked at his companion.

The smell of sexuality is in the air, he said.

Pensively, Ochorowicz breathed in the air around him. Why did Richet look almost guilty? He wouldn't get physical with a woman like Eusapia, or would he? No, Eusapia was more Ochorowicz' taste. Not that he didn't adore the elegance and refined flirtations of society women like his wife, but when it came right down to it, he found them too damn demanding. They distracted him from the important work that needed to be done. They kept you from concentrating on the big questions. They didn't take anything seriously that wasn't closely connected to their personal comfort. He wished he'd never married. Marriage is the biggest drag on scientific ambition. Once married, women think that your every thought should belong to them. Apart from a few anomalies, you can't raise women into higher spheres. How many Marie Curies were there? Marrying someone like her might have worked. You'd actually be able to discuss matters of importance. She wouldn't have considered flying machines a joke. But then he probably still would have needed the warm bodies of simpler women for balance, release of tension, and quick revitalising of his senses.

The men didn't notice that Eusapia gleefully refilled their glasses and encouraged the maid to bring additional jugs. Following his own thoughts, Ochorowicz concluded that no doubt about it, Eusapia was his style. Like those chambermaids and barmaids who had no qualms providing quick and easy thrills without exacting demands on wit and sensitivity. They didn't come collecting interest on their investment. That's what was good for science: uncomplicated sex that invigorated your body and left your brain free for creativity and invention.

Her powers must stem from redirected sexual energy, Ochorowicz proclaimed, more intense than intended.

The two colleagues openly scrutinised Eusapia. She grinned, immediately grasping the direction if not the exact meaning the conversation had taken. As the men were well disposed toward her that evening, and since even Richet had a reasonable knowledge of Italian, they spoke mostly Italian, and for the rest, Ochorowicz made the effort to translate chunks of their conversation for her.

You want to see? she said. Before the men could respond, the table cloth billowed out. Raps exploded through the room and echoed like drum rolls. The curtains at the windows swung in and out despite the fact that there was no breeze. A ghost face shone into the rapidly darkening room. Whitish hands waved from the window. When the men turned their backs to Eusapia to get a closer look at the hands, she landed, seated on her chair, with a soft thud on top of the table, knocking over Richet's wine glass and squashing a loaf of bread.

I can't believe it, Ochorowicz cried out. Did we witness an elevation?

New strange noises came from the window. The men leapt out of their chairs and ran to inspect this newest occurrence. Nothing. The curtains hung limply. When the men drew them apart, they only saw the darkness of the night and a slight shimmering of the moon. Just as Eusapia had anticipated, the men were so focussed on the action near the window that she was able to execute her crucial next manoeuvres. By the time the men turned around, they found Eusapia and her chair on the floor again.

What happened? Richet asked.

But Eusapia, who sat slumped in her chair, did not respond. Only after the men started nudging her did she finally straighten up. She rubbed her eyes as if awakening from a trance.

The ghosts have spoken, she said and stood up, swiftly leaving the room.

It's absurd, Richet said. But it's true. Things are happening. We have seen it with our own eyes. I can't deny it any longer.

When Ochorowicz explained to Eusapia later that Richet didn't actually believe that the essence of a brain could survive through death and decay, Eusapia screamed out loud in dismay.

Just think, Ochorowicz went on, according to Richet, personality depends on a specific brain. That's the reason why it necessarily ceases to exist when a person dies.

Is he crazy? she shouted.

My mother lives on the other side unaltered, with her brain intact. When I'm dead, I'll find her, and we'll be together forever. The same goes for all the people I love. Should any of us die, we shall find each other fully intact.

Eusapia didn't like Richet's way of thinking. Even after Ochorowicz had left to work on one of his projects, she continued to grumble. How could anyone assume life would ever end for good? Surprisingly though, it was Richet who was the most curious about her phenomena. He never doubted that some of them at least were authentic, just like he never doubted the intuition that led him to his scientific discoveries. Whatever grew out of her body during séances, he studied with rapt inquisitiveness, while at all times adhering to the strict rule not to touch any medium's supernatural emanations so as not to endanger her life. He used serious-sounding terms he had coined himself to name psychic phenomena. She had been surprised to learn that the word ectoplasm that Giorgio had explained to her originated from him. The unexplained happenings around her and other mediums, for which people came to see her, he called metaphysics. Eusapia loved to repeat those big words that scientists, journalists, and other educated people all over the world had adopted. They sounded so much more important than how she would have described what she was doing. She couldn't get enough of Richet describing her phenomena in scientific terms. Sometimes she thought that all those impressive words made her brain vibrate. When this happened, images and visions shot through her mind that made her creative and therefore alive.

How could this same Richet frighten her with his insane views of death? Eusapia was eager for Raphael to distract her. Yet, the unsettling conversation left her worked up.

What is it, Eusapia? Raphael asked.

Do you believe your mother and brothers are fully intact on the other side just as they were on this earth?

Of course, I do. What are you saying?

I think I'm losing my bearings. Richet and his island are messing with my head.

No, you're too strong for that. Trust in yourself.

Eusapia started to relax when quietly approaching footsteps forced Raphael to jump out of bed, his eyes sharp and alert, his movements fast and precise, as he made his well-planned exit through the window into the open. Eusapia cursed and stretched wistfully. Unfamiliar cheerful voices from the shore caught her attention. The peculiar shuffling of feet stopped, then started up again, almost inaudible, gradually fading. She assumed that the person outside her door had left to respond to the calls of the visitors.

After a few more minutes in her cosy bed, Eusapia pulled herself up to check out the new arrivals. Both Richet and Ochorowicz, as well as the lighthouse keeper and his young wife were at the beach, where a smallish boat had dropped off the visitors from England. Their noisy greetings had Eusapia in stitches. French was bad enough. But what those English men did to French was beyond mistreating human ears. To tune out this mashed-up ugliness, she examined the physical appearance of the men. She knew that the tall one had to be the scientist Oliver Lodge. Tall? He was a tower, a majestic tower at that, a few years over forty maybe, the upper part of his head a bald gleaming dome. Eusapia was impressed. Beside him, the second visitor, somewhat older than the rest of the men, almost disappeared. Frederick Myers, a founding member of the Society for Psychical Research in Britain, stood with a vague smile, looking insignificant. While she took an immediate liking to Lodge, she had reservations about Myers. She would have to be careful. From Ochorowicz she had learned that both men firmly believed in life after death. Good news, she thought initially, because that belief puts contacting people on the other side in the realm of the possible. The men's mission was to obtain information and clarification, which they did with unfettered hope. Eusapia sighed. The not so good news is that they expect the impossible. How much simpler to deal with someone like Ochorowicz who assumed her powers had to do with redirected sexual energy! That she could understand. She also understood why people wanted to remain in contact with the people they lost. She wouldn't have survived without speaking to her mother and Gianina and her family. But to suppose that moving curtains, tooting trumpets, waving ghost hands and glowing faces contained messages from dead relatives and friends made neither rhyme nor reason! You'd assume that with all their education and brilliance, they would have come up with something more sophisticated.

Ochorowicz had explained to her that spiritualists accepted this less than satisfying communication from the beyond because establishing contact was at its beginning stages. They expected it to evolve from the rudimentary to the complex, and lead to elaborate conversations and discussions in the future. As was the case for finding cures for diseases and developing new designs for flying machines, even imperfect starts held great promise and provided the basis for unexpected advances and breakthroughs.

Eusapia had to bite her tongue not to respond. More often than not, it was better to swallow what you wanted to spit out. Knowing what she knew about rappings, elevations, and moving objects, she was convinced that spiritualists focussed on all the wrong elements. Where would that lead them? It's not my problem, she thought contemptuously. If I had been sent to school and raised on books and cultured conversation and given the chance to become a doctor or professor, I'd certainly concentrate on more worthwhile projects than so-called psychic phenomena. People who insist on believing things that don't make sense get what they deserve. If I could earn a living any other way, I would. Unfortunately for all involved, that's not possible.

Host and guests moved unhurriedly under the blazing Mediterranean sun, delighted to be on this island, filled with anticipation, expecting to experience manifestations and vistas beyond their imagination. We will open a window on eternity, Myers thought, and his vague smile became more authentic.

He edged to Eusapia's side, suddenly less guarded and tense, compelled to put words to his undaunted optimism, There has never been any doubt in my mind that the soul survives. But to actually have proof, I can't wait to see that.

Eusapia looked at him with big eyes, wondering what his serious mumbling was about, but getting the idea of it. Ochorowicz who walked right behind them translated for her. She nodded gravely. Inside she shuddered. The expectations were too high. Proof of survival? If the dead did not talk to him like her mother talked to her, how could there be proof? If people's hearts did not let them see, hear, and feel the communications from the other side, why would stupid tables and cheap instruments be able to do so? Despite her misgivings, Eusapia let a promising smile slowly cross her face. Myers stared at her as if transfixed. Buoyed initially by his trust in her ability to provide answers to haunting questions, Eusapia could not afford to savour her relief. His all-consuming fear that in the end she was nothing but one of the many cheats he had encountered on his search for truth almost choked the air out of her. That, Eusapia could not accept. Whatever she thought of herself, she had grown accustomed to people around her admiring her powers. Even traces of doubt were demeaning.

She wanted to shake the skinny man beside her, thought better of it and, with a hint of a smile on her lips, directed calming rays toward him that slowly warmed him until he relaxed.

It's a privilege to be in your company, he said, letting the peace of the island and his resurrected hope for illumination and clarification drive away darker thoughts.

Yet, for some reason Eusapia wanted to get away from him. The man had barely arrived and already he was wearing her down with his nervous intensity.

She was so relieved when Lodge joined them, that she wanted to throw both arms around him and waltz around the island. She almost did. Despite his formidable appearance, he seemed uncomplicated and good-natured, the type who might try everything at least once, with the curiosity of a child who needs to explore whatever is in his path. At the moment, she was the object of his cheerful and utterly judgement-free scrutiny. There was no pressure in his interest. His salvation didn't depend on a positive outcome of this investigation. No, she simply had become his newest toy. He wouldn't be able to rest until he knew its inner workings, with the process being at least as rewarding as the results.

Be gentle with him, she heard her mother's voice. If there were to be great sorrow in his future, he will need the connection to the otherworld to handle grief. Give him a positive experience so that he can build his own visions to find comfort.

Eusapia stopped walking. Mammina, this is getting too serious. I'm here to have fun and make a living. Michela looked at her daughter with concern. Mammina, you know I'm not an angel. To that, Michela said simply, You don't need to be an angel to help.

Is something wrong? Lodge asked as Eusapia kept standing at the same spot.

Oh no, she said, and instantly recovering, she added, Professor Lodge, I just realised that we all are on earth for a reason, each of us has a purpose.

Lodge agreed, but did not feel it necessary to inquire further.

At that moment, Richet called out, Why so solemn, my friends?

Eusapia grabbed him and twirled him around.

Who says solemn?! she shouted. Let's make merry! Let's have wine. Lot's of good dry wine!

No objection to that! the men replied. Great idea!

Yes, Eusapia agreed, splendid idea. She had caught a whiff of alcohol on the English men's breaths when they first arrived, not wine, not beer, something stronger, either whiskey or Scotch. With four men intending to watch every one of her moves during the séance, an extra dose of alcohol could only help the visions she was expected to conjure up. If her comfortable life was to continue, the evening needed to be successful. She was no slacker when it came to her work. She would give them what they came for!

Richet's wine was good. His cheese and fish were good. Everything coming from this man is good, Eusapia thought with admiration as she looked around the table and listened to the English men recount the adventure of their journey. The way Eusapia understood it, they had left the train at one of its many stops to have a drink and for unexplained reasons, missed the departure. During the latter part of their trip, Myers insisted on

285

stopping again, this time in the historic town of Avignon to see the palace of the pope and the famous old bridge before it crumbled away. Eusapia was glad that Ochorowicz provided her with extra explanations. She had no intention of being the silent outsider at the table. Often, she would jump up from her chair and blare out her own stories in such dramatic fashion that their content was pretty much obvious. But Ochorowicz' animated translation was a big help. If the material sparked his interest, he could be dramatic too. What better person to retell the stories of her life: how her mother died and her father was murdered. No one was more capable of adapting to the mood of the audience one of her many versions about the dying Signor Pellegrino who talked to her through the closed door, about a secret lover and a girl born on a mountain, little Maria who died because she was too weak and famished to fight disease, Anna who disappeared and was never found, the Siamese twins, the dwarf and the giant who were forced to live in flea-infested freak quarters. Raphael however was off limits. He belonged to her and no one else. As for her other stories, she made sure that her listeners visualised every detail, heard the emotions in the voice of each relative or acquaintance she wanted to bring alive in front of them, that the audience breathed in the specific aroma of each episode. But if the men wanted to distinguish truth from fiction, they were on their own. Eusapia revelled in ambiguities, and adherence to facts came last in her list of priorities.

Eusapia Palladino became the magnetic centre that drew all eyes. For this evening at least, she was able to wrestle the attention away from Richet, whose wide-ranging knowledge and interests, facility with words, and ingratiating manners kept everyone under his spell. Tonight, she was the celebrity. Who else had special powers? So what if they were great scientists? She was the mystery. Mystery beat brains any time. Look at me, she shouted when she felt their thoughts drift.

The well-mannered men instantly apologised, Sorry, Eusapia, we're all eyes and ears.

And they were! But she would not rest until she outdid previous performances, and the men responded with stunned interest. Good, good, my friends, she whispered. Very good.

As she looked up, she unexpectedly faced the young lighthouse keeper's wife Melanie who was serving them. Melanie was a jolly woman with the air of a child in a candy store. Laugh-lines spread happily over her face. Her lips were trembling so hard that she had to bite her lower lip to stop herself from hooting with laughter. Eusapia was outraged. How dare she! Me-la-nie, she screeched, and Melanie jumped, turned, and fled out of the room, her shoulders shaking, though not from fear as Eusapia had intended, but from a desperate effort to repress a violent explosion of laughter. Eusapia glowered after her.

Don't mind her, Richet said soothingly, you must have spooked the simple girl. She is not used to mediums.

Eusapia said nothing. She couldn't possibly explain to them that Melanie's mind functioned pretty much like her own. I'll talk to you later, Melanie, she decided. There is a good chance we'll be friends before tomorrow is over.

Bits of conversation, lively exclamations and Eusapia's unabashed burps erupted against the evening clamour of cicadas as the night stealthily shrouded the island in darkness. Two candles flickered on the console in the back of the room, throwing a whitish gleam on the perpetually moving faces and flitting hands. Under the natural cover of darkness, threatened

287

only by a few unexpected moonbeams, Eusapia gleefully anticipated miracles that she hadn't been able to produce in prior sittings. Richet accompanied his friends and Eusapia to her special séance table. They all sat down, pinning their personal hopes on the coming events. Except for the crackling of some trees nearby, the rustling of a few night critters and the continued thrumming of the cicadas, the room was still.

It takes time and patience, Richet cautioned the others.

Ochorowicz started singing a hymn in French. Richet, though remembering some of the words from his childhood, kept silent while the two others joined with the English version of the familiar melody.

After a while, when nothing happened, the voices petered out long before all the points of Eusapia's psychical constellation aligned properly.

Music, she ordered. Do you want the ghosts to come? Do you? Sing!

Obedient but tired — especially when it came to the English men who had a long journey behind them — they started up again, with no fervour at all, but audible enough for Eusapia's purposes.

She didn't like the way Myers watched her hands. Even Lodge, despite his tiredness and his raised alcohol level, seemed to watch her with a multitude of eyes from the most unusual positions, vigilant of her slightest moves. She didn't have to worry about Richet and Ochorowicz. They had already witnessed her powers. But those damn English men! Eusapia sighed. She hadn't slept well the night before and felt tired. Performing without being in full command of her faculties was dangerous.

288

Finally fed up with the impertinent stares of the visitors, she snapped. The table rose frantically.

Stop it, Myers shouted, you're cheating! I saw you use your leg.

Idiot, Eusapia screamed, wilfully oblivious to the sobering effect her outburst produced on him. It's your job to control my hands and feet. Don't you know that suspecting me of fraudulent behaviour is a sure-fire prescription for me to do so? You put the notion in my head. And since it's extraordinarily taxing to produce authentic phenomena, I then follow the voice in my head that tells me to spite fools like you and use my foot to move things along.

Don't get mad, Eusapia, Richet tried to calm her, It's our job to get the experiments right. Why don't we start over? None of us will think of ways for you to cheat.

I will try, Eusapia said, still in a huff, I will try to get over the insults you heap on me. I will concentrate on my connection with the other side.

The men sang in low voices.

Suddenly, the table rose, not more than an inch, but it did rise. They all saw it. Then raps exploded from the walls around them, behind their backs, in front of them, but the loudest, almost like cannon balls, came from the window. The men were halfway out of their chairs when a sudden noise from behind Eusapia startled them.

I don't believe it, Myers exclaimed. A full materialisation. It must be John King.

I am John King, a deep voice sounded out from behind Eusapia who had trouble keeping a straight face. But she did. She didn't even turn around.

What is your message? she asked.

In lieu of an answer, more canon ball raps sounded from the window.

Everyone turned toward the noise. When Myers looked back, he shouted, Oh no, we're losing him. John King is dematerialising.

The men jumped up from their chairs.

Sit down, Eusapia screamed and was immediately obeyed. The raps at the window intensified as if they had a message. Then, to her surprise, the ghostly white face of a young woman appeared, glowing unearthly for a few seconds before vanishing in unexpected hurry.

When the men wanted to rush to the window, Eusapia held them back with her commanding voice, Do not disturb the ghosts.

A moment later, she collapsed in her chair, spread out seemingly unconscious.

We must help her, Lodge said. The poor woman is overwhelmed. Again, she was carried to her room, but this time the men decided it was better to let her rest. Anyway, they wanted to search outside the house to see whether they could spot anything unusual. What had happened just now? There was no one else on the island besides them. Under those circumstances, could there be anyone audacious enough to deny the reality of another dimension that had manifested itself in their presence?

In the warmth of the island, Myers's mind slowly opened up to Eusapia's powers. She had seen the almost mystical hunger in his eyes, his gaze directed toward the universe in search of just one vision, one familiar voice that seemed to echo in his heart. He was more convinced than ever that the afterlife would bring back lost love, and reunite with heavenly passion what should have remained united on earth. In amazement, Eusapia watched his eyes glaze over during her séances, his spirit strangely removed from his present company, transported into spheres where he could finally find fulfilment.

Lodge is so different, she concluded. He watches as attentively, with a conviction that was as assured as Myers, but more earthly, almost mundane. No, Lodge had no mystical tendencies. She wouldn't be surprised if he pictured the afterlife as an exact replica of his very comfortable present lifestyle, a place where he would sit in a circle of friends and relatives, absorbed in discussion, enjoying foods cooked to perfection, stiff drinks and strong cigars just as always, except for an otherworldly intensity of delight and refinement. To Eusapia, such an image had a certain appeal. She too appreciated food and drink. But from her talks with her mother, she knew there was no need for food or drink to be happy once they were reunited.

As was the case after all productive séances, Eusapia kept herself apart to restore her powers. It always took her a while to overcome the exhaustion and physical malaise that followed her performances. Leave those men to their scientific stuff! That's where they should have put their efforts to begin with. When she learned that they were up at the crack of dawn, she wasn't surprised, but still couldn't get over it. Discussing, measuring and throwing their fancy ideas around, they acted as if someone had put them in charge of changing the course of the universe.

Eusapia was not stupid. She grasped the impact that brilliant minds like theirs had on new inventions and knowledge.

Ochorowicz pointed out to her during an impromptu visit to her bedroom that the island fertilised the mind. But he immediately forgot about this idea. His purpose was to get his bit of sexual gratification, which Eusapia offered with no ill will. This time she hoped he wouldn't take too long as she wanted to be with Raphael and no one else. Ochorowicz was in no rush to leave though. Despite the quick and easy execution of the physical aspect of their encounter, now that it was over, he wanted to remain in her bed and relax. Unhurriedly, he took up his initial conversation, When you're here with other brilliant men, he said, every word has the capacity to challenge traditional notions. One of us raises a topic. It is immediately discussed, expanded, analysed, and then, in the blink of an eye, out comes a completely new train of thought that may alter the direction of science and culture. Eusapia normally felt flattered when he talked to her like that. Not today. She tried hard to curb her growing impatience. She already knew what he was trying to tell her and had understood a long time ago that each moment those guys were left to their professional endeavours would be more worthwhile than any time spent at her séances, a truth she could barely admit to herself in private, and certainly vehemently denied in public. So despite her need for attention, she did not interfere with their work. Under the present circumstances, this suited her own plans perfectly. She wanted Ochorowicz to leave without delay. Stay away my friend, she silently pleaded, and all of you, keep busy as long as you can, because I have Raphael here with his muscles of steel and comforting magic.

Watch out, Eusapia said to her husband after their latest romp, as they boldly left the house.

Don't worry, he responded, those scientists might discover invisible realities, but don't see what's under their noses. They live in a higher system of logic. Even if they tried, they couldn't lower themselves to our level.

Eusapia laughed. Well, I like it down here. Right now I couldn't think of anything more perfect. We have delicious wine, delicious food. And I have you. Nothing can beat that.

Don't forget travelling through France. Years ago, would you ever have believed in such a possibility, Sapia?

Never, Eusapia answered. But now, Raphael, let's grab what's due to us. And if possible, we give some of what we grab to those who can't grab their own.

Eusapia had barely finished her sentence when Raphael's eyes widened. Just in the nick of time, he rushed up the tree beside them without a sound, his brown shorts and tanned body pressed against the trunk in an almost seamless blend.

Hello, my dear, a distracted Richet called out on his way to the house to pick up yet another instrument for the project he was working on with Ochorowicz and Lodge. He passed barely a few meters from where she was standing. He pointed toward the shore where he and his friends carried out their newest research. Do you want to join us?

I'm sorry, Monsieur, I'm still trying to recuperate. Soon, she said haughtily. Soon, my psychic powers will be restored.

Eusapia walked to the other end of the island and suddenly saw Melanie sitting on a rock near the sea, with a piece of cloth in her hands. She was sewing, her two arms flailing about as if in mockery of an actual sewing woman. You'd suspect her to break into a wild dance at any time or to throw her sewing over the cliff and take off like one of the seagulls above her.

Hello, Eusapia called out and plopped down beside the young woman.

Hello, Melanie responded in French full of energy and excitement. Should she take cover? She tried not to laugh, which was her natural tendency when she was unsure what to expect.

Eusapia stared at her. Friend or foe? Could she be certain?

The women sized each other up, eyes and gestures doing the talking as neither spoke the other's language. Low and behold, they understood. Yes, yes, no, are you sure? Eusapia's communication improved steadily. Grinning, she put her arms around the girl.

Fantastic, she shouted and burst out laughing.

Melanie vigorously echoed her hollering and sentiment.

Wait, Eusapia said.

She extricated herself from the tangled embrace. The enjoyable luxury she had experienced since travelling suddenly compelled her to share some of her unexpected good fortune.

Here, she said as she searched in one of her deep pockets and brought out a brooch of a bird, pressing it into Melanie's hands. Melanie couldn't take her eyes off the jewellery. Her laughing eyes suddenly filled with tears and Eusapia understood that the girl had never seen such a superb piece up close. Gingerly, Melanie held it in her left palm.

For me? she signalled questioningly with her fingers.

Yes, for you, Eusapia responded, nodding emphatically. The poor girl couldn't move. Her emotions were too strong.

It had been a long time since Eusapia had felt so content. Giving is the only act that truly makes a person happy.

Impulsively she put her hand back into her pocket and pulled out a gold ring with a small ruby. She handed it over very fast, afraid of changing her mind because that ring was among her favourites. By now, Melanie was sobbing. She took the ring and with her hands drew a small child in the air, then she held her treasure against her stomach, pointing, For the baby, for our baby, she said.

Yes, Eusapia said, for the baby, pressing a kiss on the woman's stomach which was still flat but radiated with promise.

Melanie picked up her sewing. Her wild movements seemed gentler and more rhythmical.

Happy? Eusapia asked, dramatically pulling up the corners of her lips.

A bright smile spread over Melanie's face. Yes, very happy, she responded.

A noise from the other side of the island intruded into their newfound closeness. Both their heads craned forward to glimpse the action through the trees. Three of the men were tugging on some old tool intended for God knows what purpose. The young women caught each other's eyes. Their laughter, suspended for a moment, finally rang out boisterously, waves of hilarity rippling through their bodies, tears of mischief drenching the collars of their blouses.

Friends, Eusapia said, interlacing her fingers with Melanie's.

Friends forever, Melanie answered and repeated it slowly to herself as Eusapia made her way toward the cottage.

At supper, the men looked at Eusapia with renewed expectation. Go to hell, she thought, I've given you enough. Weren't the phenomena at the last séance spectacular, with faces appearing at the window and the possibility of special messages

295

swirling in the room? Admittedly, the messages weren't getting through completely, but that was because of the men's meagre psychic capacity.

It's your fault, Eusapia shouted. Your ears are closed to what the departed are telling you. The only people you listen to are yourselves.

Eusapia's voice became louder and shriller. She meant what she said too. A simple woman like her had no trouble hearing her mother and understanding every word she said. So why were those educated men unable to capture a single word sent from the beyond? It's not their ancestors' fault, who surely talked as clearly as her own relatives and friends. I think these men are unable to open up their souls unconditionally. They're incapable of tuning into the minds of others, including the people who left this earth. Why, when it's so easy, Eusapia thought, why don't they get it? Why do they need their stupid instruments to measure things that are unmeasurable? Why this crazy obsession with writing down every word uttered, even if it doesn't make sense? Why?

What were those men doing now? Eusapia stared at them indignantly. They had suddenly disappeared into a parallel world.

We should let Lombroso know about our new theories, Eusapia heard Richet say. He took out a sheet of paper and brought his ink pot and pen to the table.

Richet looks elegant when he's writing, she thought. He looks attractive whatever he does. The three other men watched as he wrote and added pieces of information she did not understand, but knew had nothing to do with her.

I want to say hello to Cesare, too, Eusapia screeched.

The men treated her as if she were acting crazy. Eusapia pointed to herself and made exaggerated signs of writing. Richet ignored her, too absorbed in his own ideas. So did Oliver Lodge, who was right up there with him, adding, correcting, deliberating. Only Myers and Ochorowicz noticed the woman's rising agitation.

Don't worry, Ochorowicz tried to placate her, you'll be able to write your name at the end of the letter. But even he was caught up in the mounting excitement of the two other researchers who looked as if they were in the process of solving an age-old riddle.

All of a sudden they quieted down and stared satisfied at the sheet in front of them. Both Richet and Lodge were nodding.

Now, Eusapia said.

She wants to sign the letter, Ochorowicz explained.

What for? Richet asked.

He is my friend! Eusapia shouted and grabbed the pen.

Ochorowicz soothingly pushed the ink pot toward her. At the same moment, Oliver Lodge, who sat beside him, made an unexpected movement. The ink pot jerked up, then down, and ink splashed in an energetic flow toward Eusapia.

No, she screamed, no, no, no. She stared at her hands which were spotted with black ink. Eusapia jumped up like a madwoman. It's bad luck, you'll see, it's a terrible sign. She grabbed a napkin and rubbed at the spots. Part of the ink came off, but most of it stuck to her hand like black glue. Melanie brought water and soap and with a brush tried to get rid of the spots. To no effect. Eusapia stormed out of the room into her bedroom.

Leave me alone, she screamed as the others followed her. You bring shame on a medium! No medium can work with stains on her hands! Don't you know that? You're ruining everything.

She shoved them rudely out of her room.

Stupid scientists, she grumbled. She dunked her hands in a bowl of water that Melanie had left on the narrow table at the back of the room. She threw soap into the water. Then she waited. What was she going to do? She glared at the spots as if to remove them with the power of her eyes. Did they start to fade? Carefully, Eusapia examined her hands. Exasperating dark patterns remained. As soon as she put her hands near the kerosene lamp, the ink came alive, mocking her attempts to remove the stains. Even under the gentle light of a candle, the dark smudges were conspicuous. I have to remove those marks, Eusapia muttered. I can't give another performance before my hands are as shining clean as ghost hands. And I can't put those damn scientists off much longer. They're set on getting another series of phenomena.

Please let me wake up with the scorch of those stains gone, Eusapia murmured to no one in particular before falling asleep with her hands in the bowl of soapy water. Right away she started dreaming and found herself watching her stains grow bigger in the middle of a séance. The ghost hands floating through the air were so tainted that the audience screamed with disappointment. Those are not ghost hands, the men and women shouted, they're your hands, Eusapia, see the spots on them, they're your spots. The audience wanted their money back. But Eusapia held on to her coins. The sitters started grabbing at her harder and harder until she was pulled into sitting position and woke up, sweat streaming down her body.

Why do I let stained hands provoke such a crisis? She couldn't help being completely preoccupied with her stains. What a pitiful melodramatic approach to life, she chided herself. Being abandoned by Giorgio or leaving my daughter back on the mountain, that's something to get worked up about, not this. But here she was now, helplessly fixated on nothing more than ink stains on her hands.

Eu-sa-pi-a, she suddenly heard a whisper through the door, which she recognised immediately as the excitable nasal voice of Melanie. Eusapia rushed to open the door. Melanie brought a small pail of water and a container with some weird looking cream or mush.

Special, very good, Melanie said, pointing to the cream.

Thank you, Eusapia exclaimed and stuck her hands in front of Melanie. The young woman wasted no time. Out of one of her pockets, she pulled a rag and a brush, and spread the white stuff over Eusapia's ink-spattered skin. After letting it work for a moment, she drenched the rag with water and rubbed the spots until they paled away under her magic touch. Eusapia grabbed her friend in a jubilant hug.

You saved my life! Thank you!

The girls laughed.

Perfect! Melanie called out.

Yes, my friend, absolutely perfect!

Melanie pointed to the séance table Eusapia had brought to her room. Now the table can rise again, she gestured enthusiastically.

Eusapia looked at her, smiling, and sat down beside the table, staring at it seriously as if to command it to rise. Then all of a sudden, she slipped her foot out of her shoe and raised it in plain sight. On top of her toes, the table negotiated a steep elevation. This lasted a mere two seconds before Eusapia's straight face broke up and a cheery bellow escaped her mouth, while the table came unceremoniously crashing down to the floor.

Bravo, shouted Melanie, who joined in the roar. The women threw themselves on the bed, rolling around, and like little girls stuffed their faces into the pillows to muffle their unstoppable giggling. Lucky for them, the men were down at the shore, deep in discussion over one or the other of their newest inventions, unaware of the ruckus in Eusapia's room.

Despite the clean hands, the evening séance turned into a disaster. Again it was Myers who with his insidious comments threatened to prevent the occurrence of new phenomena. Eusapia didn't have a moment's peace. His sudden mistrust pasted itself to every one of her movements. Something that sticky couldn't be shaken off easily. Somehow she had to change Myers disposition. Where had she gone wrong? What provoked him into treating her like a fraudster? Nothing came to mind. It's hard to deal with indefinable suspicions, even more so if they had to do with religious sensibilities. From the beginning, she knew that this was going to be a problem. The religious ones expect too much. They yearn for inspiring mystical experiences and want to be uplifted into higher spheres. Well, why come to her then?

Myers and Lodge would be better off going back to their churches where the candle light was purer and the incense made you soar. She knew because she had gone to several Christmas Eve masses. She had cried over the beauty of the ceremony and felt an unfamiliar tugging in her heart. She had sat there and hoped the good feelings would last. But when the service ended and the crowd pushed her out into the street, she came crashing down to earth. She didn't belong and felt lonelier than ever before, mourning a life she couldn't embrace apart from a few superstitions she had adopted as part and parcel of Neapolitan life. Lodge and Myers, on the other hand, belonged in churches even though they sneered at the thought.

Too much dogma, Ochorowicz had translated for Eusapia during one of the evenings when such subjects were discussed. Dogma, he said, answering the question in her eyes, dogma means that a pope makes declarations of truths that are not to be challenged.

And you're sure God didn't give him those truths? Eusapia asked.

Ochorowicz' scorn almost blasted out of him. Why would God give truths to the followers of one religion and not to others? But, he added, better leave this subject alone and concentrate on contacting the dead.

Eusapia cringed. Ochorowicz' disparaging tone was as vexing as Myer's mistrust.

I have to pull my thoughts back to the task at hand, which is this séance, she decided and wondered where her mother was. You always were the one I could count on reaching when I needed someone. Why keep away now and refuse to talk to me and these scientists when you could be the solution to my

301

problems? The strange thing with the dead is, Eusapia continued musing, that humans have no power over them. They come and go as they please. It's impossible to devise a system to rein them in or make them work to your advantage. They were what they were. Their love — and Eusapia had no doubt they never cease to love the people they were close to during their lives — this love took on such foreign characteristics that Eusapia did not even attempt to understand it. What mattered was that her mother loved her. Eusapia was sure to be one day reunited with Mammina in an all-embracing love. The most persistent traces of suffering would be erased as if it had never occurred.

My dear Eusapia, Richet's slightly impatient voice reached into her daydreams. Eusapia opened her big eyes fully and gazed into his, then spontaneously grabbed him for a liquidy smooch. Her strength seemed to leave her. She slumped onto his chest, where she remained for several minutes before straightening up. She looked around the room at the four men as if she had no idea what just happened.

Eusapia struggled under a mounting pressure to produce. Expectations in the room were high for various reasons. But in the general hope that she may succeed, Eusapia spotted flickers of doubt and suspicion that didn't augur well. She needed to get out of this room before it was too late. Some evenings did not lend themselves to séances. This was one of them.

Bad feelings are in the air, Eusapia chanted in an impersonal voice. No spirits will come near us.

I don't believe you, Myers protested.

Eusapia knew that at this moment he wanted her caught. He wanted her exposed as a fraud.

You, Eusapia screamed at him. You're the problem.

302

Start your séance, he commanded.

Not with you here!

Let's be civil, Richet intervened. We're all here with open minds.

Not him, Eusapia screeched, pointing at Myers.

Even Myers, Richet responded calmly. He more than anyone else wants to find a door to the beyond.

Eusapia listened, wondering whether it was safe to produce some phenomena. Suddenly, the table ascended in uncertain jerks and jumps.

You're cheating again, Myers said, his voice trembling with disgust. I saw you.

Stupid pretend-expert, Eusapia growled, flinging herself at him, Why don't you make sure I can't cheat?

We all try, Lodge said, pleading for a truce.

All of a sudden, Eusapia saw the men's eyes turn to Richet.

What's he doing? she marveled, watching spellbound as Richet seemed to be involved in an experiment of his own. Ochorowicz had explained hypnosis to Eusapia, the power of one mind over another. That she understood. She didn't need fancy words. If she concentrated hard, people's minds followed her into regions otherwise inaccessible to ordinary mortals. She could bring them to meet loved ones on the other side. If scientists wanted to call this hypnotism, so be it. Eusapia stared at Richet. She couldn't help admire his unshakable concentration. He is stronger than me, she thought, slightly taken aback. Richet held the men's attention. There was no escape. Eusapia stood on the sideline. He was not going to drag her into his sphere of power, no matter how tempting. Intrigued, she watched as he seemed to mesmerise his colleagues.

That's when they started seeing spirits, relatives and friends. Eusapia gasped. She wondered whether Richet was pulled into his own vision. He seemed totally unaware of reality, or was he?

Eusapia didn't interfere with what was happening in front of her. She listened with fascination to their exclamations, My aunt, my dear cousin, Leo, my friend, my dearly beloved! It suited her that her sitters saw spirits without her doing. After she decided that the men had received their fill of otherworldly communications, she sent the table shooting into the air. Trumpets started playing. Bells rang through the room.

Then, all of a sudden, dead silence, except for the alert breathing of the men.

Eusapia stood up.

There, she said. Do you believe me now?

Myers was too overcome with emotion to respond. He reached for Eusapia, who grabbed his hand and squeezed it warmly.

It's a privilege to meet again those who have left us, she said.

It is, Myers replied, his voice trembling, but Eusapia had already left the room.

A privilege, Myers repeated to himself, a wonderful gift from the heavens.

Richet looked at his friends silently. It was one of the rare evenings when all four men followed their own thoughts and the room did not hum with lively discussion.

From that evening on, it became easier for Eusapia to produce phenomena. Even if Myers caught her cheating, he would not fall back into doubting her psychic powers. He would chalk those incidents up to moments of weakness and exhaustion. A medium, loath to disappoint her sitters, would compensate by cheating. Sometimes a medium would cheat because of impatience when it took too long to set the right conditions.

I'm sorry I doubted you, Myers finally told Eusapia.

I have to shoulder part of the blame, she responded. I know I have a tendency to cheat. I shouldn't let myself be tempted to make my life easier.

Don't worry, Myers said, I understand.

Eusapia thought it wise to leave the conversation at that.

When the men left the island four days later, their belief that invisible forces manifest themselves in Eusapia was confirmed, each man defining those forces in his own way. Only men like them — whose minds were open enough to explore uncharted territory — possessed the brilliance and intuition to envision new dimensions in the scientific and metaphysical spheres. They were the innovators and new prophets. Despite ridicule and vicious attacks, they would not falter in defending their new truths. A small boat carried them back from an island of revelations to a world of uncertain realities and complicated questions of faith and knowledge.

England, August-September, 1895

9

WHEN EUSAPIA ARRIVED IN LONDON, she already wanted to be back home. Something in the air gave her a chill even though it was warm. Not even the familiar face of Frederick Myers, who had come with his wife and an interpreter to meet her at the train station, would cheer her up. As they travelled the last stretch from London to Cambridge with her, the skies tore open. Rain poured down and shrouded the landscape in a dismal grey. Maybe the only reason to see the world is to appreciate the beauty of your own country.

Terribly dreary and depressing, she sighed, indicating the foggy grey landscape around her with a discouraged swerve of her arm.

Don't worry, Eveleen Myers tried to reassure her. Once the rain stops, England is green and bright.

Oh, Eusapia responded without enthusiasm. She had come to a dead country. As the carriage drove them toward the Myers' residence, the streets were empty except for a few black umbrellas hurrying along. She closed her eyes and ignored the inquiries and well-meaning comments of her companions. Only when the carriage finally stopped did she bother to open her eyes again. It was still raining.

The Myers brought her into their house, where the housekeeper served hot tea and some sort of sandwich cake with a strawberry jam and butter icing between its two layers. But England had already destroyed Eusapia's appetite. Since she wasn't in a mood to talk either, she accepted to be led to her room, where the unnatural cleanliness and prim arrangement of the furniture and pictures felt like a reproach. She fought to quell a growing sense of apprehension. Through the closed door, she heard the Myers whisper and knew they were whispering about her. Dismayed, she threw herself on the bed. At least, it was comfortable enough. After just a few seconds, she fell asleep, grateful to forget her present circumstances.

A knock on the door interrupted her nap.

Eveleen quietly opened the door and made a sign for eating.

Yes, Eusapia responded, I'll be there in a moment.

Seated with her hosts around the table, Eusapia stared doubtfully at the plate in front of her.

Roast beef with gravy, said the interpreter, who had stayed to facilitate the interaction between the Myers and their guest. Mashed potatoes, carrots, he added helpfully, wondering why she seemed hesitant to even touch the food.

Eusapia finally took a bite.

No damn taste, she grumbled. Surprised by the smiles around her, Eusapia realised that the interpreter had given a more polite translation. She too smiled now. And since she was starving, she took another bite, and then a whole series of bites, imagining that she was eating pasta with tomatoes and garlic. She drank the tea pretending it was Chianti.

I'm glad you like the food, Eveleen said.

Eusapia looked at her and beamed. Yes, different taste, English goodness! When she saw the warmth in the English woman's eyes, she softened and for the first time looked at her closely. Beside her husband Fred, Eveleen looked fresh and real, with a touch of the dramatic, an irrepressible urge to be different from anybody else, her dress recycled and ingeniously transformed into a fantastical creation all her own. In short, a woman who stood out and would not be ignored. Eusapia nodded approvingly.

Thankful as well that the rubbernecking gaggle of boys and girls hanging about when she arrived had disappeared, Eusapia proposed to cook an Italian meal the next day. Get the ingredients, and I'll surprise you. Despite her non-existent cooking skills, she was set on producing Italian flavours. Even the worst Italian meal would beat what the English served up.

But our housekeeper can cook an Italian meal if you like, Myers said.

Eusapia stared at him as if he were out of his mind.

Only Italians can cook Italian meals, she said with such ferocity that Myers knew better than to contradict her.

The longer Eusapia stayed with the Myers, the more fascinated she became with Eveleen or Effie, as her relatives called her. When the woman's full voice rang through the rooms, Eusapia's eyes automatically swerved to Myers. Even with his two feet planted on the floor, he seemed to go against the law of gravity, floating up into higher spheres, deliberately removed from reality. If he didn't react to his wife's call, she'd smile and raise her voice a few decibels. Soon enough, a few fidgety tremors would run through his body and he'd come floating down from his mystical heights back to earth and to his family and friends. Only a powerfully earthy woman could accomplish such a feat. Despite Effie's strength, there was tenderness in her gestures and admiration in her eyes. Eusapia pictured her holding a rare bird in her palms, delighted as a child at its potential to fly to the skies, but also confident she would keep it securely in her hands so that everyone around her could enjoy its unusual twittering. Myers did not appear to object. His wife was the engine of the family who kept things rolling along their rightful path, and he respected her for that.

Mixed in with Eusapia's fascination was a certain weariness. She couldn't stand it when Effie studied her with unabashed curiosity. To her credit, Effie was less intrusive than some of the other Cambridge women, whose soul-searching gazes sickened her. Eveleen's eyes lingered on surfaces. She saw shapes and lines, shadows, lights, and texture that she wanted to capture on camera. Since her marriage with Fred, she had developed into an accomplished photographer and impressed Eusapia with the ease she handled camera and subjects as she directed husband and daughter into a harmonious composition. Eusapia too was asked to pose for a portrait and was flattered that it showed the passion in her eyes and the splendour of her hair without giving away her secrets. But when Effie wanted to take pictures during a séance, just thinking what the amount of light needed to take pictures would do to her séance infuriated Eusapia.

Don't you know that such light might kill a medium? she shouted, lecturing Effie about the foolishness of her intentions.

What really incensed Eusapia though was the sudden distance that developed when the Sidgwicks came to visit. She had met the philosopher and founder of the Society for Psychical

Research Henry Sidgwick and his wife, the mathematician and school principal Eleanor Sidgwick in France once before. Rarely had she taken such an immediate dislike to someone. Eleanor or Nora, the thin, tough-as-nails little woman had flung her mistrust and suspicions at her from the moment they met. This rigid fool had vetoed an endorsement of Eusapia's psychic powers and insisted on additional proof. She was the reason that Eusapia now found herself forced to undergo a psychic investigation on enemy territory.

Eusapia recognised the bond between Nora and Effie, which she could have accepted if it hadn't been for the hostile dimension to their unity. They formed a wall of exclusion around their special club of well-bred, morally superior women. In this milieu, even Effie's extravagant hats and frilly sleeves lost their splendour, as if the sober respectability in the room shrunk their proportions and bleached their colours. Eusapia turned toward the men, whose lips twisted up in half-smiles, the watchful company of their wives inhibiting a more expressive and hands-on reception. Is it possible to have the slightest fun around here? she groused.

Since Eusapia had come to doubt already that the English air allowed for even a shred of merriment, she took measures into her own hands. Boldly, she pulled Henry Sidgwick toward her and kissed him fully on the mouth. She didn't have to turn around to see the shocked disgust on Nora's face. It bore into her back as if it had come alive. To spite her, Eusapia kissed Sidgwick a second time. Now, that's a kiss you probably didn't experience before, she thought, satisfied with her own audacity and revenge on the judgmental woman who had dared to humiliate her in France. Myers had to be approached more

311

carefully. He appeared immune to advances, always giving the impression of being otherwise occupied, like yearning for experiences no living woman can give, pining for a dead lover, someone more present to him than his wife. Trying to reach him would be a waste of time.

I guess, we'll see you at the séance in two days, Nora said in passably good Italian, cutting the visit short.

Two days, Eusapia confirmed with her fingers, glad to get this horrible woman as far away from her as possible.

At the sight of tomatoes, garlic, basil, olive oil and dried pasta, which the Myers had secured with the help of the Italian ambassador's wife, Eusapia's spirits lifted. She grabbed one of the aprons hanging from hooks on the wall near the sink. Hastily, she threw it over her dress, then went searching for pots and pans. Cupboard doors flew open. There! She pulled out a big pot and filled it with water. On the stove it went!

No, no, no, whimpered the horrified cook who watched Eusapia's every move. Not like that.

The moment Eusapia heard the cook's voice, the past rushed back at her. She stared at the woman so hard that the cook's features melted and spun and finally hardened into something completely un-English. In the blink of an eye, the cook had turned into the Cattalani housekeeper and thrust Eusapia right back into childhood. There was no escape from this spell. As if no time had passed and she hadn't grown up, Eusapia turned back into the anxious, revengeful, desperate girl she had been, presently stuck in a new nightmare.

The cook resolutely withdrew the pot, took an iron lifter to remove one of the lids from the stove, and stoked the fire inside the opening. In reply, Eusapia got hold of what looked like a frying pan from another cupboard. The cook wouldn't let her continue and immediately snatched the pan out of her hand and replaced it with a heavier one. Eusapia spooned lard into it and finally managed to fry her onions and garlic. Later she added the tomatoes, and some basil, while in the high pan to her right, the boiling water started to soften the pasta.

The familiar garlic-onion air around her appeased her to some degree. Her homesick heart expanded and at last relaxed. If food smelled like home, you could survive. Neapolitan melodies popped into her mind and immediately went out into the open full throttle. She sang so loud and high that some of the glasses started to vibrate and the housekeeper almost backed out of the room, grumbling helplessly, Lord have mercy, this foreign creature is turning my poor kitchen into a disaster zone.

Eusapia anticipated an attack by the housekeeper, who eyed her apron as if to rip it off to recapture her status as chief cook and take back her pots and pans. But Eusapia needed to bring her meal to its glorious conclusion if her body wasn't going to shrivel up in this damp country. More garlic. More pepper. She stirred. She grasped one of the spoons beside her, scooped it full of sauce and shovelled it into her mouth.

Perfect, she exclaimed.

Before she could dunk the spoon back into the sauce for a second helping, the housekeeper tore it away from her, shoving another spoon into her hands, her face red with indignation. How disgusting could this stupid Italian get! No one licks and dips again, certainly not a dirty foreigner! For heaven's sake, don't they teach them cleanliness and manners in other countries. The housekeeper's murderous eyes had little effect on Eusapia, who just wanted to bring Naples with its blue sky and energetic bustle to England!

Still, the woman beside her annoyed her to no end. When again she came too close, watching like a hawk, Eusapia dipped her spoon into the sauce and flung its contents toward her so that a spray of red splotched the white apron in dramatic fashion.

The housekeeper screamed. Tomato stains! How would she ever get them out! She took off her apron, ran to the sink, and let the water rinse off the mess. When the stains resisted her efforts, she moaned but persevered.

Good riddance, Eusapia thought, only too pleased to have found a way to keep the housekeeper occupied and unable to poison the atmosphere.

The Myers picked at the Italian meal with about as much enthusiasm as Eusapia could muster for the English fare. Every forkful of food seemed loaded with apprehension, spiced with the horror stories their housekeeper had told them. Was it safe to eat the pasta? Unseemly visions of germs and ringworms destroyed their appetite. But like all the English people she met, the Myers were polite. Just dull and so much harder to understand than her fast-talking fellow Neapolitans, Eusapia thought, and was fully aware of the serious handicap this presented when proof of authenticity was at stake.

Eusapia realised that she needed to take special care with the finicky Myers, who made her sweat by his mere presence. After all the progress she had achieved with him on Richet's island, she saw his conviction fritter away quickly. Without the Mediterranean sun and wine, and in reaction to the negative response to his report, in which he confirmed the authenticity of

314

the phenomena she produced in the South of France, doubts had reawakened in him over the months. Suspicion crept back into his heart as if it had never left. Not that he ever doubted his soul would survive after death, but Eusapia became suspect again. The fiery lava in her eyes left him cold. More subtle attempts to gain entry into his psyche pushed against locked doors. He stared at her not with contempt yet, but increasingly critical.

Then there was Nora trying to poison Myers against her while pretending to keep an open mind. The two were huddled at the other end of the room in grim conversation. Keeping them in her sight, Eusapia saw Myers become more and more agitated, and the notion of fraud that Eusapia was convinced Nora was trying to instill in him seemed to take hold.

Eusapia's priority was always to gain her sitters' trust. If they doubted her special powers, her séances were doomed to fail.

Having to deal with Nora was bad enough, but Effie was turning into a bother as well. She now insisted on taking pictures during a séance. I don't see how taking pictures could hurt you, she complained one time too many.

Eusapia stormed out of the sitting room into her bedroom. That Effie was going to be the death of her. She and the dreadfully correct Nora. Men are so much easier to handle. A certain look, a certain touch, and they became malleable like putty in her hands. Eusapia did make friends with a few women, but the caution if not disdain she encountered right and left, and the whispered badmouthing behind her back made trust difficult. Yes, they gave her credit for being a powerful medium. No, they did not want to be otherwise associated with the woman they considered vulgar and illiterate. How much Eusapia preferred the men! Most were in awe of her and fully expected to find a few moments of gratification in her presence. Eusapia was generous. She gave freely to anyone who opened himself to her powers.

The séance scheduled at Cambridge would not be business as usual. If Eusapia failed to convince the members of the Society for Psychical Research, her reputation would be ruined. When months ago her good friends from Île Roubaud submitted their report to them, there was one member, Richard Hodgson, who more than anyone questioned the findings of the report, criticising the controls of her arms and legs as inadequate and suggesting that trickery was at the origin of her phenomena. Hodgson couldn't be dismissed outright, since he was considered a trustworthy investigator, sent by Sidgwick himself to work on psychical files in the new world. Richet had been outraged that anybody dared to question his observation and research skills after he had conducted so many séances with all the necessary precautions, and considering his unparalleled standing as a scientist. No matter how much the participants at the séance in France protested, Hodgson's reaction cast doubts on Eusapia's authenticity.

She needed to erase those doubts about herself and the critical faculties of her brilliant friends Richet, Ochorowicz and Lodge. Not even the righteous Myers deserved to be dismissed as naive, especially as he had put so much work into his positive report regarding her psychic phenomena. If I want to save my skin in the looming showdown, I have to be in top form, she exhorted herself. In the privacy of her room, she stretched and twisted and contorted arms and legs with brutal tenacity to counteract the stiffness that had crept into her limbs since arriving in England. She went for a sprint through the least travelled neighbourhoods that Effie had shown her in previous days. The hours passed quickly but without endearing England to her in the slightest. It was drizzling again. The place seemed deserted. With the unpleasant weather affecting her spirits, she worried that she was not up to the task and that Cambridge might become her undoing. Fear of failure doesn't bring you close to a country. She seemed incapable of establishing even the frailest of connections to this land.

The light pouring through the window into the séance room startled Eusapia. The illuminated faces of her sitters took on sinister airs, taunting her with their gleaming surfaces, screaming bloody vulnerability at her. She glanced perplexed at her hands fluttering like small white birds. That meant her face must be glowing like a full moon out of the shadowy darkness of the room. Never allow such contrast! It's deadly. Impatiently, she pointed to the curtains. Draw them. After an instant's hesitation, Sidgwick pulled them closed, leaving the room in quasi-darkness. Only the lamp on the note taker's desk gave off a weak sheen. Slowly, the sitters grew accustomed to the dark, and the familiar faces of partners and friends became recognisable again.

Eusapia asked for hymns. At once, Effie's unselfconscious voice rang through the room, while the others joined in more timidly, the Sidgwicks grudgingly. But they all sang. As experienced investigators, they considered it their duty to establish optimal conditions for phenomena to occur. Singing was one of them. Researchers, who approached séances with closed minds and cynical attitudes, impeded the manifestation of

317

psychic powers. Despite Hodgson's suspicions and his criticism of the report from France, the four sitters anticipated an extraordinary display of supernatural phenomena. Myers had experienced such occurrences on the French island, and they all trusted the instincts and observation skills of Richet and Lodge, two of the most brilliant and imaginative scientists of their time.

When Nora closed her eyes in concentration, a familiar quivering started in Eusapia's fingers like a trigger to proceed with the séance. Be patient, she warned herself, the price for misjudging the timing is excessively steep. Effie's voice was still too clear, her eyes too observant. Henry Sidgwick's eyelids twitched slightly, a sign of undivided attention. Let those sitters sing their hymns a lot longer, she thought. As the voices trailed off, Eusapia snorted, her arms dramatically waving upwards to get the sitters to turn up the volume. Obediently, they sang louder.

It was time for her to go into a trance. As soon as her body started squirming, the singing fizzled out. Eusapia urged them with animated gestures to keep singing if they wanted the séance to be successful. Myers agreed that music is a spiritual conduit, and spirituality is at the origin of any meaningful connection with the otherworld. Carried by the music, he sought hope and illumination in the communications from the beyond. His wife, on the other hand, just wanted action. Waiting was easier with at least part of her body or mind occupied. Projecting her voice did the job as well as anything and gave the moribund chorus a few more gasps of life. Everything about singing appealed to her, the sounds, the rhythms, the heaving of her chest, her tapping toes. With her photographer's instinct and sharp eye, she perceived even in the dimmest light the mystical shroud that suddenly

318

covered her husband's face, the rare uncertainty in Nora's expression, and Henry's tentative look of remembrance. Eusapia caught that look too. She went beyond Effie's purely visual observations. Sidgwick was most likely on a journey back to his childhood faith, reliving the sense of loss that the rejection of his religion brought with it, and seeking to replace the void with new values and meaning. Funny, Eusapia thought, watching Effie drift from observation to observation, we both get so involved in what we do that we hypnotise ourselves, and by doing so, constantly gain new insights. She knew she had to be careful. But sizing up Effie's state of mind once more, she decided that if ever phenomena were to occur tonight, this was the moment.

Again she felt the familiar prickling in the tips of her fingers and the almost unbearable tension in her lower back. Her body started twitching and her arms, which were controlled by Myers and Sidgwick, first shook, then jerked free.

Myers objected. What's the point? You're squirming out of my hold any chance you get.

Eusapia pointedly ignored him. Her eyes began blinking in an odd staccato rhythm while he struggled to hold on to her hand. Watery sighs almost drooled out of her mouth.

The light is too strong, she complained, grimacing as if in severe pain. Please, turn the light down. Soft red light is better for mediums, it's better for spirits. Please.

It was Nora who got up and changed the lighting. By the time she sat down again, both Myers and Sidgwick exclaimed that strange hands were poking and hitting them. Just as Nora tried to get a closer look at the two men, the table rose to the accompaniment of a few trumpet sounds.

319

Effie was rapt with excitement. God Almighty! Things were happening!

Eusapia lifted her eyes to the ceiling.

Come into this room, souls from the beyond, speak to us, she implored whoever seemed on the verge of materialising.

Every one stared up. A sudden thud redirected their focus. A little table, which had been standing at least five feet behind Eusapia, lay now upside-side down on the séance table, pinkish flowers poking out from between its legs, so fresh and covered with dew or rain drops that they must have been cut only moments earlier. The sitters didn't have time to admire the flowers. Eusapia collapsed, thrashing about as if she had a seizure.

Water, Nora said, and rushed out of the room.

Henry Sidgwick turned the lights back on. It was Effie who steadied Eusapia's head between her hands to prevent injury, releasing it only when the medium's body had calmed down under her efficient care. The men carried Eusapia into the guest room and laid her on the bed to let her recover and restore her powers.

Effie covered Eusapia and wiped the pearls of sweat from her forehead before she and the others tiptoed out of the room. Amazing, she exclaimed. Who were the spirits talking to us through all those phenomena?

One day we'll find the answer, Henry Sidgwick said. Do you think Hodgson would still doubt Eusapia's authenticity if he had participated in this séance?

No one answered. They all tried to recall as many details of the séance as they could, and on Nora's suggestion wrote down what they remembered. Before they had time to put their

320

observations on paper, the doorbell rang and after a few seconds, the housekeeper led Richard Hodgson into the room.

Eusapia, who could hear the hullabaloo and guessed that the visitor had finally arrived, thanked her good fortune for his late arrival. It would give her time to check him out. Through the door she heard the group jump right away into a discussion in which her name played a prominent role. She couldn't understand much, but she heard Hodgson's loud voice in attack mode and Myers' mounting a defence that was too shaky to be convincing.

When Effie called for breakfast the next morning, Eusapia ignored her. After calling and knocking several times, Effie opened the door, and stared at the figure that lay as if in a stupor, unsmiling and pale on the bed. Worried that something was seriously wrong, she put her hand around Eusapia's wrist to measure her pulse.

Nothing wrong here, she mumbled. With well executed pantomimes, she asked Eusapia whether she wanted breakfast to be served in bed. Finally, Eusapia reacted. The sharp shaking of her head indicated an unmistakable no.

You want to join us? Effie signalled.

This time, Eusapia nodded, but otherwise remained unresponsive.

Practical as ever, Effie took hold of Eusapia and sat her up, pushed her legs over the edge of the bed, and supported her back with pillows so that she wouldn't fall backwards. She took some water from the nearby enamel basin and washed Eusapia's face, gathering from her expression that she did not object. Effie continued her procedures, combing the black hair and dressing Eusapia in competent movements.

Do you want me to guide you?

Taking the dejected nod as a yes, Effie helped Eusapia to her feet and, supporting her arm and her back, brought her to the dining room where the men were so absorbed in the stories their visitor told them of his troublesome voyage across the ocean that they did not hear the women enter.

Look who we have here, Effie interrupted them as if introducing one of her children.

The men jumped to their feet. Eusapia stared listlessly at the floor, her eyelids drooping.

I think she is still too worn out from yesterday's séance, Effie reminded them. Let her eat in peace and give her time to recover.

The men agreed and immediately resumed their conversation as if there hadn't been any interruption at all. Eusapia watched them and suddenly felt Hodgson's disparaging stare on her. Her mood darkened. She wanted to be back in Naples, hear the banter and shouts across the streets, feel the warm sun on her hair and skin, buy macaroni from the street vendors, fill her lungs with pungent odours, but most of all, simply feel part of the action around her in a city that accepted you warts and all.

Hodgson turned back to his companions and again dominated the conversation. Eusapia heard his voice and then Nora's in translation, Imagine being one of the few lucky travellers not getting sick in a storm that whipped the ocean liner about like a toy. Add to that drama the sounds of roaring water, howling winds, screaming passengers, impatient commands of the ship's first mate, and the constant moaning and retching of the seasick. Yet there was something powerfully riveting in this spectacle . . .

No question, Eusapia thought, secretly studying the ruddy face of the tall man across from her, he would not fall sick easily. Bursting with vitality, he was her age, his stamina and robust health equalled hers. She listened to the drawling sound of his voice, so different from that of her English friends. They must speak different in his birth country Australia. Or maybe this was American English. Interestingly enough, Hodgson's didn't look like someone who put his nose into books, even though he was so obsessed with philosophy and poetry that he had been drawn to study at Cambridge because his favourite poet had studied there. My God, what kind of person would choose a university to commune with a dead writer instead of seeking the best place to exchange ideas with living students and teachers?

Eusapia barely touched her food, knowing that she had squirreled away enough bread, cheese, and cake to tide her over to the next day.

Do you want to lie down again? Effie asked solicitously as she worried about Eusapia who had sunk into herself, looking small and vulnerable on her chair.

Eusapia shook her head. It was part of her job to gather as much information as humanly possible, and she certainly couldn't miss the opportunity to pick up clues from an animated group. To her amazement, even Nora and Effie were completely drawn into a lively conversation on philosophy and ethics, which left Eusapia free to observe at her leisure. Nora, who took the floor at length, forgot to translate. With a vastly improved arsenal of English words, Eusapia had counted on gaining at least bits and pieces of new insights. At this point, though, nothing intelligible oozed from the talk around the table.

Then, with a shift in tone and subject, the words J.N. Maskelyne, which without doubt had to be a name, burnt themselves into her brain. J.N., Eusapia mused, it sounds like initials, which she thought was possible as she had heard of one or two other people, artists or writers, being called some weird letters. There was a sudden uncomfortable pause when Sidgwick first mentioned Maskelyne. The women glanced at Eusapia not in their usual, open way, but almost embarrassed. The uneasy pause lasted for just a second before the voices took off again, with forced vivacity as if to hide a ruse or worse. Eusapia fumed. Those damn English plotters who thought they were above everyone else. Who was this J.N.? The two letters had an ominous ring to them. Why couldn't there be a single language? Despite understanding more English than anyone suspected, she struggled to grasp those important facts and innuendos that were crucial to an effective séance. All of a sudden, she had enough. With her arm shooting melodramatically toward her room, she made it clear she wanted to be escorted at once. Effie was at her side instantly and guided her back to her room, where Eusapia threw herself on the bed. What am I going to do? she asked gloomily, waiting in vain for an answer from her mother, who hadn't shown herself yet in England.

Eusapia wasn't the type to be kept down for long. After a lazy day, with supper served in her room, followed by a good night's sleep, her fighting spirit came back. She jumped out of bed and threw her arms into the air. Bring on the challenge, Hodgson, she dared the contrary Australian American. She stretched confidently. Yes, her arms worked as they were intended to. Her legs too were strong and precise as usual. As long as she kept her confidence, she'd be able to produce convincing séances. Few surpassed her ability to draw people into her world. Rich and brilliant men and women succumbed to her spell. Even Richet, who mesmerised his companions at dinner conversations, had been impressed by her commanding presence during séances.

Before Effie could come knocking on the door, Eusapia proceeded to join the group in the dining room. A quiet murmur kept her from entering. She recognised Sidgwick's and Hodgson's voices. To her chagrin, words combined incomprehensibly in the low-pitched flow of English mumble-jumble. But one of her smart and well-travelled Neapolitan friends had made it his mission to drum into her head the English essentials a medium needed when accepting invitations into enemy territory. Over and over he repeated: magician, fraud, illiterate, trick, or then on the other hand, authentic, psychic and supernatural. Together with the tone of voice, that knowledge became an invaluable tool to determine whether she dealt with friends or foes. The need for appraising her situation jolted her at least minimally out of her early-morning drowsiness. J.N.? That's this Maskelyne person. Did they just say magician? Eusapia couldn't be sure, but warning signals went up all around and inside her. She tried to absorb additional information, but was interrupted by approaching footsteps. She let her purse drop and bent down to pick it up.

You're up already? Effie exclaimed, Come sit down with us and have a cup of tea.

Eusapia charged into the room.

Good morning! she exclaimed and the vigour of her voice sent the air spinning.

She looked keenly into everyone's eyes, except for Nora who barely got a cursory glance.

Hello, Signor Hodgson!

Hello, Signora Palladino, he responded, watching Eusapia closely.

Eusapia studied him in turn. Would he respond to her powers? She held his gaze a while longer as if to hypnotise him into submission. Too hungry to continue, she sat down and energetically dug into her eggs.

A lively conversation started up, with everyone pretending not to notice Eusapia's lack of manners. Let them, Eusapia thought defiantly. Give me one good reason to give up the enjoyable, lax and hands-on Neapolitan eating style. She gleefully grabbed bites of egg with her fingers and noisily chomped down on her food. In the corner of her left eye, she saw Nora wince. That prissy, disapproving little nag! Eusapia turned directly toward Nora and waited until the woman tilted her head toward her. Then she burped as loud as she could straight into her face, twice. Nora kept her composure, but soon excused herself and left the table while Eusapia scraped clean her plate, realising at once that this hadn't been her shrewdest manoeuvre. Why did she let Sidgwick's wife get under her skin? Nora provoked a reaction in Eusapia just by breathing the same air. To hell with that woman! Now Eusapia was reduced to checking out Hodgson without the benefit of translation.

When news came that J.N. Maskelyne was delayed, the investigators decided to go ahead with a séance that evening despite his absence.

Eusapia agreed emphatically. This trial run was crucial. Dealing with two extreme skeptics at the table simultaneously was too much to handle without thorough preparation. After tonight, she'd know better how Hodgson's examination techniques worked and whether he was at all susceptible to her psychic powers.

Until tonight then, my dear Signora Palladino, Hodgson's said, smoothly covering his eagerness to unmask Eusapia as a fraud.

Until tonight, she snarled and refused to look at the man who tried to hoodwink her with his false politeness.

The sudden discord chilled the room.

As always, Effie was the one to take the edge off the situation. I'm sure we won't be disappointed, she said with a voice that harboured no mistrust or ill feelings.

Eusapia's face brightened a bit. Sometimes, Effie was all right, especially when Nora was out of the picture.

The conversation took off in different directions and Eusapia had a chance to watch and dissect the interactions around her without arousing suspicion.

At the séance, Hodgson was seated to Eusapia's right, and Sidgwick to her left. Nora sat beside Hodgson and Effie between Sidgwick and Myers. The interpreter acted as note taker and was placed at a separate table with only a small red light illuminating his pages. Eusapia could feel Hodgson's growing impatience beside her. As last time, Effie started to sing, summoning a meagre following. Her strong voice rendered the hymns unerringly and with fervour. She loved to belt out her songs. Far from being taken aback by Effie's unselfconscious religious conviction, the others almost envied her for her uncomplicated faith. She had no doubts. She loved her church and she loved her religion. Most of all, she loved to sing. Eusapia smiled. Michela would be pleased. She too had found refuge and hope in the church choir. But this was not the time to indulge in memories.

Eusapia had her hands full with Hodgson and his continuous flashes of negative thoughts. Dammit, she thought, this guy destabilises the atmosphere in the room. Breathe slowly, breathe fully, she chanted soundlessly, reaching deep inside herself with a concentration that rarely left anyone untouched. She needed to have the right vibrations in the air in order to pull everyone into her sphere. Only then could she produce psychic phenomena. Now what is this? Eusapia thought as she noticed Sidgwick rubbing up against her thigh under the table, which wasn't like him, since he didn't have a flirty fibre in his body. To all appearances, both Sidgwicks lived uncomplaining outside the realm of sexual desires and didn't seem to miss anything. So why was he pretending? It's another of their ploys, Eusapia inferred, another of their annoyingly stupid traps they set for her. But she'd better not let her temper fly or give away that she was on to them. She began to writhe in typical pre-trance mode. Instantly, the breathing of her sitters accelerated in anticipation.

Someone pulled my beard, Sidgwick exclaimed.

Eusapia saw her suspicions of Hodgson confirmed when he let go of her hand on purpose. He was out to get her. Ah, she thought, do you think I'm stupid? She firmly encircled his hand with hers. By no means would he be able to say that it was her hand that poked and pulled people.

Ouch, Hodgson's cried out in surprise. Something hit me in the back.

Bene, molto bene, very good, everyone murmured in Italian. As they must have been instructed to do, Eusapia assumed. To lull me into believing that my mediumship would go uncontested. But they won't succeed because I am the best there is. Growing up, I had nothing to be proud of. Now I do. I have more talent than any other medium, which means money and fame, and everything that comes with it. No one is going to take that away from me!

Myers was the only one remaining silent. He looked apprehensive and Eusapia knew that she was in danger of losing his trust altogether.

There was no time for reflection. Her phenomena had to occur now.

Ouch, Hodgson yelped again. Everyone had heard the slap. On my head, of all places. And the strength of that thing!

That thing? It's a ghost, Effie objected, awed by the spooky and rather gloomy ambience in the room. Some foreign substance had seeped in. Why not a gentle ghost? Why not a happy one? Effie asked rather loudly. In her mind, the world on the other side was as cheerful as her present circumstances.

Hodgson glanced bemused at the capable and practical woman across from him and wondered what could inspire such sweet visions of heaven.

At that moment the table jumped.

This time, the *bene's* and *molto bene's* sounded more genuine.

Even Hodgson was impressed. Eusapia had blown a little hole into his cynicism.

Lights travelled through the room like shooting stars. A cold breeze blew out from the front of Eusapia's head. Suddenly, limbs grew out of her body. The sitters gasped. The tension in the room increased. Eusapia had the sitters under her spell, in a sort of twilight zone where it was difficult to distinguish reality from hallucination. Would she dare call on her spirit guide John King to make an appearance? She quickly assessed Hodgson's mental state. His cockiness was gone. She could see he was baffled. Yes, she would bring John King into the séance room.

John King, she exclaimed.

Watching her arm movements and her expression, everyone understood she was beseeching him to materialise. It didn't take long for a dark figure to rise behind her. Before she could put any questions to him though, he had disappeared.

Eusapia collapsed into a heap, emitting disconcerting cries of pain or satisfaction, as she often did when coming out of a trance. She threw herself into Sidgwick's lap, pushing against him. He did not extricate himself, and again attempted to bring his rusty flirty side to the fore to keep in her good graces.

Fed up with this spectacle, Nora decided it was time to accompany Eusapia to her room. After a curt good night, Nora left the bedroom so that Eusapia could restore her powers. Eusapia trembled with exhaustion. She attempted to listen through the door to the conversation of her English sitters, but was unable to extract many clues. Only Hodgson's voice resounded over the din. His barely hidden frustration made Eusapia smirk. He gave zero credence to her powers, but had been thoroughly stumped by her powerful performance and so was unable to explain her trickery. But Eusapia knew he would not give up until she was defeated. She had already figured out that including Maskelyne was his idea. If he couldn't denounce her tricks by himself, he would bring in experts that would.

Eusapia threw herself on her bed, only to jump up again. Nausea shook her body. As often, after the extreme exertion the demonstration of her powers required, her body was racked with pain, and an acidic stream of greenish vomit left her weak and low-spirited. Tonight was worse than usual. How on earth was she supposed to hit the mark the next evening if already this Hodgson guy got her that tense? Tomorrow she'd have to deal with the mysterious J.N. Oh Lord! What if he was a magician? Magicians were her worst nightmare, holy terrors compared to the docile academics and scientists who tended to accept what they saw at face value. Magicians saw right through her tricks if she faltered the least bit during her performance. Tomorrow, she needed to keep at least one of those two cynics out of the room, a manoeuvre she had accomplished in the past, but doubted she could pull off this time. The seemingly amenable Sidgwick was set on having Hodgson and J.N. in the room together, and if that was his plan, they would be there. She knew better than try to change his mind. Please let me survive the next séance, Eusapia prayed.

Fatigued and despondent she fell asleep into a world of monsters the size and ferocity she hadn't experienced since her childhood. They corralled her and squeezed her into a smaller and smaller space. She could barely breathe. She woke with a scream when big sharp jaws were about to clamp down on her.

Eusapia lay wet and shaking. She knew those monsters well. The smell of defeat crept into the room. But having survived a childhood like hers, she would not let herself be trampled down again. Tomorrow, she would show them.

To Eusapia's disappointment, J.N. Maskelyne did not show up the next day. She groaned. All last week and especially

331

yesterday, she had mentally and physically prepared for his arrival. Her eyes darkened. All that expenditure of physical and mental resources for nothing! She couldn't afford to do things for nothing.

What's wrong, Eusapia? Effie asked, concerned for her state of mind.

Eusapia glared at her without answering. Effie decided it was best to leave her in peace. Still, the furtive glances being exchanged in the room felt like an attack.

An oppressive heaviness took hold of Eusapia. From the day she arrived in England, she had felt it nestle in her and slowly take root. Now it took over. Was it the grey sky? Was it the food? With every day, producing phenomena became a bigger strain. Eusapia resented how hard she was forced to work just to ensure she had food, clothing, and lodging. Who said people were created equal? Some had it all and some were doomed from birth. What if Henry Sidgwick and Nora had been forced to grow up in her world? Poor Henry. She couldn't see him survive the hardship and depravity of her own childhood. Tough, emotionless Nora might actually have been able to shoot back the taunts of the children, and stare down the insults in the teacher's eyes, even rise to the status of best reader, best everything, and put the stupid teacher in Minervino to shame. Contrasting Henry and Nora with herself did nothing but intensify her desolation.

Eusapia attempted to give additional séances. She sat among the sitters, heavy and dark. None of her arms or legs would move. Nothing appeared, nothing levitated. Though she appreciated how well she was paid for participating in scientific investigations and knew the consequences of not producing as expected, she had lost all motivation to go on. While sitting and staring, her old performances played in front of her, over and over, always the same thing, the little table rising, curtains billowing out, instruments tooting, ghost faces and hands appearing. And for this repetitious nonsense she had to twist herself into excruciatingly painful contortions, swallow objects, regurgitate them, pull out her ingenious contraptions from all parts of her clothes and body without raising suspicion while at the same time use every one of her mental faculties to hypnotise her sitters and keep them mystified. She couldn't do it anymore.

The disappointment among the Cambridge investigators was palpable as it became clear that the investigation was a waste of time and money.

When a séance finally took place, it was a meagre type of event, and Eusapia found little to cheer about overhearing the chatter afterwards. The words fraud and cheat came up over and over.

It's becoming more problematic by the day to believe that you haven't been cheating all along, Myers said accusingly to Eusapia during breakfast. He seemed distraught. Had Hodgson been right to question his report and doubt his critical faculties? More than likely, the manifestations on the French island had nothing to do with psychic powers. But how could brilliant scientists like Richet and Lodge be taken in by a vulgar charlatan? Their extensive professional experience had trained them to investigate and sharpened their observation skills. Both scientists were convinced that Eusapia was genuine.

The following morning, Eusapia was surprised to see a blue sky and a golden sun. It's a sign, she thought. I can't be defeated. I'll show them.

With that, she started practising and preparing again.

Now where is this J.N.? Eusapia wondered when the group gathered again. She was angry that she still had no idea what he was about. Her snorting and hissing brought the conversation to a halt.

What is it? Nora asked brusquely, not even disguising the disdain she felt for the so-called medium.

There she went again, this woman with two brains, no heart, and completely dried-up emotions, except for her efforts to advance the higher education of women. She was rubbing Eusapia the wrong way like only she could. Higher education? Why talk about that when millions of people like Eusapia didn't even get the chance to learn the basics. But Eusapia could see that this fixation on higher education was deeply personal for Nora and came out of a strong sense of injustice. It should have brought them closer. The way Eusapia saw it, if Nora had been a man, she'd be as renowned as her brother-in-law for whom she did mathematical work, or as Richet and Lodge. Across the gulf of differences, she vaguely understood where Nora was coming from. Yet she couldn't stand her.

What is it, you ask? Do you really care in a human type of way? Eusapia screamed at her.

Nora refused to be drawn into a quarrel.

Piss off, Eusapia shouted, and stormed out of the room.

Even the dull English air was preferable to being cooped up in a place where people like Nora tried to ruin her. With the sun shining, the air that even out here was fouled up with Nora's obsession to unmask her should become breathable again. This woman had concluded from the beginning that Eusapia was a fraud, but was forced to rethink her position when certain phenomena defied explanation and she had to wonder whether Richet and Lodge were right. Could nuggets of genuine mediumship be found among the cheating, trickery and vulgarity? Eusapia hollered contemptuously into the fog. Under the circumstances, she had actually done well. She would give her all in the coming days to protect her livelihood. With her humour improving, she sped along the streets. Amazing, how encouraging a bit of sun can be.

Suddenly, Eusapia felt a familiar tugging at her heart, one she had ignored for too long. When she dared to look up again, she saw Celestina waving faintly, as if she had given up hope her mother would acknowledge her. But Eusapia wanted to see her daughter more than anything else. And there she stood, full of vitality, a dynamic young woman of twenty-four already.

Celestina! Eusapia cried out, and pain and longing twisted together with the guilt she had tried to bury all her life. Celestina, I'm here, Eusapia added hesitantly because she did not believe her daughter could ever forgive her.

Celestina smiled and blew a kiss to her mother.

Come down here, Celestina! Let me see you up close.

But Celestina remained on the sunbeams. She smiled once more, waved, and then was gone.

Later that afternoon, Eusapia's ears perked up when the name Damiani came up in a conversation, yes, Damiani, Mrs. Damiani, daughter. When Eusapia had a moment alone with the interpreter, she questioned him about Signor Damiani and his family.

Oh, said the interpreter, they just arrived back from a vacation in Italy, their daughter's fifth trip to Italy, but her first to Naples where her father was born. I wish they had accepted Signor Sidgwick's invitation to attend the séance, but no, they left for the country in a sudden weird type of urgency, explaining that they're just here for a change of clothes and then had to be off to other parts of the country.

Did their daughter like Naples? Eusapia asked carefully, emptying her voice of all emotion.

Oh she loved it, the interpreter answered, and Eusapia could see that Celestina had made a powerful impression on the interpreter. Suppressing her impatience, she waited for additional information.

What a stunning young woman, the interpreter said admiringly. A ball of fire and vivacity. Intelligent too. She speaks four languages. Everyone was commenting on how easily she assimilates and analyses everything she looks at.

I wish I could have seen her, Eusapia said wistfully. Could you come back, Celestina, she implored the skies, and didn't care that the interpreter stared at her fearing for her sanity. Could you come back?

There was no response.

When Eusapia made her entry into the séance room that evening, she was depressed and panting, and her bad mood spilled into the room like manure. She could almost see her sitters holding their noses. To hell with them! This was one evening too many with the same group. She knew that the real test was somehow connected to this Maskelyne person. Yet there she was, forced, no matter her personal circumstances, to produce phenomena night after night, trapped in a tiresome and dangerous situation where the initial amazement had worn off.

Sidgwick intoned calmingly, If we did anything to offend you, we're sorry. It certainly wasn't our intention.

Never mind then, Eusapia snapped. Turn down the light. It's too bright in this room. Do you forget how sensitive ghosts are to light?

Sidgwick, with his back to Eusapia, had barely turned down the light when the table rose ferociously into the air, swung backwards and forwards and, amidst the astonished cries of the sitters, to the left and to the right before it came crashing down to the floor to the angry tooting of a trumpet and the harrowing screeching of mandolin strings. Then the commotion stopped abruptly. A fraught silence filled the room, and was disrupted only by the laboured breaths of the medium. Eusapia fell toward the left, where Sidgwick had sat down again, her arms and legs jerking, her eyes rolling, and an icy breeze emanating from the white tuft of her hair. All of a sudden, she became so still that Effie and Nora rushed to her side. She did not move again. Sidgwick and Myers carried her to her room and laid her on the bed. Still no movement. Concerned, Effie checked her vital signs.

She is alive, she said simply. Let her rest.

Before Eusapia fell asleep, she heard the beginnings of an animated discussion through the closed door. She picked out the word authentic and greedily latched on to it even though she couldn't be sure of its context. Eusapia needed this word to help her get through the night. One of how many thousand nights without her daughter? Celestina slipped in and out of Eusapia's consciousness, leaving her in such turmoil that she couldn't sleep for hours. How could she have missed meeting her child? I got what I deserved, she concluded sadly. But slowly, Celestina, floating through the common air they had breathed in earlier in the day, brought some unexpected peace. She seems to be doing well, Eusapia mused. So something good has come from me giving her to Giorgio.

When Maskelyne finally arrived the next afternoon, Eusapia felt refreshed. Her skin tingled. A new challenge! She was up to it. She could handle anything coming her way, even a magician. But was he a magician? The uncertainty bothered her. Experienced investigators like the Cambridge group included skeptics and fraud debunkers in their investigations to lend credibility to their work.

Signora Palladino, J.N. Maskelyne said with a flourish, extending his long animated hand toward Eusapia.

No doubt, this is the hand of a magician, she thought, and the certainty of her knowledge made her mind jingle.

Mostly though, it was his expression that gave him away, his happily searching eyes. She knew he didn't miss a detail of her black heap of hair. No, he took in every strand, every single hair, worse, every pleat and fold in her clothes as a means or tool for magic, quickly judging its potential during a performance. He broke her down into components as if she were a machine designed to execute various manoeuvres.

Hello, Signore, Eusapia greeted him, her head spinning. If her fate hadn't been in the balance, she might have enjoyed his company like a sudden sun ray from Naples. Sometimes, she tired of the academics with their sense of self-importance and self-entitlement, their convoluted reasoning and expectation that the world should adapt to their ideals. They didn't have a clue what it meant to rub one's nose in the stench of abject poverty and struggle amidst the hollowed faces of hunger. How could they understand people whose most pressing goal in life was to survive?

Eusapia openly stared at Maskelyne. He was nothing like her Raphael. Look at this guy in his expensive suit. A rare magician who made it big! Did it affect his heart? When she scrutinised his face, he stared right back, intrigued by her interest. He still has the drive, she thought. There he stood, full of energy, ready to jump. He must be close to sixty, but looked twenty years younger. His hair was still mostly black, elegantly slicked back. His moustache was a splendid statement of confidence, and she saw right away the usefulness of its bushy growth for a magician. She started to enjoy this.

Pleased to meet you, she said, and gripped his hand.

She laughed when Maskelyne resorted to a blank expression. Who do you think I am? she thought. But she was not mad at him.

Suddenly, Maskelyne broke into laughter himself. A certain camaraderie developed between the two. But Eusapia knew it was no friendship. They remained fierce competitors in a contest where you had to crush the opponent to come up the winner. For her, the outcome would determine whether she kept or lost an adequate income. No way would she ever go without a decent bed and the comfort of food and drink again. She'd better get her act together. Eusapia scrutinised her challenger and caught him doing the same. His level of energy amazed her — one of those guys who gets by with three hours of sleep a night. She imagined him jumping out of bed with new ideas, running toward a heap of material and putting mind and body to work with the same concentration as Raphael. But given his obvious wealth, he'd be able to get all the help and material he needed. Not like her husband who had nothing to his name. How can a magician become so rich?

What do you do for a living? Eusapia asked in a bantering voice, camouflaging her curiosity, and keenly aware of the secret glances among the group.

I own a theatre, Maskelyne said.

He shows movies in his theatre, Nora added. Not only that, he produces them and improves the apparatuses used to make them. In fact, he is an inventor.

Impressive, Eusapia said. So he was acquainted with a whole plethora of mechanisms. He would be a formidable adversary.

That evening, Eusapia refused to leave her room for supper or even for the planned séance. She held her belly with both hands and moaned. I'm too sick, she said.

Her hosts had no choice but to postpone the séance to the next day. This gave Eusapia more time to prepare. One mistake she never made was underestimating her detractors.

When the séance finally took place, Maskelyne was seated to Eusapia's left and her friend Lodge, who happened to show up at the Myers' by chance, to her right. Grateful for a friendly soul at her side, she smiled affectionately. She could count on him. On her left, Maskelyne started to fidget. What was he trying to do? It wasn't the moment to start doubting herself. She hit the table with the palm of her hand, then surreptitiously knocked three times. In response, soft knocks answered from the back of the wall like echoes. Eusapia glanced over to Maskelyne and caught the flash of smug triumph on his face, this cruel satisfaction of the cat that ate the canary. He immediately wiped the smirk away, but not fast enough. She wanted to scratch the contempt off his skin and squash his brain! His attempt to trick her into a false sense of security with an innocuous smile failed miserably. Let him be, she thought. Concentrate on your task. Make the table rise. Slowly, it started swaying, but remained on the floor. There was unusual pressure coming from Maskelyne's side. This man was seeking to ruin the evening. She tried again. Table rise, she said. It moved an inch or two sideways. But again, there was obstruction from Maskelyne's side. Eusapia had enough.

Stupid toad, she screamed in Neapolitan, you dreadful snake, stop that nonsense.

Maskelyne, who had been told in advance to go along with any request of the medium in order to facilitate the manifestation of phenomena, nodded sheepishly. From then on, he behaved himself. The table rose suddenly. It swerved, teetered for a moment, then came dropping down, but did not hit the floor with a bang as Maskelyne had expected. It gently moved back to its original position on the ground. Eusapia could hear his brain whir trying to figure out her moves.

Everyone waited for John King to arrive. Nothing happened. Then a smattering of trumpet sounds rang through the room. Except for the defiantly sexual moaning of the medium who leaned heavily against her friend Lodge for comfort, no other noise could be heard. The sitters waited. When Eusapia's agitation finally lessened and her head rested calmly against Lodge's chest, she did not move for a long while. Suddenly, she jerked up and menacingly pointed her finger at Maskelyne.

You useless louse, you frighten the spirits away.

She took Lodge's arm, and he guided her courteously to her room.

Another séance was set up for the next evening. Lodge, who had to leave, did so expressing the expectation that Eusapia would make up for the poor showing the night before and replicate what happened on the French island, where supposedly the real thing was produced.

How was she going to do that with Maskelyne at her side and without the support of her friend Lodge? Why did Maskelyne have to infect everything with his malicious intent to discredit her? No magician should be allowed into a séance room, except for your most loyal friends. She wished her husband Raphael were present to help her conjure up unforgettable and baffling manifestations. Here in England, she was on her own, apart from an accomplice who secretly rendered services that cost her an arm and a leg. But alone or not, she had a job to do.

To complicate her life, Eusapia felt Myers attitude toward her cool rapidly, his original doubts flooding back into his fickle soul. Was she a cheat? Had she fooled them on the French island? He turned away from her in disgust. Her swearing, lack of manners, overt sexuality and the strong body odour emanating from her during séances assaulted his refined senses. Eusapia shuddered. There he was, slave to the unattainable, floating up again in that impossible sphere where perfect love promised to fulfil his desperate yearnings. Judged from those heights, she was the lowest of creatures, an affront to his mystical expectations. If it weren't for Myers' otherwise endearing personality, she would have hated him. As it was, she let her innate generosity flow toward him and his compulsive need for contact with the otherworld. In that respect, she understood him. If she were prevented from communicating with her mother, she'd be lost too. She could identify with him. And yes, she had something to offer.

When Eusapia first laid eyes on the handsome young man who accompanied Maskelyne to the next meeting, so similar to him, with the same eyes and mouth, undoubtedly his son, she could have shouted for joy. Young blood exhilarated her. It added excitement to her repetitious performances, new ideas, and different ways of looking at life. He too was unlikely to be an academic. This pleased her even more. Maybe it was possible to have fun again. Impatiently, she pulled Nevil Maskelyne to the chair to her right, then leaned heavily against him. Taut, strong muscles! A musky smell. Tobacco breath. His sparkling eyes filled with relaxed amusement. He displayed none of the fanaticism of the typical debunker like his father or the famous Houdini who was every medium's nightmare. No, Maskelyne's son seemed harmless, which made him even more desirable, although she wondered whether she wasn't already intoxicated with the sheer maleness of him. Leaning against him, she greedily absorbed the warmth of his young blood, which coursed through his body in splendid freedom.

Lower the lights, Eusapia screeched. Just before the room turned dark, she could see Nora's nasty eyes bore into her. That shrivelled old witch, she won't ruin the bit of gratification séances bring with them. Virulent young men were a pleasure Eusapia wouldn't pass up even if the world came crashing down beside her.

Nevil, she whispered, and then forgot everything else for a few minutes. She didn't care what anyone thought. At this moment, the success of her séance meant little compared with the exhilarating feeling of being alive.

Eusapia's moaning grew stronger.

She must be getting into her trance, Sidgwick's voice rolled through the room, commenting on the progress of the séance in a manner that could not have been more matter-of-fact, while Nora had half a notion to leave the room.

This time, the table rose straight up and remained suspended longer than during previous evenings. Again the little wicker table to her right landed upside down on the séance table. The concert of instruments, accentuated by exploding raps and their echoes, vibrated intensely in the ears of her sitters. Eusapia was in her element. The *bene's* and molto *bene's* carried her along. Too easy, she thought, but pushed the thought away. No undue physical pressure or hindrance from Maskelyne, which was good, or was it? she asked herself.

Be careful, another voice urged as the table rose again.

For once, Eusapia just wanted to produce her phenomena without second-guessing herself. But maybe young Maskelyne beside her distracted her too much to be careful. She convinced herself that he wasn't part of their plot. The old Maskelyne, however, and by now "old" was the only term she used to describe him although he was robust enough to easily keep up with her, this old Maskelyne was a nuisance. His mere presence spoiled her evening. Don't let him out of your sight!

Turn the lights down if you want John King to appear, Eusapia commanded.

Dutifully Sidgwick did as told until only a weak red gleam came from the note taker's desk in the back of the room. She didn't even have to look at old Maskelyne to feel the continued intensity of his observation. The spirits left him alone, while Myers and Sidgwick exclaimed that strong hands poked and prodded them. Nora cried out when a hard object whacked her on the head. Nevil Maskelyne let people know that there were hands all over his body. Eusapia smiled. John King was doing well.

Do you want to see spirit limbs grow out of my body? Eusapia asked Nevil Maskelyne.

That's what I'm waiting for, he responded eagerly.

But promise on your life not to touch them. Contact with any body part could cause convulsions and lead to my death.

You can trust me, Nevil assured her pleasantly.

Then stand two feet behind me.

Nevil placed himself in direct line to her back. The feeblest beam of light illuminated her shoulder. Eusapia sat very quiet for a moment. The room was now completely silent. Suddenly, Nevil could hear the medium blow gently. An extra hand grew slowly out of her shoulder, then withdrew immediately. Again it appeared and disappeared.

Can you see the limb well? Eusapia inquired.

I do, Nevil confirmed.

He watched until Eusapia slumped into a heap and became unresponsive. For fear of missing crucial details, he sat down beside her again.

Bring me back to my room, she requested plaintively. As she seemed unable to walk, Nevil carried her back and laid her on her bed.

Without warning, her strong arms pulled him toward her body. Taken by surprise, he fell on her. Her hot lips melted his. Her fire breath seared through him. As footsteps sounded near the bedroom, Nevil was released from her embrace and pulled himself up. By the time Nora and Effie entered the room, Eusapia lay unconscious on her bed. Nora touched her and checked her pulse.

Don't worry, Nevil said, I think she is still very much alive.

Are you sure? Effie asked.

Very sure.

The mischievous tone of Nevil's voice reassured the women. They all left the room to give Eusapia time to restore her powers.

Eusapia immediately fell into a deep sleep, but woke up again barely an hour later. Lying in bed, her arms crossed behind her head, she became aware of the excited twittering of voices through the door. The investigators had remained in the séance room to discuss the evening. Refreshed from her sleep, she sat up and listened. She had expected the humming of approval after a rather spectacular show. What were they saying? She couldn't make out individual words, but was shocked by the unpleasant jarring in the voices, which could only mean disaster. Why? What had gone wrong? It must be old Maskelyne. She should have resisted Nevil's inviting body and kept her eyes on his father at all times. Eusapia felt a sudden urge to assess the situation more closely. Cautiously she left the room and eavesdropped from the hallway, but was too agitated to process even familiar English words that could have explained the meaning of her hosts' grumbling and blathering. To make sense of conversations, she had to see expressions.

As she glanced unseen through the slightly opened door, she saw old Maskelyne, who was wearing a skirt like hers that covered his legs, give a demonstration with her séance table, all the while explaining and instructing Nora to turn the lights on and off, so that he could contrast the tricks. And what a difference light and darkness made! Maskelyne used his wrists, fingers, thighs, feet and toes to expose how she raised the table in different manners, repeating his feats with the light completely dimmed to hide his movements, talking more dramatically to show the investigators how easily she distracted them and how their talking or singing covered any noise from her actions. After the table was raised, with him leaning backwards, still distracting everyone, he was slowly pulled back into an upright position by the table which slipped back down to the floor. When he leaned back again, he was able to extend his arm to the seemingly out-of-reach little wicker table behind him and pulled it toward him, lifted it with his teeth and placed it upside down on the table. He knocked on the table, and with his hand skilfully skipping over the wooden plate, produced answering raps, not as expertly as herself, but well enough to explain how the sounds were produced. Eusapia could read outrage and anger in her sitters' faces. Myers wiped sweat from his temples, and his body trembled. Nora shook her head in livid silence. Sidgwick gave a small speech Eusapia couldn't understand. Her eyes were fixed on Nevil Maskelyne. Oh no, not him. How could he! Using his father's props, he sat with his elbows on the table, his hands resting calmly. When Nora turned on the light, it was clear that the hands jutting out of his jacket sleeves and looking amazingly real in the darkness were fake. Nevil proceeded to also illustrate how Eusapia had squished her free arm under her blouse to her body, then let it protrude out of one of the many openings of her clothes as a spirit limb. His demonstration was poorly executed, but frighteningly accurate.

Infuriated by his betrayal and desperate to create a new mystery, Eusapia took hold of a vase on the console beside her, raised her arm, aimed for the miserable group of people and released the vase, which flew spinning toward the middle of the table. Before she heard it shatter into pieces, she raced back into her room and onto her bed. With the strength of her willpower, she calmed her heaving chest. When the door opened, she lay motionless as if unconscious.

She is in bed, Eusapia heard Effie whispering.

Nora just grunted as they approached.

She is barely breathing, Effie added in a low voice. There is no way she could be behind this latest incident.

Relieved, Eusapia fell back asleep. When she joined the others though, she was greeted with frosty politeness. What's wrong now? she thought, frowning.

Regrettably, we have come to the conclusion that your phenomena are consistently produced by trickery, Sidgwick addressed her in a tone that trembled with the graveness of the situation.

Eusapia flew into a rage.

What are you talking about?!! If there has been any cheating, it's because I haven't been controlled properly. It's your fault. It's your fault, she repeated and pointed her finger accusingly into one face after the other.

It's our opinion, Sidgwick continued, that besides cheating in your conscious state, you never fall into a complete trance. Everything about you is pretence and fraud.

Eusapia, who saw her livelihood disappear, flew at old Maskelyne, clutching and pulling his hair in murderous fury. It was young Maskelyne who extricated his father from her grip.

You fools, Eusapia screamed, just because I cheat when given the opportunity doesn't mean I'm a not a medium with powers few others possess. You'll regret your decision. One day, you'll beg me for forgiveness. With that, she snatched her plate and extra bread, and stomped back to her room.

Luckily, she already had an invitation from two of Richet's friends, who were both in London at the time: Colonel Albert de Rochas and Dr. Xavier Dariex, the editor of the French journal for psychical sciences. While Eusapia remained holed up in her room, Effie, who had the softest heart of the gang, brought her food on a tray. Eusapia ate but refused to talk except for screeching the name of Colonel de Rochas.

Colonel de Rochas, she repeated over and over. Colonel! Colonel! Now!

The meaning was clear. So why wasn't he here yet?

Maybe we could go for a walk? Effie suggested, and with clear and precise gestures indicated walking outside.

Colonel! Eusapia insisted.

When he finally arrived with Dr. Dariex, she grabbed the men by their arms.

Take me away. Please, take me away from these people, she beseeched them frantically and pulled them out of the house, the housekeeper running after them with her suitcase.

At the residence of Colonel de Rochas, Eusapia took back her life and her optimism even though she had been declared a fraud by the Cambridge contingent and feared that the repercussions on her income and opportunities might be severe. In this new location and in friendly company, phenomena occurred with ease again. Eusapia was in her element. When she

349

heard Colonel de Rochas describe psychic powers as exteriorised motricity, she looked pleased. Yes, that's what it was. Dr. Dariex took copious notes. His readers were hungry for new information. Notions like ghostly protuberances and exterior motricity would catch their attention and counteract the negative impact of the Cambridge investigation. Society wasn't done with metaphysics yet. The circulation of his journal would still increase and the satisfying tinkle of coins continue. Eusapia and the two French men had a good time, worthy of extensive celebration with unlimited food and drink. Excited conversation rose and swirled joyfully around the room.

Those Cambridge people, Eusapia and the men complained, how could anyone expect authentic psychic powers to manifest themselves in their presence when they display such unprofessional and insensitive behaviour? They deserved what they got. To witness psychic phenomena, you had to display the professionalism and faith of people like themselves or Richet and Lodge. De Rochas, Dariex and Eusapia nodded sombrely, took their glasses of wine and drank to their own genius and to their new and eternal friendship.

Fate had sent Eusapia's way these two like-minded, nonthreatening men, tasked to resurrect her from the Cambridge debacle and tend to her scars. She remained a full two weeks in their company before leaving with them for the continent. Reassured by the turn of events, Eusapia knew she had nothing to fear. She'd survive. She could leave this damp and strange country with her income secure. Bye Cambridge, goodbye forever, England. Hello to renewed and successful fraternisation with ghosts.

Paris, 1898; Genoa, 1901;
Paris, 1905-1906

10

EUSAPIA ARRIVED IN A PARIS WHERE the academic world responded to the steady rumours of Dr. Charles Richet's interest in spirit phenomena with a mixture of fascination, disbelief, mockery and cynicism. His reputation as a scientist was too stellar to write him off as crazy. It was such that some colleagues happened to wonder whether he could be right. Others thought it best to indulge him and his ghosts. The least charitable ones called him a lunatic in private without however losing respect for his academic brilliance.

Richet was not immune to what his peers thought of him and wanted to prove them wrong, especially after the Cambridge fiasco. No one would make a fool of him. After all his scientific breakthroughs, there was no justification for anyone to question his convictions concerning psychic phenomena. The world would learn that his sharp intuition necessarily led to the truth. Even if some of the experiments with mediums were not as conclusive as he made them out to be, and trickery was rampant, there was no doubt in his mind that invisible psychic currents existed. If his critics had been privileged enough to witness occurrences like those on Île Roubaud, they too would believe in Eusapia's authenticity. He would never give up on his mission to cross scientific boundaries and discover new phenomena, name their properties, categorise and explain them to less intelligent and perceptive scientists. His superior intellect and openness to new ideas in any field let him perceive presences not explainable by the physical laws he knew so well. Nothing in the world, not unsuccessful experiments or crooked mediums could deter him from his bold convictions. His colleagues owed him at least the respect of taking the possibility of new truths seriously. He would not fail in persuading them that metaphysical dimensions were there to be explored. More academics needed to join the ranks of those investigating these new frontiers.

Eusapia was contentedly seated in Richet's library, her eyes alive with a warm, wine-induced glow. But she didn't need the wine to understand her friend. Why would anyone doubt that you could communicate with the otherworld? Not if you knew first-hand that your dead mother comforted you when you needed her. Yes, the departed stayed with you. Even Richet with his crazy ideas had to acknowledge that once a human being died, something lingered behind. One day, Eusapia thought, he'd have to realise that it's more than just particles left suspended between life and death. He'll get proof of a full-fledged afterlife.

While Eusapia tried to catch a quick glimpse of the world beyond, Richet wondered what the properties of a dead person's invisible remains might be and how temporary they were. As rudimentary as the knowledge of the afterlife was at this point, once uncovered and understood, it bore the possibility of revealing unknown aspects of the universe.

Eusapia smiled at Richet. She liked him. He never questioned her. When she had a bad séance, and doubts about her mediumship arose, she was convinced that he'd do anything in his power to help her phenomena along because in the end this served a greater truth. Whenever she needed a push, she expected that push to come. She never talked to Richet about it, or asked for anything. But as long as he was around, tables would rise and his colleagues and friends would see supernatural phenomena. It was a fortunate coincidence that she and Richet had similar hypnotic powers, and his power of suggestion matched hers.

Salute, she said.

Santé, Richet replied, and gave an enthusiastic toast to the success of her séances in his nasal yet strangely melodious Italian.

The energy of Paris almost compared with Naples. Still, the sky was not as blue, there was no Vesuvius and no Mediterranean Sea. But Eusapia had to admit that you could have fun in the French capital. Richet introduced her to fabulous bistros. She loved the Jardin du Luxembourg: its fountains, puppet theatre, bee-house, actually everything about its happy to and fro. She never said no to a stroll along the Seine or through the Latin Quarter. When they happened to go by Notre Dame Cathedral, Richet did not stop.

I want to see the church again, Eusapia said.

You want to pray? Richet asked, a note of incredulity in his voice.

I want to pray and I want to see.

See what? Richet asked without noticing that Eusapia felt insulted. It was beyond him to envision that an uneducated

353

person like herself could appreciate stained glass windows or the impressive experience of space and light and shadows in a cathedral.

I want to see, she repeated stubbornly.

With all his knowledge, Richet could not figure out where the hurt in her voice was coming from. Reluctantly, he accompanied her into the cathedral. To her dismay, he did not feel the need to point out architectural details or explain the history of the building as he had done last time when one of his colleagues was with them. Okay, Eusapia thought, her resentment mounting, if that's how you see me, I won't explain anything either. Richet seemed in a hurry to leave and continue their round of bistros. That was more at her level. Cathedrals belonged to another sphere. He would come back here with Myers, whom he expected to arrive in Paris any time now. Myers with his culture and mysticism would make the visit a worthwhile experience. Clearly recognising how Richet delegated her to what he deemed her rightful place, Eusapia continued to sulk. His gallantries, and the good wine and *coq au vin* he ordered to appease her, failed to pull her out of her black mood.

I'm sorry if I upset you, Richet said, trying to stop her from banging her glass and the bottle on the table and shooting daggers with her eyes,

Eusapia could see that he had no clue what her tantrum was about. Even if she explained, he wouldn't understand. It's strange how the most educated people can in some ways be so clueless. She wondered how he would have related to her friends from the travelling show. Would he have seen beyond their more unusual features or the dark skin of some of her friends? Right now, she doubted it. Despite this sudden realisation, she calmed

354

down. Cut him some slack, she admonished herself. You depend on his good will.

After two more glasses of a full-bodied Bordeaux wine in which she detected Neapolitan flavours like almond and peach, but also hints of pepper, thyme and licorice, she felt better. How could she forget that his weakness made her strong? It gave her the power to exploit it to her advantage. She raised her glass again.

To science, she said and laughed sardonically. Richet neglected to ask her for an explanation, presuming that her toast was without significance.

When Myers arrived in Paris, Eusapia stayed out of his way as much as possible. She couldn't deal with his wounded expression, his dying-deer eyes staring at her full of accusation. He was still upset with her. Not that he came out and said so, but his closed-off stiff body couldn't give a clearer message. Except for a lukewarm hello, he avoided talking to her. To him, she was a common cheat who played with the noblest and deepest human emotions. Nothing could be more sacrilegious and despicable. Eusapia looked at her friend Richet. He almost imperceptibly shook his head, meaning that this was not good at all. Lucky for her, Richet too hoped for Myers to keep an open mind and to agree to a re-examination of Eusapia's phenomena. She may have cheated in Cambridge, but on his island, she had been genuine. Myers, lighten up, Richet seemed to say, here is your chance for authentic communication with the otherworld, don't throw this opportunity away without a serious second look.

For all his efforts and intense discussions on metaphysics, Richet made no progress. Myers remained resistant. Richet decided it was time to bring in a spiritualist friend of his as reinforcement. This friend, a medical doctor, was similar in character to Myers, more importantly, both men had suffered great loss, Myers his first love, the doctor his young wife. As expected, the two men took to each other from the instant they met and trust between them developed quickly. Myers admitted that he found it impossible that anyone could find perfect love twice in a lifetime. Any subsequent love could only be a poor substitute, one that provided companionship at best, but never again the deep feeling and connection that fully unites and transports you to a higher sphere of consciousness. The doctor agreed without reservations.

I need to reconnect with my wife, he said. Do you think there is any chance that Eusapia, despite all her vulgarity and cheating, might have the power to establish connections with the otherworld? If our love is so supernaturally strong and our loved ones respond with the same intensity, don't you think that the paths of those feelings are fated to meet at some point and that even the poorest excuse of a medium could constitute a conduit for reunification?

Myers wavered. Was it possible? No. Thinking of Eusapia's blatant lies and trickery, he saw no redeeming aspect that would allow for such a possibility.

But if we lose hope and give up, don't we betray our love? the doctor asked in a voice that trembled with sadness.

As Myers was turning the question in his head, the doctor was called away to an emergency.

Richet, who had remained silent during their whole conversation, took Myers by the arm. His doctor friend had sowed the first seeds. Now it was up to him to nourish those seeds and make them grow.

Eusapia watched the two men strolling down the street. She counted on Richet being persuasive as always. What were they doing now? Myers stopped and just stood there, suddenly motionless, listening attentively to Richet's speech. Eusapia had seen Richet draw his listeners fully into his symphony of words many times. Under his baton, the words expanded and under his lead almost danced to the spot he had intended from the beginning. Since she had never been able to understand much of his discourse without translation, she always focussed on his eyes. They alone made the spectacle worthwhile. As if they were instruments of magic, they made people shiver and believe that they were given entry into the intricate workings of the universe.

While Eusapia reflected on Richet's interactions with others, the men disappeared. She didn't see them again until late in the afternoon. Myers seemed more relaxed, even upbeat. The dead have a chance again, Eusapia murmured to herself. She looked at Myers with her dark, intense eyes. Though still on edge, he held her gaze. She could feel that if she gave him reason and encouragement, he might want to trust her again.

It was her turn to do the persuading. She effectively recycled her tried-and-true excuse that unbelievers in the room weaken her strength so much that phenomena can only manifest themselves through fraudulent means. Then she promised Myers that from now on she'd invest her whole being into establishing a link with loved ones and rather admit defeat than use trickery in her next séance.

An unexpected lone tear rolled down Eusapia's cheek because she couldn't give Myers what he needed. He must have heard the sincerity in her voice. His scowl slowly disappeared. Richet was right: this woman deserved another chance.

It was rare that Eusapia went into one of her séances with such apprehension. But Myers' desperate need for otherworldly communication put the fear of God in her. She did not want to hurt him. He might be uptight, but he was a good man. Good men were rare these days. Better take care of the few that were left.

Richet pressed Eusapia's hand and she could feel that he wanted to reassure her. Don't worry, he seemed to say.

Eusapia asked Richet to draw the curtains and dim the lights. The room darkened drastically, but they still could make out each other's faces.

Sing, please, Eusapia requested.

Myers intoned the first notes of a hymn, but without the leading voice of his wife, he faltered. Richet, who refused to sing, called his housekeeper to do the job. Despite her good voice, Eusapia wasn't pleased. What was listening compared to singing? She needed her sitters' minds occupied. To her relief, Myers was wholly engaged by the pure, childlike voice of the housekeeper who, in stark contrast to Eusapia and her crass antics, led him mercifully away from everyday unpleasantries. While patiently awaiting the manifestation of spirits in the room, he marvelled at the innocence of the woman's rendition. He knew from experience that music itself was capable of elevating humans.

We're getting closer, Myers said reflectively.

Richet nodded.

Eusapia watched the two men carefully. Nothing escaped her, not their slowed-down breathing, not their increasingly relaxed expressions. She pulled the heavy window curtains together to cloud out the last bit of brightness and gradually turned down the lights until the only visibility came from a soft shimmer of red light in the far left corner of the room.

The time for falling into her trance had come. Eusapia squirmed. Unearthly sounds came out of her mouth. Myers winced. A tad of refinement would be more conducive to a spiritual experience. He sat stiffly, his legs firmly planted on the floor, his hands gripping the seat of his chair as if he could be thrown off.

A-a-an-nie-ie, Eusapia whispered in a hoarse voice. It took only this one word, the name of a woman whose importance to him he was sure no one was aware of, to throw Myers off balance. Gone was the controlled dignity. A tremor shook his body as if he were a rag doll. He remained upright in his chair by sheer willpower.

The table rose triumphantly and came down swaying and dancing. The curtains of the cabinet billowed out and swung back. Hands grabbed and poked the two men. A head rested on Myers shoulder. After pressing a gentle kiss on his cheek, it disappeared. Myers couldn't refrain from crying out in pain, tormented anew by his unrequited love for which there could be no peace except in death.

Eusapia absorbed his pain. She felt with him.

A second kiss lit on Myers' cheek. Eusapia thought she saw a trace of a smile on his face.

A trumpet played softly and a mandolin played a simple tune.

Then it was over. Richet turned the lights back on. After a few restless gasps for air, Eusapia quieted down. Neither of the two men moved or said a word. Without looking, Eusapia had no doubt that Myers was sitting hunched, his elbows on the table, his forearms supporting his head, his face buried in his hands. Richet took Eusapia's pulse. He touched her face to find out whether she was feverish. He seemed calm, almost serene.

Later he helped Eusapia to her room.

After he left, she could hear the soft murmur of the two men.

I hope Myers found what he was looking for, she thought, confident that this was the case. She smiled to herself and thanked the late Annie Fairlamb for the indelible impression she had made on Myers during her short life. It always helps to have allies on the other side.

When she awoke the next morning, she had the usual, after-séance upset stomach and sore throat, but otherwise opened her eyes to a world that looked friendlier and more promising than she'd experienced since Cambridge. She stretched luxuriously. She wanted to stay in bed and have breakfast served in her room, though the aroma of freshly brewed coffee tempted her to join the men. The bits and pieces of their conversation reaching her through the walls sounded positive, confirming her assumption that she'd done well the night before. An hour later, there was a knock on her door and Richet entered.

Don't move, he said, I'll have breakfast brought to your room.

You don't want me out there? Eusapia asked, a touch of bitterness in her voice.

You did so well, Richet tried to appease her, you might want to let the glow of last night do its magic. Your presence might contrast with the emotions yesterday's phenomena evoked in our friend Myers. Let him savour this special moment for as long as possible.

Eusapia knew exactly what Richet implied.

Well, all right then, she responded and requested five croissants and a big pot of strong coffee as compensation.

Eusapia wondered what Richet told Myers about her physical and mental state. But then it didn't matter, as long as Myers turned into a believer. For a moment, flashes of anger surged up in her. Treating her like a common cheat! Those Cambridge people! The mere thought of them made her gag. Who did they think they were? Not only did they have this sense of being born superior, they felt entitled to die superior too. Furious to the bone, Eusapia spit on the floor. She was mollified when the housekeeper arrived with the coffee. Its effect was immediate, like a drug it stopped the running commentary in her head and calmed her down. From one second to the next, a smile pulled up the corners of her lips. Ah, food! Only a person who'd been hungry too many times could take such pleasure in the smells and tastes of food! She devoured the croissants and pieces of cheese heartily, washing them down with big gulps of coffee.

What did Myers say? Eusapia asked Richet when he dropped in a few hours later to see how she was doing.

He felt a comforting presence in the room that could not come from an earthly source.

Eusapia nodded.

Do you want me to give another séance tonight before his departure tomorrow evening?

No, I think the last one made an impression on him that would be hard to replicate. You should take this time to rest and regenerate your psychic powers.

Is Myers fully convinced now?

Well, he seems to believe that channels to the otherworld were opened through your mediumship and that for a few moments some sort of communication got through and reached him in the form of a poignant presence more compelling than any words.

Eusapia looked at Richet, trying to figure out what he thought of Myers' experience. His eyes gave nothing away, except maybe a bit of relief over Myers' conversion.

On Richet's advice, Eusapia remained in her room. She did not see Myers before his departure. However much she would have liked to bask in his newfound approval of her, she had to admit that absence had its advantages.

Eusapia's next stop was the home of Camille Flammarion, a leading astronomer and one of France's most popular authors. She had met him several times and couldn't wait to see Flammarion's flashing eyes that exploded with life and excitement. Even his copious hair and beard made dramatic statements. His body connected people to the skies and, just like hers, was a channel to mysterious worlds. A remarkable man, she had to admit.

This way, please, Flammarion's wife Sylvie said, as she led Eusapia into their library. Eusapia had never seen so many books in one place. In Angela's room there were two books. Giorgio and Richet had over fifty each for sure. Here the walls were made of books! Volumes and volumes of books, one beside the other, covering every inch of the wall. Sylvie noticed Eusapia's shocked gaze.

My husband's brother is a publisher, she said simply.

To Eusapia, this was no explanation. Who wrote those books? Who read them? Besides Giorgio and Richet and a few other academics, she had rarely encountered people who put their noses into books, except for the Bible, which was different and didn't count.

Sylvie tried to pull Eusapia along. But as if turned to stone, Eusapia did not move. She tuned into the stories of those pages with their emotions of beauty and horror. Behind the covers of those books was life. She distinctly heard the clamouring, the whispered seductions, grievances, laments, and Giorgio-style grand ideas. The messages from the shelves reached her more clearly than those from the dead.

Eusapia? Sylvie asked, touching her arm as if to wake her up.

Excuse me, Eusapia grumbled, keeping up a facade of politeness, but annoyed that anyone would dare to pull her from this strange world of jiggling letters and words.

If you want to read any of the books, please let me know and I will make the necessary arrangements, Sylvie said. The insincerity in her voice offended Eusapia and she stomped ahead in dismay. Why did Sylvie have to make it so obvious that Eusapia, whom she clearly considered illiterate, was out of place between the walls of books? Why could she not even entertain the notion that Eusapia was drawn to this strange world? Eusapia spit on the floor as if throwing down the gauntlet.

It was Sylvie's turn to take offence.

What's wrong? she asked coldly.

Eusapia didn't answer. She continued staring at the books and at the bookshelves with their designs of stars, moons, zodiac signs, and astrological instruments. Many people she knew became spooked when offered a glimpse into the world of the dead. To her, these walls of books were much more haunting. They made a cruel statement of closed off worlds to which only the rich and privileged were given keys.

363

Eusapia plonked down in the middle of the room.

To hell with the books, she screamed, while the woman beside her flinched. Leave me alone.

Sylvie wrung her hands, not knowing how to react. When the minutes passed and Eusapia remained planted on the floor, she discreetly left the room to get her husband. Flammarion was able to convince Eusapia to get up and prepare the cabinet for her séance. He did not understand her agitation or what she was complaining about in a shrill voice and in her strongest and most expressive Neapolitan dialect.

That night, Eusapia's phenomena presented themselves quite differently than in previous séances Flammarion had attended. Gone were the gentle touches and kisses, gone were the smiling apparitions. Threatening raps exploded from the walls of books, then echoed from opposite sides. A cacophony of sounds swirled in vicious circles through the room. Nothing soothing, nothing uplifting. The mandolin jumped on the table where all four pairs of strings snapped in two. From the table it shot straight to the top of Eusapia's head and remained swaying there for an eternity before crashing down to the ground behind Sylvie. The next moment, the empty walnut chair behind Eusapia landed on the table. A trumpet tooted garishly near the window. Flammarion and his wife had barely time to check what caused the ruckus, when the chair took off from the table and, diving toward Sylvie, almost crushed her foot.

Why are the spirits so angry? Sylvie asked, terrified.

They must reflect the medium's mood, Flammarion suggested. That's the only explanation I can think of. I've never seen them like that before.

Is John King here? Flammarion asked into the darkened room, but received no answer.

Eusapia started writhing, and her moans rattled through the room. Sylvie grabbed her husband's hand across the table for reassurance. The next moment, his hand was yanked away from her as Eusapia's body fell on Flammarion, pushing him backwards. His wife gasped. Neither husband nor wife moved until finally Sylvie resolutely stood up and turned on the lights. Flammarion extricated himself from the tight embrace of the medium and propped her up so that she wouldn't fall. With the help of his wife he guided Eusapia to her room and laid her on her bed. They watched her for a while, hesitant to leave the room for fear the ghosts had caused serious harm to the medium.

On her return trip to Italy, Eusapia's smile came back. After the disaster in Cambridge, she had redeemed herself in London, then in France. The support of Richet, Myers and Flammarion guaranteed a continued stream of academic and rich visitors with their endless supplies of money, food and drink, providing her with the means to save a few otherwise doomed youngsters from a fate like Maria's and Anna's, and allowing her to hand out bread and blankets to frail and old homeless people. Most of all, Eusapia simply rejoiced in coming home to her country with its sun, sea, volcano, tasty food, heavy Chianti, and the laughter and heated discussions of her own people. Here, she understood every word again with no effort. Her pronouncements, insights, jokes and insults were not lost, and she had no need for an intermediary who probably misrepresented everything she said. In Naples, before she even finished a sentence, repartees sallied forth, and she could rally back with even wittier and more provocative retorts. Eusapia's pulse quickened. She'd rejuvenate the moment she set foot on Italian soil, cheerfully skipping through the streets, her brilliant black hair bouncing, her roguish eyes spewing lava again as if in cahoots with Vesuvius itself.

Nothing could erase the hatred Eusapia harboured toward Cambridge and all it entailed. Yet, staying abroad gave her a new appreciation for her country. Everything she needed was right here. Her stories about the strange food in other countries and the eccentricities of the people there kept her audience entertained. Whether rich or poor, it certainly was good to be Italian and to live in a country where the language was the twin of music.

Eusapia made a decent living. With the years, however, her sitters badgered her for phenomena not seen before and, when they didn't come forward, customers became scarcer, though she still managed to avoid hardship.

A surprise invitation from Dr. Enrico Morselli, neurologist and director of the Clinic of Nervous and Mental Disease at the University of Genoa, perked Eusapia up. He invited her to his laboratory for eight months of thorough testing. She knew that she had to thank Richet for this new opportunity. His testimony carried weight. He needed friends and colleagues to believe in her and wanted them to corroborate his own results. Even if Eusapia's phenomena happened to be less convincing when others investigated her, his friends would give her the benefit of the doubt. Since Richet had seen the real thing, they would ascribe less than satisfactory performances to exhaustion or negative outside interference, or to a temporary loss of psychic power. Eusapia knew also that Richet counted on her to meet expectations. She would not let him down.

Eusapia had met Morselli before when another famous Italian, the criminologist Cesare Lombroso, examined her. Morselli must be almost exactly her age, maybe a year or two older, certainly not past fifty. She looked forward to seeing him again.

Well, hello, my friend, Eusapia exclaimed joyfully, good to see you again. She studied him closely. His hair had thinned and receded a bit, but with the exception of two grey strands was still black. His bushy moustache, chiselled into sharp points, still made a strong statement of authority, contrasting oddly with the modest and kind expression of his eyes. Eusapia openly stared at him. Ochorowicz had told her that Morselli had written an important book on suicide. Suicide? She hadn't known about this when they first met. She broke into a cold sweat. Suicide was not something she ever wanted to think about, not after what happened with Raphael's friend Mario. Why would Morselli want to tackle such a painful subject? To help people in crisis? She hadn't realised that Mario was in trouble. Would Morselli have been able to prevent his death? She doubted it.

Why so serious, my dear Eusapia? Morselli asked. Don't you remember me? Didn't we have good times together?

Enrico! I don't know what came over me just now. I'm overjoyed to meet again, Eusapia exclaimed and exuberantly threw her arms around him and kissed him vigorously on the mouth.

Morselli chuckled.

You haven't changed, Eusapia. You're exactly the way I remember you.

367

And you like what you see?

Remembering his position as a serious researcher, doctor, and director of a mental institution, Morselli took a small step backwards and said in an unexpectedly measured voice, I can't wait to work with you again.

As the two of them strolled through the narrow alleys and streets of the city, Morselli took pleasure in Eusapia's enthusiastic exclamations. Genoa was a port city like Naples where you could watch the ships set sail or dock in the harbour all day long. Standing in the shadow of the old brick lighthouse The Laterna, Eusapia listened to Morselli explain that it was the tallest lighthouse in the world and the most famous landmark of the city. They walked slowly along the shore. Eusapia impulsively took off her shoes and dangled her feet from rocks or ledges into the water wherever possible. Morselli couldn't believe his eyes. Here of all places! In the harbour! No other woman he knew would be audacious enough for such extravagance. To Eusapia, the sea seemed alive with an almost mystical promise. It made her new.

I'm whole again, she stated when she withdrew her feet from the water. Come on, Enrico! Feel the power of nature. Neither the wooden desk nor the four walls of your library will renew you. No, it's here, where water and air meet, and purity and filth come together in a strange concoction that we are reborn.

Morselli smiled. What an odd woman, he thought, a disconcerting stream of conflicting emotions slithering through his body.

When they sat on a rock to rest, Eusapia jumped back up, then knelt down unselfconsciously and pulled the shoes off his feet.

Come on, Morselli, feel what it means to be alive.

She shoved him in front of her to the edge of the water. When he hesitated, afraid of the slippery patches and treacherous waves, she gave him a push so that he almost fell. Shaken, he stood in the water, not knowing what to do next.

But when Eusapia stared at him expectantly, he couldn't help but see the glowing reflection of the sun in her eyes.

Isn't life wonderful! Eusapia burst out.

Morselli, who hadn't taken his nose out of his papers and books for months as he struggled with new ideas on psychiatric treatments, suddenly felt free, as if a load had been taken off his shoulders. He felt the blaze of the sun, he smelled the saltiness of the water, he experienced the gentle breath of the wind in his hair.

Yes, he responded, as if awakening from an eternity of dead sleep. Yes, he repeated, yes, yes. Still slightly confused, he didn't know whether he imagined Eusapia's watery hands all over his face, tracing his lips, his moustache. He wasn't sure whether she was actually touching him in the most startling places or if he was under a spell. True or not, his body soaked up the new experience, starved for the intoxicating nourishment it couldn't remember receiving before. When he looked at Eusapia, she seemed to contemplate the water, the air, and the sun. Yet he felt her hands all over his body. He didn't want this feeling to end.

Enrico? . . . Enrico?

What? he finally responded.

You like it here?

I do, he said.

This time he was sure that Eusapia put her hand on his arm. Her face was very close.

369

I'm happy you're showing me the city, Eusapia confided. She pulled the bewildered man back on top of the rock where they could sit down. She knelt down, dried his feet with her skirt and slowly put his shoes back on.

Do you want me to give you a séance tonight? Eusapia asked after a sumptuous meal of beef and macaroni that they washed down with a bottle of red wine.

I would like that very much, Morselli agreed eagerly. He had received letters from Charles Richet, Oliver Lodge, and William Crookes, three of the most esteemed scientists, detailing the phenomena Eusapia was able to generate. While admitting that she often resorted to fraud when not properly controlled, they made it clear that in their view most of her phenomena were authentic. As a bitter skeptic of paranormal phenomena, Morselli couldn't wait to see with his own eyes what Eusapia had to offer.

Eusapia prepared her cabinet.

How are we going to do this? she asked. How will you be able to exert proper control all by yourself?

Don't worry, I will know if you liberate an arm or a leg to produce your phenomena.

Are you sure? she asked, uncertainly. Maybe you should invite a friend or a neighbour.

No, I don't need diversions.

As you wish, Eusapia stated curtly, but make certain you control me without fail. I want to ensure that tonight you see the real thing.

Don't insult me, Sapia, I'm an experienced investigator.

Very well, then, Enrico. Let the show begin.

She sat so close to him that her body pressed against his.

Feeling me this way, she explained, you will notice right away if I use a hand or foot fraudulently.

Morselli refused to sing or allow any other distractions.

I need to hear the slightest bit of noise or rustling.

So Eusapia sat quietly beside him until the potent mingling of their body heat put both of them into a new phase of consciousness.

It was time for her trance.

Soon, among her wriggling and fidgeting, Morselli was poked and prodded. What was going on? He held both her hands firmly in his own. But there it was again, a shove in his back, then suggestive strokes in the groin area. In a sudden explosion of raps, tooting, and chirping, the table rose. A cold breeze blew in his face from the spot of white hair on Eusapia's head. Strange lights flitted through the room. Morselli suddenly felt awed. Was this real? More likely, Eusapia was hypnotising or tricking him. Did the wine impair his judgement? Or were higher forces at play? He stared at the woman beside him and at her two hands now pressing down on his right hand. It was impossible that she could have freed one hand or both and artificially created the unexplainable occurrences around him. Eusapia moaned, slowly emerging from her trance and collapsing into Morselli's lap. When she opened her eyes, she did not seem to know where she was and who she was with. Her arms suddenly jerked up, gripped Morselli's head and pulled him toward her, as he willingly followed her lead. This is the real phenomenon, she thought elatedly, his body connecting with mine.

The next day, Eusapia remained in her room. It was only the day after that she let Morselli coax her to join him in the dining room.

We should have another séance, he said eagerly after she had devoured everything on her plate in record time as if it were her last meal.

My dear Enrico, Eusapia said, placing her hand demurely on his, my powers have left me. I have tried to recharge them, but I feel empty and unable to find any psychic substance.

How can that be? Your powers were so strong the other night.

Maybe I'm exhausted. I'm not thirty anymore, Enrico.

Just take your time. I want to experience all your phenomena.

It's not that easy, Eusapia responded.

But on Richet's island, you were able to produce phenomena day after day. What's different now?

Who knows the intentions of the universe? Eusapia said gravely, maybe another medium was given the task to take over and fulfil the promise of the early phenomena.

Morselli understood that there was no point insisting. He would give Eusapia all the time she needed to recuperate. As a researcher, he was known for his patience. So it surprised him how anxious he was to attend another of Eusapia's séances. It can wait, he thought, but suggested that she'd give it another try in the evening.

Eusapia looked at him with her expressive eyes and shook her head.

Tomorrow then, Morselli heard himself plead.

I think I'm finished. It feels as if I'll never again be able to call up spirits.

Don't say that, Morselli interjected passionately. I want to study your phenomena. I want to know everything about them.

As the days and weeks went by, there was no sign of Eusapia's powers re-emerging.

I'm sorry to disappoint you, Eusapia said on one of their many excursions through the city.

I trust that your powers will reappear, Morselli responded.

While he was waiting for a change in her present condition, Eusapia explained to Morselli all the phenomena that happened on Richet's island and in the libraries and living rooms of other important men like Oliver Lodge and Camille Flammarion.

Enrico, Eusapia said, sometimes the powers are very strong. The table rises almost to the ceiling. Instruments start playing in concert, the guitar accompanying the trumpet, drums rolling, violins calling for the spirits to appear. In this turbulence of sounds, John King materialises, bringing messages from the departed. In his wake, spirits of the deceased find entry into the séance room. Many times, friends and relatives of the sitters, often parents or children, get through to their loved ones. Do you know how much comfort they bring to the ones they left behind? At times, they look at their relatives in silence, other times, they touch and kiss them. Their presence is overwhelming. It affects everyone in the room. Cold and hot air flows out of me as if to acclimatise the spirits to this world. Lights flicker all over the room. You hear the thumping of raps and their echoes.

Eusapia gazed into Enrico's eyes. His expression was animated. He could see the phenomena as clearly as if they were happening around them right now. His eyes glazed over in awe, he stared at the woman. What was she capable of? He remembered the long descriptions Richet had sent him from France. Oliver Lodge's words reverberated through his brain. From what Richet said, even the disappointed Myers, who had declared Eusapia a common cheat in Cambridge, even he had to revise his negative opinion and accept most of Eusapia's phenomena as authentic.

Feverishly, Morselli wrote down every word that came out of Eusapia's mouth. So many phenomena! It was incredible. As he wrote and continued writing, her descriptions started to take on fantastical proportions. He decided to categorise her phenomena and came up with thirty-nine varieties. The more time he spent with this curious medium, the more he became convinced that extraordinary occurrences took place in her presence.

With detailed letters arriving from France and England from scientists and other important people he held in high esteem, the pages of Morselli's notebook filled up with amazing speed. He could see the outline of a book forming right in front of his eyes. He wrote and read, and reread, and analysed. Eusapia filled in the gaps.

Do you want to know what happened at Colonel Albert de Rochas' house? Eusapia asked excitedly, her wide-open eyes fixed on a scene long past that seemed more present than anything else in the room.

I rose out of my chair, Eusapia exclaimed dramatically. I slowly rose toward the ceiling. I remained suspended above the table for at least five minutes. There I was, between floor and ceiling, my body as if on fire, bolts of lightning shooting out of it. When I looked down at my arms and legs, they were glowing with a strange golden light. Around me, ten different instruments played, and the wicker table danced. It was unreal.

Morselli stared at her in fascination, then hurried to write down her words. He didn't want to miss a single detail.

Eusapia all of a sudden fell silent. She crumpled into a fragile heap. Morselli had to prop her up in order to keep her sitting upright on her chair.

What is it? he whispered.

But there was no response. Eusapia looked exhausted as if the whole episode had happened this very moment. Morselli hailed a cab to bring her back to her living quarters and helped her into the carriage. She leaned against him as if unable to support her own body. Her left hand rested heavily on his thigh. Morselli didn't dare to move. When they arrived at her apartment, he guided Eusapia to her room and her bed. Afraid for her mental and physical wellbeing, he stayed with her to make sure she would not succumb to seizures or violent outbursts of hysteria.

When Morselli worked on his book the next day, he looked at all the material he had already accumulated. He might not have seen most of the phenomena with his own eyes, but to him they were as real as if he had observed them himself over and over again. Blank pages automatically filled with the vivid visions playing in front of him. He could see it all. In the presence of Richet, Lodge, Myers, even himself, the medium Eusapia was producing results he wouldn't have thought possible. Her phenomena fell into six major categories: mechanic movements involving contact with the medium, telekinetic movements executed without any contact, altered gravity of objects, sounds and signals, unexplained appearance of objects, and materialisations and ectoplasm. Despite Morselli's disappointment at Eusapia's temporary loss of powers, he felt revitalised. His book took shape without effort. There was nothing more exhilarating than starting a new project. Nothing made him feel more alive. His brain buzzed with ideas. His body felt twenty years younger. He already saw his book in the hands of his readers. *Psychology and Spiritism.* Yes, that was a respectable title. He would pull it off. What had possessed him to let the fear of running out of ideas paralyse him completely during the last few years? Why had he been convinced that his creative juices had dried up? Now he couldn't wait to get back to writing. When Eusapia said her goodbyes, he had fewer regrets than expected. It was the right moment for her to leave. He would be too busy with his project to entertain her.

Good luck, Enrico, Eusapia whispered, and for the last time burned her eyes into his. For a moment, Morselli felt pulled back into her aura of secrets and mysteries, only to realise almost instantly that the world of empty pages and scholarly erudition had an even more powerful hold on him.

As soon as Eusapia arrived back in Naples, she miraculously regained her powers. Well rested after her relaxing and rejuvenating stay in Genoa, she went about her business as a medium with renewed confidence. It was high time to be back. Deprived of Eusapia's generosity during her absence, two fragile old acquaintances had died. Several children suffered the same fate or had otherwise disappeared. Eusapia was most heartbroken that her little friend Claudio, an artistic eleven-year-old boy she had befriended during the past year, had died in excruciating pain after gnawing chicken bones he had picked off a pile of garbage. The loss of the orphan boy hurt almost as much as the loss of Celestina, who at least was still breathing and had a good life with Giorgio and his wife. Eusapia was grateful that Raphael was in town to console her because he too knew what loss was.

It's not your fault, Eusapia, he said. You can't watch over everyone.

Eusapia always could depend on him even if they saw each other only once or twice a year and he had moved on to other women and had children of his own to worry about. He never asked for anything. Since the birth of his first child, the plight of other children, to which he had turned a blind eye before, suddenly became a source of distress. When Eusapia wanted to give him money for his family, he would tell her to use it for the less fortunate.

He still liked to eat and drink. Whenever they were together, they went out and ordered all their favourite foods.

This time, he left most of the food untouched. Eusapia sensed an unusual heaviness like a cloak draped around him. She looked at him with concern. Something was wrong.

What is it, Raphael?

I don't want to take advantage of your generosity, Sapia.

I know that. What do you need?

My second daughter, Giuseppina, has been in an accident and lost one of her legs. I made her crutches so that she can get around, but she can't do any physical work anymore.

My God, Raphael, that's terrible. How old is Giuseppina now? Fourteen?

Fourteen in two months, and what a bright child she is. Regrettably, the schooling she got from the teacher in our village is worthless. A good education is Giuseppina's only chance now, and she'd succeed if given a chance. I'm sorry I have to ask for help. I should be able to provide for her myself.

Raphael, my friend and husband, we were brought together to support each other. Come back after your performance. In the meantime, I will give as many séances as I can and put the money aside.

You shouldn't have to do that, Raphael said, his voice raw with emotion

But I want to. I want to see Giuseppina embrace the future with hope.

You don't know what that means to me.

Come back soon. I'll be waiting for you.

Eusapia plunged into work. Giuseppina's wellbeing depended on her. Cripple or not, the girl needed to learn to fend for herself. If Eusapia had a say in it, Giuseppina would receive an education. Maybe she'd be able to work in an office later on. Eusapia called on Carla, a highly intelligent girl from her neighbourhood who had received her teacher's certificate but couldn't find a job. If Eusapia paid her salary, would she teach Raphael's daughter and any other children from the village he thought might benefit from extra teaching? Of course she would. To put her knowledge to use and not starve, how could anyone say no? And who knows where this experience might lead.

Before Raphael and Carla left for his village, Eusapia sold part of her treasure, then sent Carla shopping for books and other school material, as well as clothes for Giuseppina.

Teach well, Eusapia said, but no encouragement was necessary. All Carla ever wanted to do was teach. Her enthusiasm would give Giuseppina reason to see beyond her missing leg.

There was a new glitter in Raphael's eyes. His daughter had a chance.

Long after the two had left, Eusapia indulged in visions of Giuseppina reading and writing and, most of all, smiling. Thinking of the young girl evoked memories of Celestina. For Eusapia, Celestina would always remain a child. But no, Celestina — or Rosa, who might have become Rose or Rosy by now — was a grown woman who had already turned thirty. God Almighty, time passes, Eusapia thought and shuddered. During all the years gone by, every living cell in her had been waiting for a call from her daughter. It had never come. She hoped this was because Giorgio and Lillian gave her all the support she needed. Celestina? Eusapia called out into the air. Celestina? Her daughter did not appear. She did not answer. Eusapia tried to home in on the faraway spot that held her invisible daughter. She wanted reassurance that there was a smile on Celestina's face. But as much as she tried, she could not fill the blank space in the air.

Eusapia worked hard. Most of Naples knew who she was. Sitters once again came from all over town, awestruck by Eusapia's display of psychic powers. Her spirit control John King often added a darkish dimension to her séances. Materialisations of other spirits were more likely to bring joy or consolation. They would stroke her sitters' faces, kiss their cheeks, even their lips, and whisper sweet words into receptive ears.

Money flowed. Eusapia ate well and drank with abundance in the company of her friends, though she could never turn a blind eye to the outstretched hands on the street. The misery in peoples' eyes opened her wallet. She understood their sad stories without words. There were days when the injustices in this world seemed so crass that she fell back into her old habits. Why should her rich sitters have so much and others starve beside them? In those moments, watches and brooches disappeared again and were traded to feed additional mouths. There were days when she spent all her money on food for the hungry and was left eating dry bread. But as long as enough chunks of bread filled her stomach, she had nothing to complain about. Why should she, knowing that she was still capable of earning a living for the foreseeable future? She never missed a payment to Carla, and received good reports back about her teaching.

So it went, her pockets full some days, empty the next. Fate would take care of her. It came as no surprise when a messenger reached her with an invitation from Richet to come to Paris and participate in meetings with several famous scientists. Was she up to it, the messenger asked. Was she? No doubt! Life in Paris was easier and much more lucrative compared to any revenue she could generate here. Meeting up with Richet would be like a holiday. All her Neapolitan money could not buy the fine wines Richet served and the luxury he provided. Giving séances in his presence was less stressful than anywhere else. When he was in the room, her powers soared, Somehow his honour depended on the positive outcome of her séances.

When Eusapia arrived in Paris, the day was neither sunny, nor rainy, nor grey, nor stormy. It was something in-between, indefinable, unlike the roaring action in the city, which had a definite energy to it. The city squealed, it screamed, it hummed. It swirled and scooped Eusapia up, pushing her along streets that by now were familiar.

Paris was like an Italian city, a place that allowed you to breathe. Richet had said it was the city of love and romance. Eusapia sniffed. Yes, something was in the air. If not love, then at least sex, hot and tantalising sex, which was a good first step. Not many people had the luxury to engage in real romance. It seemed a prerogative of the rich. Love she had seen, even among the poorest. What she had with Raphael, was that love? Maybe not love per se, but all the same a relationship that she wouldn't trade for anything. There was caring. They could count on each other. Even apart, they were carried by mutual support. In the arms of different partners, they never forgot each other. Love? No. That was beyond either of them, she thought. They weren't born under such a lucky star. Paris itself wasn't up to being the city of love. It made promises it couldn't deliver.

Setting foot into Richet's library again felt like coming home. Despite the books, which she viewed as testimonies to a higher world, impenetrable to her, unique to Richet, the room took her in without question. Her feet automatically led to the corner where she usually hung her curtains to make a spirit cabinet. Yes, she reflected calmly as she examined the furniture and books with proprietary pride, Part of this belongs to me. Why she would entertain such thoughts, she did not know and did not care. It only mattered that she felt at home in this room, which was supposed to be way out of her league. She was happy to be here.

Richet, who had been at work and in meetings all day, entered the library with panache, as if Eusapia was the first order of the day. During supper, he explained his plans.

We have our work cut out for us. You will meet with some of the foremost scientists of this century like Pierre and Marie

Curie. With all the recent discoveries in scientific fields, it's paramount that we achieve breakthroughs in the metaphysical world as well. We need the most competent scientists to explore the unrealised potential in people to communicate with discarnate entities through as of yet undiscovered channels. It takes a pioneer like me to point out the initial direction and to open new worlds to people. The more scientists start working in this domain, the more progress we'll make.

What do you want to achieve?

Knowledge. And progress.

Eusapia felt a tingling warmth mount in her. She liked it when Richet talked as if her work were a contribution to the world. Maybe he was right. One day, everyone would be able to communicate with the dead. What solace it would bring to people if they could remain connected with friends and relatives who passed on! Just as she remained connected with her mother, so would everyone else be able to talk to their loved ones in the otherworld. Eusapia herself would be able to reach more people. She always wanted to know how the little girl Maria was doing. Was she happy now? Was Anna with her? At present, there were only a very few people who talked to Eusapia: her mother, and Gianina's family. And she had seen Raphael's mother and brothers once. But no one else. Not her father. Not Signor Pellegrino. What were the hidden channels Richet was talking about? Was there any chance that she actually had unknown powers to open the longed-for communication with the otherworld? She pinched herself. Don't be ridiculous, she sneered silently. She was only too aware how her world functioned. In all her endeavours as a medium, not once did she catch a glimpse of something metaphysical, as Richet called it so mysteriously. If anyone wanted to know the simple truth, she could give it to them stripped of all mystery, a miserable heap of cheap tricks.

Are they nice people, those Curies? Eusapia asked.

Bright and quiet.

When anyone talked of bright women, it always brought the censorious Mrs. Sidgwick to mind. Please God, not another one like her, Eusapia mouthed. I couldn't take it.

Madame Curie was nothing like Mrs. Sidgwick. When she was introduced to Eusapia, she fixed her intelligent, curious eyes on the Italian medium without prejudice. Eusapia could feel her intense determination not to miss a detail. Every facet of the visit would be registered in Madame Curie's brain, instantly organised and dissected.

What did the woman hope to gain from this encounter? Eusapia asked herself. Madame Curie wasn't a typical spiritualist, but rather a curious woman open to new ideas and intrigued by Richet's convictions.

While Richet introduced the two women to each other by summarising their accomplishments, Madame Curie and Eusapia continued observing each other. Suddenly, Eusapia detected dark specks of pain right in the middle of the other woman's eyes, sitting precariously exposed among the particles of extremely focused scientific interest and ambition. It's the sort of pain only the loss of a child or a miscarriage can cause, Eusapia thought with sudden tenderness. Zooming in on the pain, she saw the story of loss expand. First, everything was blurry. The woman in front of her was very private, too proud and reserved to reveal ancient hurts and sadness. Eusapia wondered why she felt this strange connection to a woman so different from herself.

Accompanied by the sounds of Richet's voice explaining the workings of séances, she waited for further insight. All of a sudden it dawned on her that this was a woman who like herself had to grow up without her mother, at least for part of her childhood. That's what it is, Eusapia thought and felt a closeness she'd rarely experienced with other women. She is a survivor, from another background, but someone who had to fight to get where she is now, just like me.

The two women gave each other a quick smile.

How would she deal with Madame Curie without exploiting her pain? Eusapia asked herself. She had to make a believer out of this woman without Madame Curie's child or mother materialising, that much was clear. Would she be able to create a convincing atmosphere? Eusapia sized Madame Curie up once more. Her first impressions had been right. This woman too wanted a better world for everyone. More justice! More opportunities!

This way, please, Richet said, leading the two women into his library. They had barely moved a few steps when the housekeeper brought a Polish friend of Marie Curie's into the room. Eusapia greeted her politely, but with no special interest. This one was like any of the many sitters she had met. It was Madame Curie she absolutely wanted to have on her side for personal as well as professional reasons. She wanted to give the best of herself to a woman she had come to respect at first sight, a woman she liked and judged worthy of her finest performance.

Sitting at the table, Eusapia applied herself more than in a long time. The room was already darkened. The Polish friend sang with fervour some hymns in Polish, alone, since Madame Curie made no sound. Her eyes were riveted on the medium beside her. Eusapia had put her hands on the women's hands and could feel their feet against hers. It was important that she knew the exact position of her sitters' hands and feet. She glanced over at Richet who sat quietly beside Madame Curie, her hand in his. He looked confident. Eusapia must be on the right track. She slowly sank into one of her so-called trances. Her body temperature rose. Drops of sweat squeezed through her pores.

Eusapia noticed Madame Curie register every detail. The woman's focus on scientific observations that she would validate later against Richet's precise measurements suited Eusapia. The table could ascend, and it did so energetically at least three feet. Up there it hovered for two seconds and then came sliding down to the floor. Madame Curie gasped, while her friend cried out fervently, Jesus, Joseph and Mary. Before Madame Curie had time to absorb this phenomenon, sounds of flutes merged into an eerie medley. Simultaneously, an eruption of unspecified pops and twangs cascaded through the room.

Eusapia repeatedly felt her illustrious sitter's hand tremble. Good, she thought. All is as it should be. The small wicker table rose, then floated toward the séance table. Slowly it descended and came to rest upside down in the middle of the table. The two women were still staring at the wicker table when phosphorescent lights glided across the room. A cold breeze sent a shudder through Madame Curie's body. Eusapia perceived astonishment, even awe in the woman beside her. Filled with a sense of satisfaction, Eusapia let escape a sigh. She had competently produced her phenomena without unnecessary crudeness. As she slumped down on the table, she could hear

Richet say, She'll be coming out of her trance momentarily. We will have to let her rest. She needs to restore her powers.

The dynamics at the next séance were quite different. Madame Curie was accompanied by her husband, Pierre Curie and a colleague from the Sorbonne. When Eusapia first saw Pierre Curie, his quiet strength and intensity quickened her pulse. He was different from the men she was naturally drawn to, but for some inexplicable reason he aroused her emotions. If it hadn't been for Madame Curie, who stood unpretentious but confident beside him, she would have thrown herself at him, just to find out whether he could make the meaning of life clear to her. Somehow she thought he was capable of anything. But Eusapia had her honour too. As soon as she had taken a liking to Madame Curie, her husband became off limits. This didn't prevent her from keeping a close eye on him. He was probably a few years younger than herself, not as young as his wife, but not quite fifty. His body looked lean and must have been strong at some point. His chestnut brown hair was greying fast. Suddenly, Eusapia winced as she read his face. Beside the kindness, intelligence and remnants of a rather robust constitution, shadows drew dark symbols on his face. When Eusapia examined them closer, she saw sickness and, no, she didn't want it to be true, something more ominous, why did she always have to look so close? Why couldn't she just forget about the messages on people's faces? Did it help anyone? No! Did it make anyone happy? No again. But Eusapia had to acknowledge the shadowy scribbles no matter what. Sickness they said. I don't want to see anything else, Eusapia thought desperately. But there it was, not just sickness, but death, rapidly approaching and inevitable.

Madame, she heard Pierre Curie's voice. It's an honour to meet a medium of such renown. My wife was intrigued by your phenomena. And our esteemed colleague, Charles Richet, has always believed in you.

Eusapia smiled warmly at both him and his wife. These two people accepted her as their equal. Very different from even her friend Richet. Though she liked Richet very much in general, she had no illusions about their relationship. In his eyes, she was situated on a completely different plane, so low that outside her séances he barely saw her. His real universe comprised top scientists and well-bred people only. Despite her reputation as a famous medium, in his presence, she was constantly made aware of her modest origins and lack of education. She had seen him in action. He'd never be able to appreciate anyone with a different kind of intelligence. Or skin colour for that matter. She'd watched him squirm out of an encounter with black people as if he feared contamination. A flicker of anger rose in her. But she squashed it resolutely. She owed her good fortunes to this man. Thank God she met him. More than anyone, even Ercole, he had been her ticket to fame and comfort. She took the excellent wine and food he served as his token of respect, yet was never blinded to the fact that he kept her happy for his own purposes.

When the first sounds of one of Richet's records, his newest and most prized acquisition, floated out into the room from his gramophone, Eusapia sighed blissfully. Every time she heard the tenor voice of her beloved fellow Neapolitan Enrico Caruso, she thought she was in heaven. Richet had played the record for her previously during one of her repeated attacks of homesickness. It was a miracle to be away from home and still be able to hear the lyrical and seductive sounds of Italian virility. For a moment she forgot to breathe. Oblivious to the Curies and Richet, she let her soul be filled with Naples' brilliant sun, the dark rumble of Vesuvius, and the enthusiastic love-making of her men. An unusually tender, amorous smile played around her lips.

I've never heard anything as stirring as this rendering of Puccini, Madame Curie echoed everyone's thoughts. The wonders of art and technology overwhelmed and excited them. Instead of turning their attention to the séance, they continued listening.

When the music stopped, they slowly remembered the purpose of their meeting. Richet restarted the record as no one in this group would sing. Though entranced for a second time by the tenor's voice, they made a conscious effort to stay with the business at hand. Pierre Curie was seated at Eusapia's left, Richet to her right, holding the hand of Madame Curie, who sat opposite her colleague. With the music carrying her along, Eusapia fell into a trance almost right away. But it wasn't time yet. For a few moments, she leaned backwards with her eyes wide open, pressing hard on the hands she was holding. She waited until she had the full attention of her sitters, then she relaxed, sitting demurely in her chair, this time with her head bent. When all eyes were on her, she remained in this position without any further movement. A medium's main quality is patience. No matter how long it takes, you have to wait for the right moment. It was good to have Caruso around and let his golden voice lead people into regions that would have been out of reach without his music. Pierre Curie, whose traits turned dreamy with the sound of the first notes, already was at the tenor's beck and call, following his moods and inspirations. Even Madame Curie looked softer than usual, as if the music had the power to peel away one of her many protective layers.

We're getting there, Eusapia thought. It's almost time. She stared up at the ceiling. Her mother wasn't there. No one was there at all. But she kept looking. Slowly the eyes of her sitters followed hers, trying to catch a glimpse of the invisible signs and symbols Eusapia seemed in the process of deciphering. It was at that moment that the table rose, higher than most times, four feet maybe. Eusapia herself was amazed at the table's unusual power. For a second it remained in the air but then descended as fast as it had risen. The sitters couldn't suppress their surprise. Pierre Curie grabbed the table with both hands, just as a blue flower landed in front of him. Everyone held their breath, waiting for additional wonders.

Nothing more happened. Eusapia, still in trance, threw herself about, sometimes landing on Richet, though barely touching Pierre Curie. A quick glance at his wife instantaneously firmed her resolve not to betray the bond that had so easily been forged between the two women. Eusapia crumpled into herself while her sitters waited. When she stayed motionless, Richet explained that her powers must be more exhausted than expected.

We'll have other séances, he said, and the Curies and their colleague concurred.

Most of the séances took place at the Psychological Institute in Paris. When Eusapia complained and said the library was much more congenial to spirit presence, Richet agreed. However, he added, you can't overestimate the prestige the institute lends to your work. She had to admit that the scientific nature of the place raised the stature of her phenomena to a different level. Nothing could beat the strange looking instruments that were supposed to measure everything from her pulse, blood pressure and weight, to wind currents in the room, magnetic fields, and electric currents in and around her body. There were instruments that recorded the paths of objects moving without direct contact. Telekinesis is what the scientists called it. Scientists also established that she caused molecular vibrations in objects at a distance from her. She loved those important sounding words. It was tempting to get caught up in the excitement and believe that she was at the centre of new discoveries. Such measuring and recording could go to the head of even the humblest of mediums. To her, this whole hoopla was just another aspect of securing an income and gaining more power to change lives. If you had money, you could save people and animals. Her job here in France was not only to build up her ability to be independent, well-fed, clothed and housed, but also to acquire the means to pull others out of their misery. The scientists were not going to ruin her mission. On the contrary, they would serve as perfect allies in her quest. For this to happen, all cells of her body had to work at their optimum and in perfect harmony. Concentration, she exhorted herself, undivided concentration and superhuman physical exertion. Do or die.

Not every séance went well. Some of the French professors were as irksome as their English counterparts. The present evening was especially exasperating.

She's cheating, they sneered, does she think we didn't notice that she freed her hands? She is the one touching us, not ghosts. Definitely, it's her, they jeered, gloating, talking not to her, but about her as if she weren't in the room, treating her like an insignificant freak. On they went. I saw her use her foot to raise the table. She swung her leg backwards behind the curtains to pluck the strings of the guitar with her toes.

When the professors' French voices spiked and the content of their complaints was painfully clear even to an Italian, Eusapia screamed at the top of her lungs, What's wrong with you? It's your attitudes that prevent the real phenomena from occurring!

Disgusted, she banged the table with both her hands.

You no-good stupid academicians! You should know by now under what circumstances metaphysical activities can occur.

Don't overreact, my dear Eusapia, Richet said, trying to calm her down. They don't mean any harm. They want to understand.

Understand!?? The hell they do!

My dear friends, Richet addressed his colleagues, I ask you to excuse Eusapia's blatant tendency to cheat. Long ago we established that like so many other authentic mediums she resorts to easy ways of producing phenomena when not properly controlled. No one among us in this circle can imagine the extraordinary mental and physical stamina a séance demands of a medium. Since I first experimented with Eusapia Palladino on Île Roubaud where her most astonishing phenomena occurred in abundance and with ease, she has aged. Calling up even a fraction of the power she once had is a great achievement for her nowadays. Today is worse than ever. Under the circumstances, we'd better cancel the rest of the séance and postpone it to a later date.

Eusapia, who got the drift of most of his explanation, was grateful for Richet's unfaltering ability to say the right words at the right time. When even his well-chosen words were greeted with grumbling and mocking sneers, she exploded.

Stop it, she screeched and stormed out of the room and out of the building into the street where she called a cab to drive her back to Richet's apartment.

Eusapia refused to hold any séances for over two weeks, and Richet had to serve some of his best wine to keep her in Paris. He coaxed her into staying with the promise of specially selected sitters for the next meeting.

You'll invite the Curies?

No, we should not overexpose them. We need additional corroboration of your authenticity. I wish we could invite Arthur Conan Doyle. You could not find an author with greater credibility. What other author has scientific training and is able to create such a sharp-minded detective like Sherlock Holmes? No one would dare criticise him for being deceived by fraudulent mediums. And he is a spiritualist of deep conviction. Unfortunately, he is otherwise occupied.

Eusapia shuddered. Did she hear right, did Richet say detective, fraudulent mediums?

Oh, don't worry. He would believe in you and your phenomena. No doubt!

If not him, who else then? Eusapia cried out, even more agitated than before.

You have to calm down, Eusapia. Just because some people raised doubts doesn't mean you have lost your credibility. Show them your unique talents. You know you have the power. So use it. Use it wisely.

The two men Richet invited were two distinguished elderly scientists, a M. Leblanc and a M. Maillet. The first thing Eusapia noticed was their spectacles and very thick lenses, which instantly made her well disposed toward them. Though retired for years, the men were still active and their voices vibrated with the success of their younger years. These days, they acted mostly as emissaries of goodwill and encouragement. Mentors, students called them. Teachers at heart, who could not help but be positive. Their task was to build, not destroy. Eusapia took to them immediately.

At present, one of the gentlemen was seated to her left, the other to her right. Richet sat beside M. Leblanc, an expression of confident expectation on his face. Again the poignant voice of Caruso sounded through the room.

The two men dutifully held Eusapia's hands. In no time their spectacles disappeared under an upside-down black bowl on the table. The professors did not seem to notice. In fact, their eyes closed as time went by. The music is bewitching them, Eusapia thought, then corrected herself, No, supernatural powers are gaining entry into their souls.

Suddenly the figure of a slender girl materialised behind M. Leblanc. The girl, bathed in glittering light, bent to kiss the top of his head, then as if in a slow dance moved toward M. Maillet, kissing him on the cheek. Neither of the gentlemen uttered a sound or made the slightest movement. As quickly as the girl had materialised, she disappeared. Simultaneously, the table soared into the air and remained floating longer than Eusapia had managed before. As it descended, the sounds of a guitar, then of a trumpet, mixed precariously with the sounds from the gramophone. Again the table rose, but at once came crushing down on M. Leblanc's foot while lights blinked and floated from wall to wall and from floor to ceiling.

When darkness returned to the room, Eusapia threw herself back in her chair, her arms flailing. She moaned and sighed, then slowly came out of her trance, looking confused into the sweat-laden faces of her two sitters.

Where am I? she asked, frightened.

You're coming out of your trance, Richet said. Let me bring you to your room so that you can collect yourself and restore your powers. As he guided her to her bed, he congratulated her on her séance.

Your mediumship was at its best tonight, he said without looking at her.

The success of the evening provided a reprieve. Compensating for the numerous cynics and skeptics, the two esteemed older scientists, together with the world-famous Curies, lent renewed respectability to the medium. She had succeeded in reviving interest in her special abilities. When Richet translated for her a few days later the main points of a newspaper article lauding her unquestionable authenticity and incomparable mediumship, the cloud over her head lifted. Her appetite soared. The wine tingled in her veins and she purred like a cat with happy contentment.

Yes, yes, yes, life is good! she exclaimed and salivated at the increase in fees her new standing would bring with it. She thought of Raphael's daughter. Her future would be secured. The hopeful faces of the many waifs and abandoned elderly under her wing smiled at her. Besides giving in to visions of better lives for people she cared for, she drooled at the idea of plentiful seafood, pasta, pizza, and, oh yes, maybe a bottle or two of Richet's famous wine that would accompany her back to Italy. She merrily smacked her lips. No more poverty for her, ever! Step by painful step she had freed herself from the shackles of her wretched childhood. She looked up to the sky. There was her mother Michela.

Are you proud of me? Eusapia asked.

Her mother answered, I'm just glad you survived.

Eusapia wanted more. Are you proud of me? she repeated in her most insistent voice.

Again her mother simply answered, I'm glad you're alive.

Eusapia was annoyed, This is hopeless, she grumbled and looked away. Maybe at another time, her mother would be more appreciative of her accomplishments. Why are you so damn demanding? Eusapia cried out.

Softly, she heard her mother's voice whispering not from the sky but from deep within herself, Because I have faith in your potential.

Then it was quiet.

Eusapia pleaded for more. But her mother was gone. She had said all there was to say. It's not enough, Mammina, I need more, Eusapia begged, but knew that all the answers she needed were in her own heart waiting to be acknowledged.

Despite her newfound confidence, Eusapia dreaded to go to the Psychological Institute. The atmosphere wasn't right. Drafts from the windows disturbed the tranquil rise of the temperature in the room. Instead of warmly wafting back from the walls, the air ricocheted from them like ice bullets, shooting cold unease into the sitters. Together with the ever-present swirls of scientific skepticism, this unease turned into a mixture frustratingly resistant to Eusapia's dramatic mediumistic powers. Complaints about her cheating multiplied. Contempt intensified. When Eusapia saw sitters talk to Richet, she didn't have to understand their words to know that it was an attack on her integrity and personality. The quick angry flickers in Richet's eyes revealed that it was also an attack on his judgement. What was he doing wasting his time and talent on psychic phenomena and blatant cheats like Eusapia Palladino? Some of his friends wanted to whisk him away from her, pull him out of this sea of folly in which they thought he was drowning. Those attempts galled him most. How dare they question his sanity, and isn't that what they were doing? Hadn't he proven his worth a long time ago? He expected friends and colleagues to follow his lead. He was the one the world would remember as the pioneer of metaphysics. His intuition and leadership were necessary steps in the advancement of mankind. Suddenly, his irritation vanished. He wouldn't give up that easily. Animatedly, he described the phenomena he had witnessed during Eusapia's earlier years.

Yes, he admitted, it is possible that her powers are waning rapidly with age. Even at the height of her powers, she had a tendency to cheat when her stamina and concentration weren't strong enough for telekinetic movements, full-sized materialisations or the growth of ectoplasmic limbs. But don't be fooled, besides the common tricks, you cannot help but notice pearls of an extraordinary and unexplainable nature.

The response to Richet's speeches was not unanimous. At times, colleagues succumbed to his powers of persuasion, and Eusapia saw uncertainty creep back into the faces of some of his challengers. At other times, they shook their heads at his incomprehensible convictions. Worse, she witnessed numerous academics storm out of the Psychology Institute in disgust. That she hated. When it happened, Richet would sink into deep resentment. The grief and hurt he felt inside would manifest itself in his face and voice. He became distant and distracted for hours until all of a sudden, he'd open a new bottle of wine and say, We'll show them.

Eusapia realised that a certain laziness in her preparations for the séances was partly to blame for the mounting criticism. How did she let things slide like this when she knew very well that the currency of success was all-out physical and mental training? With this insight, she tried to overcome the foggy tiredness that had crept into everything she did. She pulled herself out of bed earlier again than in previous months. Behind locked doors, she now practised with a determination that bordered on obsession in order to increase her speed and accuracy in moving, lifting, descending, concealing and bringing forth objects. But even when the Curies came back for another séance, she barely managed an elevation of the table of an inch or two, a wobbly two inches at that, a jerky rise followed by an immediate descent. She was lucky the table didn't topple over. The only thing she could bring herself to produce was a crushed flower with half its petals missing.

Don't worry, Madame Curie consoled her at the end of the séance, we were privileged to experience incredible phenomena before. Even with your exhausted capacity, the table still rose today and a flower landed in our midst. It's inconceivable that trickery was involved in the occurrences we witnessed.

I agree, Pierre Curie added, and Richet stood beside them, quiet and attentive, nodding.

Eusapia was aware of letters going back and forth between Paris and London.

I'm keeping them informed, Richet explained. They need to know that even world-famous scientists like the Curies believe in you. I'm telling them about the seesaw success of your séances, but I make sure that they understand that despite your frequent cheating, authentic phenomena do occur.

Eusapia smiled. Whatever Richet did was fine with her. He was on her side: his side was always her side as well. What would it take to open the minds of the members of the English Society for Psychical Research? Their Cambridge decision stood firm. Sometimes, Richet frowned when he received the responses to his letters. Lately though he looked more upbeat. The Curies carried weight. Even the English couldn't ignore their conclusions.

Every time I write, Richet said, I exhort them to keep an open mind.

His perseverance paid off. One day a letter arrived, advising him and Eusapia that the Society was considering a new investigation, preferably in collaboration with Italian investigators, in the city of Naples at a date still to be determined.

Excellent, Richet said and Eusapia could see that he felt somewhat vindicated.

Good, Eusapia added. Splendid. Finally, she would be given an opportunity to live the good and well-remunerated life of scientific investigation in her home town. It was so much more fun in a place where people talked her language. Let's see what the future holds, she said confidently, and Richet responded with a quick warm glance. The interest in psychic investigation was being kept alive. It was only a matter of time until new insights would present themselves to scientists with open minds. Richet and Eusapia both could look forward to new and favourable developments.

Naples 1908; Trip to America, 1909

11

INITIALLY, THE RESPONSE of the English Society for Psychical Research filled Dr. Charles Richet and Eusapia with great optimism. As time went by and no action followed, frustration replaced excitement. Many times, the Society members reverted back to the position they took during the Cambridge investigations that had unmasked Eusapia Palladino as a fraud. Other times, they relented. If eminent researchers besides Charles Richet, especially the Curies, had come to believe in Eusapia's authenticity and ruled out fraud in several instances, then maybe, a re-examination was warranted. It took two years though before the society decided to send a new team of investigators to Naples to settle the question of Eusapia's mediumship once and for all.

One of the investigators, the young, half-Eusapia's-age Hereward Carrington, who had lived in America since his early adulthood and worked for the American Society for Psychical Research, emphatically endorsed a second examination of the medium based on the scientific community's immense interest in this medium. His own qualifications as a trained magician, experienced investigator and already popular author made him a perfect candidate for this task.

In the end, the team consisted of Hereward Carrington, the former magician Wortley Baggally, and Everard Fielding, a psychical investigator for the English Society. If anyone was qualified to re-evaluate the disgraced medium, it was this group of energetic fellows whose curiosity and expertise equalled the medium's.

The news that she'd be dealing with young investigators thrilled Eusapia, but also exponentially raised her challenge. Not to worry though, the titillation of younger blood and bodies was worth the risk. She tried to remember what she had heard about Carrington. Apart from his reputation as a charming conversationalist and something of a ladies' man, she clearly remembered the Sidgwicks mentioning his extensive training as a magician and unparalleled capacity to catch fraudulent mediums. Eusapia sighed. Was he as fanatic as Houdini? No, he can't be that bad, she reassured herself and immediately added, but I'd better be careful. And the two other fellows? Alarm bells went off when she learned that the second was also a magician, a very skeptical one at that. Only Fielding was a different breed. From what she recalled, he came to spiritualism after a crisis of faith caused by the death of his sister Clare. It took years and a second tragedy, the death of his brother Basil in a boating accident, before his professional interest in spiritualism evolved into a personal quest. That should mean, Eusapia inferred, that he is looking for some sign from the otherworld. He was her best hope, the weakest link, the one member of this team who might have a stake in a positive outcome of the investigation. A connection to his brother might help him cope with his grief. Her heart overflowed with empathy. Reaching back into her own suffering, to that raw corner where, over the more than fifty years

402

since her mother's death, strength and caring had slowly taken root, Eusapia was intent on using that strength to try to lessen his pain.

Weeks went by without additional news. Eusapia was disappointed. Scientific investigations were so much more satisfying than ordinary séances. She craved the respect scientists displayed when they believed her phenomena were authentic. As soon as their tools and notepads came out, she felt raised to a different level, a pedestal almost. The scientists saved her from the dreadful vision of impending dissolution into nothingness. Their continued attention lessened the despair she felt during her frequent walks through the cemeteries of Naples where the neglected tombstones of forgotten citizens or the skulls and bones of the unnamed poorest filled her with gloom. Thinking that she'd be doomed to oblivion a few years after death threw her into distress. Celestina will have no memories of me. Raphael might die before me or soon after. My friends will mourn for a short period of time and then go on with their lives as they should. Eusapia even feared that she'd never be reunited with Mammina. Though she constantly talked to her mother, there were moments of darkness when she felt contaminated by Richet's views and started to doubt that the essence of a person continued to exist after death. Were there any spirits? Who was she talking to when she saw Mammina? A purely imagined ghost? Her conscience?

Mother, she said into the air, are you real?

Mammina looked at her with compassion and love as if to console her, but never answered the question.

Whatever reassurance Eusapia could find came from the scientists and their stenographers who recorded every detail of her phenomena and every aspect of her bodily functions. Something of her would remain, and at this point a stack of papers dedicated to her phenomena was better than nothing. People might call her illiterate, but there she was living on in journals and books. Even if I don't make it to the otherworld, at least all those passages and paragraphs written about me will carry my memory into the future.

Eventually, the first two members of the team arrived at the Hotel Victoria where they established temporary quarters for the investigation.

It's about time, Eusapia screamed when she received the news. Let the fun begin.

In a hurry, she put on her green silk dress and her yellowish hat. She couldn't wait to catch a glimpse of the young men and assess the difficulty of the task ahead. Richet had described Carrington as an impressive young man with a sharp mind, too shrewd for his own good. Somehow, this tidbit caught Eusapia's fancy. What did it mean though? Would it be to her advantage?

Carrington might be a magician by training, Richet had said and then continued, but he picks up the principles of science as quickly as my more advanced students. He loves physics and chemistry, but is too lazy to fully engage in science. Eusapia paused, Now what was the meaning of that in this context? Another sentence, this one from Myers, floated into her brain, He is a populist. Without hesitation, Eusapia added, I think that means he loves money, easy money. She smiled. More likely than not, she'd find this Hereward Carrington to her taste.

Everard Fielding recognised the medium as soon as he caught sight of her. He had seen her in pictures and the Sidgwicks and the Myers had described her to a tee. This dramatic woman with her expressive eyes and voluptuous body could not be mistaken for anyone else.

Eusapia felt exuberant watching the men approach. Her eyes lingered longest on Carrington. What's his game? she wondered excitedly. Never mind, she could play with the best of them. A quick smirk twisted the corners of her lips upwards for a second. Carrington looked straight at her and continued smiling as if he hadn't noticed, but the cunning spark in his eyes made it clear that they were on to each other.

How are you? Carrington asked solicitously.

Superb, Eusapia answered, and yes, she felt good. Life suddenly fizzed with interest, promising that her job could once again be more than the drag it had become over the last few years. Not that she had lost her abilities, but she found it increasingly difficult to pull her phenomena out of this deepening sea of boredom that threatened to suck her to its bottom. Out of necessity, the performances and pretence had to continue with no end in sight if she wanted to live.

One glance at Everard Fielding confirmed her speculation that he'd come to the table expecting a sign. She wanted to bring a twinkle back into his eyes and humour into his heart. He had been known for his jovial smile and easy laughter. Now, there was not even a trace of joy left. In his attempt to make sense of the drowning death of his brother, he'd sought to connect with him by whatever means necessary. If a medium presented even the slightest possibility to open the channels of communication, he'd grab this opportunity with both hands. Fielding looked at

405

her from out of his despair, with hope and pain twisted into an aching knot. Eusapia took his hand in both of hers. Fielding made no gesture to withdraw it. The warmth of her hands brought comfort, and the sincerity in her eyes a soothing promise of authenticity.

The room where Eusapia's séances were to be investigated was situated on the second floor of the Hotel Victoria between the rooms of Carrington and Baggally, who was expected to arrive shortly. Eusapia inspected it thoroughly, asking to be left alone for the afternoon to assimilate the atmosphere of the room and the building. Though the first séance was only scheduled for two days later, she wanted to set up her cabinet in advance.

The spirits have to become familiar with a room before they make their presence known, she said to the men, who took her word for it.

Eusapia's hired assistants brought the séance table, her special chair, and chairs for the sitters, black curtains, lamps of different intensity, a three-legged wicker table, and musical instruments to the hotel, setting them up according to her instructions. As soon as this was accomplished, she asked to be left alone and seated herself in her chair behind the table. For a while she just stared into space, until — with a slow movement of her head — she assessed the room, evaluating hiding places for a small assistant and essential instruments and objects. She etched the slightest detail into her brain. Behind locked doors, she stretched with abandon, first her arms, second her legs, swinging one after the other straight up so that they touched her ears. If anyone had seen her like that they would have thought they were hallucinating. She didn't know herself why her limbs bent into impossible positions and slithered like snakes. She smiled. Her left leg slipped easily out of her heavy shoe, swinging backwards and finding its way to the drum behind the curtains. Most objects were in reach just by using this one leg in one of her mind-boggling stretches. Adding her extendable pole, she was assured that nothing behind the curtains was inaccessible. She turned down the lights and looked at the table. Within seconds it rose and descended. This spectacle continued non-stop for the next hour and a half. When the table finally came to rest on the floor and remained there, Eusapia smacked her lips in satisfaction. All this exercise had barely raised her pulse, and her chest did not heave. Everything was under control.

Eusapia looked up to the ceiling and saw her mother watching her calmly. I guess I haven't shown you anything new, Eusapia said. She looked more closely at her mother whose black hair and rosy complexion shone with health and youth.

Oh, mother, Eusapia sighed, remembering with disgust the grey hairs she had pulled from her own head in the last few months, I'm growing old.

This time, her mother came down from the ceiling to sit beside her, You're doing well, Eusapia. And you will continue to do well because there are people whose lives depend on you.

Despite a sudden tiredness, Eusapia sprang up from her chair to take her mother into her arms. But Michela had dissolved. One day, Eusapia thought, I will be able to hold you. For now, she had to be content with inhaling the air that had surrounded her mother just moments earlier. With each breath, Eusapia drew new strength. Don't worry, I'll be ready for the séance, she said, and left the room without looking back.

By chance, she met Carrington in the hallway. Again he inquired in his broken but expressive Italian about her wellbeing.

Eusapia couldn't help notice the unabashed expectation in his voice. Not that Carrington had much in common with those of her customers whose needy hunger for spirit manifestations made her almost uncomfortable. But she could see that he clearly wanted something. What is it? Eusapia thought. There was nothing of Myers' fervour in him or Lodge's simple belief. His talent for unmasking fraudulent mediums was no secret. So why didn't she feel threatened? On the contrary, his presence made her feel as much at ease as her dear friend Richet's, and that was rare.

You seem to expect a lot from my séances, she finally said.

Oh yes, he answered, chortling, Great things, Eusapia, fabulous phenomena.

The two stared at each other. Their eyes locked, and in those few seconds, their communication was effortless. Thoughts bounced back and forth at the speed of light. Despite the wait-and-see attitude that remained, the first impression on both sides was positive. They needed no words to confirm that they had the same objective. If they delivered on their unspoken promises, the results of their unlikely partnership could only be advantageous.

The evening of her first séance with the two English men was filled with a strange tension. Eusapia ate with them, but refused to talk. Carrington explained to Fielding that she must be in preparation mode. In spite of her silence, she loomed large at the table, dominating as if she had grown to five times her size. The two men started a conversation between themselves, but were unable to ignore her. Every few seconds, they glanced at the woman and quickly turned away again to avoid her brooding eyes which seemed to chastise everything said and done. The men tried to forget about her, but could not tear themselves away. What was that disconcerting power? How was it possible that they were pulled into her sphere with little or no resistance? Up to this point they had been secure in the knowledge that no woman had more control over them than they decided to give her. The much older Eusapia revealed a different reality. She was more than their match. Not willing to play by men's or women's rules, she lived by rules uniquely her own. No matter how much the men were aware of her game, they were unable to foresee her moves. Thus the tension. Thus the incomprehensible attraction.

As Eusapia sat in front of her cabinet, a few minutes before midnight, the room crackled with anticipation. Carrington sat to her right. Despite their understanding, she feared he could turn on her at any time if she slipped up. Everard Fielding was seated to her left. Eusapia didn't even ask the men to sing. Instead, she had instructed her assistants to set up the gramophone the hotel had made available and put on the Caruso record Richet had given her as a parting gift. Its impact never failed. Not a single person could escape the seduction of the tenor's voice. With Caruso singing, Eusapia fell slowly into a trance. The men had to wait more than an hour before the first object tentatively moved just as the music stopped. Eusapia's dress bulged out at various places to the sound of loud, hollow rappings. Softer raps responded, followed by the faint swish of the black cabinet curtains billowing out, at times flaring out so far that they covered a hand, an arm or even the head of one or the other of the two sitters. The table rose slightly, and after tilting precariously sideways, descended. Several partial levitations followed. With sudden vigour, the table rose straight into the air. Nothing more

409

happened. Eusapia lingered in her trance, falling into Carrington's arms, enveloped in a pungent cloud of hot air, her body undulating in almost sizzling waves, until she finally regained consciousness.

It takes time for phenomena to become stronger and materialisations to occur, Eusapia explained in a calm voice as she tried to compose herself. Spirits have to get to know the sitters before feeling comfortable enough to reveal their presence.

A slight shudder ran through Fielding. Even Carrington, who was well informed about the details and nature of Eusapia's phenomena, couldn't help but be intrigued. The scarcity of the evening's manifestations didn't deter him. She had produced whatever it was he expected. Their vague understanding was not in jeopardy. Eusapia knew she needed to protect it at all costs because somehow in the end, there'd be a prize of some sort. Of what this prize consisted, she dared not guess. Yet, she had no doubt it was useful.

The next séance had a similar feel to it. As she watched Carrington and Fielding in endless discussions afterward, pouring over their notes, comparing and making adjustments, she found no peace. It worried her that Fielding's face still fluctuated between hope and disappointment. At the third séance, he stated excitedly, I don't think the foot control is as perfect as it should be.

To Eusapia's dismay, Carrington concurred, You're right, Everard, we have to make absolutely sure that Eusapia doesn't substitute a foot or a hand for the other.

True to impulse and habit, Eusapia screamed at Fielding as time after time he questioned everything she did. He'd better stop calling for more light! But in the same way Carrington agreed with Fielding, Eusapia found herself giving in to his demands, suddenly realising how Carrington's mind worked.

John King, she informed her spirit guide, we will increase the light.

But unfortunately for Fielding, King thwarted her efforts in every circumstance.

No, no, darker, darker, he instructed.

No matter how hard Eusapia tried to convince him to improve the lighting, in the end she had no choice but to do his bidding and turn it down.

When the third member of the trio arrived, the dynamics shifted. Full of enthusiasm, Baggally greeted Eusapia. He loved full-bodied women with generous curves. Eusapia responded in kind. She'd make sure her spirit control would ask for particularly low levels of light tonight.

Contending with suspicious scrutiny from her sitters, Eusapia decided to be prudent and wait an hour for the first object to move, then produced with great efficiency her usual series of phenomena. At the end of the séance, as was her habit with many men, especially those of Baggally's character, she enlaced herself in a tight embrace with him and later on extracted herself, chuckling and pleased that she still had the power to hold men in thrall, even those half her age. In Baggally, she had woken a dormant volcano. Fielding too struggled to keep his composure. Only Carrington appeared collected, but even he couldn't hide his fascination and the glint of shrewd appreciation in his eyes. The unspoken understanding between her and Carrington held, strong enough to promise benefits way beyond a usual business arrangement.

During the sixth séance, Baggally complained in a burst of outrage about the substitution of hands and feet.

It was Fielding who placated the agitated Baggally.

According to Richet, he explained quietly, the unfortunate fact that Eusapia cheats when provided the opportunity does not preclude authentic phenomena from occurring under different circumstances.

She clearly cheats, Carrington concurred.

Eusapia jumped at him, fuming with rage, but softening when she recognised that despite indications to the contrary their implicit pact was not threatened.

I beg you to calm down, Signora, Carrington pleaded. Why don't we try the same routine again, except this time with your ankles and feet bound together?

You're not tying me down, Eusapia screamed.

I think it would be in your interest to allow us to do so, Carrington responded.

As you like, Eusapia growled, accepting the challenge only because of the devious reassurance in his voice. But not now! she shouted in a new fit of rage. She stormed out of the room and refused to see or talk to any of the three men for four days.

At the next séance, Carrington asked Fielding to secure Eusapia's legs and arms with ropes. Eusapia arched her back in fury and flexed her muscles. Her eyes spewed venom. It took Fielding forever to tie the cord and sit down at his usual place. Eusapia waited bad-humoured in her chair. To prove one's mediumship was challenging under normal circumstances, with extra constraints impossible. In contrast to her previous performances, she sat without moving. Why make the effort to produce phenomena if the investigators only wanted to destroy her? She heard Carrington cough. As she shot a furious glance at him, she saw warning signals flash in his eyes. What was that about? He was the cause of her troubles. After a second glance, she suddenly felt less tense. Slowly, she started the motion of going into a trance. Her body vibrated with small convulsions. With each turn and twist, her confidence grew. She almost cried out loud in surprise when the first raps sounded through the room. She watched the little wicker table move toward her. Thank you, Carrington, my precious spirit, she mouthed silently. An instant later, the wicker table rose grandiosely into the air and completed its trajectory with an unhurried descent onto the table.

I should check whether she is still secured properly, Carrington said suddenly. The others agreed. After tying the ropes in a different manner and very much to Eusapia's satisfaction although she objected in her shrillest voice, he went back to his place.

Eusapia now fell into a deep trance stage. The room came alive with unexplainable occurrences, so many in fact that it felt as if more than one medium were at work. The men were poked and prodded. Ectoplasmic protrusions grew out of the medium's body and with supernatural energy played instruments at a distance, rang bells and hit the drums. Lights blinked throughout the room.

When a spirit apparition made its entry into the room, Fielding almost fainted. He clearly noticed a resemblance to his brother. Before he could utter a word or ask questions, the apparition had disappeared and did not reappear. Only partial materialisations manifested themselves after that. Hands of

413

different sizes and colours stretched out of the cabinet, touching and stroking the sitters. The table rose and rose again. Sometimes its movements were jerky, other times it descended with elegance and style. Fielding was breathless. Was the spirit control John King trying to transmit a message from his brother Basil? Did Basil offer forgiveness even though Fielding had failed to save him? Even the magician Baggally was impressed. There was no way an ordinary person, especially with arms and legs securely tied, could produce this type of phenomena. These were the manifestations of supernatural forces. He had been able to duplicate many so-called mediumistic manifestations. But what happened here was impossible. He felt stumped and afraid. Could it be true that spirits existed and that they made their way back from the otherworld into ours? Baggally shook his head. It's impossible, he thought. Yet . . .

When the lights came back on, Eusapia remained in her trance, sprawled immobile on her chair. Carrington took upon himself the task of removing the ropes that tied her limbs. Pondering improbable facts, the men searched each other's faces for confirmation and maybe interpretation of their own experience.

Nothing will be able to erase the powerful impression of this séance, Carrington said. I'm at a loss for words. After the cheating in the previous séance, I never expected to be truly convinced that Eusapia produces authentic phenomena. But who can doubt it now?

Fielding nodded in agreement.

Carrington asked Baggally to guide the weakened medium back to the bedroom they had rented for her for the duration of the investigation. With his left arm supporting her back and his right arm holding on to her arm, Baggally led her down the hallway. As the pair disappeared behind the door of Eusapia's room, Carrington and Fielding continued staring into the dark for quite a while. They finally decided to go for a brisk walk before calling it a day. They needed to clear their thoughts.

For two weeks, Eusapia stayed away from the men. Not just because she firmly believed in the saying that absence makes the heart grow fonder, but also to give her sitters time to relive her last séance. Experience had taught her that without interference or additional stimulus, the colour of a memory intensified with each emotion-charged recall. With every retelling, the levitation of her table increased. In fact, people became convinced that the table had risen more than four feet into the air. They even remembered it floating up to the ceiling. Blurry features crystallised into more recognisable faces. Doubts about the identities of spirits disappeared. Who'd dare deny any longer that channels of communication had been established? Individual perceptions evolved into everyone's experience. Yes, that's what the sitters had seen with their own eyes. Eusapia smiled. Like a gardener, she watched the seeds she planted take root, grow and become viable plants or trees. When it came to séances, her patience was unmatched. It was her best kept secret, and she made the most of it.

Day after day, Eusapia informed Baggally and Fielding through Carrington that her powers were too exhausted to be called upon for another performance. It was imperative to lower the men's expectations. Fielding's out-of-control hopes for a brother-to-brother conversation needed to be manoeuvred carefully. To let him continue on the path of unfulfillable expectations was unsafe for him and for herself.

415

Everard, she addressed him when she finally emerged from her room, her voice full of concern, I wish I could reach your brother, but my powers have left me. We're still at the beginning stages of spiritism. In the not too distant future, you might be able to establish a more satisfactory communication. But at the moment, I'm unable to do so. I'm truly sorry.

It's not your fault, Fielding responded. Maybe tomorrow, you'll feel stronger, he added eagerly.

I doubt it, Eusapia responded in her saddest voice. While you yourself witnessed authentic powers the other night, those powers are not developed enough to consistently reach the otherworld or to build on a communication once the first contact has been established. You are a few years too early, Everard.

Could you try though?

I will but only if you promise not to get your hopes up. I can't bear to disappoint you.

Even the slightest sign will bring me closer to my brother. That's all I want, to feel his presence for just a moment.

Eusapia sighed. Fielding was hard work. It was so much more fun to deal with Baggally or Carrington, who didn't need the tiring engagement required for Fielding. Not to mention that sometimes it took all her energy to deal with her own losses and she had none left to soothe someone else's grief. Besides, his world was too removed and different from hers. He had more in common with Myers. Grief had rendered them similar. Too similar, she thought, they'd be even less able to reach out to each other than she was. While she might not be able to help, she was at least not so wrapped up in herself to be unaware of their plight. Those two lived in bubbles without ever completely connecting with the real world. However nice and decent, they shut family and friends out and made it nearly impossible for ordinary humans to reach them.

The next day's séance started tentatively. Eusapia felt wary. She sensed the men scrutinise her every move. When she asked for the lights to be turned down a notch, Baggally protested. She countered by requesting that the lantern in the back of the room be covered with red tissue paper. Again Baggally refused to accommodate her. But Carrington argued that the dimmer light might facilitate materialisations, and Baggally finally relented. Eusapia wondered whether his intense concentration was directed toward the movements of her hands or the curves of her body. Could she relax? She was especially nervous, as she had been unable to smuggle her assistant into the room. When suddenly loud raps sounded through the room, she almost jumped. Before she could fall into a trance, the table rose. She just had to stare at it and wave her arms to direct it. It swayed to the left and to the right, it floated up and down. She asked the table to stop moving. Immediately it stood motionless on the floor.

Spirits, I ask you to bring us sounds of music, Eusapia commanded.

A few seconds later, two or three instruments started to play.

Amazing, Baggally exclaimed.

Eusapia saw Fielding stretch out his arms as if beseeching his brother to make his presence felt.

Spirit, Eusapia said into the darkness, if you're a relative of someone in this room, I implore you to touch this person. A short moment passed. Then Fielding, who sat beside Carrington, cried out in astonishment.

A hand is tapping me on the back. Brother, he continued, please talk to me.

The spirit remained silent. Fielding however took comfort from additional pats on his back.

During the following séances, similar occurrences took place. Quick appearances of materialised spirits, mostly apparitions of hands only, white, dark, large and small hands. Loud raps and echoes from all corners. Tooting horns, sweet chords of the guitar. Blinking phosphorescent lights. What a woman, the men mused. Fielding kept aloof from the group. It was the first time since his brother's death that he felt at peace. His brother hadn't disappeared into nothingness. He had begun a journey to a higher level beyond the reach of human comprehension where his intellectual and emotional faculties could broaden and open so that at some point he'd find a way to respond to the calls of those left behind. One glorious day, communication across their different worlds would be possible.

I think, Carrington said, it would be best if Everard were the one to write the report of our séances here.

Baggally agreed. More than any of us, Everard experienced the depth of Eusapia's powers. We all felt presences from the other side. But when it happens to be your brother, it transforms you.

Everard accepted to write a first draft. I'll base it on my notes and on the transcript of the stenographer that Eusapia provided for us. The two of you will make additions and correct any inaccuracies that might have slipped in. I'll intend to be a worthy witness of the extraordinary occurrences that have taken place, Fielding promised, I'll prepare a work of scientific rigour and gratitude.

Solemnly, the men shook hands. They had travelled to Naples to unmask a fraudulent medium and came away with life-altering experiences that affected each of them in different ways.

We owe it to this woman to make her known all over the world, Baggally said.

That's my opinion too, Carrington responded. Never before have I come to believe in the reality of metaphysical occurrences. In my previous encounters with mediums, I uncovered fraud at the core of every one of their manifestations. Not so with Eusapia. I have to accept that she has special powers.

His two colleagues murmured agreement.

We should be able to define those powers, Carrington added. I wonder, he went on, whether I should take it upon myself to become her manager. As you said, Wortley, she should be known. I could introduce her to the scientific community in America.

That's a great idea, Baggally said. Talk it over with the Sidgwicks and other members of the English Society for Psychical Research. Once they get acquainted with our new insights and revised judgement of Eusapia's mediumship, they might support such a trip.

I'll certainly think about it, Carrington agreed. There are times, he continued his thoughts silently, when it's wise to unmask those trickster mediums who lurch at every corner, but at other times it pays to take advantage of the spiritualist tendencies of society and hook up with a powerful medium like The Great Palladino. A quick calculation of what Eusapia's séances might bring in and the percentage that would fall to him, especially if he arranged the lucrative scientific experimentation sessions, made such a proposition almost irresistible. In addition,

419

the European and American psychical societies would have ample reason to finance his continued investigation of all metaphysical phenomena connected with Eusapia, and to remunerate him for the meticulous record keeping that this implied. Most appealing though, there would be enough material for a new book. The more Eusapia Palladino was known, the more such a book would sell. Ah, to have money and live the lifestyle he deserved!

The other two men looked at Carrington, waiting for a more definite plan.

Well, Baggally said when it didn't come forward, I wouldn't have missed this experience for the world.

Fielding felt no need to add anything, but was gratified that his brother had made himself felt and would accompany him back to England.

I think, Carrington announced, I won't be travelling back with the two of you tomorrow as planned. I really should stay a few weeks more and investigate the possibility of a partnership with Eusapia. The men went out for supper and drank to a future with new-found possibilities.

Eusapia drove a hard bargain. Her financial skills took Carrington by surprise. Like most of his colleagues, he thought of her as a talented medium without education, culture or the ability to make decisions for herself. She set him straight immediately. Yes, she wanted to travel to America. Yes, she couldn't wait to cross the ocean in a big ship. Yes, she was ready to see a new part of the world where, from everything she was told, you could even find Italian food. But, my dear friend Carrington, don't underestimate my worth. Carrington had to settle for far less than he had anticipated. Still, if they were successful in their venture, their partnership was bound to boost both their fortunes. With the main aspects finally settled, Eusapia asked a neighbour to cook a feast that they washed down with two bottles of wine. In the following days they roamed the streets, stuffed themselves with pizza and chunks of beef amidst constant discussions about the upcoming trip. Carrington assumed his self-defined duties as manager on the spot. Working hard to make good money, they passed the time in style while waiting for the blessing of the English Society for Psychical Research, which arrived three months after Carrington had sent his request to London with Fielding and Baggally.

We're set, Carrington exclaimed.

Hooray! To success and triumph in America, Eusapia toasted, and they drank until even the smallest cloud on their way to comfortable stardom had been chased away.

After many unexpected delays and snags, they finally left Naples in October, a trusted Neapolitan translator, as well as a female assistant in tow, stowed away in another corner of the boat as if the two pairs were unconnected. The weather was unusually cold for this time of year. Bundled up in a woollen coat, Eusapia looked out on the grey ocean and wondered whether her excitement was justified. Ever since she glimpsed an ocean liner when she arrived in Naples as a young girl, she fantasised about being a passenger one day. To be on the Prinzess Irene was a wish come true. The motion of the waves made her come alive. As the fury of the wind amplified, and fellow passengers became listless and green in the face, she walked around with renewed energy, holding up much better than the younger Carrington. Motion sickness was not something she'd ever encounter. Her stomach was strong. She smirked as she poured tea for her friend.

Here, drink this. It might get you back on your feet.

Carrington groaned. He was less ill than most other passengers who kept throwing up over the railings. But the stink of their vomit and the retching noises around him churned the already heaving remainders of lunch in his belly. God, how long was this torture going to last? And to be outdone by a woman, a much older woman at that! It was as embarrassing as if she'd drunk him under the table.

Finally, the weather cleared. Life became more bearable for a few days. As soon as his stomach settled, Carrington's entrepreneurial ambition kicked back into gear. In no time, he helped Eusapia set up a small cabinet in her booth and advertised her presence. Many of the seasick travellers battled with irrational fears. Fear of death pervaded the ship like cold fog and put a damper on the voyage. Would they make it? Would family and friends survive this trip? A medium might have the answers. With no need for coaxing, the travellers filled Eusapia's booth, paying respectable fees for short séances.

Working with limited space, she quickly adjusted her performances and limited herself to transmitting comforting messages of safe passage to fellow Italians mostly. Many sitters came back for repeated reassurance. Over and over they needed to hear that their boat would not sink and they wouldn't succumb to sickness and die. With a steady stream of customers, Eusapia's and Carrington's money supply was secured for a while. When the last sitter of the day left her cabin, Eusapia and Carrington lovingly touched their small piles of money. Their partnership was destined to bear lovely fruit.

A reporter on the boat, a certain Signor Rossini, circulated with unabashed curiosity. He too saw an opportunity for making extra money.

Be careful, Carrington advised her when Signor Rossini wouldn't leave her alone.

But Eusapia was not afraid. She knew how to deal with people, and Rossini fell exactly into the category that suited her best: handsome, vain, and overconfident, with an insatiable appetite for sex and money.

Come to my booth, Eusapia said. You deserve an exclusive interview.

The two met after a late supper. Her guest brought scotch and rum, which Eusapia poured for a quick get-acquainted round of toasts. As they continued knocking back shots fast and furious, Rossini's eyes beamed like signals from a lighthouse.

Signor Rossini, Eusapia started.

Oh call me Beppe, the man responded with smug familiarity as if they had known each other for years. Eusapia, who truly appreciated Rossini's single malt scotch, pulled herself together. You had to be careful with reporters, who were very different from the easily duped academics. Contrary to the honest naivety of many scientists when it came to the twilight zone, the reporters she had come to know remained alert and never abandoned their hunt for juicy tidbits regardless of how drunk they were.

Eusapia watched the contents of the bottles disappear rapidly. Rossini's tolerance to alcohol might surpass hers. She'd better be careful. Almost imperceptibly she turned down the lights until only a small lamp threw a reddish sheen over the room. Yet she knew that Rossini had noticed and was as watchful as at the beginning of the night.

Do you ever cheat, my dear Eusapia? Rossini asked, gazing soulfully into her eyes, so close that despite the scotch on her breath she could smell the rum on his.

My dear Rossini, Eusapia responded, every bit as passionate, it's inevitable. I can't bear to disappoint my sitters when my powers are low. Why go through the demanding mediumistic effort if tricks do the job? No one can imagine the exhaustion the production of authentic phenomena leaves behind. It takes me days to recover, she confided, her body leaning against his. My dear friend, it's not very often that I trust someone enough to tell it as it is, but you seem like one of the rare people worthy of complete honesty.

Rossini now stared at her as if under a spell.

I'll show you, she said in such a low voice that he had to move even closer to hear what she said.

Eusapia took his hand and pressed it to her left breast.

You feel that? That's my heart going wild under the stress of producing phenomena.

Rossini said nothing. For Eusapia, the mounting temperature of his body was response enough.

Look carefully, she instructed. She moved the table slightly from one side to the other. See my leg?

Rossini tried to see what she was doing.

See? she repeated.

He slowly turned his head to watch up close and saw her leg neatly balancing the table.

I do it so well, she added, that very few detect the fraud. But sometimes, I get caught and people get extremely angry with me.

You shouldn't cheat.

That's easy for you to say. I would show my sitters the real thing every time if I could, but that's impossible. For you, I'll do my best. If I can't produce the real thing, I will not pretend. You might need to be patient though because it could take me a while . . .

That's all right. I don't mind waiting.

As he displayed no religious tendencies, she did not ask him to sing. Chattering, shouting and even some drunken singing seeped through the cabin walls and provided much needed background noise. Ten minutes passed, half an hour, an hour, and nothing happened. Eusapia could feel the alcohol in her blood. She shouldn't have tried to outdo him. She was paying the price, while Rossini looked remarkably fresh for the advanced hour. She moved closer to him again, feeling his leg pressed against hers. The rest of his body was almost touching hers with just space enough between them to create an exhilarating tension, which she hoped would soon produce effects. She gave a sigh that made Rossini shudder. Well hello, she said to herself, everything is as it is supposed to be.

Concentrate, she instructed Rossini. This time, the table will rise by itself.

Rossini stared at the table.

Before it rose in jerky movements, hands poked him in the back and soft lips kissed him on the cheek. The drum rolled. Sounds of a guitar sounded faintly from the back of the room. In a swift movement, Rossini turned around so as not to miss anything. As he glanced in the direction of the sounds, he suddenly felt the table jump up at least four feet into the air, then briskly descend. Despite his quickness, he only caught a glance of the rapid descent. He still felt Eusapia's leg pressed against his.

425

Before the séance, he had been sure that she was cheating. His job was to discover how. Now he started to wonder whether the claims of her authenticity were true. Loud raps interrupted his thoughts. Weak echoes from all four walls seemed to mock his doubts. He waited. By now Eusapia seemed in a deep trance. From time to time she moved as if her insides exploded. Rossini wiped his forehead. Sweat dribbled rapidly down his cheeks and neck. He felt as if unearthly powers were dragging him to promises of another world. All of a sudden, Eusapia's arms grabbed him so tight he thought she'd strangle him. Yet he did not want the séance to end or extricate himself from her grasp. For a moment, she loosened her grip, but not for long. The next squeeze pushed him over the edge. He cried out and lost consciousness for a few seconds, and after an instant was fast asleep. When he awoke two hours later, Eusapia was lying stretched out on her bed, still in deep trance, with her blouse open and nothing under it. Rossini could not take his eyes off her chest. He moved closer as if drawn by magnets. Just for one moment, he wanted to rest his head between those two soft mountains. He hesitated. But two strong arms grabbed him and in a wild tangle of limbs, in an explosion of shouts and cries, he lost consciousness for a second time.

It was Carrington who helped Rossini to his room and lent a sympathetic ear to his gibberish. While he couldn't make much sense of what Rossini said, he had no need for words to understand. This was one awestruck man, a confused cynic who couldn't come to terms with what had happened in the cabin!

Carrington knew he couldn't afford to let this opportunity slip away. He settled down in the chair beside Rossini. He would stay there the whole night if that's what it took.

I know it's hard to believe, Carrington admitted in his most genuine voice, I myself still have trouble believing that here is a woman with actual powers. Never before have I met someone like her. I came to Naples to unmask another cheat. Yet, here I am, looking dumbfounded at phenomena that cannot be explained by trickery.

Rossini was silent now, listening, as if Carrington handed him a lifeline with his words.

I'm sure, Carrington continued, that as a journalist you must be as much of a skeptic as I myself. You have seen too much fraud to believe in supernatural occurrences any longer.

Exactly! Are you convinced that Eusapia Palladino is authentic? Rossini asked slowly as if he couldn't trust his own voice, but heartened because the man beside him did not think him a fool.

There is no doubt in my mind anymore, Carrington responded.

How is this possible?

Carrington looked at the man gravely, but said nothing.

I saw it with my own eyes, Rossini continued. How did she do it?

Carrington did not respond. He was patient.

What powers are at play?

It makes you question all your assumptions, doesn't it? Carrington said pensively.

Rossini looked at him without answering.

Carrington could see the man's mood shift from questioning his own sanity to an "I know what I saw" attitude, and from there to the troubled excitement of a reluctant convert. He should leave the man to his own reasoning now. He could see that Rossini needed time to absorb the impact of the séance.

Eusapia smiled as Carrington gave her an account of Rossini's reaction.

Well done, she praised him. I wonder what he'll cable to America.

I think we'll get some fine publicity out of his new insights, Carrington responded.

I was powerful yesterday, Eusapia said, grinning.

What did you do?

I called on the highest powers to make their presence felt and touch Rossini's doubting heart, Eusapia said, and her laugh rolled through the cabin like a series of explosions. Carrington guffawed when exuberant echoes answered from the walls.

Every day, Carrington prepared letters and cables for newspapers, universities, societies and acquaintances, to be dispatched as soon as they docked. Rossini didn't disappoint them, either. Clever descriptions of the supernatural part of his experience filled page after page and would go to his own newspaper as well as one or two others. In addition, the late-night séances left most sitters with unforgettable impressions and the urge to let other people benefit from this once-in-a-lifetime occasion. Not everyone has the chance to meet La Palladino on a boat like you, Carrington would remind the satisfied customers. Now that you have, make sure your friends and relatives are aware of what they'd miss if they failed to take advantage of the many opportunities in New York to visit Eusapia. Here is my contact information so that you can find out where to send your loved ones.

428

What Eusapia loved most about Carrington was his convincing manner, his unbeatable expression of sincerity. He was good for business. He would bring her fame, money, delicious food and excitement. Cheers, my friend, she exclaimed, raising her glass in an appreciative toast.

12

WITH PUBLICITY PUT IN MOTION from a distance, Eusapia entered New York with fanfare. Despite the drizzly grey November weather, she moved invigorated to the rhythms of the loud noises of the city as if they were music. New York seemed to know and welcome her. She snatched newspapers from the hands of paperboys because the vision of her signature in print fascinated her. This was more supernatural than any of her own phenomena. When she discovered a picture of herself, which Carrington must have sent to America from Europe long before their departure, she could not put the paper down. Imagine, she was that famous!

I put my faith in you from the beginning, Eusapia said to Carrington, but never in my wildest dreams could I have foreseen how utterly irreplaceable you'd be.

Thank you, Carrington said pleasantly, you're not bad either.

Did you make final arrangements for the investigations?

In my opinion, Carrington responded, a nice, slow build-up with private séances would best advance our cause.

But that won't pay as much.

Believe me, this introductory period will pay off, the more the news of extraordinary occurrences spreads, the more you'll be able to charge, even for the scientific investigations.

Eusapia acquiesced. No need to worry with a promoter as shrewd as her friend. What was good for him was good for her and vice versa.

Carrington rented an apartment for Eusapia on 34th Street, not the neighbourhood she had expected but a place with its own rewards for sure.

You're in luck, he said, the people living here always seek novel excitement. Spiritualism will rouse their interest for sure.

But I like professors, Eusapia responded, balking at the idea of being reduced to a curious vaudeville act.

The more diverse the audience you're able to convince, the faster your reputation will grow. And don't worry, I'll send you professors too, Carrington tried to placate her.

The satisfying effect of the initial fanfare wore off quickly. What did the Americans want? Carrington thought it wiser to stick with Italian immigrants whose real or make-believe preoccupation was to plan their trip back to their homeland. Speaking and hearing her colourful language in a country where grey mumblings sputtered from people's mouths boosted her confidence. Her fellow Italians never grew tired of her. When she threw in a few lucky numbers for success in business, love life and especially betting ventures, their adoration and respect skyrocketed. Eusapia almost purred with pleasure when her countrymen and women invited her to their homes and treated her to Italian food and wine.

Even Signor Giuseppe Bonfiglio, ballet master of the Metropolitan Opera House, and his wife whom she had met on the Prinzess Irene during her trip across the ocean, invited her to their home. They wanted to see more spirits. They wanted to relive the dramatic emotions they had experienced during previous private séances with the medium. In Eusapia's presence, spirituality, sensuality, and pure fright swirled through and around them in a fantastic dance. Unusual rhythms and apparitions, punctuated by frantic drum rolls and galvanised by impassioned callings from unearthly creatures, whipped them into a frenzy. Everything the Bonfiglios and Eusapia desired during those evenings happened effortlessly as if the world existed solely to satisfy their needs.

Sometimes Eusapia wondered whether the American Italians were the same as the Italians in Italy. She was sure that their psyche changed in the new country and the American air altered one or two dimensions of their personalities. Eusapia couldn't put her finger on it. Maybe they had to be a different breed to begin with to be able to embark on such an adventure. Apart from economic considerations, which she knew to be powerful motivators, she couldn't think of any reason to leave family and friends behind and say goodbye to the blue sky and Mediterranean ambience of their homeland forever to seek a new life in an unknown country. Yet, once arrived, these immigrants fell into diverging camps. Many reinvented themselves, shook off the shackles of the past and ignored that they were born under unfavourable circumstances. They prospered and discovered an energy in the new country they could not have developed back home. Others though could not hide regret and dashed hopes, a dispirited longing for relatives back home. What they had left behind in the old country slowly took on the proportions of a lost paradise. None of the gains in America could ever make up for their loss. Eusapia knew that some of her learned friends would theorise for hours about the essence of immigration. They would categorise and reformulate and redefine with complicated words. She just observed. With a keen intuition, she picked up clues and interpreted them as she saw fit, astonished at her compatriots' curious suspension between two worlds. Whether happily adjusted or sadly uprooted, they always had their feet in both worlds, never a hundred percent sure where they belonged and with whom they identified most. But that seemed the fate of first-generation immigrants from anywhere, Eusapia continued her thoughts. She had to know such things if she wanted to gain entry into her sitters' hearts. It established a first connection and made it easier to conduct successful séances.

Eusapia didn't linger on this reflection. She was a doer, not a thinker. It amazed her that some academics spent their lifetimes thinking about issues that for her were crystal clear. She knew about people, their goals and motives. To her it was an ability you learned like talking or walking. While practising her profession, she came to realise that she was faster in picking up clues than most anyone, including those claiming to be psychologists and experts in human nature. Even though she sometimes envied those fortunate enough to grow up with books and brainy notions, she felt contempt as well. What was the value of an education if it didn't teach you to see what stared you in the face?

If Eusapia had been given a choice, she would have chosen only expatriate Italians for her séances, now that she knew them. It was so much easier and so much more fun to speak without need for translation. In Italian or Neapolitan, every word added drama and mystery, every sentence was an integral part in the successful production of inexplicable phenomena. Remove language, and you take away the soul of a performance. Be that as it may, Carrington showed her no pity. He expected her to be just as successful using her eyes and hands, and the help of her interpreter.

You're familiar with those conditions, he said. It never prevented phenomena from occurring before.

Don't you see that I'm getting older? Eusapia cried out plaintively.

What does that have to do with it?

She stared at Carrington as if he were joking. Don't you know that my powers too will wane just like any aging person's abilities?

Eusapia sighed with frustration. She needed double the preparation and recovery time than twenty years ago. Now that she was over fifty, every bone and limb in her body ached for hours if not days after a séance. What she'd give to turn back the clock! She hadn't lost all her powers though. Even at fifty, she could still turn up the heat anywhere, but especially in a darkened séance room. Eusapia grinned. Life was still fun. She wondered for a second how she'd scrape together a living five or ten years from now, but declined to dwell on troubles looming ahead.

Enjoy the good times while they last. Let's bring on the American professors, she almost shouted.

That's the spirit, Carrington responded. Don't worry, they'll love you as much as the Italians.

Despite her aging body, Eusapia experienced a sudden surge of energy. She wasn't finished yet. The future promised great things.

The session with her first set of professors played out to her satisfaction. Even Carrington congratulated her. The men were bewildered. Was it possible that dead friends and relatives tried to contact them? Were the strange currents in the air signs of supernatural presences?

When however the youngish psychologist Hugo Munsterberg arrived at her quarters with his mentor, the psychologist William James, Eusapia itched to throw him out the door. He was bad news. That much was clear from the moment she spotted him standing there in his confrontational broad-footed stance, scorn ostentatiously displayed on his face. It didn't matter that William James compensated for his colleague's rudeness with soothing warmth.

Outraged by Munsterberg's preconceived opinion of her, she shouted, pointing at him without making eye contact, My powers shrink in his presence. He is inimical to everything I stand for. I will not give a séance for a man who disrespects me and my profession.

I beg you to change your mind, my dear Signora Palladino, Carrington appealed to Eusapia in a calming tone.

Eusapia had already opened the door and threatened to either storm out or give the no-good Munsterberg a kick in the ass.

Signora, William James said, it would be a great honour for the two of us to witness your phenomena, especially since my friend Richet gives strong credence to your authenticity.

His sincerity pacified the enraged woman, but not enough for her to agree to a séance.

After catching James's imploring glance, Munsterberg stated evenly, If I have offended you in any way, Signora Palladino, I'm sorry. I'm a scientist who has not had the privilege to come across so-called supernatural phenomena. I promise to attend this séance with objectivity.

Despite his apology, her hatred of him intensified. His words, rapidly spit out in a slight German accent, hit her like the commands of a drill sergeant. An overpowering instinct to flee the premises tensed up every muscle in her body. Against her better judgement, she remained. Munsterberg had thrown down the gauntlet, and if he thought she wouldn't take it up, he'd better think again. She would not leave this challenge unanswered.

Eusapia saw to it that the séance room was prepared even more carefully than usual. Appreciative of the help Carrington provided in setting it up, she slapped him merrily on the back. As soon as the men were seated, Eusapia asked for the lights to be dimmed. In the soft sheen of one four-candle-power red bulb and a two-candle-power white bulb, and in the resulting blurring of features, merely the familiar traits of close friends and family members would be recognisable. The two men's foreheads shone almost ghostly in front of their receding hairlines. As Eusapia entered into her trance, she kept a sharp eye on Munsterberg. Nothing escaped her, no movement of his fingers or arms, no undertone in his voice. William James was easier to handle. Thankfully his approach to the supernatural was unbiased. He watched with an open mind, fully engaged in the moment. Eusapia liked to listen to his concise comments. He was never mistaken in how high a table rose, how many ectoplasmic limbs she displayed, where sounds came from, and who had materialised during the séance. When she heard Munsterberg sneer at James' accounts, her revulsion grew so acute that she nearly barfed over his black suit. Though she couldn't follow most of what he said, its meaning came across stark and rude. Not even his professional respect for James mitigated the contempt he felt for any fool who believed in spiritualism. She was only too able to understand the meaning of his impatient speech, *What does it matter what you think you see? All that counts is what actually happens. Don't you recognise this woman for what she is, a master of deception and undeniably a champion in her field?*

Even the ever polite James bristled under the insults of his young colleague.

Let's keep a measure of impartiality, James suggested, *and see what the rest of the evening brings.*

Agreed, Carrington replied.

The men took a break until, more than an hour later, Carrington led everyone back to the séance table. Eusapia perceived this as a sign that the real test of her phenomena had come. Yet, she sat motionless and silent, as if transplanted into a different universe. She made the men wait for another hour before she initiated preparations for falling into a trance, never letting Munsterberg out of her sight. The table stirred. Musical instruments gave sporadic serenades. Loud raps sounded from every corner of the room. In spite of the darkness, she could detect a sudden confusion in Munsterberg. She was on the right track. Though he still had the alert breathing of one of those self-proclaimed debunkers of mediums she disliked so much, she detected the slightly sour smell of frustration exuding from his armpits. Her confidence increased. Phosphorescent lights glided through the room and flashed from various spots. Cold breezes from the white tuft of hair in the front of her head sent eerie drafts toward her sitters. Eusapia could see Carrington give an almost imperceptible nod. The table rose again, higher than before.

Four feet, William James called out.

Fresh flowers landed on the table.

I'm being poked, William James stated in a muted voice.

A hand slapped me, Munsterberg exclaimed, and now someone poked me in the back.

A head appeared above Carrington's shoulder, lingering for a moment. After pressing a loud kiss on his cheek, it disappeared quietly.

Eusapia slumped over the table, quiet for a few seconds, then writhing as if in pain or under the influence of other powers.

The two psychologists sat awkwardly beside her, unsure whether it was appropriate to say anything, and not too sure what was going on.

Finally, Eusapia quieted down. Carrington led her to a sofa where she could stretch out comfortably and recover from the enormous expenditure of psychic energy. He also handed her the customary cup of tea she demanded after each sitting to soothe her throat and stomach.

What do you think? James said to his colleague as the lights went on.

She certainly puts on a show, Munsterberg uttered, a trace of anger in his voice.

Did you see her cheat? James inquired.

No, I didn't. She is good at what she does.

Couldn't you admit at least the possibility of unexplainable phenomena occurring in this room? James suggested.

The only thing I'll give her credit for is her immense talent as a performer and fraudster.

Scientists need to keep an open mind, James admonished him, since they are the ones with the necessary imagination and creativity to explore unknown territory.

Munsterberg threw his hands up in frustration.

Will you at least come to one more séance? James pleaded.

Munsterberg balked at the suggestion.

Come on, James encouraged.

All right, then, Munsterberg said, giving in rather reluctantly. Let the chips fall where they may.

Carrington scheduled a new séance for the eighteenth of December. What a blessing that Munsterberg had not figured out how her phenomena worked, Eusapia thought gratefully. However, no one had ever accused her of a false sense of security. This man was out to get her. It seemed to rile him that he had been unable to unmask her immediately. An intelligent man like him incapable of catching her at her tricks! Now that he had been dragged into this affair, he would not rest until he could say triumphantly, Ha, I told you so. Eusapia grew angrier by the minute. Why should she have to perform under such disagreeable circumstances?

Arrange for a séance with nicer company, she screamed at Carrington. I've had it with Munsterberg.

What impression would that create, Eusapia? I've never seen you shy away from a challenge before, and I don't think I need to underline the importance of this next meeting.

Eusapia let out a shriek, stormed into her room and slammed the door shut behind her. People do get older, she thought, I get older. The séances take too much out of me. It was such a walk in the park when she was twenty. At thirty it was even easier. She was at the height of her powers, a perfect mix of talent and experience. At fifty-five, she needed to rely more and more heavily on the mental aspects of her profession, on words, expressions, and especially drama, to make up for her decreasing physical prowess. She wanted someone to give her a break. *What's happening to me!!? I've always been able to take care of myself and will continue to do so even if it kills me. I'm not done yet. Too many people depend on me. Raphael's daughter, homeless orphans and sickly old people. Don't forget the legions of starving and beaten animals.* Now that she remembered again what was at stake, she pulled herself together. *Whatever it takes, I will deal with Munsterberg.*

In the meantime, Eusapia gave a series of séances at Columbia University. Several times she was caught cheating, but couldn't be written off entirely. Too many phenomena remained unexplained. The scheduled séance with Munsterberg was to take place at the house of Professor Lord who was a friend of both spiritualists and their opponents. Carrington approved of him, which reassured Eusapia. Still, she couldn't shake the feeling of dread that invaded her body the moment the date was set.

Hello, Signora Palladino, Professor Munsterberg said, *how do you do?*

Eusapia cringed at his formal politeness and fretted at the horrible trap hidden behind its smooth curtain.

Hello, Signor Munsterberg.

That was all Eusapia would force herself to say. Not wanting to give anything away by the tone of his voice, Munsterberg too kept silent.

To Eusapia's relief, Professor James arrived at that point and diffused the tension. The two colleagues chatted cordially for a few minutes. James, who spoke Italian, took care to include Eusapia in the conversation. With every passing minute, her mood improved and her misgivings lessened. Complete ease though was elusive. As she looked around casually, but aware of the slightest change, she noticed the level of James' expectation and Munsterberg's nasty cynicism rise rapidly. Eusapia knew she could not afford to wait for a more propitious constellation of their conflicting approaches. No, every minute lost would add to their hazardous mix of explosive differences. Already, a small but ominous shadow began to cloud their friendly chatter.

I hope, James urged his colleague, that your scientific training and curiosity will guide you during this séance and allow you to attend it with the impartiality it deserves.

I shall look at the phenomena as the rigorous scientist I am, Munsterberg responded rather tersely. To diminish the sudden discord, he added quickly, We both will.

Focusing on secret preparations for her phenomena, Eusapia nonetheless caught the almost imperceptible frown on Carrington's face. He's worried, she thought. Why? Except for the tense politeness in the room, she had not much to go on. Should she withdraw? It was evident that Carrington had noticed her hesitation. He clearly did not want her to bow out now. On the contrary, he was nudging her on. After a last glance in his direction, she accompanied the two scientists to their seats on the right and the left of her table. They sat down quietly as if not to disturb the strange currents in the room. At the last minute, Professor Lord, who had been delayed by an unexpected

442

messenger, joined them as well. He sat down beside William James, opposite Carrington.

Again, unusual feelings of dread knotted in the pit of Eusapia's stomach. Something was off. The problem didn't originate from James or Lord, whose facial expressions contained nothing she hadn't seen before. As expected, the culprit was Munsterberg, who had been obsessed with sabotaging her from the beginning. What made him more dangerous today? The obvious smugness on his face? She didn't think that was new. But when she saw the glint in his eyes, she was certain he had something up his sleeve. She watched more closely, but his face was suddenly set in stone. Apart from that momentary glint, Munsterberg was in full control of his emotions, shielded by an invisible armour that prevented her from picking up further clues. Eusapia let out an exasperated sigh, to which Carrington responded with a meaningful clearing of his throat. She tried to concentrate. This séance business was becoming too damn demanding. She just wanted to sit in a loud Italian restaurant and eat Italian food and drink Sicilian wine. Another suggestive cough brought her back to the business at hand. She couldn't afford to fail.

The sighs and moans that followed were part of her ritual for falling into trance. Eusapia thrashed about more than in previous séances. She was aware of every current and wrinkle in the air. She took in James's hopeful observation, Lord's detached attention, Carrington's quivers of nervousness, and most of all Munsterberg's nasty caught-you attitude. I can do this, Eusapia encouraged herself. I'm able. I'm talented. I'm La Palladino. But for the first time in years, her confidence abandoned her. She waited in vain for the exhilarating tingling in her fingertips that was a sure sign of her readiness to perform. Confident or not, though, she had to produce.

Slowly, the table rose an inch, but immediately thudded down again. A minute later, it rose two inches and floated gracefully back to the floor. The intensity of the currents in the room increased, rushing toward her from all sides. James and Lord were touched by floating hands. Nothing happened to Munsterberg except for a slight breeze from the top of Eusapia's head that strangely cooled the right side of his face. Lights flickered throughout the room, and a flower fluttered down on the table. It was time for the little wicker table to march toward the group. Eusapia breathed in deeply. She leaned forwards covering her end of the table. Before a new phenomenon could occur, a bloodcurdling scream shook the walls and threw the whole room into chaos. The scream came from Eusapia whose foot was caught as if in a vice, with someone or something hanging on to it with merciless determination. Lord jumped up from his seat and turned on the lights. There it was for everyone to see: Eusapia's foot in full swing backwards toward the wicker table, gripped in midair by two strong hands attached to a man in black clothes lying on his back on the floor. This creature must have snuck into the room unseen and unheard during her séance to examine from close-up what was happening in the dark. Eusapia tore her foot out of his grip and stomped full force on his chest until Carrington pulled her away. Shrieking and swearing in her starkest Neapolitan, she lunged at Munsterberg, whom she knew to be the real cause of her debacle.

This time both James and Lord held her back. You cock-a-hoop son-of-a-bitch! Eusapia screamed, plunging into hysterics. She was so enraged that she tore herself free from the men's hold and punched her enemy in the chest. Again she was subdued and brought back to her seat.

I guess your answer is obvious now, she heard Munsterberg address his colleague James, each word understood perfectly as though it were screamed in Italian instead of his hideous English.

James responded only with a slight nod. He looked as if the life had been drawn out of him.

Eusapia offered to continue with her séance. It couldn't get worse. Chances were she could redeem herself. James did not respond. He didn't even look at her. She repeated her offer. This time, Carrington shook his head.

I don't know what happened, he said, looking perplexed. It must be her age. I have seen spectacular phenomena in Italy. So did Richet in France. Maybe her powers have left her for good.

You must be kidding, Munsterberg interrupted. What does it take for the two of you to acknowledge that this woman is a common cheat like all of those so-called mediums? Let my assistant explain to you in detail what he observed from his vantage point under the table.

James looked offended. He had to acknowledge that in this case Eusapia perpetrated blatant deceit. Did his colleague have to rub it in his face? Although Munsterberg suddenly was careful not to gloat too openly, James felt insulted and could not subdue the resentment that sprouted up in him like an unsightly weed. Eusapia took solace from his mounting exasperation. He'd never forgive Munsterberg for humiliating him with his high-handed actions. What an ingrate to throw doubts on the judgment of his former mentor! James would forgive him even less for the mocking account Munsterberg was sure to deliver to the

445

scientific community with much glee and self-congratulatory satisfaction.

Why don't I ask the cook to prepare a light meal, Lord suggested, and we will discuss what happened in a more pleasant setting.

Unfortunately, I have to put the finishing touches on a manuscript that has to go to the publisher tomorrow, James replied.

He stood up and said politely goodbye to everyone, even giving Eusapia a nod, and left hurriedly.

Carrington seemed in no mood to make conversation with Munsterberg and came up with a flimsy pretext for leaving immediately.

I will drop Eusapia off at her quarters, he said.

On the way to her hotel, Carrington refused to talk to her. He sank into a foul mood, which kept Eusapia quiet for once and careful not to ignite an already incendiary situation.

Alone in her room, she flung herself on her bed. She'd had enough.

Carrington didn't show up or send any messages for days. She doubted that a good ending to her stay in America was still in the cards.

Eusapia avoided opening the New York Times over the next few days. Even if she was unable to understand an article in full, she had always been obsessed with picking out loaded words that clearly expressed judgement or praise and had been taught to her in Italy as preparation for her trips abroad. She craved the reenergising mix of baffled compliments and stunned respect. These days she didn't have to look to know that the press was negative, the words nothing but condemnation.

In the wake of her disastrous séance, she had no desire to go out and see anyone. She kept busy stuffing herself with pasta and sweets. Over and over she sent her assistant out in search of tasty meals prepared by native Italians who didn't have to be asked twice to provide the renowned medium with her favourite dishes. The food helped calm her restless body and cool her incensed brain.

What now? Eusapia asked herself, but already her old spunk arranged to jump back into action. Rising above darkness and depression, and after restless reflection, she decided to resume work with or without Carrington. She couldn't afford to leave America penniless.

In her next move, she sent out her Neapolitan interpreter, this time to announce that she would begin giving séances in her private quarters this very evening. While this was a comedown, she accepted it, unhappily to be sure, holding her nose, but aware that in her situation she couldn't be picky. To get up when she was down and fight adversity was a necessity and second nature. Not only did she always pull herself up again, but once she got going, she thrived on the challenge.

The one-on-one séances proved successful. People who sought her out respected her and needed her help. As always, she figured out in the first moments what her sitters came for. Even those she couldn't stand, the conceited rich who rolled in money without ever lifting a finger, Eusapia knew how to satisfy. She looked at them with big mysterious eyes until they trusted her and she could bilk them for all they were worth. From the moment they set foot in her quarters, it was just a matter of accurately interpreting clues and details. Luckily, she could rely on her interpreter for more than just translation. No medium,

447

and no magician for that matter, can function without trustworthy and capable collaborators.

Eusapia's empty pockets gradually started to fill up again. In no time, her friend Carrington was back, organising, making publicity, and scheduling. When they put their minds together, they were a formidable team. United in their need for money and fame, they soon regained entry into circles where new opportunities abounded and good wine flowed freely.

I knew you couldn't stay away, Eusapia said to Carrington

As different as they were in their demeanours, they had a rare understanding of each other and despite their frequent quarrels could not afford to betray their fragile bond. Still, the Munsterberg episode remained a thorn between them.

Never dwell on what could have been, Eusapia suggested. Always search for new roads to your destination.

They eagerly visualised those roads and places until they turned into viable possibilities. Eusapia and Carrington were ready to resume where Munsterberg had rudely interrupted them. They would show him who had the last laugh.

With fresh energy and hard work, they enlivened the uneventful winter months. Eusapia leapt at the chance to meet other mediums and magicians. She saw through every trick and ruse at once and stole ideas right and left. The exchange confirmed that no one matched her powers. Ha, she commented to herself, imagine pulling myself up from a childhood like mine and managing to capture the interest of the rich and famous. Who would have believed they'd take me seriously? Only rarely did resentment creep into her voice. Yes, she sometimes let her imagination run wild with scenarios where she was born under different stars. Life should have been easier for her and others like her. It wasn't right that all your time and energy got used up in the struggle for survival. It still made her livid to think that talents and intelligence had little to do with your prospects in life. No, what became of you depended mostly on money and the standing of your parents. If anyone as much as touched on this subject, she flew into a rage. Injustice, she shouted, but cut her outbursts short because in her world more immediate struggles required attention. Sometimes though, her outrage was too strong to be controlled. Damn the cruelty that lets some live in luxury and makes others starve or suffer in horrible misery! When she had her rages under control again, she threw herself into her work. Make money, she told herself, that's what gives you power. The more money, the more opportunity to change lives. And by God I hope that the people I help go on to do the same for others. She believed in the domino effect that Giorgio had explained to her a long time ago: Piece by piece, the world will change for the good, until at last and at least the physical needs of people are met. As it was, she put her mind together with Carrington's, who had his own dreams, aspirations, and reasons for accumulating money and fame, but was instrumental in helping her inch toward her immediate goal of replenishing her pockets.

Following the crushing blow by Munsterberg, academics still came to visit Eusapia, just not in an official capacity.

Given that we can't change what happened, Carrington said, we should at least take advantage of the unexpected benefits of the Munsterberg episode. Who says you can't benefit from notoriety?

Eusapia couldn't argue with that. She had lived by this philosophy her whole life, not by choice really, but in response to the calamities that befell her over the years. Only the rich can afford to live honourable lives, she defended her actions even to herself, trying to push away images of good honest people she had met who subsisted on the absolute minimum. Then there was Gianina, who had little and still gave, Lucia and her brother who kept barely anything of what they earned for themselves. Okay, you don't have to be rich to keep your integrity, she admitted. But if you have to be born poor, let it be in a family that struggles together and takes care of its members so that hardship can only make each of them better and stronger.

Right now, her priority was not to think, but to make money since hers was running out again. So she continued meeting whomever she could. She had aspired to higher company, but ever since she hit fifty and especially since being stranded in this unfriendly country, her expectations plummeted. The stamina and flexibility needed to produce high-quality séances made themselves scarce. Her previously never-ending supply of energy dwindled. From time to time, one of her knees acted up with arthritis, which didn't prevent her yet from carrying out her acrobatics, but made them unpleasant. The same was true for her back, which throbbed with discomfort. As she didn't feel up to performing at a high level, she couldn't be choosy when it came to her clients. The academics who came to her now, openly or in secret, were for the most part less interested in her mediumistic powers than her feminine attributes, which even now she still used to great effect. She had no qualms meeting their needs. It took less effort than producing top-quality séances, and those sitters left in general more satisfied. They'd go into

450

their community with great testimonies to her abilities and would come back repeatedly. However weakened she was, she still was able to provide comfort and consolation, even encouragement and a few light moments. That was the one aspect of her profession that filled her with pride. Sometimes she felt like a saviour. She knew she had brought back people from the abyss, especially men. She might not be a psychologist by training, but she was one at heart, a good one at that, she thought, better than most she'd met because her intuition and observation skills were sharper, and her mind quicker when it came to processing and analysing matters of the heart.

I'm going to introduce you to my friend Howard Thurston, Carrington responded to her constant questions about his recent mysterious meetings and comings and goings.

Who is he?

One of the most famous magicians in the world.

Oh no, you don't, Eusapia exclaimed, furious he would expose her to more danger. He hadn't kept Munsterberg away, and now this!

Eusapia . . .

What devil possesses you to send a magician my way? Eusapia shot back. I chose you as my manager to protect, not to destroy me. What happened to the scientists? Did you lose their trust? Did you ruin our chances?

If you'd stop for a moment, I could explain. I guarantee you, Howard Thurston will endorse you.

How do you know that? Divine insight???

Something like that. Certain things are better left unsaid. We've done well together working in this manner. If you value this partnership, then you'll keep your faith in me.

You better not disappoint me! Eusapia screamed, but had to admit that Carrington's wicked smirk inspired confidence in her. She had detected this expression numerous times before, and every single time, the execution of their plans progressed without a hitch.

As soon as Eusapia caught sight of Howard Thurston, she breathed easier. An instant familiarity sprang up between them as if they had known each other all their lives. His dark hair and eyes gleamed and evoked strong memories of her magician husband Raphael. Eusapia could not help sighing. The lines in Thurston's face told stories of long-ago adventures, replicas or twins of hers and Raphael's on their tours through Italy. It wasn't just a similar storyline they had in common, but also the background, the emotions, and the constant struggle for physical and professional survival. Like her, he was treading a fine line between good and bad, full of good intentions, not above swiping what he needed or brazenly lying to get out of tight spots or carry out seemingly impossible ventures. Thurston might be famous now, but she saw that he too had suffered his share of misfortunes. Only his obsession with magic, his unerring way with words and his inexhaustible energy had allowed him to survive. She smiled knowingly and received the same smile back. Carrington was right, she did not need to worry. Cheerfully, she accepted the challenge in Thurston's eyes to prove herself worthy of his support.

Yes, my friend, she exclaimed. I will show you all I have. You won't be disappointed.

Carrington was thrilled when he saw his friends get along so well.

It's time for the séance, he reminded them.

He put on a record she hadn't heard before. Nothing religious. In fact, it sounded like circus music.

Thurston swayed enthusiastically to its rhythms and melodies. The gramophone fascinated him to the point he almost forgot the séance. His curiosity knew no bounds. A technical advance, a record he was unfamiliar with and he was in heaven!

Extraordinary, he exclaimed, and already saw this same music underscore some of his performances.

All of a sudden, his eyes widened in strange anticipation. He could sense that the performance was imminent.

The table rose. Thurston's face furrowed. Seeing his puzzled look really got her going. She had heard of people writing important exams before being approved by their profession. This was her big test. When it came to her professional pride, the academics did not count. The seal of approval could only come from Thurston or someone like him. Not in a long time had she invested so much of herself in the outcome of a séance.

The table rose again, accompanied by mandolin chords and the clear sounds of a trumpet. Bracelets, necklaces, and watches sailed over Eusapia's head and slowly floated down on the table as lights blinked in every corner of the room. John King materialised in front of them, an imposing ghostly figure that produced a few sentences in an eerie-sounding English.

Thurston was taken aback by the mention of his dead mother. And how could the medium or her guide know about the sailor who sporadically appeared to him in his dreams with predictions of things to come? No one knew about this. But King elaborated and managed to confuse the great magician, who since his early childhood had been a romantic at heart.

The séances ended with the materialisation of other spirits gently poking and kissing Eusapia's new friend.

Suddenly she collapsed, lay immobile for a minute or two, then in a sudden movement sat up straight.

And? she asked expectedly.

Congratulations, Thurston said, talking to her as if he had met his equal, I am impressed.

For the rest of her life she would treasure this moment.

Eusapia, you're in for a treat, Carrington announced, because I present to you one of the two great performers of magic. You've heard of Houdini, the king of escapes. Tonight you'll see the king of cards perform just for you.

In front of her eyes, Thurston produced the trick of the rising cards, which had made him famous all over the world. One after the other, the cards rose, stayed suspended in the air for a few seconds, then disappeared into nothing.

Do it again, she exclaimed.

So Thurston did, over and over as Eusapia begged him for more. His presentation was spectacular. Knowing a great deal about card tricks, she wanted to figure out his sleight of hand. No matter how carefully she watched, she only had an inkling of how the cards seemed to rise on their own.

Again, she commanded.

That will be it, my dear, Thurston responded. Eusapia wondered whether she had been on the right track with her conjectures, but realised at once that this might be exactly what Thurston wanted her to think.

You're good, Eusapia exclaimed. Thurston bowed. She could see that he too savoured her compliment.

When she thought the show was over, she heard a sudden jingling of bracelets, necklaces and rings and couldn't believe it when the jewellery she had used in her own séance appeared from out of nowhere and settled on the table in front of her. Thurston gleefully rubbed his hands, but simultaneously assessed the value of the loot with the gleam of someone who understood its worth and could appraise it to the last cent.

He buys and sells, Carrington said casually.

Oh, Eusapia said, giving a last glance at the American jewellery with just a tinge of regret, why don't you keep this as my gift to you.

You're extremely generous, Thurston answered and quickly stowed the bounty in one of his many pockets.

They're good pieces, Carrington said quietly, sometimes they become even more valuable if they're reset.

Of course, Thurston responded quickly, all the jewellery I buy and sell is reset.

After spending most of the week together, the three had formed a close bond. To cement their friendship, Thurston offered to put an ad in the newspapers as a testimony to her authenticity, offering a thousand-dollar donation to the charity of a magician's choice if he succeeded in producing Eusapia's phenomena under the same conditions she did, a feat he declared impossible from the outset.

Charity? Carrington asked. That's a good one!

Eusapia flashed a smile. The charity idea was brilliant, plus how clever to demand that the conditions be the same she had to submit to!

Most magicians didn't accept Eusapia as one of their own. On the contrary, they saw her as a brazen rival who took advantage of people's grief and made a mockery of it. In the eyes of those magicians, she shamelessly exploited recent loss for financial gain. They hated her for encroaching on their territory by unethical means. Many magicians made it their mission to unmask those phony mediums. In Cambridge, it was magicians who dealt Eusapia an almost fatal blow. Neither she nor Carrington wanted to be reminded of it. The fallout from that episode followed her, some people would not let her forget it.

Now, two magicians by the name of Rinn and Davis challenged her in New York to another session, offering her a thousand dollars of their own money if they were unable to detect fraud in the production of her phenomena. To everyone's surprise, Eusapia accepted the challenge. A séance was scheduled to take place on the 22nd floor of the New York Times Tower, with the Times carefully stating that their only role in this affair was to provide a locale, not to give support to one or the other of the two sides.

While at first the two groups seemed to agree to each other's conditions, they plunged into acrimonious haggling almost immediately. Eusapia stormed back and forth through the room, glaring. No one succeeded in appeasing her. Did they think she was stupid? Carrington had told her that Professor Jastrow, who her enemies wanted to be among her sitters, was one of Munsterberg's friends and out to get her for sure.

Under no circumstance do I tolerate the presence of Professor Jastrow at any of my séances, Eusapia insisted furiously. His personality prevents an even minimal production of genuine phenomena. He'd doom me to fail even before the séance gets under way. Either he is out, or I am.

How could they expect her to submit to his prejudiced approach? His unkind tactics would ruin any séance he attended, not just hers.

In the end, Jastrow withdrew. That left Rinn and Davis to deal with. On the positive side, Carrington and Thurston would be at the séance. Were they sufficient to counterbalance Rinn's and Davis' negative currents?

If you want to make sure that no one is aiding me, she shouted at them, I want to make sure that no one is impeding my phenomena either. Even at the height of my powers, it would have been impossible for me to direct the forces in the room to levitate a table if grown men were heavily leaning on it to prevent it from rising.

We'll just observe, Rinn responded good-naturedly. It is important however that you be put in a canvas sack, provided by myself, that will be laced up to your neck in the back and can only be opened by cutting. In addition, this sack will have to be fastened to the floor. Only in this way can we be assured that you don't use your arms or legs.

Beat it! Eusapia thundered. You don't want me to succeed! Once, I consented to be in a sack back in Italy. You know what happened? It made the spirits stay away. I was not able to produce any phenomena because the currents between me and the forces that manifested themselves in the room weren't allowed to flow uninhibitedly. You want nothing to happen? Is that your goal? Then yes, I should be stuffed in a bag. But if you are serious about observing phenomena, my arms and legs need to be free.

After Carrington brought the group back to order, Eusapia acquiesced to be tied but with at least eight to twelve inches of slack between her ankle and the chair leg and another eight inches between her legs. Conditions were proposed by one side, discussed and rejected by the other. Proposals flew back and forth.

You make it impossible, Eusapia scolded, full of indignation.

Oh yes, Davis replied smirking, if there is control, nothing happens, if there is no control, you cheat. Then you blame your cheating on the investigators, saying they didn't control you properly. What's the point? Reconsider, one thousand dollars is a formidable sum of money. It's yours for the taking if you convince us of your authenticity. We even agree not to use the sack. We will only tie your legs and hands. I personally will do you the honour.

Eusapia glared.

You will not touch me! Even your breath harms me. Yet, there I am still allowing you to be present. You will not tie me. This task has to be done by someone else because you don't understand the difference between bound and tied. Never will anyone bind me, but I agree to be tied as specified earlier.

You will produce at least four of the eight phenomena mentioned in the Times? Davis asked.

What is the matter with you people? Eusapia screamed at the top of her voice. I cannot promise. With genuine phenomena you can never promise. You can only hope that they will occur.

By now the climate was tempestuous, with both sides frustrated by unacceptable conditions.

Eusapia suddenly grabbed the arms of both men.

Go away, you two, go. I don't want your money. I will give a séance in the New York Times Tower as I promised, but not in your presence. I will give the séance for the scientists out of my love for science, and listen to that: I will forgo all remuneration!

With strong arms, she shoved the two men out the door. Carrington was unable to intervene.

Keep your money, she shouted behind them, I'll do it out of my love for science.

Her séance was well received. No one tried to undermine her. All her conditions were scrupulously followed. Again, she was able to produce her magic under just a shimmer of light. Quite a few of the scientists, even some non-spiritualists came away from the evening wondering whether there was a supernatural dimension to her performance. Carrington was satisfied.

Well done! he complimented his partner.

On this high note, Eusapia answered, I want to leave New York. I'm weak with homesickness. I need to hear and talk my language, breathe in Neapolitan smells, live among fellow Italians.

The timing is good, Carrington agreed only too quickly, hitting a raw nerve with Eusapia, who increasingly resented the way her stay in America had turned out. We salvaged our reputations at least in part, Carrington continued as if unaware of her reaction, We can go about our future business with our heads held high.

Naples, 1910

13

A STRONG WIND seemed to add to the power of the Prinzess Irene and propel it faster through the dark waves toward Naples, creating a merciful distance between Eusapia and America. Looking back at her stay, Eusapia's blood pressure rose. Nothing had gone her way. In the end, even Carrington seemed in a hurry to get rid of her. While she knew he'd continue to defend her in public, he was the one who caused her the most misery and hurt feelings. Where was he when she waited to board her ship? It was just like him not to see her off. There he went, already busy promoting other, more lucrative propositions and taking up his work at the American Society for Psychical Research again. How dare he devalue their friendship this way after all the money he made off her séances! Even when the scientists had turned away from her, she brought in the dough. That merits at least a smidgen of gratitude and gentlemanly courtesy. She should have known better. Carrington was obsessed with keeping his options open, cleverly playing both sides of the spiritualist spectrum. He singled her out as special and at the same time unmasked as many unprofitable mediums as possible. Eusapia spit out in a rage. Never put your trust in a person who speaks from both corners of his mouth.

Traitor, she screamed into the wind.

After she had spewed that word out of her system, her blood pressure began a shaky descent to normal. So did her frustration. She smiled uncertainly when she realised that the wind was dying down. Well, she grumbled, bad memories won't keep me down. I'll take comfort from the good ones. America obviously was not without satisfying and triumphant moments. Immediately, snippets and chunks of stories flashed up inside her, waiting to shoot into the open and keep friends, family and future sitters back home spellbound. But for now, those stories were still too raw and in need of transformation to make them fit for public consumption.

To Eusapia's surprise, Raphael was waiting for her at the harbour. Every so often, very rarely now that he was older and had settled down, he performed in Naples and roomed at her place. No other welcome could have restored her mood as instantly and completely.

The angels are still on my side, she exclaimed. So is the Virgin Mary, and my mother, and Celestina. It's an encouraging omen you're here, Raphael!

Eusapia threw her arms around him. As she embraced him, the familiarity of Naples and its inhabitants flooded back into her. From the depths of her dark eyes, a stream of Vesuvian lava prepared to rise and pour out in a shower of golden sparks.

I'm still alive, she declared, life flowed back into me with the first breath of Neapolitan air. Nothing can break me, not even America. I remain The Great Palladino.

Raphael smiled as if in pain. In her excitement, Eusapia had failed to notice the signs of distress in her friend. It took only a moment though before the enormous sadness in his smile stopped her enthusiasm short.

What's wrong, Raphael?

When he couldn't speak, Eusapia became alarmed.

Is it Giuseppina?

No, Raphael finally answered, his voice flat and cracking.

Who?

My wife, Raphael responded, his grief unchecked now. Her heart gave out, just like that, without warning.

Eusapia held on to him until he quieted and finally straightened.

Shaken by Raphael's news and worn out from her voyage, Eusapia asked a friend who lived in her building to throw some food together. It was clear from Raphael's drawn face that he had barely eaten or slept in days. His shirt hung loose on him and his pants threatened to slip off. Realising how frail he was, Eusapia worried that he'd disappear into nothingness without warning. I will nurture you back to health, she pledged. Soon the tempting smells of cheese, basil and tomato filled the room. Despite Raphael's brave efforts to force a few morsels of food down his throat, Eusapia had no illusions about the daunting task in front of her. She watched him anxiously while the room vibrated with the presence of strong powers. Her own mother approached behind Raphael's chair with a promise to help him find the way to a more hospitable place. His mother and brothers were already waiting for him. Eusapia expected his wife to appear at any moment, but for now saw no sign of her. The slightest pull from her might be enough to whisk Raphael away right in front of her eyes. Eusapia blinked. When she opened her eyes, he was gone.

Raphael can't be alone at this point, Eusapia told herself. She jumped up from her chair and stormed out the door. Where would he have gone? In spite of her tiredness, she raced from one street corner to another, without luck.

She rushed toward the train station with its many dark corners and niches where someone could hide his grief. A sudden thought stopped her. She had never seen him enter a church during all their time together, but now remembered him telling her that his wife had a very strong faith and that notwithstanding his initial reluctance, he too learned over the years to take comfort from it. Was it possible he had sought refuge in the church near Eusapia's place? She entered the building which — as if out of compassion for poor souls like him — stood unlocked. Feeling her way around in the semi-darkness, she spotted him thanks to the faint sheen of moonlight that squeezed through the window. He was sprawled out in front of the Virgin Mary, asleep, his face still wet from tears. Eusapia did not have the heart to wake him. Here, saints and angels would help her watch over him. Quietly she sat down in a pew. Too exhausted from the voyage to hold herself upright any longer, she decided to lie down beside him. As she did, she slung a protective arm around him and fell asleep instantaneously.

At first, Eusapia was still too asleep to react to the exclamations and loud prayers that suddenly reached through her drowsiness. She could feel a circle of agitated people surrounding the two of them. Her only reassurance came from recognising that her arm was still on Raphael in the same position as she had put it before falling asleep. Raphael did not stir but felt warm. Carefully, she opened one eye for a second and saw the priest drawing crosses over their bodies.

No, she cried out in fear of being buried alive, her scream pulling Raphael out of his sleep. They jerked up simultaneously. Invigorated after her sleep, Eusapia jumped up and pulled Raphael into an upright position. She put her arm behind his back and pushed him briskly toward the side exit. The flustered churchgoers started to pray louder to cleanse their church of impurities. Eusapia could hear fear in their voices as well. Everyone knew her at least from reputation and would not take any chances. She might put a curse on them if their actions displeased her. Rushing outside, Eusapia realised that the group of churchgoers was not pursuing them. Only the asthmatic breaths of the priest trailed behind. His flailing arms drew crosses in the air, setting in motion breezy currents that provoked goose bumps on her arms and neck. But even the priest gave up his pursuit after a few seconds. Eusapia marched Raphael safely up to her apartment where he lay down again and fell back asleep, unable to face being awake.

Raphael found no peace in sleep, but received at least the strength to go on another day. Eusapia noticed a tinge of colour in his cheeks, though he barely touched the coffee and pushed bread and cheese aside. Taking care of him took her mind off the humiliation she had suffered in America. It forced her to put off plotting revenge and indulging in stupid reactions that could only worsen the situation.

We'll get through this, Raphael, she said supportively.

He burrowed his head in his hands.

He needs fresh air, Eusapia thought. Given his unreceptive state of mind, she simply grabbed him from behind, stood him up, then pushed him in front of her out the door, down the stairs and into the clear May sun. Raphael mechanically put one foot in front of the other. She still marvelled that he had made it to the harbour to reach out for help. Seeking me out was an affirmation of life. When he lacked the strength to go on, he put his trust in me.

They walked for almost an hour. Raphael was slowing down. She did not let him stop. If his soul resisted the pull of life, she'd call on his body to reconnect him to this world. Even if physical pain was his only sensation, it was a start. Resolutely she dragged him along until at long last she let him rest on a rock at the Bay of Naples. She spread out a child's blanket she had stuffed into her bag. As she helped him sit down, his chin slumped to his chest, and he fell back asleep. She had to prop him up. The weather was too cool to let him rest for long, and she had no extra blanket to cover him. As they continued their walk, Raphael suddenly woke up more completely. Through this half-awareness, his eyes opened wide and full of darkness. He walked by himself now. Eusapia kept close watch as he trudged along, railing against his woes.

He grimaced and screamed, No, no, no. It's not fair. Over and over he screamed. People stared. A stranger approached to offer his help, but she shooed him away.

Eusapia looked up at the sky. She remembered how Raphael's mother and brothers had materialised from a group of white clouds to console him when the recounting of their deaths tore open old wounds. This time, she searched the sky in vain. She kept waiting, but Raphael's family did not appear, neither did his wife. Maybe Eusapia had become too old to perceive or sense the departed. Not even her mother or Gianina were visible.

The mother of my children was a good woman, Raphael said.

I know, Eusapia responded and didn't just say it to make him feel better. Acquaintances who knew Raphael's wife described her as a woman with a big heart and an endless supply of goodwill.

Day after day, Eusapia pulled Raphael out of the house. She relied on the passing of time to smooth away the sharpest edges of his grief. But she was certain that fresh air, sun, and walking were the tools to start the difficult process of healing. She forced herself to be quiet, waiting for Raphael to confide in her. He wasn't ready. Apart from instances of uncontrollable screaming, swearing and sobbing, he brooded in silence. She did not push him to talk. But soon she became restless and unable to walk and keep quiet. One morning, she poured out her own adventures and misfortunes. Even when he did not react, she continued with her familiar torrents of speech and explosions of gestures, believing they had the power to call him back to the present and ground him in reality. She persisted and pumped more and more colour and passion into her stories. As Raphael learned to cope with his grief in miniature steps, she confronted the galling bitterness her stay abroad had left in the pit of her stomach. Could articulating her problems make them more manageable? Or did each additional outpouring intensify them? Whichever was true, she had no choice in the matter, she was a talker. Silence had never worked for her. She had never known anyone to heal in silence, not in Naples for sure. No, talking to Raphael, even if he didn't hear a word, was her way of coming to terms with what had happened in America. She wished Raphael would respond. How long would it take for him to hear her again? Steadfastly she continued. One month went by, two months passed. On a hot July day, as they walked along aimlessly, Raphael suddenly stopped. He looked at her with sad, but clear eyes.

Are you okay, Sapia? he asked in an almost natural voice.

Eusapia was too surprised to answer. She threw her arms around him and held him tight.

Thank you God, she murmured over and over. You had mercy on my friend. Now hold on to him. Never let him slip away again.

From that day on, Eusapia and Raphael started once more confiding in each other, tentatively at first, even doubtful that this attempt at communication would succeed. Yet it was a small sign of normalcy, a slow return to a connection as familiar as breathing. It was Raphael's turn to talk about his wife, stories and details Eusapia had heard before. But she now listened as if she heard them for the first time. Raphael's wife had always been up before anyone else, cooking, washing and cleaning with a big smile and a happy voice, busy sharing stories and gossip that drew the neighbourhood into their kitchen, making it the hub of the whole area.

Eusapia began to catch glimpses of Raphael's wife. Gradually those visions solidified and filled the space around them. The woman accompanied Raphael and Eusapia on their way through the streets of Naples. At first, Eusapia had to get used to this togetherness. But as she recognised the emptiness that the loss of Raphael's wife had created, she reached deep down into her well of natural generosity to include his wife. Both struggling and determined, she soon accepted this new task. A raw kindness began to flow toward her friend and his wife. Raphael smiled gratefully. He understood and appreciated her sacrifice. Eusapia sometimes had to close her eyes to keep the most intense visions of his wife away. Despite all her generosity, seeing the woman too clearly would have been unbearable. This too, Raphael understood. Linked together arm in arm, the three marched forward.

As Raphael regained some of his strength, he ventured out on his own. Eusapia watched him walking down the street, his long arms thrashing the air in uproar against God, and the world, and the cruel circumstances of his fate. Recovery will take time, she thought, but at least he is alive enough to react. It didn't matter what he did as long as he awoke from his stupor. Even eating a piece of cheese without being prodded or biting into a fruit would have been an improvement. Until now, she had to drag him out of bed. If she hadn't led him forcefully to the table and placed the food right before his eyes, he wouldn't have eaten. For him to leave the house was progress. A small step only, but Eusapia clung to the hope that other steps would follow. Most of the time it's those barely perceptible accomplishments that lead to new paths, she told herself. Raphael is strong. When he sees life trace new trails in front of him, as uncertain as they may appear, he will start out on his journey with courage.

Eusapia was not surprised when a few days later, Raphael said goodbye.

It's time, he said simply.

Eusapia knew what he meant. Though still skin and bones, he had recovered sufficiently to remember his responsibilities. He had to think of Giuseppina, her older sister and younger brother. Instead of helping them cope with their grief after the sudden death of their mother, he'd not only abandoned them but caused them additional grief. He couldn't understand now how his despair had robbed him of his senses and driven him away. He had abdicated his role as a father. He could not make up for that, but at least he would try to pick up the pieces. From now on, he would face the future together with his children in the hope their mother would continue watching over them. Eusapia followed his inner monologue without the need for words.

Go Raphael, your children are waiting.

It wasn't with her that Raphael belonged even now. They had known that since he first brought Eusapia back to Naples. Yet they also knew that in their separate lives they were more united than if they lived in the same apartment, that their souls were inextricably linked and that no physical distance between them would ever change this.

Before Raphael left, she packed a lunch and snacks for him. In the bottom of his shoulder bag, she put most of the money that was left from her American tour. Raphael needed it more urgently. But she did not want to spoil their goodbyes with thoughts of money and awkward thank-yous.

Eusapia accompanied Raphael for the first two hours of his trip. Before she turned around, they held each other for a long time, taking a last bit of comfort from each other.

Come back soon, Raphael, Eusapia said, praying she would see him again.

I will, he answered, and quickly walked off.

She stood watching until the last speck of him disappeared in the distance. If I had special powers, Eusapia thought, I would use them now to send him the strength necessary to overcome his loss and be there for his son and daughters. But since she had no faith in her own powers, she crossed herself three times and entrusted his fate to higher powers.

Raphael's departure left an unnerving emptiness. As soon as he left, the horrid memories of her downfall in America returned to eat her alive. Since her return, the scientists had stayed away to protect their reputations. No one wants to be associated with failure. For now, that's what she stood for, spectacular failure, fraud, and vulgarity. Eusapia fumed. How dare those people sit in judgement of her? Vulgarity? She had seen what was going on in high society. Why was their behaviour more acceptable than hers? Were they less obsessed with sex than she? If some of the wives had the slightest inkling of what was taking place behind their backs, they might take their frustration out on their husbands instead of her. Fraud and lack of integrity? That must be a joke. How was it more honourable for academics to fill page after page with unscrupulous inventions to prove their theories? Why was it so much worse when she resorted to trickery to satisfy her clientele? Oh, she read those men more easily than they read their fancy books. As much as she hated being judged by others, she had long ago decided to turn their low opinion of her into an advantage. People who mistake a lack of schooling for inferior intelligence become so careless with their secrets that they throw about invaluable bits and pieces of information. If those scientists realised how much power their ghastly feeling of superiority gave her! Yet, it still maddened her when some of those swellheads sprouted half-truths if not outright fabrications in their important books right in front of her because they considered her too illiterate to care what they babbled about. The success of their books enraged her even more. If she were to read books, she'd be careful about what to believe. Books of truths stood on the same shelves as books of lies, and it would be a hard task to distinguish between them. It was better to trust

471

your own judgement and understanding of the world and of people. But while she kept mostly a low opinion of books during her whole life, she was always curious why people wrote. She quickly realised that just like in her own profession, money and fame were potent motivators. She did meet pure souls as well — that she had to admit — scientists who were guided by their thirst for knowledge, by imagination and creativity, or their need to help others. But she'd bet that a significant proportion of the academics she knew cheated their way into powerful positions the same way fake mediums achieved fame. If she hadn't seen it with her own eyes, she wouldn't have believed it. They took such pride in acquiring their precise instruments. Yet the instant they held them in their hands, they were apt to manipulate every aspect of their experiments to register whatever they wanted them to register. Again, how was that different from what she did? Since she needed those scientists, she didn't scream her outrage into their faces or show that she was on to them. The only outlet for her frustration, the one she always resorted to when she was riled up, was to spitefully spit on the ground, then stare at them accusingly.

It's your bitterness talking, she heard her mother's voice.

So what? Eusapia shouted. It's the truth.

She could see that her mother had no intention of answering. All of a sudden, Eusapia saw her in a new light. Without the blurred boundaries between dead and alive that allowed Eusapia to imagine Mammina as part of this world, her mother clearly was not a flesh-and-blood person. Otherwise she would have responded, maybe even shouted back. But the dead have the advantage of wisdom. Mammina wanted Eusapia to work out her problems on her own. If her mother had yelled, Eusapia could have yelled back louder and drowned her out with a few ear-splitting screams. Mammina's silence left her uneasy.

Eusapia looked disheartened down at her aging body. She lifted the left leg, then the right leg straight up to her nose and back. She swung one after the other sideways to pull her favourite trinkets from the top of her dresser. She could still do that. But her movements were slower than twenty years ago, energy-sapping efforts rather than the exhilarating fun she experienced when she was young. Again, she swung up her legs. She'd be surprised if other women her age or even young ones could demonstrate such flexibility and expertise. Still, how long would she be able to continue to work?

So don't talk to me, Mammina, if that's how you feel you should treat me, she screamed in the direction of the dead people who had vanished a while ago. Forget it, she continued at the top of her lungs, aiming the words at anyone who would listen, but at her mother in particular. Eusapia stormed out the door. She needed air. She needed noise. She needed the sun. Unfortunately, she had no such luck. The sky was clouded and threatened rain. Eusapia started to run, pushing people out of the way, ignoring the barrage of insults in her wake. She only slowed down hours later when her breath became laboured. Even at this less frantic pace, she sped past most people on the street, young people included. As for men and women her own age, no one kept up. Eusapia winced. God, they look ancient, undeniably over the hill. Some of them barely kept themselves upright. Instead of feeling relieved to be in better shape, she shuddered. Those people held a mirror in front of her. You're getting old. You're finished.

Eusapia stopped.

Oh no, I'm not! she screamed furiously. If I have learned anything in life, it is to never give up. I grew up fighting to stay alive, I'll grow old fighting.

She started running again, turned around and ran the whole way home.

As she fell exhausted on her bed, she smiled. Don't count me out. I still have some fire left in me.

She looked up to the ceiling and saw her mother hide a little smile. Eusapia smiled back. She knew she would have good dreams tonight.

Life slowly returned to normal except for painful bouts of arthritis and migraines that increasingly added misery to Eusapia's days, bogging her down and leaving her to ache for an end to hard work. Despite those setbacks, she continued working, with less and less pleasure but with her ingrained tenacity. Over the months, she gradually built up a clientele again.

The time came when she had no choice but to appeal to the understanding of her sitters. With age, she told them at every séance, mediums become increasingly sensitive. Simple beams of light turn into weapons. The only way for mediums to protect themselves from getting hurt is to turn down the light more than was necessary in younger years.

So far, the sitters accepted her justifications.

Trips abroad, she intimated, are becoming detrimental to my connection with higher forces. I refuse to travel any longer. Only when I'm grounded in my native country can I activate my mediumistic powers these days. Words and thoughts in Italian are stronger than in any other language.

No Italian disagreed with this assessment. Eusapia stared at her sitters through the darkish air. Some of them shifted uncomfortably. Catching her eye might expose them to danger.

Watch and sing, Eusapia commanded. Hypnotised by the command, the sitters looked at her expectantly. Before anyone could intone a note, invisible hands strummed the guitar in the cabinet and unseen mouths tooted on trumpets. Anxiously, the sitters stared at the black curtains. Would John King materialise? Would he send messages?

Suddenly, the young woman to Eusapia's right screamed, Over there! Over there!

As the other sitters turned to take in this new development, they exclaimed simultaneously, Heavenly Mother! Too stunned to say more, they watched spellbound as a figure materialised right in front of them, then suddenly disappeared with barely a swish.

After seconds of intimidated silence, the sitters came to life.

A miracle, the woman beside Eusapia exclaimed. They now all talked at once. Not only had they witnessed a materialisation, but they swore that at the same time faces had been peering out of the cabinet.

I know I saw my dear sister! the same young woman piped up again, in tears and overcome with emotion. My little sister hasn't changed at all. She still wore her first communion dress.

Yes, a man agreed. I saw her too. I could see she wanted to say something.

I could see her lips move, an old woman added.

Could you make out what she said? the young woman asked feverishly.

She said she is happy where she is now, the old woman answered without hesitation.

The young woman grabbed Eusapia's hands.

Make her come back, she begged. I want to talk to her.

Next time, Eusapia answered, I will try again next time.

Without compunction, she pocketed the extra money the sitters pressed into her hands. In her mind, spiritual hunger rated way below the hunger for food she had seen over and over, so extreme that it could only lead to death. Those were the people she cared about and who needed her. I'm just a breath away from their fate, she reminded herself. Misery quickly sends you over the edge, and the hand of God, which was supposed to hold you, is too slow to catch you. Misery has the strongest hold when it grew up with you. It never lets you forget what it looks like and that it is merely two steps behind no matter what you achieve in life. Tremors of unease rippled through her body. Yet, she remained thankful and took it as a sign of mercy that somehow her dead mother had been allowed to stay with her and give her the strength to survive the worst. Over the course of the years, Eusapia had been surprised to learn that only one in ten million is born with seeing eyes. She knew that it was this gift of seeing her mother that had saved her and now obliged her to take on responsibility for those who were less fortunate.

Eusapia used the bit of leftover American money to buy bread and blankets, which she distributed the same day. It did not prevent her though from using some of the coins to buy a few bottles of heavy wine. In the company of four good friends, she drank herself into a feeling of contentment that was intensified when one of her many long-time friends decided to stay the night. Real peace came over her when she drifted asleep knowing that his warm body would still be there when she woke up. Just before sleep took over, she wondered how Raphael was doing.

Even in times of meagre income, Eusapia resisted wishful thinking. Get off your ass, she hounded herself. Wasting time on what-ifs never improved your lot. Forget the scientists. So what if they avoided her? She would make do with whoever showed up.

But when word reached her that Everard Fielding wanted to book another session with her, she beamed. I'm not over the hill yet, she thought. Maybe I'll be able to regain the trust and admiration of the academic community. She refused to indulge in memories of the good old times when scientists made her the centre of attention, and money, food and wine flowed toward her in never-ending streams. Still, she couldn't help wondering whether her good fortunes were about to return.

She enthusiastically ran toward Fielding when they finally met. As soon as she turned her attention to his friend William Marriott, her heart sank. She unerringly recognised him as a magician. Why couldn't Fielding have brought another spiritualist? she thought, very much taken aback, but intent to face the situation head-on and calmly. Fielding greeted her in an unpretentious manner that made up for the insolence of choosing a magician as his companion. He had always been one of the good guys. She could see that he seemed stronger than last time and less consumed with sadness. The artificial smile that had remained frozen on his sad face even during the most difficult months had thawed and become more genuine. His eyes were less clouded. Though he clearly wasn't over his loss, time had worn away the sharpest edges of his grief. Fielding breathed freer. Life was pulling him back. He remembered that he was on earth to fulfil his destiny. No matter what life demanded of him, he had a duty to respond with courage.

The fee is still the same, Eusapia continued, collecting the money before her visitors could change their minds. Given that they belonged to the class of the privileged, they certainly had the means to pay her what she deserved. Coughing up a hefty fee without haggling was a way to show respect. Despite her seeming confidence, Eusapia was nervous.

Unfortunately, I'm all booked for the next few days, she explained, not letting on that she felt it necessary to put in a solid practice before calling on spirits in the men's presence.

When the two men arrived for their séance, she had to steady her nerves. She determined that Fielding had grown even stronger than she had assumed at the outset. As she had always liked him, she was happy for his good fortune but worried about the implications for her séance. She had no illusions about his friend Marriott whose cynicism dripped off him like sweat on a hot day, a very different character than Fielding's previous companions Carrington, who from the beginning of their encounter set his sight on becoming her manager, and Baggally, whose sexual appetite was more than obvious. This guy Marriott, no, she could not trust him! Eusapia insisted on having some of her friends in attendance.

You must be kidding, Marriott yawped, rejecting her demand outright, For the money we paid, we expect a private séance.

Eusapia focussed her warmth and sympathy on Fielding, asking about his health and state of mind, but couldn't get much more than a quiet "fine" out of him. She recalled every detail of their last séance. If she reproduced that séance tonight, would it have the same effect? Eusapia searched his darkish eyes in vain.

478

Not good, she thought. She blamed his defensiveness on the response to his report of their previous séances, which had met with harsh criticism and outright mockery. Non-spiritualist scientists and journalists wrote it off as a joke. Some called him a naïve dupe. Others, gentler ones, speculated that grief over the death of his brother had robbed him of his critical faculties. Carrington had told her all about it, how the insults had hurt their friend, who not once through the whole ordeal faltered in his belief in her. She should take comfort from that, but she didn't. A strange gleam in his eyes alarmed her. Yes, he wanted to believe. Yes, he wanted to reconfirm her authenticity. But he would do so with a clear mind.

Marriott was worse. He looked ready to pounce. His one-track mind put Eusapia on guard. There was a man with a mission. He wanted to make her pay for taking advantage of his friend when he was at his most vulnerable. While Eusapia respected his concern, she hated the man for denying even the possibility that she had helped Fielding overcome his grief. Without her intervention, he would have been considerably less able to cope with the death of his brother. She gave him hope when he needed it most. False hope, she expected Marriott to retort. This man gave her zero credit for trying to help. So be it, she thought and steeled herself for a difficult session.

There he was already fussing and clamouring for more light when she needed the room to be darker than ever. Marriott finally refrained from forcing the issue, but his contempt seeped into the room like cold dampness. Eusapia struggled to find a point of connection with this man. She couldn't discover recent or even ancient grief in him. If he had lost someone close to him, the death had touched him little. She couldn't even sense a lost love. Because he has no passion, she concluded harshly. Restlessly, Eusapia moved around in her chair. To her relief, Fielding had not changed since their last encounter, except for his improved health and outlook. Despite the accusations of incompetence levelled against him since the publication of his report, he held on to his beliefs. What he had experienced during her séance in 1908 was real. Not once did he second-guess her or wonder whether the unusual phenomena had been produced by trickery. For that, Eusapia was grateful. He would watch carefully this time, but without preconceived notions that she was a fraud. Would she dare evoke his brother? Not during this session, not before she'd laid her groundwork.

Again, Eusapia tried secretly to dim the light. Marriott kept further objections to himself, but tensed up, fully alert to what was happening around him, too vigilant for Eusapia's type of powers. Fielding sat impassive. She couldn't assume though that he was less watchful. In a daring move, she turned up the lights to their maximum.

Watch the table, she commanded.

Marriott stared at her disdainfully. Do you think you can dupe a magician like me? Eusapia could hear the sneering in his head. What was she supposed to do?

Both your bodies are inimical to authentic phenomena, she said. I don't know why. Two years ago my special powers seemed to awaken in your presence, Everard.

I remember, he said curtly.

Again she tried to dim the light.

Why does it have to be so dark? Everard asked.

I don't know myself, Eusapia replied, but from experience I know that special manifestations are most likely to occur when the glare of the light is softened.

Okay, it's time to let us see something, Marriott urged her on.

Eusapia knew she had to come up with some phenomena.

Your foot is out of your shoe, Fielding said reproachfully.

He grabbed her leg which had swung back toward the cabinet.

Oh, Eusapia said, don't mind that, I have to stretch before I can fall into a trance.

Moments later, she started to moan and writhe in her chair, throwing her body around, and landing on her sitters numerous times. There was no response from either of the two men. They remained watchful. Music, she said. She asked Fielding to put on a record, and was grateful for its immediate effect. At least the seductive sound of the newest Caruso arias calmed the men.

Suddenly, the table rose a few inches.

I saw you use your leg, Marriott snarled in disgust.

Sorry, my friends, Eusapia excused herself, I'm not feeling good tonight.

She closed off the session and turned the lights back on. Let me rest for a while on the sofa, then I'll try again. I'm too exhausted right now.

Take your time, Fielding said kindly. We'll wait, don't worry.

Eusapia caught the faint flicker of hope in his eyes, a plea for another encounter with his brother.

She sprawled out on the sofa and soon was lost to the world.

Signora Palladino, Fielding finally called out after two hours had passed, will you be able to continue with your séance?

She moved uncertainly as if unsure of where she was.

My friends? Are you still here? Of course, I will give my séance. You paid good money for it. Even without money, I would want you to witness occurrences that cannot be explained by cold logic. Come back to my table.

Marriott and Fielding took their places on each side of her.

As before, Eusapia desperately tried to dim the light without drawing attention.

When an object in the cabinet started to shake, Marriott said dryly that she had used an extendable pole to move it. When a wicker stool took a few hesitant steps toward the séance table, he accused her of using her leg again.

Poor Signora Palladino, Fielding said when he was poked several times in the back and on his head, it's not your night. It's clear you used your own arm. Why, my dear friend, why do you have to cheat?

Eusapia looked at him with her dramatic eyes, willing him to cut her some slack.

Everardo, you know I was able to produce materialisations last time. You know all about my powers.

I know, Fielding said simply. I remember well.

I tried very hard tonight, Eusapia conceded, I just have nothing left in me. I can't summon my powers.

Don't worry, Fielding said, still grateful for the peace he had found during his last visit.

I haven't seen anything yet, Marriott said stubbornly. You're a cheap fraud with no credibility whatsoever.

Oh, no, Fielding defended her, she is much more. But age must have caught up with her and prevented supernatural powers from manifesting themselves.

Then give us our money back, Marriott said roughly. No one should have to pay for nothing.

Eusapia glared at him.

Let the poor woman be, Fielding said to Marriott. I'll pay.

They left, with Marriott grumbling all the way.

You should have seen her last time, Eusapia could hear Fielding's fading voice in an attempt to calm down his friend. She did have special powers. I know. I was there.

Watching her visitors disappear in the distance, Eusapia had the feeling that her life or at least a big part of her identity was walking away with them. She tried to call it back, but it had irrevocably attached itself to the men.

Sometimes, people have to let go, Eusapia heard her mother's voice.

Why, why should I?

Because you understand the cycles of life.

No, Eusapia responded crossly, I was born a medium, and I will die a medium.

Isn't it your experience that, at some point in your life, you have to take leave of your former self to concentrate on new aspects of your existence?

Other people might do that, yes, but not me.

Eusapia tried to catch her mother's answer through the noise of the street, but there was no answer.

You don't believe me? Eusapia yelled into the air where her mother had stood just moments earlier. When again she received no response, she complained defiantly, That's just like you, Mother. Why don't you believe in me? No real medium loses her powers as she grows old. I won't either, you'll see.

483

EUSAPIA TRIED HARD to put the humiliating experience in America and the disheartening séance with Fielding and Marriott out of her mind. She couldn't afford to contemplate an end to her career, and did her best to keep fear at bay. Successful or not, she had to work.

Wilfully ignoring her dwindling money supply, she went to the newspaper office nearby and ordered a big ad for three days running. She needed to put her name back into circulation. Soon, interest in her séances rekindled. Some of her former clients came back.

Oh, Signora Palladino, they said, don't lose sleep over those full-of-themselves Americans and their lies. We have seen with our own eyes the extraordinary manifestations that occur in your presence.

Thankfully, word about her latest disaster hadn't reached her sitters ears. As Eusapia experienced loyalty and renewed adoration, her old contempt gave way to appreciation. Adjusting to the ravages of age on her body, she shifted her emphasis from physical phenomena to more theatrical verbal productions and turned her psychological skills into a profitable tool. Her sitters still needed physical signs to believe that links with those lost to the otherworld had been established. To Eusapia's relief though, what they wanted most was simply advice on everyday problems.

Signora Defferari, Eusapia would say, or Signor Scipione, I understand what you're going through. She didn't just say so to make them feel better, she did share their feelings, and sitters willingly opened up to her. She had heard more stories and secrets, seen more hurts and betrayals over the years than seemed possible for one human being. She instinctively knew when to say, You have to talk with your husband about this, or Never mention what happened to anyone else. Sitters trusted her more than their priests because she was practical and made sense. They would not clam up for fear to shock her with the sordid details of their stories and did not feel it necessary to restrict their accounts to the least scandalous parts only. Confronted over the years with every aspect of human vice, cruelty and other ugliness, Eusapia was well placed to predict the consequences of certain actions and point out the results of alternative moves. She started to throw in a few lucky numbers again with her usual performances, which the sitters snapped up with greedy expectancy, not doubting their importance for a moment. No other city was as crazy about numbers as Naples. Neapolitans used whatever she pulled out of the air to determine dates for weddings or departures to other countries. Most of all, the numbers were needed to put luck on their side when playing the all-important weekly lottery. Everyone needed luck when it came to money, and Eusapia was the most likely to give it to them.

Am I ever glad I thought of using the numbers, Eusapia congratulated herself. Nowadays, not even music or unidentifiable noise was as propitious for the manifestation of physical phenomena as her sitters' obsession with numbers. As long as the sitters' attention was hooked on them, anything could happen. Tables rose straight up in the air with a rapidity that took attendees by surprise. The abundance of ectoplasmic limbs growing out of her body filled the audience with wonder and fear. When no one looked, Eusapia gloated in satisfaction. If the scientists had written her off, that was their loss. The renewed success and accompanying financial benefits rejuvenated her. Fewer hairs turned grey on her marvellously full head of hair. Apart from the familiar tuft of white hair that had singled her out since childhood, her hair was still black in the back and minimally grey in front. She pulled her silver-plated hairbrush through her hair, determined to ward off unseemly aging. *Black hair, black eyes, my two best features.* If she were a wizard, she'd put a protective spell on them. But she was a simple medium. She knew about ageing and about changes. *I'll be ready when nothing can hold them off any longer,* she thought and relaxed.

No matter how badly one stumbles or even falls, Eusapia murmured, *there is always a way of getting up.* Months went by. The bitter aftertaste from her latest trip slowly dissolved. She looked down from her window to the street where people with baskets walked toward the market and back. *I still can pay for my apartment, and meat, and a few treats, and a fancy hat every so often,* she said. Through the colourful garlands of clothes drying across the street, she happily caught exuberant snippets of Neapolitan dialect. The vibrant noise called out to her, swirling together with the stench from the sewers and mouth-watering aromas of food in a strangely potent mixture. People like her thrived in this intoxicating chaos. She wouldn't want to be anyplace else. She rushed outside to be part of Naples' everyday life. She too wanted to leave a mark on it.

Stepping out briskly, with the ever-present curious, admiring, or frightened eyes of the people from her neighbourhood fixed on her, Eusapia listened to the little cogs in her brain turn and whir. She gave a quick salute to three men sitting lazily on the ground, hunched against the wall of an apartment building not too far from hers. They squinted up at her expectantly. Did she have any of her out-of-the-ordinary, beyond-drudgery tasks for them? Any job would do to fill their empty stomachs, but her projects came with unexpected wrinkles and fun. Eusapia shook her head. Not this time. But soon enough she would call on their services again. Don't worry, she called out encouragingly, there will be work again. She gave them a few centesimi to buy melon slices. These men were agile, strong, and most of all cunning, the type she liked. If for any reason her instructions needed to be adjusted during a séance or when ferreting out her sitters secrets, she could count on them to come up with their own quick-witted solutions. Oh, she liked to see them in a good mood. People and especially these men rendered the best services when they were happy — as long as you didn't allow them to pull the wool over your eyes, which they would if given the chance. More innocent persons might fall prey to their cunning, but not her, and they respected her for that.

Further down the street, a crowd of young children surrounded Eusapia. For all their ebullient chatter, they could not suppress the chafing hunger in their bellies. Without thinking twice, she reached for half of the few coins she felt comfortable bringing along without fear of being robbed clean, and handed them over for bread, which the children almost tore out of the

488

vendor's hands. Eusapia sympathised with the pitiful anger in their eyes that so closely mirrored hers as a child. Pain and outrage gripped her at once. No child should go without food. If she had envisioned giving up her profession and stretching out her savings over the coming years as a fitting reward for working hard all her life, she now had to reconsider. Her much-loved vision of a hassle-free life in relative comfort suddenly revealed itself as a grotesque delusion. People had no right to turn a blind eye to the desperation around them. Fighting against abject poverty and wretchedness in the little ways she knew gave her purpose. Everyone needed a purpose in life if they didn't want to end up depressed and disillusioned. That much she could tell from working with countless numbers of sitters. While most of her energy was taken up trying to meet her own needs, she never turned a deaf ear to the plight of others. She did not have the gift or capacity to mount big campaigns against the injustices of this world. But in her own neighbourhood, in everyday life and during her séances, she did her best to make a difference, convinced that her few good deeds somehow multiplied and her more dubious behaviour did at least not harm anyone.

People might describe her as vulgar, conniving, cheating, and untrustworthy — and she had to admit to a few unsavoury acts — but she took satisfaction in knowing that her intentions were mostly good. Eusapia had never been one to wonder what motivated or triggered her actions. So why the unlikely reflection and fuzziness? It must be the hotter-than-usual embrace of the Neapolitan sun and the especially intense promise of the blue sky that led to unpredictable trains of thought. On ordinary days, she just lived, pushed along by a continuous series of spontaneous actions and reactions. Whatever was required to

489

survive, she'd do without hesitation. If there was fun and games, she played. If a drama developed in front of her, she flung herself into its centre. But today, under the scorching sun and paralysing heat, a sudden unexpected breeze teased her senses and stopped her in her tracks. It must be old age that gives people the wisdom to pause and wonder instead of jumping headlong into action, Eusapia continued her musings.

Hello, Signora, a wisp of a kid shouted, swiping a loaf of bread from her basket and scooting off down the street.

Hey you, little bastard, she screamed, running after him. In no time, she caught the half-naked boy by one of his arms. What do you think you're doing? she scolded, thrilled by her own speed and agility.

The boy glared, his eyes bulging, his chin in a stubborn jut.

I asked you a question.

Still no answer.

You! Answer me!

The boy squirmed, assessing his chances for escape. Nil, he thought, and his fierce stance dissolved. I haven't eaten in three days, he said grudgingly.

Eusapia saw in his eyes that he spoke the truth. Why didn't you ask me for the bread?

The boy said, I didn't think you'd give me some, or you would have made me work for it. And I'm too tired and too hungry to work.

Eusapia let go of his arm. The bread is yours. Share it with some other poor devil.

The boy looked at her in disbelief. He touched the bread and then Eusapia, convinced that his hunger played cruel tricks on him.

I am real, she reassured him. If you're here when I return, you can come to my apartment and eat more. Once you get your strength back, I might have some errands for you to run. The boy jumped up and down with eagerness. I'll be waiting for you, he squealed.

When Eusapia came back two hours later, the boy was nowhere in sight. Other boys hovered around the area, bigger and stronger guys with big fists and bully faces, which explained why the boy stayed away.

Signora, one of the older guys shouted, we heard you have money.

Eusapia was in no mood for their shenanigans. There was no hunger in the eyes of the big boys, used as they were to snatching with force whatever they wanted if they needed it or not.

Shove off, she screamed, fully aware that they'd resort to violence if she resisted. She had dealt with many brutes in her life. She would not cower in front of these either. At this stage of her life, she was still feisty enough to try at least to stop them. Don't ever come near me again.

The boys gasped. In the habit of getting their way, they pressed in on her. But in one energetic swoop, their caps disappeared from their heads and went flying into the street. Torn between bringing this crazy woman to her knees and saving their prized possessions, the boys finally scooted after their caps, cursing Eusapia, but almost relieved to get away from her. Something was not right here. An old hag was not supposed to get the upper hand on strong guys like them.

Eusapia stepped out vigorously without fear of being followed. She knew the power of her eyes. Like other aggressors before them, these hoodlums backed off like cowards. Despite

491

her easy win, bad memories dampened her mood. She'd never get used to bullying. Because bullies sniff out weakness in humanity itself and hack away at it. When the weak and helpless get attacked, everyone loses. Eusapia spit on the ground. She wished she could shake sense into these guys. But that was asking too much. Now where was that young boy? Eusapia never saw him again.

As the days went by, the children of Naples began to draw her eyes as if daring her to tackle challenges that even the most skilled politicians and champions of change were unable to solve. She saw the children wave their arms and could have sworn that their taunts and pleasantries were pleas for her to employ her special powers on their behalf. But her powers were failing and her income was drying up again to a trickle that barely kept her living comfortably. Eusapia growled at the children, Leave me alone, there is nothing I can do for you. She still handed out whatever food she could spare, which was a fraction of what she could offer in better days. With age, her justification for diverting items from the rich to herself and the poor and weak had lost its enraged fervour. When she watched all the thieving going on around her, and there wasn't much that escaped her trained eye, her own activities became harder to defend. On some days, though, the wretchedness of abandoned old people left to die, or of children too emaciated to combat even minor illnesses, would whip her back into action and drive her to reallocate money, food and other goods as she saw fit. But if at all possible, she stuck to a more lawful course of action, scheduling more séances and working ten times harder for a fraction of her former fees. Whenever she gave one of her watered-down séances, she made it an iron rule to weave the hungry faces of the poor into the fabric of her productions and materialisations. She embedded them in the numbers that promised to bring luck in upcoming lotteries. Three, Eusapia would call out, three sickly children, walking in front of you, not like normal children, no, like ghostly occupants of another world. Three, lucky number if elevated into that status. Redemption is necessary. When the sitters asked after the séance what that meant, she mostly let them figure it out themselves. But often, she had to help them along. What it might mean, she'd say emphatically, staring right into the core of their souls, you will receive only by giving. Feed them and any other combination of children or old people, and the sums of their groupings will bring luck. Eusapia was sure her words were not in vain. Generous actions often followed her séances. The sitters would come back, and she could see a soft shimmer in their eyes. Moments later they would tell her that they had fed a few or many hungry creatures since their last séance. I see your actions give meaning to your life, Eusapia would say. The sitters looked bewildered for a second, but the sentence stuck and made sense. Eusapia knew she had started a good thing not just for the poor, but for their benefactors as well.

In spite of her relative success and a sense of achievement, when it boiled right down to it, Eusapia was tired of her mediumship. She wanted someone to take over. Like a magician handing his baton to a successor, Eusapia wanted someone to follow in her footsteps. Not an adult for sure, but one of the young girls who like her as a child had no outlet for her talents and intelligence. Soon after this newfound realisation, Eusapia started her search. No matter what occupied her mind, she kept an eye open for the right combination of physical flexibility and stamina, of a quick mind and dramatic expression. There was no shortage of undiscovered talent on the streets. You have an amazing voice, Eusapia said to a stern-faced teenage girl, whose voice warbled toward her with an almost challenging audacity. The girl never acknowledged her. She was caught up in her own world of song and music with no chance of opening it up to a wider audience. Another girl danced circles and loops around the medium, graceful and needy, following her down the street. I know that type, Eusapia thought handing her a centesimo, then moving decisively away from her. She's a butterfly fluttering from one flower to the next, not what's needed in my profession. After months of wandering the streets, Eusapia realised that her talents might be rarer than she thought. They had always seemed pretty ordinary to her even though her shrewd business sense would never have allowed her to admit this in public. To survive the competition, she needed to stand out from the run-of-the-mill group of fraudulent mediums as the special one with authentic powers. Eusapia smacked her lips, then laughed out loud, but immediately became serious again. Nowadays, her only wish was to benefit from her career as a medium by transmitting her knowledge to an apprentice for part of that new medium's income. She was due for a rest.

In the face of increasing fatigue, she soldiered on bravely, all the while keeping her eyes and ears open for the perfect successor. She had believed that age was to blame for the decline in her income, but accounts from Italy and other countries told another story. The scientists had not just distanced themselves from her, but from other physical mediums as well. Pure trance mediums fared slightly better because fraud was harder to prove. While pure trance mediumship held little appeal for an athletic person like Eusapia, stiffening limbs and a slowing body pushed her to move in that direction. She couldn't say no to easier money and the more satisfying response she could elicit with dramatic, even incomprehensible prophecies, rather than her usual physical phenomena that had become mediocre at best. But even her enigmatic predictions progressively lost their lustre. While, yes, there always were a few poor souls filling her living room, eager for advice and consolation from the otherworld, Eusapia could not overlook the change in the air. She tried to identify its source, hoping to adjust her performances accordingly, but was unable to do so.

Out of the blue during this time of reflection, Raphael's former travelling companion Tomasso with his copper brown hair turned grey but still bouncy dropped in to see her. He had travelled the world for over forty years, living by his wits as a performer, salesperson, medium, preacher — whatever seemed most lucrative at the time. His recent experience gave him the confidence to state point-blank that the time for mediumship had come and gone. Spiritualism, Tomasso elaborated, had been a necessary bridging mechanism. He went on to explain the past with a spiel she had heard before about new insights of science and dogmatic beliefs of religion, loss of faith and unavoidable feelings of guilt, painful voids and the hopeful message of spiritualism. However, Eusapia's friend continued, we've entered a new epoch, and the new generation growing up with less certain beliefs feels free to either reject religion completely or on the other hand reconcile the seemingly incompatible systems of religion and science by interpreting the Bible in new ways and by establishing a more mature relationship with Christianity. Eusapia listened carefully, though it was her own daily reality she trusted most. Unfortunately for her and other mediums, this change in attitude could only lead to the abolition of their profession. She sighed. Couldn't that have waited another twenty years?

My friend, she asked, do you think it's possible for a potential successor of mine to continue in my steps for one more generation?

No, Tomasso answered bleakly.

I think you're right, Eusapia conceded, but how can I accept this? How can anyone accept that their time has passed, their ideas and talents are outdated and have to make way for new ones?

You don't have a choice if you want to survive without bitterness.

Eusapia looked at her friend in dismay. He was right, of course. But there went her cherished idea of mentoring right out the window.

Don't be mad at the messenger, Tomasso said.

I'm not mad, Eusapia growled, I'm struggling to remake myself.

Good!

If not a medium, then what? Eusapia asked. Mediumship is the only thing I know.

I'm not worried, her friend responded, giving up your mediumship does not mean giving up the skills that go with it. You're still strong, cunning, and quick-witted, with an unerring intuition for what the person in front of you is all about.

While that may be true, Eusapia responded, don't you think it becomes harder to reinvent yourself at sixty when reality has depleted your energy and taken a big bite out of your optimism?

Tomasso smiled reassuringly. He knew it was only a matter of time until Eusapia's zest for life would kick in and lead her in new directions.

After it sunk in that she'd never be a mentor, Eusapia fell into a downward spiral. Her strong breasts started a noticeable descent. Her once flat belly ballooned. Prominent strands of her hair turned suddenly white. During her most recent séance, she dropped her extendable pole twice. When the table started to rise in front of her sitters, one of them screamed at her not to use her leg.

It's called cheating, the man continued to berate her, and the other sitters chimed in with similar reproaches. Distressed by her own clumsiness, Eusapia shuddered. Not only were her limbs not obeying her commands, her voice was not up to the task. Her sitters left unsatisfied.

What frightened her most, neither her mother nor Gianina nor any of the other people who normally brought her comfort in tough moments showed up.

Why are you abandoning me? Eusapia shouted, staring into the air, while Tomasso looked at her with concern.

Mother? Gianina? Where are you?

There was no response. Only the voice of her friend reached darkly into her thoughts, When I told you spiritualism was finished, I meant it, he said firmly.

I'm not worried about spiritualism. It's my mother and Gianina we're talking about.

Tomasso shook his head. You can't be serious, he said disparagingly. You don't believe in that stuff, Eusapia. Listen to yourself. This doesn't even sound like you.

But Eusapia, who by now was frantic, grabbed him by his collar and unceremoniously marched him out the door.

Don't come back, she said. I should have known that you don't understand a thing about me.

She slammed the door shut behind him. What a relief to get rid of such an unpleasant presence! She could breathe again. At that moment, she saw a flicker on the ceiling. But that was all it was, a mere flicker. For Eusapia though it contained hope. First a flicker, she thought, and later the whole manifestation. They'll be back. I have confidence in them. I'll see them soon again.

As the days went by, Eusapia put all her concentration into calling up her dead relatives.

Don't rob me of this one satisfying and useful gift I have, she said and wondered who she was talking to. I need you, she continued, but her words fell into an unresponsive hole.

Eusapia stared into the grey nothingness with increasing discouragement. Even a woman as determined as she was could not reach spirits who didn't want to be contacted. Eusapia pulled herself together. Never give up, she mumbled. This has been my motto all my life. I'm not going to change it now. One day, the spirits will reveal themselves again.

Fresh air and exercise, that's what I need, she told herself. She started a strict regimen of vigorous walking. While her mood slowly improved, her hair continued to turn white. She tried not to think about her mother. Yet every so often she stared hopefully at the ceiling or the sky, where she saw nothing but an ordinary ceiling and an ordinary sky.

All her life, Eusapia had given advice to people. What did she have to say to herself now? Not much. Whenever an answer prepared to present itself, she refused to see or hear it because she did not want to be told that her mother had never been more than a figment of her imagination.

Three weeks later, Tomasso called on her again, knowing that Eusapia was not one to hold a grudge against an old friend for long.

What do you want? she snarled.

To renew our friendship.

What friendship?

Oh, come on, Eusapia. Don't be like that. Anyway, listen to me before you write me off. I have a proposition for you that you won't want to refuse.

What proposition? Eusapia asked, curiosity getting the better of her.

She invited him into her apartment for coffee.

Shoot! she ordered before he could take his first sip.

Well . . . Tomasso started, then paused, afraid she might not be ready for what he had to say.

Well what? Eusapia barked. You don't strike me as the dithering type. So let's get this over with. What do you have to offer?

Okay then, here it is: Like me, you need to make money somehow. Our old sources are drying up faster than spit under the Neapolitan sun.

Eusapia wanted to shut him up, but kept quiet.

I found a new opportunity, Tomasso went on. It's not glamorous, but it will pay our bills.

Our bills?

We'll need to work together since neither you nor I have enough money to do it alone.

You want to take me to the cleaners?

Now come on. You know me. I won't take more than you would take if you were the one making the proposition.

Eusapia laughed. She did know him, and he had more in common with her than she cared to admit. But just like her, he was loyal to his friends.

Let's hear it.

It's a shop, not anything special, in fact it's in poor condition, and the merchandise is of questionable quality, but it's stuff people need.

You want me to work in a shop??

To start with, yes. You'll have your former assistants whip the place into shape. We'll hire some help. If we do well, we should get an acceptable return on our money. At some point we'll hopefully be able to watch the shop run itself with competent people that we put in place.

It's not my idea of fun.

The shop will grow on you.

You don't believe that.

Do you have a choice, Eusapia? Jump into this enterprise before all your money is gone. I had intended to settle down with my long-time friend and partner, but he died three years ago. I simply don't have enough money left to enter this venture by myself.

Where is your shop?

Not too far from here.

Eusapia and her friend walked companionably along the seven blocks to the street where the shop was located.

That dump?

I told you we'll fix it up.

Eusapia assessed the shop in one quick glance: peeled-off paint, broken shelves, a discouraging accumulation of dirt, and a very visible infestation of rats and various types of insects. She also saw potential. The location was perfect. The merchandise of everyday household goods fitted the needs of the people in the neighbourhood. If they managed the store properly, it would attract passersby as well. Eusapia saw herself standing behind the counter, a vision so improbable that she would have rejected it out of hand in her younger years, but didn't entirely hate it now.

I'll work my butt off, Tomasso said.

What's the profit-sharing? Eusapia asked.

Fifty-fifty, he answered, except that you have to provide sixty percent of the start-up money because I simply don't have it.

That's not fair.

It is! Because without me this opportunity would not exist. I'll make it worth your while.

Eusapia looked at him seriously. Had wandering the world for so many years changed him? No, she decided. I can still trust him.

I'm in, she said.

We're in it together then, he replied, and they immediately used their skills to acquire the shop for a bargain price.

Since her friend had no fixed address at this point, he ended up staying at Eusapia's apartment and soon became known as her husband. The nature of their relationship came as a surprise to Eusapia. Unlike most men she met during her lifetime, her sensual, dynamic, and energetic friend had never shown any sexual attraction to women. Nothing had changed in this respect. But she enjoyed his presence, his infectious smile, his crazy schemes, the fantastical stories of exotic places. His not negligible cooking skills perfectly satisfied her cravings for tasty food.

I'm glad you came to Naples, Eusapia told him.

As much as both Eusapia and her friend sought to present the image of a typical hardworking couple, the dramatic expression of their eyes and movements made them stand out. Men, women, and children openly stared at them. Eusapia wondered whether their eccentricities would keep people away. But no, customers flocked to the store fully convinced that the second-hand clothes, buttons, spools of thread, scissors, etcetera contained special powers that could not be found in other stores. Neither Eusapia nor her friend tried to convince them otherwise.

Partnership or not, Eusapia felt no need to make adjustments to her spontaneous acts of generosity. Like all her closest friends, Tomasso was generous at heart. Seeing her give away clothes and even money brought a smile to his face. He himself was not given to part with items at the first sign of need, but watching Eusapia in the unexpected role of Good Samaritan and not objecting made him feel like a better person. His task was to make sure their income remained stable so that the giving could continue.

Eusapia and her friend worked from dawn to dusk.

Who would have thought I'd adjust to this work? she asked

I did, boasted her friend. I wouldn't have asked you otherwise. I also knew I needed you at my side to survive in this shop.

And how are you holding up?

Better than I thought. It is surprising that after years of thrills and drama, the two of us can enjoy everyday lives.

So their lives continued, more ordinary than they had foreseen, but overall satisfactorily.

Don't we look almost idyllic? Tomasso asked in his irrepressible optimism.

You mean downtrodden, Eusapia responded, but couldn't help join in his laughter.

Yet, Eusapia felt sudden pangs of stress in the pit of her stomach when she looked at her partner. His outward gaiety belied an unsettling tiredness that crept into his movements. No matter how much he tried to hide it, he could not convince her that he was okay.

What is it, Tomasso? she asked, repeatedly.

My dearest friend, he answered, in a deceptively jaunty voice, we all have our aches and pains. Why talk about it? As soon as we start belabouring them, we've become old. I'm not that old yet. My heart and brain are still filled with fascinating ideas and thoughts, even dreams, and that's what I want to talk about. Please respect this one wish of mine. Yes, I'm nearing seventy, but in my heart, I'm still twenty and full of wonder and hope for what's to come.

Eusapia smiled. She expected no less of her friend. Her approach to life was the same. And while every day he had to pull and push himself more, they grabbed life with the zest and excitement of youth.

That's why I want to be with you, Eusapia, Tomasso exclaimed.

I'm so happy that fate brought us together, Eusapia responded. For the first time in her life she felt at peace.

Eusapia knew the time had come to hire more permanent help. Right away she thought of Isabella and her husband, who had helped a friend of Eusapia's clear out an apartment of an old relative and had done so with boundless energy and great honesty. Yes, oh yes, said the young couple, happy to have work at all, but especially pleased to do the type of work where even their six-year-old twin sons Arturo and Francesco could be useful.

As Tomasso grew weaker, he kept upbeat. Eusapia saw his skin grow sallow and his feet and arms heavy and less coordinated. But out of his weakened body shone such courage and acceptance that Eusapia took strength and kept going. How does he do it? she wondered. Even when he collapsed beside her, he seemed to keep smiling. The doctor looked serious and prescribed dried herbs, crushed roots and awful smelling drops for his heart and lungs. Tomasso sat in a big chair with cushions she had hauled up to the apartment, his left arm clutched to his body, his left leg stiff and unresponsive. Yet the radiance of his face remained not only undiminished but grew as if already he saw truths and wisdoms unknown to living people.

Now I understand what you mean when you say you see your mother, Tomasso said, and looked happy. Your mother came to visit me too.

Why can't I see her anymore? Eusapia asked plaintively.

You will, Eusapia, you will.

Eusapia looked up at the ceiling. She detected no sign of anyone she knew.

But Tomasso's expression was reassuring, and there was no way she would ever doubt him.

Day after day he took his medicines, not the ones the doctor prescribed but the ones he had brought back from his travels. She kneaded his arms and legs. She massaged his body to give him strength. She fed him little pieces of melon which was the only food he still tolerated and enjoyed. Since it was impossible for him to climb stairs any longer or even walk by himself, she often sat him up in bed and, when she felt strong enough, loaded him on her back and carried him for short distances. She brought him to the window and propped him up so that he could watch the busy life in the streets. Not once did he complain.

All in all, I had a good life because all the way through I was lucky to meet friends like you, Tomasso said quietly one day when he knew his time had come. Thank you, Eusapia.

Eusapia couldn't respond. She did not want to let him go. His hand lay in hers.

Your mother will be back when it's your time, Tomasso said, the last words barely audible.

When Eusapia dared to look at him again, she realised that he had left. She kept the fingers of her left hand interlaced with his, and with her right hand gently closed his eyes.

The sadness that engulfed Eusapia after his death threatened to suck the life out of her. But Tomasso had also left his presence and the gift of his courage in her apartment and her heart.

If he could accept death, so can I, Eusapia told herself every day.

She expected him to come back and console her like her mother had done until recently. But neither her mother nor Tomasso showed up. Yet Eusapia did not feel alone. Wherever she went, her ancestors and friends went with her, unseen, but unmistakably there. Strangers and acquaintances on the street made way for them. Without seeing, they knew. Eusapia knew too. Through the connection with her lost loved ones, she found steps to doors that were, if not open, at least unlocked.

Every day, Eusapia went to her shop to check up on Isabella and her husband who had bravely taken on new responsibilities during Tomasso's progressing illness. Nothing fazed their unwavering enthusiasm. Eusapia could hear their yelling as soon as she turned the corner two blocks from the shop. Even their twin sons Francesco and Arturo could be heard hollering. All that noise seemed to be beneficial to their work. The shop was cleaner than other stores in the neighbourhood, always well stocked, and filled with customers who heartily took part in the animated back-and-forth banter.

As soon as the twins would catch sight of Eusapia, they ran toward her.

Hello Signora Palladino, they yelled.

Before Eusapia could answer, they'd twirl her around until her strong arms grabbed them and somersaulted them backwards and forwards. It did not astonish them that a sixty-year-old woman had this amount of strength. She wasn't just anyone. She was the Great Palladino.

More, more, they shouted when she finally plopped them on the street.

Boys, leave Signora Palladino alone. She must be sick and tired of you.

But Eusapia smiled. Never would she get tired of those two kids. They could make the sun shine around her even when it was raining.

Next time, she promised.

The boys went back to work helping their father unload boxes from a cart or sweep the floor.

506

Eusapia had never found proper students for her mediumship. When it came to Tomasso's and her shop though, she'd struck gold with pupils who already surpassed her own skills, a whole family of talented merchants.

The only thing she had to do was help out when she felt up to it, and collect her part of the money. The generous compensation she gave the family kept them happy and worry free, but there was something much deeper that connected them, a rare sense of belonging together.

When the twins visited her in the apartment, they enthusiastically begged her to show them magic tricks. The boys' bright black eyes shone with interest, curiosity and wonder, but both of them increasingly turned to their parents for inspiration. Eusapia understood that the boys took exactly the paths they needed to follow. She smiled as she saw their faces turn serious when they counted money with their father or pleaded with an old teacher who lived in the neighbourhood to teach them letters and numbers. With the help of their teacher, they learned to construct neat columns and rows that clearly indicated quantities and price. There was pride all around.

Life is as it should be, she said to herself.

One evening in late fall, Eusapia let herself be dragged into another séance even though she had refused to give one for months. The two women who convinced her had participated in some of her early séances. Being old and frail now, they sought reassurance once more. Eusapia had said no several times, but their insistence moved her. They had always believed in her and still did. Their faith warmed her heart. She couldn't resist their call. But when they sat around her little table in the darkened room, any power she ever had deserted her, leaving her legs leaden and her arms stiff. Why had she agreed to this? She looked at the women and was tempted to leave them with some cheap pronouncements, some trumpet sounds from the cabinet, a few moving objects. She realised that despite her lack of energy she could get away with it because the two women had become hard of hearing and much slowed down in their reactions. But a new sort of integrity prevented her from taking the easy way out.

I'm sorry, Eusapia said, there are no powers anymore.

But we can feel them, the women insisted.

Grateful for their confidence in her, Eusapia put her hands on theirs and asked her assistant to turn up the lights. The women looked at her with fearful eyes. But Eusapia smiled at them.

To the end of séances, she said, raising her arm, and to new beginnings.

The two women instantly grasped the significance of the moment. They too raised their arms.

To new beginnings, they repeated, and as they said it, they felt a fiery warmth sear through their bodies. They gasped, but suddenly felt contented, trembling with fresh hope and renewed strength.

Thank you, Signora Palladino, thank you so much, they said, and wouldn't let go of her hands.

I should thank you, Eusapia replied, you made a painful moment acceptable and showed me the value of honesty.

The women looked at her strangely moved, not sure what to make of the situation, but glad to be part of this extraordinary experience.

508

Eusapia looked back to this evening without regret. The previously unimaginable final curtain had come and she had accepted it with courage.

For an illiterate and vulgar woman like me, Eusapia said to herself, remembering all the slights and hurts she had endured in her so-called glory days, I entered this new stage of life with dignity. I showed more class than many of the scientists I met. So there!

She couldn't prevent herself from spitting on the floor, just as she had done in the past, three times in a row for good measure. Then she breathed deeply. When you're old, you don't have a minute to spare on unpleasant thoughts.

I stand here, under the sky of Naples without my mediumship, without special powers, but uniquely myself, strong and proud as always.

Eusapia invited the twins and their parents for supper. They ate and drank, and talked and laughed. They had become family. At last, in her advanced years, she unexpectedly found what she had been seeking desperately throughout her childhood. Nothing brings more happiness than this feeling of belonging and total acceptance.

The winter blew into Naples harsher than usual, strong winds reaching right down to her bones. She couldn't stand the chilly dampness. In contrast to all the years gone by, she preferred to stay indoors. She started to eat less, and stayed away from cheese and sweets because if she didn't, her belly turned into a torture chamber. Even small amounts of fatty or sugary food caused unbearable pains. Eusapia placed hot water bottles on her stomach to survive the nightly attacks. All her life she had worked to increase her tolerance to pain, and owed her success in part to her capacity to smile and not wince, no matter how much stomach, throat or limbs hurt. Now the pain woke her up several times an hour and the lack of sleep left her groggy in the morning. Instead of jumping out of bed with the first ray of light, Eusapia stayed huddled in her blankets for an hour or two more. When she finally got going, her movements were slow and tentative. Even getting dressed was an effort. If she dared venture outside, negotiating the stairs now tired her more than walking uphill for hours just a few months earlier. The first time she heard her own raspy breath after a minor exertion, she panicked. In spite of her extreme exhaustion, she pulled herself together and went to see a doctor.

My dear Signora Palladino, he said after groping the hard masses in her stomach with an increasingly serious expression, I'm so sorry.

Eusapia couldn't bear to hear him out and listen to his death sentence. His eyes clearly confirmed what she had come to fear in the last few weeks.

My dear friend, the doctor tried again, but before he could say another word, Eusapia fled his office as if by escaping she could change her fate.

Frantic and out of breath from her walk home, she slouched in her chair, her legs stretched out, her face buried in her hands. Abruptly, she straightened, then crossed herself three times. With the last doubt and hope taken away, Eusapia became calmer. How does a lifelong survivor survive death? she wondered.

By accepting it, she heard Tomasso's voice.

Where are you? Eusapia said into the dark, but couldn't see anyone. He didn't add anything either.

I'll never accept it! she shouted, suddenly agitated again. If I did, I'd be dead tomorrow.

Tomasso failed to reassure her. No one else came to her rescue. What had she done to piss off her mother? Why after all these years did she not help her now?

Feeling alone and utterly abandoned, Eusapia crawled into her bed and pulled the covers over her head. She had heard and seen enough for one day. But she could not block out the new reality. She burrowed her head into her pillow and with relief felt an overpowering tiredness take hold of body and mind. Her racing thoughts slowed down until only a vague sort of discomfort remained. Her eyes closed and, conscious of falling asleep, she savoured that short moment before the heaviness of night blanketed the last of her painful awareness.

With the first rays of light poking through her window, Eusapia was on her feet. She had work to do. She opened the cupboard containing her hats, an extravagance she had indulged in all her life. Carefully, she took each one of them out of its box and placed it on her head. The hats perked her up. Not even Isabella could have guessed that she was sick.

Okay, Eusapia said, this cute red one is for Giuseppina.

Eusapia chose two more hats for her, marking the boxes with big G's. Then she put M's, R's, and A's for her neighbours. She kept three reasonably practical hats for herself, and placed I's on the rest of the boxes for the twins' mother. She sent a young boy to Isabella asking her to come by when she had a moment.

Isabella was shocked when she was told to dispose of the hats according to Eusapia's instructions.

What's wrong? she exclaimed.

I'm dying, Eusapia replied.

Oh no, you aren't! Isabella screamed. No, never, not you.

She grabbed the boxes and started to pile them back into the cupboard.

Eusapia stopped her.

I need your help, Isabella. It's important to me.

I don't want your hats.

But you always loved them.

That's not the issue. You'll need them as soon as the warmer weather arrives and you'll want to go out into the public again.

Don't worry. I kept three comfortable hats.

You'll need them all for this year, and the next and all the years after that.

When Eusapia failed to respond, Isabella stared at her, then staggered backwards as she suddenly recognised the hollow eyes of death in the flushed face of her friend.

No, she shouted, no, it can't be.

She grabbed Eusapia and folded her into her arms as if to protect her against evil forces. They stayed like that for several minutes. The warmth of the two bodies gave Eusapia new strength and new confidence. Firmly, she extricated herself from the embrace.

Now, take the hats, she ordered, taking charge again.

Without any further objection, Isabella took as many boxes as she could carry, then came back with the twins to pick up the rest.

One more thing, Eusapia said the next morning to Isabella, my ring with the yellow stone, I want to wear it until I'm dead.

Then it has to go to Raphael for his oldest daughter. That's where it belongs.

What happens when you die? Francesco asked when he dropped by with his brother later in the day. While the twins were subdued at first, their natural curiosity took over quickly.

Yes, what happens, Eusapia? Arturo repeated the question of his brother.

You're not going to hell, are you? Francesco asked, vividly picturing flesh-burning fires and devils.

Don't be stupid! his brother interrupted, Eusapia will be up there with Baby Jesus, the Holy Spirit, and the Holy Father.

The twins seemed to like this idea.

But won't it be boring? Arturo all of a sudden asked. I mean it's like being in church forever. Even if you had the best choir with violins and flutes and a majestic organ, and the church were decorated with the most beautiful candles and flowers, who would want to be stuck there for a full day, let alone for eternity?

Now boys, Eusapia responded thoughtfully, it's what's in your heart that decides whether you're bored or not. I haven't been bored a single day in my life and I don't intend to become bored in the afterlife. I think that once you're on the other side you'll know what's important. Everyone will feel at peace.

I'd rather live, Arturo interjected. It sounds more interesting.

Eusapia tousled the boy's hair.

Anyhow, you two, you're too young to think about death.

But if you die we do have to think about it.

Eusapia sighed.

Well, she responded, that's true. I can't help you with that. You might even cry for a few days. But then, you'll go on living.

That's your job, that's everyone's job. You live and make life exciting.

Maybe you could come visit us from the other side like the dead that came to your séances.

I wish I could. But no, it'll be goodbye.

You don't want to see us anymore?

Oh, I do! If there were any way I could, I would come back. It's not in my power. But I will be there somehow, like my mother was there for me!

How?

Eusapia sighed again.

I wish I knew, she said, and became lost in her own world.

The twins, impatient with her strange mood and ready to explode with life, lost interest in the peculiar conversation. They started chasing each other around the apartment, leaping over chairs, tumbling through hallways, jumping up and down on Eusapia's bed until she couldn't stand it anymore.

Get out! she screamed.

The boys raced to the door, laughing, because her screeching voice was brimming with love as usual. Before shutting the door behind them, they shouted back, We love you, too, Eusapia. Don't worry, we'll take care of you. Mamma, Papa, and the both of us, we'll take care of you.

Isabella made all the necessary arrangements. She hired her sister to help take care of the store so that she or her husband or the twins could spend time with Eusapia.

No doctor or priest at my bedside, Eusapia instructed Isabella, but a good Catholic funeral.

What do we do if the pain becomes too much? Isabella asked.

Tomasso left me something. Here, see, Eusapia said, pulling out a tin container with all kinds of envelopes, bottles and miniature tin boxes. They all came without names but with short instructions on small strips of paper.

Look here, Isabella, I have been taking this medication throughout the last months, Eusapia explained, pointing to a light coloured box. Tomasso told me that this one is for excruciating pain when there is still hope for recovery. When the pain becomes too much, I'll change to the tin box with the blue label, intended for excruciating pain without hope for recovery. I need you to give me the contents of this tin box if I can't take the medication myself anymore. You'll continue to give it to me until it is finished. Then allow me to leave this earth with dignity by giving me this medicine here.

What is it, Eusapia?

It doesn't matter, does it? It helped Tomasso. He had a good death. This one here, see! Promise to give it to me when the time comes.

Isabella shuddered with terror when she saw a tag tied to the bottle's neck with the image of a skull and crossbones which someone had drawn on it in red. She didn't want to hear or see anything more of the box and its contents. But Eusapia made sure she understood. She made Isabella swear with her hand on the Bible that she'd comply with her wishes.

Couldn't I send for a priest at least? Isabella asked. You don't want to end up in hell. And neither do I.

Oh Isabella, don't worry. You won't! As for myself, I had to live life my own way. Now I have to die my own way whatever the consequences. But if life and the afterlife have any meaning, there has to be grace. People won't be punished for trying to live life the best they can.

Isabella could see that Eusapia wanted to add something but was prevented by a new wave of pain from doing so.

Now! Eusapia managed to get out, pointing to the box.

Isabella fumbled with the medication, then finally got a grip on herself. Decidedly, she pulled out the medicine for excruciating pain with hope for recovery. She pulverised three tablets in a small tin bowl with the back of a spoon, mixed it with some water and carefully spooned it into Eusapia's mouth. Within half an hour, Eusapia became calmer. The next day she was up and arranging her affairs. The store and a few treasures from her apartment would go to Isabella and her family. On other items she put the names of neighbours and friends. The rest of her possessions and anything remaining of her savings would go to Raphael and his family. When everything was neatly arranged, Eusapia felt a comforting tranquility spread through her.

Life's circle is almost complete, she reminded herself, looking wistfully at the rays of the morning sun pouring into her apartment.

Most every day, Eusapia pulled herself out of bed, put on her best clothes, and brushed and combed her dried-out hair until it almost shone. Even if it took her the entire morning to prepare herself, she'd do it. Sometimes racking pains interrupted this activity, but as soon as she could breathe again, she'd continue.

You're the strongest person I've ever known, Isabella would say.

Eusapia weakened rapidly, forcing her to ask Isabella to double, then triple her medication, and finally to change to the medication without hope. She was ready. She only worried that there was not enough medication left to last her to the end. Tomasso had increased his doses daily in the last weeks and taken them with increasing frequency. Never forget, Eusapia, he had warned her, once you start this medication, you won't be able to do without it.

Soon, she felt the worst edge of her pain taken off and she sank into a blissful fog. She was able to sleep for an hour. For one last time, she summoned her strength so that Isabella was able to change her clothes. Eusapia then gave the sign and watched as Isabella tripled the dose and added some wine to the pulverised substance.

By the time Raphael arrived, Eusapia was unable to leave her bed. But she knew he was there. She even noticed how much he had aged and how stiffly his legs and arms moved. Take care, my dear Raphael, take care, she wanted to say. Though the words did not come out, she knew he understood.

My dearest friend, he said, and quietly held her hand.

When the first women from her building and the neighbourhood, who had come to her apartment in the last few hours, started wailing, he heard Eusapia's faint, No, please no. He stood up and led the women out. While they seemed to wail even louder outside, their absence from the room provided some peace. Raphael knew that she wanted to say things they had never said out loud. But she was too weak.

There is no need, Eusapia. We both know how much we love each other.

Eusapia wanted to say yes, or nod yes at least, but she only had enough strength to gasp for air. Isabella and Raphael provided some relief by helping her to sit up straighter. Isabella was worried. There were just seven pills left. She hesitated, but when the pain seemed to tear Eusapia apart, she gave in and crushed them all, though giving her only part of the powder. They barely provided a few minutes of peace.

She needs all of it, Raphael said quietly.

I can't.

But when Isabella looked into the tortured face of her friend, she started spooning the rest of the mixture into her mouth.

For a moment, Eusapia breathed easier and the pain seemed less. She almost looked serene. When she opened her eyes again, she saw Raphael and Isabella. A few other friends were there, even the twins. And right beside was her mother.

You've come back! Eusapia said soundlessly.

I've always been here, Sapia, her mother said. You just didn't see me for a while. Look, we're all here. Me, Tomasso, Gianina and her family, even Celestina.

Celestina? Is she dead?

No, but she wanted to be here with you today.

Eusapia smiled. What more could she want. All the people she loved were around her or waiting for her.

She wanted to wave, but the pain became so strong that she couldn't move her hand. The faces around her disappeared into darkness. All of a sudden, she felt Isabella's face almost touching her own.

Eusapia?

Now, Eusapia said, her voice rasping and almost inaudible.

Isabella knew what she meant, but could not do what her friend wanted her to do. Eusapia started to panic, when suddenly she heard Raphael's soothing voice.

I'll do it, Eusapia.

518

As Eusapia painfully swallowed the bitter drops, her love for Raphael and her gratefulness to him knew no limits.

When she opened her eyes again, the pain was gone, the darkness was gone, and as her eyes adjusted to the new light, she knew she was home and connected to everyone in this and the otherworld.

Bibliographical Note

In order to research spiritualism, mediumship and psychic investigators, I have read many books, articles, and interesting tidbits in print and online. The following books and articles have been especially helpful: Eric John Dingwall, *Very Peculiar People*, Rider and Company, 1950; Stanley LeFevre Krebs, *Trick Methods of Eusapia Palladino*, (Reprinted from The Reformed Church Review, Vol. XIV), 1910; Hereward Carrington, *Eusapia and her Phenomena*, B.W. Dodge & Co., 1909; Hereward Carrington, "More Tricks of 'Spiritualists'", in *Library of the World's Best Mystery and Detective Stories*, Julian Hawthorne, editor, The Review of Reviews Company, 1908; Everard Feilding (also known as Fielding), *Sittings with Eusapia Palladino and other Studies*, 1908, Copyright 1963, University Books, Inc.; Deborah Blum, *Ghost Hunters*, The Penguin Press, 2006; Barbara Goldsmith, *Other Powers*, Harper Perennial, 1999; Grace Thurston, *My Magic Husband, Howard Thurston Unmasked*, A Phil Temple Publication, 2006; Alan Gauld, *The Founders of Psychical Research*, Schocken Books, 1968; Ruth Brandon, *The Spiritualists*, Alfred A. Knopf, 1983; C.E. Bechhofer Roberts, The Truth about Spiritualism, Eyre and Spottiswoode, 1932; Alex Owen, *The Darkened Room, Women, Power and Spiritualism in Late Victorian England*, The University of Chicago Press, 1989; Theodore Flournoy, *Spiritism and Psychology*, Harper and Brothers, First Edition, 1911.

The concept of criminal atavism and the terms used to describe it are based on Cesare Lombroso's *L'uomo deliquente* or *Criminal Man*, first published in 1876. Also, Cesare Lombroso's comment about being like a pebble on a beach when it comes to spiritualism is part of a letter he wrote to M.T. Falconer in 1900. Lombroso's description of his relationship with spiritualism "Who knows whether I and my friends who laugh at spiritism are not in error, since, just like hypnotised persons, thanks to the dislike of novelties which lurks in all of us, we are unable to perceive that we are in error, and just like many lunatics, being in the dark as regards the truth, we laugh at those who are not in the same condition." is taken from his article in the 1888 *Fanfulla della Dominica* on the "Influence of Civilization and Opportunity of Genius".

About the Author

R.K. Marfurt grew up in Switzerland and now lives in Ottawa, Canada. *Calling the Dead* is her first novel. Her short stories have appeared in American and Canadian literary journals.

www.ingramcontent.com/pod-product-compliance
Lightning Source LLC
Chambersburg PA
CBHW030538020726
47494CB00005B/1415